...usician who always bets on
...is debut novel *Bait* won the Arthur Ellis Award
for Best First Novel in 2014. He currently lives in Toronto with
his wife, dog and a trio of cats.

Husk

J. KENT MESSUM

PENGUIN BOOKS

PENGUIN BOOKS

UK | USA | Canada | Ireland | Australia
India | New Zealand | South Africa

Penguin Books is part of the Penguin Random House group of companies
whose addresses can be found at global.penguinrandomhouse.com.

First published 2015

001

Copyright © J. Kent Messum, 2015

The moral right of the author has been asserted

Set in 12.5/14.75 pt Garamond MT Std
Typeset by Jouve (UK), Milton Keynes
Printed in Great Britain by Clays Ltd, St Ives plc

A CIP catalogue record for this book is available from the British Library

ISBN: 978-1-405-91426-0

www.greenpenguin.co.uk

*For my parents
who raised me right*

Prologue

At a popular pub in London's Shoreditch, a striking woman in her mid-twenties leans against a varnished oak bar with a male companion. The clink of glassware and cool sounds of the Miles Davis Quintet fill the air. They drink overpriced martinis and talk business. It is her last night in the city and she yearns to be gone. Her body aches, particularly her ass. Her pelvis feels bruised, underwear is uncomfortable. The inside of her nose burns and itches from illegal substances, but she cannot say what kind. The nasal drip coats her ragged sore throat. The pub is crowded enough for a fifteen-year-old boy from a council estate to sneak inside and avoid the attention of the staff. He looks broken, red-rimmed eyes, shoulders slumped, hair erratic. When he sees the beautiful woman at the bar he approaches and confronts her.

He tells her he loves her, needs her, that he can't live without her. The woman is caught off guard, her companion even more so. The boy asks why she chose him, why she would spend two entire days with him, naked in a hotel room, taking his virginity, defiling his body, feeding him blue pills and feasting on their effect, only to leave suddenly without saying a word. The woman does not recall doing this. She announces to the entire pub that she has never seen the teen before, does not know who he is.

The boy falls to his knees and bursts into tears. He covers his face with his hands, ashamed. Only then does she notice blood soaked into the cuffs of his shirtsleeves, the suicide attempt that could not be completed until he saw her one last time.

Outside a Paris café, in the shadow of the Eiffel Tower, an attractive older woman dressed in high fashion approaches a handsome young man trying to sip his fresh Americano on the patio. She speaks sternly to him. The look he gives her in return is blank. He doesn't speak the language. When he doesn't respond she becomes irate, grabbing a handful of her breast with one hand and gesturing angrily with the other. Spittle flies from her lips. The young man leans back in his chair, trying to explain that he doesn't know who she is or what she wants, trying to explain that he's just killing time until his flight back home. The woman leans in and spits in his coffee, then slaps him hard across the face. The man just sits there, mouth agape, stunned. This isn't the reaction the woman wants, so she grabs the cup and dashes the scalding contents in his face.

The man's screams are a strange mix of pain, dismay and rage. In an instant he is up from his seat, knocking over the table, throwing all of his weight on his attacker. The woman is so shocked she barely fights back as he tackles her to the ground. Still screaming, he punches her in the mouth repeatedly until most of her teeth lie at the back of her throat in a well of blood. Then he takes her head and smashes it against the paving stones until it no longer feels solid in his hands. Straddling the body, the young man glances at the café windows and with one good eye sees the reflection of second-degree burns covering his face. He is ruined.

In an upscale Manhattan strip club a man in his mid-thirties occupies a private booth near the back of the establishment. His rugged good looks complement his height as he towers over the Asian dancers amassed around his table. Classic nineties R&B hammers out of the speakers suspended from the ceiling. A mirror-ball casts thousands of bright splinters over the naked breasts and tanned bodies that vie for his attention. He peels hundred-dollar bills from a wad and gives them out absent-mindedly, for he is no longer interested in any of the girls. His attention is focused on himself, the thoughts in his head, and the other personality that has been trying to emerge for the last few hours.

The man sits down heavily on the sofa and stares at a glass of red wine on the table before him. He slowly runs his finger around the rim, creating a hum that is instantly drowned by the club's music. His head feels as though it might explode, or implode, he can't decide. Left eyelid won't stop fluttering. A twitch develops in both cheeks. He gets up to go, but abruptly sits back down, confused, trying to think of something to say to the dancers who are starting to regard him with concern. All he can do is look at them, eyes panicked, dilated pupils in irises of soothing blue surrounded by bloodshot jelly-white whipping back and forth in the strobe lights. His mouth has dried to desert. Teeth feel as if they are grinding into dust.

One of the more nervous girls leaves as an all-out war begins to rage inside his head. The thudding of his heart brings forth sweat and tears. A bouncer enters the booth to ask if everything is to his liking. He can't help but lash out and drive his fists into the man's face, dropping the heavy enforcer to the ground before chopping one of the strippers in the neck and crushing her windpipe. The others stare in shock as the man begins smashing his face against the table, knocking over drinks, trying to shake something loose inside. The more he breaks and bruises his grey matter, the more bloated the personalities become, drunk on blood, swelling inside his skull until he is screaming. Something cobalt-blue is clenched in his grip, his rigid thumb crushing a glowing red button. He drops to the floor, slamming his forehead against tiles. The dancers squeal as fluid, running dark and thick, exits from his ears, looking like oil underneath the club's black-lights.

I

Who do you think you are? The way I hear it in my head, it's not so much a question as an accusation.

'. . . Researchers at the University of Boston announced today that they have successfully mapped the human brain. Using advanced computer technology, a virtual copy of the human mind is now a reality. Researchers say the ramifications are massive, and will be releasing further statements in the coming weeks. In light of their success, some of the world's most prominent companies have already offered to fund future research with millions of dollars in –'

I stop the recording, my reminder of the day things completely changed. It's good for me to remember my roots, my prior situations, especially with the way things have been going lately. You don't hear much about that day any more. What little you may come across is refuted as techno-myth, unsupported evidence, some premature ejaculation of the scientific community. I remember the story sank as quickly as it surfaced, relegated mostly to a handful of independent websites and a quick mention at the end of a few nightly newscasts that left viewers with: 'We'll keep you posted . . .' or 'More to surely come on this . . .'

Except no follow-up reports were ever made. Social

networks buzzed about it for half a day. Mainstream media never touched it again. Sure, a bunch of masturbating wrecks stationed at their self-built PCs howled about it for a couple weeks, fingers typing furiously, demanding updates, but radio silence pervaded until they were beaten back by their own boredom. In the wake of this great discovery the information blackout followed fast. Researchers renounced their findings, suddenly said the results were inconclusive. The initial reports were dissolved through distraction, sinking under the weight of the media's 24/7 updates of more unimportant matters. Worldwide ADD made it easy. Eventually the whole thing dried up, no trace left, as if the breakthrough had never occurred. There was a containment plan, there always had been, and it worked like a charm.

Similarly to when researchers announced the cure for cancer, claimed the AIDS vaccine, or had that undisputable clinical proof that exposure to cell phone signals and Wi-Fi fucked up your brain and body over time. Every statement immediately followed by tumbleweeds as independent studies were being bought out or gagged by the conglomerates. No further comments were made. Information became unavailable to the public. If they didn't want you to have a cure, there was no way in hell they'd let you have immortality. Why did we ever think different? Death is now optional for a prestigious few, same old natural selection for the other 99.9 per cent.

When I awoke this morning I was drenched in sweat. The residue of vivid dreams and a sense of panic slipped away with my return to reality. Snippets are all I recall now.

I dreamed of a man named Miller, a colleague and close friend who was accompanying me through a crisis of some kind. When I try to remember more, a smouldering sensation creeps over my scalp.

I'm in so much goddamn pain right now.

And you've earned it.

With everything available from pharmaceutical companies without a prescription these days, pain of any kind is rare. But I resolve to take nothing for it, at least for a while. For me, this pain is a healthy reminder that I'm not in a coma, something I've come to appreciate more and more. Standing in my bathroom, I run my fingers over the bruises on my arms.

You're a sleepwalker of the worst kind.

'Not in the mood.'

Stupid whore.

'Ah, blow me.'

Talking to myself again, a bad habit I've picked up in recent weeks. At times my brain generates these internal conversations I'm not in control of. Luckily, no one ever notices. Anyone within earshot figures I'm taking a call through the communications bud in my ear. I'm trying not to use the earpieces any more though. They cause brain tumours apparently, similar to the cancers that plagued the ageing cell phone and smart-phone generations a while back. I turn my attention to the scratches on my bicep, undoubtedly from fingernails.

Signs of a struggle.

'Knock it off.'

Signs of life, such as it is.

This rambling split in my psyche sounds smarter than me. I don't like it. Too cryptic, too poetic, too old school – no one talks like that. One crude scratch on the back of my hand looks like it might be from something other than fingernails.

Sign of the times.

The bruises on my body are one thing, the scratches another. But what's most painful is this cramp in my stomach. It seems to reach up through my torso and constrict my heart. Every time I breathe it squeezes my aorta, a baby hand of blood crushing an adult finger. I half commit to vomiting, glancing at the toilet just in case.

Can't you read the signs?

'The less I know the better.'

Learning secrets will sicken you in this business. What you don't know can't hurt you. My reflection in the bathroom mirror tells me all I need to know. I'm a regular money-maker, a beat-up beauty. So close to perfection, yet I feel so incorrect at this moment. Seven hours have elapsed since my last session ended. When I came to I was weak with exhaustion. A couple power naps since has sufficed. The initial pain I'd felt after being revived has not subsided much, however. Both my hands hurt. My left wrist feels close to sprained. There are more scratches, across my left pectoral and a slight one under my right eye. Most of the bruises are small, but I have a long dark one on my thigh that I particularly don't like. Looks like I might have been hit with a baseball bat or something.

I was on loan to a Mr Harrison in Chicago. Bit of a

daredevil, as his representative calls him. Likes to take me on adrenalin rush adventures and use me for extreme sporting apparently. By the look of things I'd say he got his money's worth. The goods are bashed up pretty good, but all of these injuries don't bother me half as much as the faded bite marks on the inside of my forearm. They're not from Harrison. They're from a client I had before, already one of my least favourites even though he's become a relatively new regular for me. He's also one of my best-paying.

I hear the front door of the apartment open, cueing me to put my shirt back on.

'You home, Rhodes?'

My roommate, Craig, walks into the den and stops. Whatever he's carrying falls from his hands and clatters on the ground. I walk out of the bathroom to see him wide-eyed and slack-jawed. He doesn't even look at me.

'Oh my God, you got the new HG?'

I nod. He stares unblinking at the brand new Holo-Graphic tabletop unit centred on our coffee table. I can't tell if Craig is displeased or just in shock. I'm sure he suspects this new toy was picked up on the black market, something that could end our lives as we know it. People like us can't have nice things like this.

'Are you fucking nuts? This could land us in the DRIFT.'

Theft of patented technology comes with a mandatory two-year sentence, usually served in conjunction with DRIFT, the Debt Repayment Initiative to Foreign Territories. If caught and convicted, we'd be shipped to Beijing and stuck on a chain gang building a new suburbia for the slants, helping America crawl out of the red, make good on its interest payments. The working conditions in China are subhuman. Craig knows this and he's not happy.

'It's completely kosher,' I say. 'You can stop shitting your pants.'

No way can I afford the latest in HG technology, but my clients can, and some of them are getting more and more generous with their gifts of late. Craig still isn't convinced.

'Dude, you can't afford —'

I hold up a hand. 'Someone bought it for me.'

'Oh.'

Craig is no fool, no matter how much I try to keep him in the dark about my business. Years ago we bartended together, but I moved on to more lucrative things and he stuck to slinging drinks. The work I do isn't for everyone. Very few can handle it actually, but it's a job that comes with many benefits. For the moment, Craig lets his worry slide, his eyes skating over the sexy piece of new tech before us.

'Christ, what are the dimensions of that sucker?'

I activate the HG with a single command. It blooms in the middle of our living room like a giant prehistoric flower. Craig takes a step back, mesmerized by the three-dimensional beauty.

'Sixty-inch radius,' I say. 'High def, twelve terabyte network.'

'Twelve?'

'The whole dozen,' I say. 'It's got an internal back-up

generator too. No lag ever, not even with the rolling blackouts.'

Craig grins, pleased with this new addition to our place. He hasn't asked how much it cost, and I have a feeling he isn't going to. He walks around the circumference of the HG, running his fingers through the edges of the projection.

'Sixty-inch radius, eh?'

'The sound on this sucker is incredible too.'

'Really?' Craig asks, stroking his chin. 'I wanna hear it. Play me something on this beast.'

'Sure.'

I take out my Liaison 7, the newest one on the market, and point it at the port sensor, round and glassy like a doll's eye. A bright blue pupil dilates in the centre. Data transmits and syncs everything on my Liaison to the system in seconds. My favourite playlist starts up. I'm a sucker for the oldies, back when a premium was put on talent, when singers actually had to sing in tune to have a career. Craig nods his head to the beat as Phil Collins belts out 'Easy Lover'.

'Nice. What song is this?'

I frown. '"Easy Lover".'

'By who?'

'C'mon, man, really?'

Craig shrugs. 'Shit, I don't know.'

'It's Phil fucking Collins.'

'Phil fucking who?'

I roll my eyes. 'Phil Collins? You know . . . the great white hope of the nineteen eighties?'

Craig shrugs again and says nothing, not wanting to get into the argument about music he knows I'm dying to have. He brings out his older model Liaison 3, and fiddles with the device nervously.

'Mind if I . . . ?' Craig asks.

I know he wants a minute or two alone with the HG. Craig's a film buff, got an archive of movies that would make the Academy jealous, all of them ripped off from the internet. His extensive collection of pre-millennium porn films, back when fake tits looked proper fake and landing strips were in style, is even more impressive. I know he wants to back them up on my system and start watching them in 3D.

'Go nuts,' I reply. 'I've got to get ready anyway. Just encode your stuff before you re-link. I don't need anyone tracing your pirated shit back to me.'

Craig nods. 'What you getting ready for?'

'Las Vegas. I'll be gone for a couple days on business.'

'Vegas?' Craig's distaste can't be disguised. 'You're Husking again, aren't you?'

I shake my head, saying nothing, avoiding eye contact. I pretend something on my Liaison screen is suddenly important and needs my full attention. The tension in the living room rises until Craig grows enough balls to start busting mine.

'Goddamn it, Rhodes. Why the hell –'

'Don't ask if you don't want to know, Craig. It's really none of your business.'

'It's illegal, man.'

'How can it be illegal if virtually nobody knows it exists?'

'You're gonna get yourself killed, you know that?'

'Really?' I say, pointing at the HG. 'Because from what I can see, I've gone and gotten us the very best money can buy.'

'Is it worth it?'

I'm not sure how to answer. Craig turns and actually looks me in the face for the first time since he's been back in our apartment. He points to his own cheek, where the scratch on mine would be.

'What happened there?'

I look at the HG and sigh. 'I guess I paid for that in other ways.'

'You gotta be more careful, man. You know top-tier clients don't want anything rough around the edges.'

He's right. Any scar, blemish, unsightly aspect to your appearance can work against you in this business. Top tier pays for perfection, plain and simple. But perfection gets harder to provide with increased demand. Sometimes clients have to roll with the punches, or go without. And none of them like going without.

'Look, I don't want to have to put an ad out for another roommate or anything,' Craig says. 'Pretty happy with the one I have.'

I give him a grin. 'I'll be careful.'

Returning to the bathroom, I strip and inspect myself in the mirror until I'm satisfied with my damage assessment. There are several things I always do before going to see a client. The first is to take a thorough mist. I step into the glass partition with a complete lack of enthusiasm. It's during these lukewarm mists before a session that I wish most for a hot shower or bath. I remember them vaguely from when I was a kid, before the global drought. Global is ironic: most of the globe had suffered water shortages long before they reached the West. Only when America was hit did it become a crisis worthy of campaign platforms and societal change. There are so many new deserts down south now. Utility costs are through the roof. More and more lower- and middle-class residences are being equipped with money-saving fixtures. Fully flowing faucets are rare, bathtubs even more so. The motion-activated nozzles installed in the sinks of modern units pour a trickle of water for only seconds at a time.

I dry off and apply lotions to skin, ointments to injuries. A third of my room consists of a walk-in closet with every outfit I own on display. I take time to consider what clothes might impress the client who will be renting my services. I decide to dress up for the occasion, suit and tie, adorn myself with subtle silver and gold, spray myself with cologne so expensive it acts more like a pheromone. The shoes alone are worth over a grand.

'Oh, I think one of your co-workers called here while you were away,' Craig calls from the living room. 'Guy named Miller, said he was looking for you.'

Scrolling through my messages, I find two from the man that frequented my most recent dreams. They are both from a couple days ago and aren't marked urgent. Anything not urgent can wait in my world, but still I'm curious. I play the first video back on my Liaison screen. Miller's handsome, grinning face is always easy on the eyes.

'I was hoping you were available for a drink or two

tonight. Shit, you're probably already unconscious, you popular bastard . . . give me a call when you get this and you've got a little free time on your hands.'

I sigh, wishing I'd been available. Scheduling my social life has become increasingly difficult with demand for my services going up so much in recent months. I play Miller's second message. He's smiling in this one too, although it doesn't look sincere. Voice seems more serious. He's all business, and I can't help but think it has unsettling undertones.

'Hey, Rhodes, I'm just letting you know that I'll be covering one of your regulars for a few days. A last-minute request came in for you, but you're already booked.' He forces a laugh. 'I'm not encroaching on your territory or anything, buddy. Baxter's orders, that's all. The client is awfully adamant that they have a rental this weekend.'

Miller hesitates, opens his mouth as if wanting to say something else, rethinks whatever's on his mind and shrugs it off.

'Take care, stay safe, we'll talk soon,' he says instead and hangs up.

I appreciate Miller's honesty, though he of all people should know me better than that. A lot of Husks can get territorial with their clients, but I'd like to think I'm not one of them. My Liaison tells me my next appointment is fast approaching. Don't have time to call my friend back. I leave Craig in the apartment to play with the new HG, making my way to a five-star restaurant where I plan to eat an authentic and thoroughly nourishing meal before upload. Steak and vitaminized potatoes are my go-to meal, with whatever vegetables are in season, if Canada or Mexico is feeling kind enough to ship them our way at inflated costs. I eat real beef too, not the lab-grown shit. It's expensive, but the benefits to my body are undeniable. Meal supplements and nutrition spread aren't consumed by the likes of my clients. The gap between what I am and what they once were must be closed as much as possible. It helps ensure quick rehiring. Healthy eating, clean living, maintaining peak physical condition: a Husk's recipe for success. The damage is done only by those who pay for the privilege. Lately, I've had trouble sticking to the rules.

Husking isn't an exact science. There are more than a few outfits trying to make a go of it these days. At best it's a pharmaceutically controlled time-share split personality of sorts. At worst it's a rough descent into a drug-addled kind of dissociative disorder. Thankfully, I'm employed by Solace Strategies, working with the best, for the best.

2

I catch a cab to JFK International less than forty-five minutes before my flight. It takes me only minutes to get through an airport. Manufactured credentials allow me to bypass biometric, backscatter and retina scanners. Security personnel are only permitted to x-ray luggage and put me through a metal detector. I'm not obliged to answer any of the TSA's questions. If they persist, the same people who influence the departments that create my identification can not only have them fired, but ruined in the process. All evidence seems to suggest diplomatic immunity, but that's not what it is, at least not the diplomat part. For all intents and purposes, I'm almost bulletproof when it comes to law enforcement.

The direct flight from New York to Las Vegas is only four hours. Regardless, I fly premium first class. The clients wouldn't have it any other way. They want the merchandise kept comfortable. I pass on the champagne and Panamanian cigars, even turn down the offer of a mile-high-club membership from one of the finer-looking stewardesses. I have to keep myself in check, be on my best behaviour. To make that easier, I sleep most of the journey and wake up refreshed upon landing.

Outside the arrivals terminal of McCarran International Airport a limousine awaits. The driver opens the door and I slip inside and sink into soft leather seats. A welcome note on the minibar encourages me to enjoy the few hours left before the session. Beside it is a plain white envelope containing a thousand in cash, my per diem. The limo takes me to the Strip and I ask the driver to let me out at the MGM. Inside, the oxygen pumped into the air of the lavish casino gives me a buzz. I walk around the blackjack tables until I see a high-stakes game with only three players. Actually, it's the sultry blonde dealer who grabs my attention, the kind of girl I can manipulate in my game. Gambling is as much about energy as it is about numbers. I lay my greenbacks on the table, soaking up the old-school feel. Cash for chips, something solid and plentiful in your hands, not pin numbers and plastic. With my first hand I split eights and watch the dealer bust on a five-card draw. I'm dealt blackjack for the next two hands. She smiles warmly at me. I like where this is going.

Within an hour I've almost doubled the per diem and had an offer to meet the dealer after her shift for a drink. I decline, because I won't be conscious by then. I deposit my winnings into my account and head over to the Emerald City, the newest, most expensive condominium on the Las Vegas Strip. Outside the building, I look one last time up and down the boulevard at the casinos, crowds and shit ton of neon lights everywhere, feeling the sensory overload of it all. I won't be seeing any more of it for the next two days.

That sensory overload is what makes Las Vegas popular for Husks. Bigger, brighter, stronger, faster; all of it appeals to my clients. The Strip hasn't changed much in years, serving as a reminder of better times for the people who come to lose the remainder of their money in acts of desperation. All the mainstay casinos are firmly in place, although some of them are struggling more than others. Some of the smaller casinos have changed names and ownership, mostly sold to rich Asians who live in the Emerald City. As I arrive a doorman draped in a Wizard of Oz getup that must be hell in the Nevada heat opens the front doors. Inside, security clears me for Mr Navarette and calls up to notify his assistant of my arrival. A security guard packing a Vector SMG rides the elevator with me all the way to the nineteenth floor and walks me to a door adorned with solid gold trim. Navarette is a new client, the kind I call *baby-billion*, one who crosses the finishing line well behind the others, but still makes it to the podium. This internet mogul has just enough net worth to buy into the market that Husks are groomed for, what we call top tier, the one per cent of the one-percenters. I check some notes on my Liaison and see that Mr Navarette has been deceased for almost a year now.

A middle-aged man, who has aged quite well, greets me at the door and leads me inside the exquisite 3,000-square-foot condo. Before he introduces himself, I already know his name is Dante, the client's attaché. He shakes my hand and adjusts his suit while offering me his credentials. It isn't long before he gets to the point.

'Shall we get started?'

'Let's have a quick chat first,' I say. 'Since you're his handler and all.'

'Certainly,' Dante says and sits down on a leather couch, motioning for me to do the same. I remain standing.

'This,' I say, pointing to my face. 'Doesn't get damaged, okay?'

He nods. 'All right.'

'Your boss can push the rest of me to the limits, but all this flesh has to heal quickly and fully. Absolutely no broken bones, no broken skin requiring stitches. Anything more than the superficial and I file a complaint.'

'Okay.' Dante's nod is slower this time. 'Anything else?'

I look around the large room adorned with antiquities and velvet, Ming vases and one small Picasso. A lamp casts soft light on another painting of a girl in a blue dress staring into a looking glass, the most mesmerizing piece in the room. Nearby, I notice an original *Labyrinth* movie poster in a polished frame, David Bowie's signature scrawled in silver marker at the bottom. Cameras cover every square inch of the place. I can only assume Navarette is watching as we speak.

'I have a couple rules,' I say, speaking to the cameras as much as Dante.

'I thought Husks didn't have rules?'

'I have a couple rules,' I repeat.

'Such as?'

'No paedophilia for starters.'

Dante's eyes widen. 'I beg your pardon?'

'You heard me. Nothing involving children. No role-playing priest to the altar boys.'

Dante adjusts his shirt collar and swallows in a way I don't like. I'm glad he's not the client.

'And the other rule?' he asks.

'Whatever he does, he doesn't make a spectacle out of it. I don't want my face splashed over the news or some funny viral video of the week. Discretion is important. I have other clients.'

Dante points to my cheek and curls his lip. 'You're already scuffed.'

'Your rate doesn't cover perfection. It covers the basics. You're renting me on my days off, my R&R time.'

Without hesitation I take off my jacket and remove my shirt. Flexing everything at once, I hold out my arms and rotate to show the bruises and scratches on my trim, but muscular figure. Regardless of the blemishes, I can tell Dante likes what he sees by the way he licks his lips. Before he can reply, a smooth voice with a metallic tinge speaks from another room.

'Bring him to me, Dante. It is time we met.'

Dante rises from the couch and ushers me to the room where the voice emanated from. Shirtless, I enter, finding myself in a low-lit study with shelves of classic fiction and fantasy on every wall. The door closes behind me.

'Please have a seat,' the voice says. 'Let me have a closer look at you.'

In the middle of the room is a desk made of metal and glass. A leather armchair sits before it. Standing on the desk is an oval flat-screen resembling an antique mirror, thirty inches tall and twenty inches wide, its circumference an intricately carved silver frame. Beside the screen sits a gold-plated data port. I sit in the chair and wait a moment. Green eyes with slit pupils suddenly appear on screen, a Cheshire Cat grin splitting the space beneath them. I'm used to a lot of strangeness, but I find this unnerving.

'Well, hello, young man,' the voice purrs.

Seeing the Cheshire Cat, I get it all at once. The Emerald City, *Labyrinth*, the *Alice in Wonderland* shit. Navarette likes his fantasy lands no doubt, growing more and more accustomed to living in the best unreality money can buy, whatever his downloaded consciousness desires. The eyes morph from cat to human and I watch as Navarette's head and torso materialize on the screen in a texture and colour scheme resembling the Picasso in his living room. It's creepy, but I still like this presentation more than the way some of my other clients greet me pre-session.

'Mr Navarette,' I say. 'It's a pleasure.'

'Hmmm, yes,' he says, looking me up and down through the two-way screen. 'It certainly will be.'

'You've got me for forty-eight hours. I assume you know the ropes?'

'I'm well-versed. You're not my first Husk.'

'May I ask your intentions?'

'You may.'

'What do you have in mind for us?'

'Well, we are in Las Vegas.'

I chuckle and roll my eyes. 'What happens in Vegas . . .'

'. . . will be a lot of gambling, followed by sex with multiple partners and constant recreational drug use.'

'Fair enough,' I say. 'I only request the proper detox medication post-session.'

'But of course.'

I sit quiet for a moment, wondering if he's as good as his word. It's pointless. You can never really trust a client. Sometimes they become evasive when met with uncomfortable silence, a sure sign of guilt. Navarette's demeanour does not change. When I feel somewhat satisfied I retrieve my Liaison and pull out two thin retractable cables. Hard-lines are needed for the next step. The amount of data being transferred is massive. Safety and security are paramount. The first cable plugs into the gold data port, Navarette smiling on screen as it clicks into place. The second has a syringe-like proboscis. I use my fingertips to find the small digital interface surgically implanted under the skin behind my right ear, a device affectionately known as the 'Ouija'. When I feel the indent, I guide the proboscis into my head until I hear the little gristly crunch through tissue that signals connection to my cortex. My Liaison begins the Husk sequence automatically. I fish a pillbox from my pocket and open it. Inside are rows of red, yellow and green; little traffic lights of gel caps, each colour coordinating to a different session duration. I select an amber one for forty-eight hours. As I swallow it I can't help but think of the David Bowie song and Dorothy in her red shoes.

'Let's dance,' I say.

Within moments I feel myself falling backwards into a dark hole woven from sleep. Another entity passes me as I plummet, travelling in the opposite direction, up toward the light. Before the all-consuming blackness envelops me I see the Cheshire Cat grinning from high above, one green eye closed in a wink.

3

You dream while you're under. It can't be helped. Sometimes it's lucid, other times it's just a thick haze you try your best to navigate. Never feels like you have any real control though. Clients tend not to sleep very much while they're renting you. They want their money's worth, every minute, every penny. It's safe to assume that your body is always on a bender. It has to be for a client to feel alive again. Using a Husk isn't real living, but it's close. Living by proxy is the best way to describe it. They say it feels like being encapsulated in a thin layer of rubber. There's a barrier between sensations, through which a client experiences everything on a duller note. This buffer can be overcome if the body is pushed to its limits. Full throttle, fifth gear, the max, whatever you want to call it. Dialled up to ten, that's when clients really feel alive again. When Husks reawake we're almost always exhausted, physically and mentally.

Your coma never feels long, regardless of whether you're on a short jaunt or the seventy-two-hour maximum. I'm in the middle of dreaming about a certain special lady in my life when I start to feel myself re-emerging. Coming back is always interesting, the minute of cross-over where your entire natural concept of consciousness is in question. For a few moments there are actually two distinctions sharing the same bio-circuitry, you and something that could be you, a shadow with its own agenda, extended déjà vu working with you and against you. It's the kind of thing you can't conceptualize, can't envisage until it actually happens. The best I can give you is likening the experience to the beginnings of a hive mind. As soon as you think you might have a grasp on it, it's gone. And then you're back, alone and awake and in pain.

Suddenly, I'm using my own eyes again and the first thing I see is the Picasso-Navarette before me on the screen. I'm back in his study, wearing an expensive, if not garish, suit that appears to have suffered through an all-night party or two. The tie hangs loose around my ragged throat. My body aches inside the smooth, soft fabric. My lymph nodes are swollen. I can tell I'm not wearing any underwear. My cock and balls are sore. I taste bourbon and cigars and vomit in my mouth. The effect of some stimulant still courses through my veins.

'That was fun,' Navarette says.

'For you,' I groan.

'That was the whole point.'

'How did the gambling go?'

'You win some, you lose some.'

His Cheshire grin returns. I run my hands over my face and check my reflection in the desk's polished glass, relieved to find I'm in one piece. My muscles are raw, but there are no cuts on the surface, no breaks inside. I unplug the cable connecting me to the data port and carefully pull the proboscis from the Ouija in my head. A subtle click I've never heard before accompanies its removal and a nondescript flash of something wretched and bloody invades my thoughts for an instant.

What the fuck was that? I think.

'We should do this again some time,' Navarette says.

'Yeah,' I say, rubbing my temples. 'I think so too.'

I'm under the impression he's used me correctly, and for that I'm appreciative. We're starting out on the right foot, mutually respectful, a solid understanding between live product and dead consumer.

'Please see Dante on your way out. He has everything you need.'

'Thank you, Mr Navarette. Do let me know –'

But Navarette is gone, the Picasso image breaking apart and fading on screen as he returns to whatever virtual world he wishes to exist in. I get up and remove the new suit that smells like sweat and sex. Naked, I walk out of the study and find the bathroom. In the oversized mirror I examine my body. There are fresh bruises on my chest and buttocks, small and sparse. The older ones from before are already yellowed and fading. There is mouth-wash by the sink. I rinse the taste of puke from my teeth, feeling a sharp sting in my gums. Then I step into the shower and soak up all the soft, hot water I don't regularly get to indulge in. Through the glass partition I see Dante come into the bathroom with fresh towels. He waits for me to finish. I get the distinct impression that he wants to join me.

'Was your boss satisfied?' I ask.

'Very.'

'Any problems?'

'None that are of any of your concern.'

I look over to see what expression he wears, but the steam from the shower has fogged the glass leaving a flesh-coloured blur where his face would be.

'I took the liberty of testing your blood at the end of the session,' he says. 'The results came back HIV positive.'

I wipe away the fog and look at him. 'How'd I contract it?'

'Dirty needle? Sketchy piece of ass?' Dante smirks. 'Who knows? Don't worry. You . . . I mean, *he*, infected me as well with it the other night.'

I can't help but wince. In my own absence I've either done intravenous drugs with Dante or slept with him, neither of which I find very appealing. I step out of the shower and take the towels offered. He's also brought my clothes, washed and freshly pressed. As I put them on, he hovers too close for my liking. When I walk into the living room he follows too quickly.

'Navarette is gone now,' I say, turning to face him so fast that we almost butt heads. 'He's not me. I'm not him. You understand that, don't you?'

Dante looks disheartened. 'Yes, I know.'

His eyes moisten and his bottom lip quivers. He becomes fidgety, kneading fingers, unsure how to deal with the emotions that are welling up inside him. I didn't think it possible, but I start to feel a little bit sorry for him.

'What was he to you anyway?' I ask.

'A good friend.'

He lets out a shuddering breath. What I do is a generous

27

mix of kindness and cruelty most of the time. I can only imagine how hard it is to get over the loss of someone when just enough of what they used to be still exists in such a way as to be considered living. With little left to say, I check my Liaison to make sure the correct payment has been deposited into my account.

'Satisfied?' Dante asks.

'Very,' I reply, looking at the amount.

'Good. I'll be contacting your firm about future bookings.'

'Wonderful. I guess I'll be seeing you again soon.'

I turn to leave, but stumble with my first step. Exhaustion ambushes me and I suddenly feel a swirl of drowsiness. How long I've gone without rest is unknown, but it's obvious I need sleep and plenty of it. I think about asking Dante for an espresso or energy drink or maybe a couple grams of coke if there is any lying around, but I don't want to stay in the Emerald City for another goddamn minute.

'Wouldn't you like the vaccine before you go?' Dante asks.

I turn back. 'Yes, of course.'

Dante tosses me a medi-pack with an ampoule of the HIV vaccine and a disposable syringe. I go to put it in my pocket, but he shakes his head with a sly smile.

'You know better than that, Mr Rhodes. Do it now.'

I do know better than to try and leave with the vaccine in my possession, a cure that doesn't officially exist for the general public. I fumble with the packet as I try to open it, fatigue making everything more difficult than it has to be.

Dante steps closer and gently takes it from me, prepping the dose with steady fingers.

'I've called you a limo,' he says as he finds a vein in my forearm and injects me. 'Anything you want, within reason, is available. Just ask the driver.'

'I want sleep,' I grumble.

'Sleep when you're dead,' he says, and then looks back to the study Navarette haunts. 'Or maybe not.'

He reaches into his pocket and pulls out another clear packet with a half-dozen red and white pills inside. I already know it's the detox medication for the drug abuse Navarette indulges in. These meds have been given to me before, though I can't remember which withdrawal symptoms they combat. I slip them into my pocket.

'One pill every four hours until they're finished,' Dante says. 'You can see yourself out?'

'Not a problem.'

Dante gives a terse nod and walks back to the study, leaving me in the living room. He doesn't look back before entering, doesn't even shut the door. Through the doorway I see him sit before the flat-screen where Navarette appeared. The framed oval remains dark. I see Dante's head hang forward, his face in his hands. Soon I hear the sounds of him sobbing.

Swallowing one of the pills, I exit by the front door of the condo. In the hallway outside the security guard with the Vector is waiting, gun in hand. I can't help but notice the safety is off. It makes me nervous. That particular gun can fill me with an entire magazine of .45 rounds in a matter of seconds. The Emerald City is wary of outsiders, maybe a little too much, but enough of the rich have been murdered by the great unwashed in recent years to warrant concern. On the elevator ride down I lean against the doors for support, my sore head pressed to the cool metal. The guard looks like he wants to say something, but keeps silent. He walks me out of the Emerald City to the limo idling at the kerb.

'You take care of yourself now,' he says as the driver opens the door.

'Thanks, I will.'

The guard shakes his head and frowns. 'It didn't look like you were doing a very good job the other night, pal.'

I want to ask him what he's talking about, but I can barely keep my eyes open. I half step, half stumble into the air-conditioned limo and slump down onto the cool leather. The driver shuts the door as I help myself to a rare single malt Scotch from the minibar. The pour is generous. I raise the glass to the guard standing on the sidewalk, even though I know he can't see much of me through the tinted windows. As the limo pulls away the guard looks on, unimpressed.

'To the airport, sir?' the driver asks through the intercom.

'Yeah,' I say, and throw back the contents of my tumbler. 'But for the love of God take the long way round.'

Less than a minute later I'm fast asleep.

4

The whole flight back to NYC I'm wide awake, much to my annoyance. Maybe I'm overtired, or maybe it's an effect of the detox medication. My body is out of whack, doesn't know if it's coming or going. Every time I start to fall asleep, my Ouija makes that odd click and some awful thought occurs, jarring me awake. What I scc in my head is appalling, but seconds later I can't remember what it was. There's no way to retain the information, almost as if it isn't mine to keep. I figure it has something to do with the change in air pressure, or maybe another side effect of the detox pill, except the first time it happened I was neither on a plane nor medicated. That bothers me. I sit in first class waiting anxiously for the flight to be over, being short and dismissive with the stewardesses when they ask if there is anything they can do to improve my flight experience. My thoughts race. it seems all I have is time to think. A sense of guilt seeps into me, though there is no basis for it. I feel like a total shit. I feel like I have to remind myself why it is I do what I do.

You see, I'm not what you'd call a skilled man. No trades or talents. I can't act, don't play an instrument. Singing a single note in tune is a personal challenge. I've got two left feet on a good day. Hell, my work ethic in general leaves a lot to be desired. What I do possess is the looks and little else. It's always been this way. There wasn't much for me growing up. My parents, good people, worked tirelessly at low-wage jobs so me and my sisters could keep pace with our peers, just enough to dodge the label of *poor*. Even when I was young I knew the family was living cheque to cheque, sometimes day to day. The fights I heard through the walls, always money, always too little of it. The constant phone calls and piles of mail, new credit card offers alongside letters from collection agencies running out of patience. First notices, second notices, final notices. Mom and Dad hid it from the kids as best they could, but they couldn't plug every hole in that crumbling dam.

There were times when it was more obvious. Conversations overheard, Dad asking friends for loans, Mom requesting emergency funds from family. Once in a while my sisters or I would answer the phone and get an earful from whoever was owed, threats being thrown around that we were too young to understand. None of us answered the front door much when the doorbell rang. We would stay quiet until the shadowed figures behind the frosted glass moved away. Sometimes our electricity or phone would be cut for a while. Mom walked out on us a few times, unable to cope, only to return later laden with guilt. Dad increased his drinking. There were times my parents didn't talk to each other for days, sometimes weeks after a bad blowout.

Somewhere in those formative years I made a firm decision not to live that way. I craved security, the kind that only fat bank accounts could afford. Instability was unbearable. The anxiety of my folks not knowing where next month's rent was coming from affected everybody. Living one bounced cheque away from the poverty line was always on our minds, driving wedges between us when we needed each other most. The absence of money somehow managed to trump all other aspects of our lives. Everything else we had, we had to spare: love, laughs, a certain liberty around the dinner table. My parents entertained every far-fetched dream their kids ever had, told me I would be someone important one day, told me to follow my gut and walk my path wherever it led. I believed them, wholeheartedly.

I did my damnedest to come out on top, played every card I could. People said study hard. I hit the books. Guidance counsellor told me to go to university. I applied to the best. Eventually I graduated with a Bachelor of Fuck-All and tallied up a shitload of school debt for my troubles as I entered a job market that was already saturated with degrees and diplomas, but lacking any real opportunities. I ended up taking whatever I could with the rest of the over-educated suckers. We, the post-secondary mass-produced, bartenders with bachelors, hostesses with honours, managers with masters, all of us employed in a tenth of the capacity we were good for doing jobs we never expected.

That's a bitter pill to swallow, especially when everything you were working toward was designed to ensure that you wouldn't end up where you eventually did. Sure, tell me I'm bitching about my First World problems, except too much of the West ain't looking like First World anything any more. We're more like Second World now, reminiscent of Cold War Russia, a military superpower with a miserable middle-class population facing few legitimate ladders they can climb and getting more desperate by the day.

So what do you do if you don't want that desperation in your life? You acquire an understanding, a moral flexibility to do something lucrative off the books, off the radar, and often in bad taste. You find that double-edged sword which doesn't scare you like it scares other people, and throw yourself on it. Husking and I found each other, one part destiny and one part design. We go hand in hand. You want to be someone rich and special in life? Well, for periods of up to three days at a time, I'm some of the wealthiest, most high-profile people who ever lived. There's an awful lot profit to be made in this business. I do what I do for the money, plain and simple.

Smooth touchdown at JFK International and I'm feeling better about myself. I apologize to the stewardesses for being a consummate dickhead and take a double espresso to go. Outside the airport I hail a cab back to the East Village and boot up my favourite eighties playlist. I'm listening to Hall & Oates's 'Out of Touch' when Ryoko calls. I love the timing. Feels like a little touch of fate.

'Hi, beautiful,' I say.

'Hi, handsome,' she replies, but it lacks warmth. 'Where you at?'

That fateful feeling takes on a darker tone. She doesn't sound like herself and I wonder quickly if it actually is Ryoko or if it's one of her clients breaking the rules by going through the contacts on her Liaison. I throw out our little codeword to make sure.

'Just on my way home from the airport, sugarplum.'

'Fancy meeting me for a drink, cheesecake?'

It's her. I breathe a sigh of relief and throw back the rest of my espresso to give me enough energy for a round or two.

'Love to. Where're you thinking?'

'How about Harbinger's in half an hour?'

'Sounds good. See you there.'

She hangs up, leaving me to wonder what's got her panties in a twist. Then I can't stop thinking about her panties, the trademark lacy pink ones that I love tearing away from her fantastic ass. The thought electrifies me, despite my exhaustion. I wonder if she'll take me for a quickie in the bar bathroom when we meet.

When I get to Harbinger's it becomes obvious it won't happen. I find Ryoko in a private booth nursing a glass of Chardonnay. She looks dark around the eyes and the muscles in her gorgeous face seem slack and tired. Otherwise, she's stunning, her striking half-Swedish, half-Japanese features never failing to turn heads. There's good reason why she falls under the *exotic* category.

'Hi, you,' I say as I plunk down beside her.

'Hi, you.'

I kiss her gently on the nose as she nuzzles up to me, resting her head on my shoulder. A beefy, balding waiter comes and I order a gin and tonic.

'I tried calling you the other day,' Ryoko says.

'I was in Vegas.'

'Working?'

'Yeah, you?'

She shakes her head. 'I haven't worked in a few days now, not since I got back from London. I think I need a little time off to be honest.'

'I was thinking the same thing.'

'Yeah, well, the boss is going to be crawling up your ass about more gigs. Demand is up again. Baxter has been calling me non-stop. I'll probably have to go back soon.'

My gin and tonic arrives and I take a long drink. It's not like Ryoko to turn down gigs, but the fact she's willing to makes me want to do the same. I need a timeout, a breather. Everything lately has seemed like some sort of masochistic marathon. Ryoko chews her bottom lip in a way that looks like she's trying to be cute. What it means is anything but.

'What happened?' I say.

'Fuck it. Forget about it.'

I reach over and lay my hand on hers. 'Ry, what is it?'

We're not supposed to talk about work. She takes a mouthful of wine, swishes it around, swallows and orders another one with a hand gesture as the waiter passes. Then she turns and looks me straight in the eye. Hers are surprisingly cold, disconnected in that way we have to be sometimes.

'The gig in London,' she says. 'The client used me to go slumming . . .'

I shrug. We've both been there before. Ryoko continues to chew her lip, hard. I worry she might make it bleed if she keeps it up. I'm about to tell her to stop when I realize she might be doing it on purpose. Damage decreases value. Cuts and marks, even slight and temporary, instantly make Husks less marketable. We can be sidelined for such. If she wants time off, this is one way to go about it.

'Before I got out of the city,' she continues, 'some kid managed to locate me. He must have been fifteen or sixteen. He just appears out of nowhere and starts professing his undying love for me. Without a doubt my client popped his cherry and broke his little heart.'

The new glass of white wine arrives and Ryoko takes to it eagerly, polishing off half. Her tolerance is shit, and she knows it, but she has this look on her face like no amount of booze is going to get her drunk this evening.

'Client must have done a number on him, because the poor boy didn't want to go on living without me.'

'Seriously?'

'Yeah.' The rest of the wine filters through Ryoko's clenched teeth. 'Kid had the cuts on his wrists to prove it.'

Her words leave a bad taste in my mouth. I gulp down most of my gin and tonic, thinking about similar situations I've had over the years. In the silence our attention drifts to a fifty-inch flat-screen behind the bar where a news anchor informs us that a young Manhattan woman has been reported missing. She's identified as Tiffany Burrows, age twenty. The photograph that takes over the screen is of a blue-eyed blonde bombshell with high cheekbones and a foolish smile. My gut tells me the broad comes from money. I immediately think kidnapping, a crime that has been happening in the US with increasing regularity. A ransom demand will turn up in a day or so, keeping to the standard set decades ago by lower-class criminals in South America. Kidnap rich kids, mail their wealthy parents a finger or an ear plus an amount to be paid for their safe return, and then wait to see whether they do the drop or send a SWAT team. The following report says two men have been found beaten to death in an alley in Hell's Kitchen. Police suspect they are the victims of a robbery gone wrong, yet another casualty of the rotting Big Apple.

When news of Occupy Central Park finally airs, the anchor downplays it almost immediately. The sarcasm in her voice can't be ignored as she reiterates the fact that the movement has no clear demands, much like the original Occupy Wall Street movement before it. The footage shown of dishevelled men and women rallied together bitterly voicing their anger couldn't be more biased. Reporters mockingly question occupiers before holding microphones up to their dirty, unshaven faces for answers. According to the anchor the number of protesters in the park is only in the hundreds, but everyone already knows it is well into the thousands.

'Damn,' Ryoko sighs. 'I can't get the thought of that poor kid out of my head.'

'Stop it,' I say, slinging my arm around her. 'Forget about it. It wasn't you. There's nothing you can do.'

'I know, I know. How was your Vegas gig?'

'Fine, I guess. A new client took me on a two-day binge of debauchery in Sin City.'

'When in Rome,' she chuckles. 'You look like shit by the way.'

'I feel like shit. Been having these strange flashbacks,

but I can never remember much, like my brain changes channels for a second when I'm not paying attention, and when I turn to look it's already switched back over.'

'It's probably nothing,' Ryoko says, but she can't hide her concern.

'Gotta go into the office tomorrow and see Baxter and Tweek anyway,' I say, running my fingers behind my ear, touching the Ouija under my skin. 'I'll get checked out, have some diagnostics run.'

'What you need is some rest and relaxation, sweetheart.'

'No kidding. Maybe I can get a week off, call in a favour and farm out a gig or two to Phincas or Clive or someone.'

'Clive?' Ryoko says with a frown, and then puts a hand to her mouth. 'Oh my God, Rhodes, you don't know, do you?'

'Know what?'

'Clive's . . . been arrested.'

'What? When? Where?'

'It happened a few days ago in Paris. I found out through Nikki. He beat some woman to death outside a café after she attacked him.'

'Christ,' I groan, feeling winded. 'Wait, was it him?'

'Yeah, it was *him*. He was off the clock. Unexpectedly ran into someone his client screwed over, just like I did, except this woman had claws apparently. She threw scalding coffee in his face.'

Ryoko and I stare at each other for a long time. Clive is a good friend of ours, one of the sweetest, nicest guys we know. Picturing him killing someone is next to impossible. I want to ask how bad the burns are, how much damage was inflicted. I know what Ryoko is going to say long before she says it.

'Clive's finished,' Ryoko says finally. 'Even if he gets sprung from jail, he's –'

There is a yell and a crash from the back of the bar, followed by the sounds of a scuffle. I lean out of the booth and see the waiter wrestling with an Asian man near the front door. Broken plates and utensils are scattered over the floor. It doesn't take me long to figure what's going on. Yet another customer trying to dine and dash. It's happening more and more all over Manhattan, hungry people with no way to pay. A few punches are thrown before the waiter drags the man to the floor by his necktie.

'I got no money,' the man yells. 'You can't draw blood from a stone!'

The waiter grabs a steak knife from the floor. 'Yeah, but I can draw blood from your thieving ass –'

In the blink of an eye, the Asian man flips himself off the floor and delivers a swift roundhouse kick to the waiter's head, sending him sprawling into three other men sitting at a table nearby. I'm getting up to offer assistance, not sure whether to help the waiter or the customer, when Ryoko grabs my arm and pulls me back down. She shakes her head, looking between the scratch on my cheek and the waiter's face that is now bloody.

'Gotta stay beautiful, babe.'

The Asian man shoulders his way through the front doors of Harbinger's and dissolves into the crowd on the street outside. The waiter gets up off the floor and brushes himself off, shaking his head, muttering profanities. Within a minute he comes to our table, blood smeared on his lips and chin, acting as if nothing has happened as he analyses my empty glass.

'Care for another, sir?'

5

When I return to my apartment in the East Village I find Craig flopped on the sofa, immersed in a first-person shooter game on the new HG. I down another couple detox pills and barely say two words to him before collapsing in my room for a solid twelve hours. Sleep is a degree away from death for the most part, brain shutting off, breath slow and shallow, body so still I could be a sculpture tucked beneath the sheets. But deep within that slumber something activates. As I lie in the dark, images float behind my eyelids, each lingering only for a moment. There are a few snippets I can commit to memory. A red light glows atop an operational device. Hands entangled in hair. A mouth opening wide in a gasp of pleasure or scream of pain, I can't tell.

When I finally awake, dawn is breaking outside my window. Soft yellow light licks the treetops of Tompkins Square Park and reveals the silhouettes of two hovering NYPD drones that have been using the cover of night to spy on the city. Naked, I sit on the edge of my bed and watch the sunrise until it hurts my eyes. My optic nerves burn afterwards, pain attributed to what festers inside my head, I think, not the light. Another detox pill goes down to combat the fallout of my earlier substance abuse, but that rotten feeling hasn't left. It's like an emotional tumour, malignancy growing in mind and spirit. Maybe I'm suffering some malady of the soul. Maybe this is the beginning of madness.

The drones move off in the direction of 14th Street before anyone can take potshots at them. I check my Liaison for fresh frequencies, turn on the old radio receiver by my windowsill, and dial into the new digits that have been released to the underground. Pirate radio has made a hell of a comeback, harder to shut down than websites. These illegal broadcasts are the only way you can get any real, unfiltered news any more. Mainstream media is so censored, you might not even know about shit hitting the fan at the end of your own street. The conglomerate–political machine would prefer it if everyone didn't feel the weight of the world's increasing problems.

As I do my stretching exercises, the broadcast reports that the old Ebola virus has resurfaced and is making the rounds in India and Pakistan. An avian flu epidemic ravages Asia, rumoured to have also shown up sporadically on the California coast. Treatment centres are opening, trying to combat the spread by isolating the infected. The vaccines for both viruses exist, this much I know, but if governments confirmed their existence they'd have one less form of population control. The Allies' conventional wars in the Middle East aren't going well either apparently. What else is new?

By the time I've completed my rigorous routine of crunches, push-ups, and dumbbell reps, the broadcast has turned its attention to America. New food shortages along the eastern seaboard have begun. Independent research has concluded that yet another FDA-approved food additive is cancer-causing. Occupy Central Park has grown too, estimates of over 20,000 in attendance now. The mayor of New York is growing anxious, pressured by special-interest groups to remove the protesters by force. Authorities are not only becoming concerned over the increasing size of OCP, but also of a collective within the movement that call themselves 'Integris', a militant faction that in the past has been accused of various crimes and provocations.

As political rhetoric takes over the airwaves I step to the punching bag hanging in the corner of my room and work on my Muay Thai. Most Husks partake in mixed-martial-arts training, perfect for maintaining peak form. Finding time for the gym has been impossible lately, but I cycle through punch-and-kick combinations until I'm satisfied that my skills are still sharp. Drenched in sweat, I turn off the radio and hit the mist. Under the fine lukewarm spray, I can't help but wish for the proper hot shower I enjoyed back in Las Vegas. I think about Navarette and Dante. I think about what the guard said to me outside the Emerald City. For a few seconds my mind isn't only mine.

Proud of yourself?

'Shut the fuck up,' I mutter.

Hmmm, fuck-up . . . appropriate.

I dry off slowly, taking note of the pains that still linger within. The detox pills are doing their magic, but my Ouija is still bothering me. It makes another click as I'm taking a leak and for a second the cerulean blue in the low-flush toilet bowl becomes a watery human eye, wide and frightened. I make a guttural noise, something primal and scared. By the time my piss splatters the floor the image is gone and I'm already beginning to forget it. In the bathroom mirror I look myself over and apply ointments to sore muscles, salves to the scratches, wondering if Navarette dropped any acid or peyote during his rental. Slipping on a tracksuit and sneakers, I take a mouthful of multi-vitamins and head for the front door. Craig is asleep on the sofa; video game paused on the HG. On the coffee table lies his firearm case, open to reveal his Glock .45 nestled in foam padding next to three loaded magazines. His gun-cleaning stuff is scattered around it. Everyone is getting more concerned with their personal safety these days. As I unlock the front door, Craig stirs and strains open his eyes, giving me a dopey smile that turns into a yawn.

'You off to work, man?'

'Yeah,' I nod. 'Off to work.'

Craig stretches, gives me a sleepy nod in return. 'Hey, look, if you ever want another job you only need to ask me, okay? Always on the lookout for bartenders . . .'

'Thanks, but I'm cool.'

'Just putting it out there,' he says, nuzzling into the cushions and closing his eyes. 'Stay safe. Don't get into any trouble.'

'I'll try.'

In the early-morning light I make my way back to Harbinger's for breakfast. The joint is almost empty as I enter. The lights flicker on and off for a minute and I brace for a blackout that doesn't end up happening. The same beefy waiter leads me to a table in the corner. His eyes are tired, face bruised from the fight the day before. I figure he's been on shift non-stop, since more businesses are running twenty-four/seven now. There is no recognition in his eyes as I ask him for a mimosa. When I order a deluxe breakfast, he proceeds to tell me that the kitchen is out of real eggs and bacon due to food shortages, but products from Modern Harvest are available. The thought of that company's 'food' makes my stomach turn, although I've had it plenty of times before. I order oatmeal instead and eat it slow, killing time until I'm sure Baxter and Tweek will be in the office. Above my table is a flat-screen that I can't see. I hear a male anchor relaying the city's official news in a deep, confident voice. After reporting on a recent spate of violent cab robberies, he reveals a 22-year-old New York native named Dennis Delane has been reported missing. Police are suspecting foul play. The name sounds strangely familiar. I slide out of my seat and crane my neck to see if there is a pic or footage of the guy, but the anchor has already moved on to the topic of sports. I notice Occupy Central Park never comes up.

A homeless Hispanic man comes into the restaurant, looking like he hasn't eaten in days, asking if he can have a glass of water. The waiter abruptly tells him water ain't free and to fuck off. I've seen this man before in the neighbourhood and remember when he had a home and a job to go to, which wasn't that long ago. The waiter isn't impressed when I take out my wallet and give the man a fifty, telling him he can have a meal on my dime and keep the change. I stay in my corner until the man gets his eats and is halfway through finishing them under the waiter's watchful eye. He looks up from his meal only once to offer me a weak smile.

A cab takes me uptown to the unlisted offices of Solace Strategies Inc. on 34th Street. There is no outside way to know where the company is, just a reinforced metal door with a keypad and a retinal scanner tucked in an alcove. I punch numbers and run my eye past the system before entering and taking the elevator up. On the top floor the doors open on a large office space decorated with polished black and streamlined silver. All furniture is made of either reinforced glass or dark brown leather. Solace Strategies masquerades as a high-end business consultation firm, but in reality they're pimps, negotiating Husks for the decadent dead with the deepest pockets.

Nikki, the receptionist, tucks her blonde hair behind her ears and greets me with little more than a nod. She looks like she's been crying, but I don't ask. We haven't had much to say to each other since we hooked up for a fortnight last year, a hot little fling that got awkward when we broke it off. Some days things feel fine between us, cordial and cool, other days are strained. Something's up for sure, but I decide to leave bad enough alone. Tweek isn't in yet, so I walk straight past his darkened control room and head for Baxter's office. Her door is wide open. I waltz right in.

'Boss,' I say.

Ms Baxter doesn't say anything for a moment, doesn't even look up. She's busy typing furiously on a tablet propped on her desk, expensively manicured fingernails clacking off the screen. Her expression is all business, make-up badly covering the bags under her eyes. I know better than to bug the boss further, so I sit and wait. The woman only thinks about two things: money and how to get more of it. Rumour going around was that Baxter herself used to Husk, back when things first got started. Nice enough lady when she wants to be, quite attractive for a cougar too, but she's got too many miles on her to rent out now.

'Rhodes, my boy,' she says finally, pulling her thin fingers away from the tablet screen. 'How did the Vegas gig go?'

'Fine, as far as I know.'

Baxter nods and smiles. 'It went very well. Mr Navarette has already booked you again for next week.'

'Great,' I reply, feigning enthusiasm.

She's onto me straight away, eyes drawing to slits as she inspects the scratch on my cheek. I should know better than to try and fake out the boss.

'How are things otherwise?'

'Heard about Clive,' I say.

'Yeah? Where'd you hear it from?'

'Ryoko. Saw her yesterday.'

'Clive hasn't exactly been a secret around here.'

Baxter sighs, gets up and walks to the window, hands behind her back, fingers fiddling with her diamond rings and gold bracelets. She looks out over 34th Street and frowns at the morning crowds running their rat race on the sidewalks below.

'Did you hear about Miller too?' she asks.

'No, what happened to Miller?'

'What I tell you doesn't leave this office, understand?' She presses her forehead against the glass, closes her eyes. 'Miller's dead.'

'*What?*'

'I'm sorry.'

'How did it happen?' I cry. '*When* did it happen?'

'Just before you left for Vegas,' Baxter grumbles. 'He died right here in Manhattan. A client tried to keep him going past three days, wouldn't come in for download, went psychotic and cracked Miller's skull against the floor of a goddamn strip club. Miller was DOA by the time the ambulance got him to hospital. This information is strictly confidential, Rhodes, so I've been informing staff personally of the situation as they come in and as needed.'

I can't find the air to speak. If I wasn't already sitting, I'd have fallen to my knees. Disbelief and despair twist around each other, forming knots in my throat and chest. My friend, my mentor, is dead. Miller was our alpha, our veteran. Everyone loved the guy. He worked at Solace Strategies long before I started; part of the payroll since the company's inception. He and Tweek, they practically wrote the operative's playbook, braided the ropes together. All other outfits in the game are riding the coat-tails of what he helped start. Unconfirmed, but we all thought Miller was the longest-running Husk in the business. The hands laced in my lap begin to tremble as tears threaten to make an appearance. My shock turns to anger just before the realization kicks in and floods me with sudden guilt.

'Oh God,' I croak. 'Miller died covering my gig, didn't he?'

Baxter turns away, avoiding eye contact. 'Don't do this to yourself. Miller was a grown man and made his own decisions. What happened was an accident.'

'Who was the client?' I demand.

Baxter glances over her shoulder at me, but doesn't answer. She can't. If she did, and it got out, it could easily be the end of her and anyone she tells for that matter. Our business has strict rules, internal and external. Rules that keep left hands from knowing what right hands are doing, and vice versa. We haven't had a lawsuit yet.

'Fine,' I snarl. 'As long as the son of a bitch kicked the bucket as well . . .'

She doesn't answer that either, which I suspect means the client may have survived, though that's not possible as far as I know. Clients and Husks share death if they try to co-exist past the seventy-two-hour mark. That's why it's so rare for that rule to be broken. Whoever was renting must have somehow managed to plug in and get out before Miller flat-lined.

'This is bullshit,' I mutter. 'We've never lost one of our own before.'

'It was bound to happen sooner or later. Inherent risks of the business. We've been incredibly lucky up until now, but a track record like ours can't last for ever. Both you and I know it. Fact is we're two employees down at the moment, and we need to pick up the slack around here.'

'What is that supposed to mean?'

'It means the demand for you just increased for the next little while, Rhodes.'

I shake my head, look down at my body. 'Boss, I'm in shit state right now, haven't had time to properly recover and heal from my last few sessions. Customers aren't going to like the condition of the goods.'

'It doesn't matter. More and more clients are willing to forego perfection and still pay top dollar. They'd rather not go without.'

'You're pushing me too hard, Baxter.'

'Rhodes, please, I need you to give me a hundred and ten per cent right now.'

'Fine,' I say with a sigh. 'Who do you have lined up?'

'Mr Winslade called for you again.'

'Oh no.'

Baxter looks at the schedule on her tablet. 'Tomorrow you're booked for another twenty-four hours with him. Your session with Mr Ichida is a go for the following day, but when you're done with him I need you to fly overseas and accommodate one of Clive's regulars in London for a couple days. His name is Mr Shaw, and we absolutely cannot lose his patronage.'

I have no idea who Mr Shaw is, but the thought of Winslade and Ichida makes my skin crawl. It's way too soon to take on more sessions so close together. Those teeth marks and scratches still haven't gone away. Neither has that rotten feeling that plagues me. Immediately, I'm back to wanting a way out.

'Boss, listen, I really think I should take a break.'

Baxter shakes her head vehemently, not having any of it. She picks up her tablet and thrusts the screen at me, showing the generous amounts I'll be making for the three gigs, despite Solace Strategies' fifty per cent cut. No Husk in his right mind would refuse the offer. I, however, haven't felt in my right mind very much lately.

'Look, if I had a little time off, it would be to everyone's benefit.'

'Deal with it, Rhodes. You're booked in Manhattan, and then you're on a jet to London. I'll give you a full day to yourself between here and there to recuperate.'

'Jesus,' I spit. 'One goddamn day?'

'Best I can do.'

I stand up, unimpressed. 'This ain't smart, boss. I'm not indestructible. If we're not careful you could find your-self down by three employees.'

Baxter nods, face stoic, but eyes softer. 'Your objection has been noted.'

We share a look that admits we both know the difficult position we're in. I scratch behind my ear, feeling the hard lump of Ouija insisting that I tell Baxter about its recent malfunctions. Before I can, she waves me away with both hands.

'I'll send details to your Liaison, Rhodes. Let me know how it goes.'

'Sure,' I say, already backing out the door.

As I leave Baxter's office I see the handsome black devil himself, Phineas, walking down the hall toward me. He wears a dark-blue suit and snakeskin shoes, dripping with style and flavour. I owe a lot to this man. He's the one who introduced me to the business, showed me the ropes. Phineas raises a hand, but doesn't grin like usual.

'Heya, mate,' he says, and embraces me.

I hold him tight. 'Phinn, how are things?'

'Not good at all, son. Some real bad shit has gone down in the last few days.'

'I heard. Baxter just told me.'

Phineas shakes his head. 'Fuck, man, Clive was just a kid.'

'Yeah, and Miller was old guard. Jesus, our company has the best rep in the biz. How the hell did we lose two Husks in the same week?'

'There's a first for everything,' he grumbles. 'How are you handling it?'

I give him a dazed look. 'Don't think it's even hit me yet.'

Phineas's green eyes lock with mine, searching to see if my emotions match his. He's royally pissed, that much I can tell, though it's the first real anger of any kind I've ever seen on him. The ire looks incorrect on his face. Phineas has never been anything but calm and collected for all the years I've known him. The man bleeds cool. That smooth English accent is easy on the ears, melts the elastic in women's underwear.

'We've got to start being more careful,' he says, drawing close and lowering his voice. 'Before you or I end up a casualty.'

'You're preaching to the choir, man.'

'Are you in town awhile?'

'Just a couple days. Two twenty-four-hour clients

back-to-back in Manhattan, then I'm covering one of Clive's regulars in London for forty-eight hours.'

I examine the impressive tailor-made suit he's wearing and estimate it cost close to five figures. I sneak a glance at the reptile footwear, thinking about how much I'd like to have this particular outfit, thinking about how much I'm still a slave to this kind of materialistic shit.

'Nice threads man . . . you on your way to a gig?'

'Coming back from one,' he whispers, making sure no one is in earshot. 'I lucked out with a new client. The lady who rented me said she wanted to see what life was like in a man's shoes, bought a whole new wardrobe. She went easy on the goods, let me keep the suit as a bonus too.'

'You lucky bastard. I had a new client too the other day, but the guy took me for a *ride*, man.'

'Yeah? How bad?'

'Got infected for starters . . .' I murmur.

'The clap?'

'HIV.'

Phineas chuckles and rolls his eyes. 'You can tell me all about it in London.'

'London?'

'Yeah, I'm over there for a gig the same time you are. Let's make sure we meet up for a pint or three when we're wrapped.'

Phineas smiles, pearly teeth shining, eyes squinting above high cheekbones. He raps my shoulder and starts past me in the direction of Baxter's office. I put a hand on his chest to stop him.

'Hey, while we got a minute, have you been having any problems at all lately?'

'Problems?'

Phineas looks at me cockeyed. With a grimace, I turn my head to the side and point behind my ear. Phineas's eyes widen when he realizes.

'With the Ouija?' he whispers.

'Yeah.'

'No, nothing. Everything's running like clockwork, mate.'

Up ahead I can see the lights have been turned on in Tweek's control room. I start heading that way and Phineas understands everything at once. If our problems are internal, they're worth the worry. His handsome features fold into a look of concern as we part ways.

6

'What's the problem?'

'I think my Ouija is acting up,' I say, and tap the thing under my skin.

Tweek frowns. 'Don't do that.'

'Do what?'

'That,' he says, mimicking my tapping. 'They're sensitive.'

'They better not be. You have any idea what my clients have been putting me through on a regular basis?'

Tweek nods. He knows better than most. The customized gel layer he personally designed to coat the Ouija with cushions a lot of impact, but the man is forever nervous about the resiliency of the technology he helped create. I sit down across from him and lean forward, tilting my head so he can have a gander behind my ear. Tweek looks, but doesn't touch. His chubby fingers fiddle nervously with the cuffs of his lab coat instead.

'What's it been doing?'

'Clicking.'

'Clicking?'

'Yeah, every once in a while I hear, or maybe feel, this click. Each time it happens I get hit with some strange kind of flashback.'

'What do you see?'

I shake my head. 'I can't remember.'

Tweek turns to one of his tablets and brings up several complex schematics of the Ouija, bright blue images with white lettering denoting aspects of them. In the top corner of the screen I see my name: Keith C. Rhodes.

'How long has it been giving you trouble?' he asks, opening a drawer and retrieving a device that looks a little like my Liaison, but larger and more robust.

'About a month now,' I reply. 'It's only started to worry me in the last week or so. All these back-to-back clients are wearing me thin. Maybe the Ouija took a bad knock or something in session.'

Tweek pulls a data cord out of the device and connects a proboscis to the end of it before passing it over to me. I slowly stab the needle into my head until the tip crunches into the Ouija. Tweek stares at his tablet screen, scrutinizing the stats that appear. Behind him, under a swing-arm magnifying glass, I notice another dismantled Ouija lying in several pieces among the technological clutter on his desk. I point over his shoulder at the tiny machinery.

'Been working on a new one, Tweek?'

Tweek turns to look at it, frowning again. 'No, that's Miller's.'

'Oh.'

'I had to sneak into the city morgue and pull it out of his head before they performed an autopsy. They're so busy down there and his melon was so messed up, I doubt anyone will notice . . .'

He trails off, removes his thick-rimmed glasses off, rubs his eyes. Tweek won't shed tears. I know him well enough to know that. He and Miller were the quintessential odd couple, always bickering, forever picking on each other. The adorable little nerd, he'll mourn the old Adonis in his own way, but not in front of me.

'Sorry about Miller,' I say.

'Yeah,' he snorts. 'I am too.'

'It was bound to happen some time,' I say, regurgitating Baxter's words.

'It never would have happened if I'd ever been able to figure out and implement a fucking failsafe for you guys.'

I nod. 'I guess we should all carry the Ejector pills on us or something –'

'What the hell good would they do?' Tweek snaps, giving me an angry look. 'When would you be in any position to take them when needed?'

'Sorry,' I say. 'I was just thinking out loud.'

Tweek's lip wobbles. 'My apologies . . . I didn't mean to bark at you. It's just that I'm the one who is supposed to be protecting you guys . . .'

Tweek's about to go on a tangent, I can tell. It's important that I get him refocused and quick. I need him working on my current problem, the reception of indistinct horrors in my head that I want to put a stop to.

'It's not your fault, Tweek. There's nothing you could have done. We accept the risks when we sign on, so don't go beating yourself up about it.'

More Baxter in my mouth and I hate the taste. It seems to appease Tweek enough to get cracking though. With a deep sigh he turns his attention back to his gear. Fingers dance over the tablet, implementing codes, executing commands. His eyes flick between the screen and the handheld device as they communicate with a series of chirping noises. An HG unit activates on his desk and projects an image of my Ouija, sections of it highlighted and dissected as it rotates slowly. Beside the HG I notice a device I've never seen before, something in a cobalt-blue shell with small tools and circuitry scattered around it.

'Running a full diagnostic now,' Tweek says. 'It'll take a few minutes. Hand over your Liaison while you're waiting. I want to make sure your software's running smoothly too.'

I unlock the Liaison and surrender it. Tweek checks it out, running scans and tests on the sequencer program. Nothing in his facial expressions suggests there is any problem. We don't speak for several minutes. The growing discomfort in the room is evident. I decide to break the silence with a whispered inquiry.

'Do you know who Miller's last client was?'

Tweek shoots me a stern look. Solace Strategies vehemently discourages employees from talking about work outside of what is absolutely necessary. Gossip regarding clients and sessions is strictly forbidden. Every pimp comes down hard on their hookers for disobedience, and we're no different. I don't care though. I return Tweek's stern look, wanting a reply. Enough seconds go by for me to realize that he doesn't know the answer to the question. Solace keeps the company compartmentalized, protecting client confidentiality even more so.

'Horseshit,' I snarl. 'Poor Miller buys the farm, and the bastard renting him gets to live on.'

'That's not possible, Rhodes. You know that.'

'Whatever.'

'Who says it's living anyway?' Tweek says with a grim smile. 'The Post-Mortems certainly don't.'

Post-Mortems: our name for those that cheat death by digitally converting and uploading their consciousness. It's probably the world's biggest and best-kept secret, but Tweek will tell you that virtual living ain't all that shit hot. Tweek will tell you that those in the VR worlds, designed by the best computer programmers on the planet, aren't having the time of their lives. Get a few drinks in him and Tweek will tell you that some Post-Mortems can't handle more than six months on a hard drive before requesting permanent deletion.

Tweek will also tell you that the more time a Post-Mortem spends in virtual reality, the less recognizable they become. After a few years of living in a server system, a Post-Mortem can often seem more like a bot than a person if they don't get out and interact with the real world enough. With a Husk, they do whatever they have to do in order to feel alive again. My job is about conforming and complying with what is desired of me. Show up and shut up for down payment and download, that's a Husk's day in a nutshell. In the past I haven't asked too many questions. Lately, I've been more inclined to.

'What's it really like?' I ask.

'What is what like?'

'Being Post-Mortem.'

Tweek hooks his thumbs into the pockets of his lab coat and searches his head for an appropriate answer. Few of the living really know for sure, and Post-Mortems don't care to discuss it much. They see it as being part of another of their many exclusive clubs or societies, membership required for knowledge. Digitization of the human brain is a one-way trip, a conversion of consciousness following a decision that must be made before flat-lining. After the process is complete, it's not your real brain any more. It's a recursive real-time copy that allows you to keep thinking, keep conscious via computer support and algorithms designed to mimic your original self from a mass of collected data. The only way Post-Mortems are able to upload to the living is through the Ouija; the converter mechanism that allows them limited visitations in the flesh.

The Ouija is one of the reasons not just anyone can Husk. Biological and digital can't work together without the right grease. That grease costs more than your bachelor's degree in whatever the fuck you thought was a good idea at the time, and three to four hours of high-risk black-market brain surgery. Just like pimps don't pay for breast implants or chemical peels, Husks have to invest in their own tech, paying out of their own pocket to put themselves on the operating table. Survive the operation, and you can work off the debt afterwards. More than a few aspiring Husks have gone no further than under the knife.

'I've heard it's like video games,' Tweek says finally. 'Y'know when you grab a five-star title and you sit down to play it and it's frigging awesome and you can't stop playing for days on end because you're so immersed in it?'

I nod. 'Yeah.'

'Well, y'know how you inevitably get completely bored of that game, no matter how awesome you thought it once was? How you feel like some shitty zombie staring at the graphics after a while, everything about it eventually becoming lame and predictable?'

'Yeah.'

'Apparently, post-mortem life is exactly like that.'

From what I gathered here and there, I suspected as much. Existing past your shelf-life, it's not really real, no matter how well your worlds are generated. Post-Mortems don't have the luxury of getting up and walking away from the game when they tire of it. Not unless they get into bed with people like Baxter, invest in the intelligence of people like Tweek, and lease someone like me.

The tablet completes its tasks and chimes twice, a sound mimicked by the other device. The HG deactivates. Tweek looks over the results posted on the screens and nods with satisfaction.

'Diagnostic complete,' he says, holding out a hand for the proboscis. 'Everything looks fine on the tech side, Rhodes.'

'Shit,' I moan, unplugging myself. 'What the hell is going on?'

Tweek lays one hand on my shoulder and lifts my chin with the other. 'The simple answer is that you're exhausted, Rhodes. Sleep deprivation might be causing you to micro-nap, or the flashbacks could be hypnagogic in nature, hallucinations experienced in that no-man's land between falling asleep or waking up. With the Husking, you're also in and out of induced comatose-like states, regularly. The Migraine Coma effect could be part of it too.'

'But I haven't had any migraines,' I protest.

Tweek puts his toys away. 'Tell me, when was the last time you had a good night's sleep?'

'Last night.'

'Well, it's probably still not enough,' he says and shrugs. 'You could also be having psychedelic flashbacks from a previous client's chemical indulgences.'

I think of Navarette. 'Maybe.'

'You need to get some more rest, take better care of yourself.'

'Not frigging likely,' I say, closing my eyes and cracking my neck. 'I'm back on the job tomorrow, and the day after that, and then I'm being sent off to work in the UK for a few days.'

When I open my eyes Tweek is standing by his desk, face deflated as he stares down through the magnifier at all he has left of Miller. He takes a deep breath and shudders. It's only then that I notice traces of blood on the broken Ouija. When Tweek speaks his voice is hoarse, threatening to descend into a whisper.

'You need to be more careful.'

7

The little lab rat's advice nags me the whole cab ride home. He knows damn well there's no way to be more careful. I don't pick my clients, don't actually do any work. I'm just the latest model for rent, the first-class deluxe edition available for test drives. Drop the car off, leave the keys, address the damage after the ride. My work goes into the detailing. Put some spit and polish on the body, wax it up, and change the oil before I'm back out on the showroom floor. With all my bookings in recent weeks, adequate time to recover has become elusive. Tweek's right. If I don't find a way to be more careful . . .

You don't want to think about it.

Riding through the streets of Manhattan, I stare out of the window. Nothing memorable out there, just more of the island's inhabitants constantly on the go, scuttling from point A to B with heads down, crowding the bases of buildings with their bodies as they suck enough fume-laden oxygen to convince themselves they're in perpetual motion. None of them realize their lives are in limbo, a mass state of arrested development. At a red light I witness a nicely dressed woman take a hot dog from a vendor and bolt up the street without paying for it. The vendor gives chase until he tackles her to the ground.

They writhe on the sidewalk, shouts and shrieks rising. A crowd gathers around them while other pedestrians ransack the hot dog cart during the commotion. Even this kind of thing doesn't faze me these days. It makes me wonder if the meaning of life is simply the challenge of living.

I'm so lost in my thoughts when I walk through my front door I don't realize Craig is in the apartment, let alone talking to me.

'Huh? Sorry, what did you say?'

Craig is still lying in the same position on the sofa, playing his video game. There are bags under his eyes, but he looks the opposite of tired. Two energy drink cans lie crumpled on the coffee table. A busted bag of potato chips lies on his lap.

'I said I can't stop playing this damn game,' he says. 'The developers did such a great job on it.'

Makes me think of what Tweek said. I look around the apartment. Pizza boxes and takeaway containers litter the kitchen counter, beer bottles scattered among them. Dishes haven't been done. A series of gunshots and explosions erupt from the HG, causing Craig to whoop with excitement.

'Graphics are freakin' insane, man, so good that you'd think it was real life. This HG is the greatest thing ever.'

I glance at the game as I grab a beer from the fridge. Craig's right, the graphics are something else. It's nice to see my roommate immersed in something other than porno for once.

'Have you been to work at all?' I ask.

Craig crams a handful of chips into his mouth and shakes his head. 'Took a little time off, but I've got a bartending shift tonight at the Rochester.'

I drink the beer quickly as I watch Craig lead and kill some players with well-timed headshots through a sniper scope.

'Nice shooting, dead-eye.'

'The noobs are easy pickings,' Craig says with a chuckle. 'What are you up to tonight, dude?'

'No plans.'

'Well, grab that girlfriend of yours and come down to the bar.'

'Ryoko's not my girlfriend.'

Craig rolls his eyes. 'Whatever.'

'She's not.'

'If she's still dating you when you're Husking, I'd call that pretty serious. Women have dumped my ass for a lot fucking less.'

His comment annoys me, but only because he's right. God knows where my dick has been over the last few years. Christ knows who my tongue has licked. What Craig doesn't know is that Ryoko Husks too. I figured he would have put two and two together by now, but he's not always the sharpest tool in the shed. Jesus, what other kind of girl would ever have me?

'I'm hitting the hay for a while, dude,' I say, finishing my beer and waving a hand toward the kitchen. 'Do me a favour and clean this pigsty up a bit.'

'I'm on it,' he replies, but doesn't move.

'Oh, and one more thing, man . . . Please don't leave

your Glock lying out on the coffee table. Keep the fire-arms stowed away, okay?'

Craig grunts in agreement as he horrifically obliterates another player on the HG with a handheld prototype weapon I've seen before in the real world, an advance in science that has been misappropriated by the military. The thought of it makes me shiver.

I retreat to my room, the gun playing on my mind. My thoughts turn to Winslade and his stock in that particular weapons technology. My client, the gun, Tweek's advice, it all makes me want to go to bed and forget about things for a while. As I lie on my mattress and drift off, the gun invades my dreams, showing me over and over in horrible detail what it is capable of doing to a human body.

The gun isn't the only thing that sneaks into my sleep. There is blood too, flowing from a source unknown, running red and thick. It turns into ketchup, the kind I always wanted at the dinner table, in a squeezable bottle like the other kids got, not in the self-serve packets that my parents habitually stole by the handful from fast-food restaurants along with mustard, relish, sugar, salt and pepper. Cheap hot dogs on my plate again, wrapped in slices of stale white bread, surrounded by these condiments packaged in small rectangular white. Baked beans and Mac'n'cheese make an appearance, reminiscent of tough times long ago. I'm a kid, eating them by the bowlful, aware of how frequently they are being served for supper with money so tight.

My parents sit at the far ends of the dinner table, heads

down, refusing to speak to each other. My sisters are quiet opposite me. Closing one eye, I look at their refracted images through the pitcher of tap water between us, making adjustments, trying to get the distortion to put smiles on their faces that aren't there. I try to say words that will brighten the mood, but no one acknowledges anything that leaves my mouth. I know all too well why my younger sister looks so unhappy, but I'll never breathe a word to anyone about it. She picks at her food and I stretch my legs under the table, trying to touch my feet against hers, never connecting, never comforting. My toes touch something else, cool and alien. We hear grunts from somewhere below and freeze. I can feel a monster crawling under the table, brushing my shins, moving away from me and toward my sister. I watch in horror as a hulking shadow rises from the floor behind her chair and looms over her small body. None of my family sees it, their eyes all cast down, staring at their plates. My sister, however, crumples in her seat. I yell, trying to warn her, watching as my shrill voice splinters and cleaves the table between us. It collapses inward, pulling everyone around it into the centre like a drain to be sucked down. In the increasing vacuum, suffocating, wondering where I'll end up, I manage one deep breath and hold it for as long as possible.

Suddenly I'm breaking the surface of a new dream. I can breathe again, and find myself drifting through my college days. The days and nights are a blur as I absorb lectures and care too much about classes taught in the bowels of a concrete jungle, convinced the education will earn me some kind of job security, some kind of respectable future if I just stick with it. Sitting in my graduation robes, I'm surrounded by screens of rejection notices while my ear is pressed to a phone, listening to a message that says over and over again: 'We're very sorry.' The phone gets hijacked by credit and collection agencies, legitimate loan sharks. Outstanding debts growl through the receiver, grilling me for my late or failed or nonexistent payments. Fancy paper in a broken frame lies at my feet, a degree majoring in compliance with a minor in gullibility. Fear grips me, fear of ending up like my parents, one foot in the gutter and one foot kicking the dirt out of some shallow grave.

Miller stands in the dark corners of my dream, silent and still. I know it's him by his height and stance, though I can't see his face. We were similar growing up, both from homes that bordered on broken. Most conversations we shared were about our poor commonalities. Miller watches knowingly, breathing in the dead air I expel. I want him to intervene and end this anxious reliving of the past. He reaches toward me, threatening to step out of the shadows. Before he can his figure fades, collected by the dark, his presence required elsewhere.

I wake to gentle hands gliding over my abdominal muscles, suckling mouth enveloping my dick that is quickly becoming an erection. A soft, playful tongue licks every inch of it as fingernails dig into my skin, scratching the surface of me in long lines. The naked body that writhes against my legs is warm and smooth, supple breasts pressed to my thighs, hard stomach brushing against my shins. I know the familiarity of this erotic touch before I open my eyes.

'Baby,' I groan.

I clench my buttocks and feel her giggle against the base of my shaft as she presses wet lips against me. The sensation makes my back arch. Grogginess slips from me all at once and I want to fuck her in the worst way. My hands reach down and grip her hair, lifting her face up from my lap so I can look into her eyes. A click behind my ear is heard, or maybe just felt.

'Ry—'

Except it isn't Ryoko looking back at me. Glassy blue eyes between handfuls of blonde hair regard me blankly. I stifle a cry of shock as I scramble backwards, kicking the sheets off the bed.

'What's wrong?' Ryoko says, wiping her mouth as she rises.

I try to catch my breath, scanning her unblemished skin, her ultra-fit body, making sure it really is her. Another vision, another memory I can't hold on to slips away, despite the seeming importance of it. Ryoko, naked in the afternoon light except for a tight blue T-shirt hiked up over her breasts, recaptures my full attention.

'Bad dream,' I mutter, rubbing my eyes.

Ryoko crawls across the bed and slides on top of me, her dark hair falling over my face as she bites my bottom lip. Hard nipples brush against mine, sending a buzz coursing the length of my body.

'How'bout I give you a wet dream instead?'

'You are my wet dream.'

'That was the right answer,' Ryoko says, straddling me. She shifts her hips a little and I'm past her tightness, thrusting inside heavenly warmth, skin to skin, no contraception needed. Ryoko can't have kids, and we take full advantage of this fact. My moans are muffled against her breasts, but hers are loud and growing. She bucks on my lap with a series of submissive whimpers until I lift her off and flip her over. We don't last long. The force of my riding pushes her body down further and further until she is lying on her stomach. Stretched out on top, I grind her ass into the mattress. She squirms with pleasure as I lick her skin slick with perspiration. I entwine her hair in my fist and pull, lifting her head so I can whisper in her ear as I drive myself into her as far as I will go.

'I love you,' I pant. 'I fucking love you.'

'I know, I know,' she says between short, desperate breaths.

This is the only control I ever have over a woman who could otherwise own me if she wanted. We slip into a heavy rhythm until we come one after another. I collapse on top of her, sliding on the cool sweat from our bodies.

'Welcome back, baby,' she says.

I pull out and kiss her before rolling off. 'Not for long.'

'Another gig?'

'Gigs,' I say. 'Baxter roped me into two local sessions over the next couple days, and then I'm off to London to cover one of Clive's clients.'

'Pity.'

'We still got tonight.'

Ryoko glides her fingers over the bruises on my chest. 'That we do.'

We lay there for a minute until she makes the mistake of asking me if I'm all spent. I grab her by the wrists and lead her from the bed to the bathroom, where I throw her into a warm mist. Pressing her naked body up against the glass partition, I take her for another round and think about how much I simply want to stay with her and forget all the work lined up. For now she's mine and mine alone, the real thing, soft around the edges, but sharp enough to see through the bullshit of bad art and love songs. Our connection is on a level most don't register. I wish there was a simpler deal between us. I wish she would tell me she loves me too. Wish to God she was my girl, but Ryoko is nobody's girl really. She'll have me over and over again though and I guess that's good enough.

Back in my room I watch her pull on her panties and jeans. All I can think is how much I want to tug them off and throw her on the bed again.

'What time is your gig tomorrow?' Ryoko asks, zipping her fly.

'Scheduled for a noon start.'

I'm about to ask what her schedule is when I remember she wanted a hiatus. It's then that I realize that Ryoko hasn't been into Solace Strategies lately, hasn't heard about Miller. She seems so content right now. I don't know how to break it to her. Waiting for the right time seems pertinent, so I say nothing. Ryoko roots through my dresser and puts on an old CBGB T-shirt of mine, knowing how much I love the look of my clothes on her. Behind my dresser is a long crack in the wall that Ryoko inspects.

'Tell me again why you live here when you can afford better?'

'All part of my master plan,' I say. 'I can't make my nest egg by spending money on frivolous things.'

Ryoko smirks. 'Couldn't help notice the new HG out in your living room.'

'That's a gift from a client.'

She raises an eyebrow. 'Someone sure is happy with you.'

I don't say anything, not wanting to bring up the topic of clients. Ryoko wants to pry, I can tell by the look on her face, but Solace Strategies' discouragement is a constant nag. Besides, when it comes to Husks and maintaining intimate relationships, casual or serious, the less said the better.

'So, your roommate was leaving for work when I arrived,' Ryoko says, tipping her head toward the living room with a smile. 'Fancy cuddling up on the couch and watching a flick on that new toy of yours?'

'I thought you'd never ask.'

8

Later that night we hit the bar where Craig works. The Rochester is packed: cheap bar rail drinks and craft beer deals. Some of the best prices you can find in the city. There is an undeniable energy in the air, one Ryoko and I feel like static. How we earn our living puts a perspective, a spin, on the rest of existence. The East Village comes alive after dark, its inhabitants throwing caution to the wind at the end of their depressed days. It's almost vampiric, the way people rise with the setting sun, leaving their homes to prowl for some form of satisfaction: flesh, fantasy, or pharmaceutical. Celebration comes one night at a time, a reward for the day-to-day. As the Big Apple rots, it also ferments. Ryoko and I soak it up. We could go uptown, spend more money, but we don't. After you've done your fair share of Husking, you want to stay away from the wealthy as much as you can. It's a comfort being off the clock; out of sight, out of mind, out of range of the things that can haunt you if you're not careful. Down here, most of our clients would call it slumming. We call it living.

Ryoko is more affectionate than usual, though I wonder about her motives. She stands close, sneaking kisses when she thinks no one is looking. Over the din of the clientele I yell another order to Craig behind the bar. Within a minute he brings us two Brooklyn brews and two shots of Don Julio.

'To Miller,' Ryoko says, raising her shot glass. 'Taken too soon.'

There was no right time to tell her about Miller, but I broke the news halfway through our afternoon movie. She didn't seem shocked, didn't shed a tear. She just sat on the sofa and kept watching the film as I explained how he died covering an unknown client of mine. Maybe there was an underlying desire to smash a thing or two in anger, but the girl kept it together. I expected nothing less. Ryoko might look soft and lovely on the outside, but inside she's a rock. You'll break against her before she even chips. We knock back the tequila and chase it with beer.

'So what did Tweek say?' Ryoko asks.

'About what?'

She taps behind her ear. 'Y'know . . .'

'Nothing,' I say and frown. 'The tests he ran say everything is fine.'

'Are you still having problems?'

Her face gives nothing away, but I can see it in her eyes, the growing concern over what has me so worried. Ryoko is the person I'm least likely to lie to, but I'll do it in a heartbeat if it will ease her worries. More beer finds its way down my throat, stalling a reply. The buzz from it further delays things, the hamster wheel slow to spin. My pause is too long. Ryoko knows I'm sparing her the truth as I speak.

'I'm fine, babe. No need to worry –'

The Rochester suddenly goes dark, every light in the

place failing simultaneously. Hoots and jeers rise from the patrons as Liaison screens glow in the black. Bartenders and bouncers call for calm. The sound of shattering glass comes, drinks hitting the floor as people get shoved. An alarmed cry follows, then a series of angry shouts. Ryoko grabs me in the dark, pulling me close. I slip a hand around her waist and hold her tight. All kinds of crazy things have happened, and have been rumoured to happen, in these rolling blackouts. When the power comes back on, sometimes theft or assault has occurred. Occasionally there is a corpse.

'I love you,' I whisper.

The lights reactivate as if on cue, and I catch Ryoko mouthing the words back to me, trying them on for size. Immediately she puts a hand over her mouth, eyes shutting shamefully over dropping her guard. She's trained herself to avoid toying with emotion. I want to tell her it's all right, that there's no need to keep me at arm's length. I try to touch her face, stroke her hair, something. She pulls away before I can, the movement slight, maybe only an inch, but enough to put some cold between us.

There is a loud yelp as a bouncer wearing sunglasses strong-arms some dude at the other end of the bar, mercifully drawing our attention away from our awkward moment. We watch as the culprit gets hauled out of the place and thrown onto the street. Craig swings by our spot at the bar.

'What happened?' I ask.

'The guy was trying to steal tips in the blackout,' Craig says. 'First thing we expect to happen around here when the power fails. Shit, we gotta stay vigilant even with the lights on these days.'

'How'd they catch him?' Ryoko asks.

I point at the bouncer. 'That guy's not wearing sunglasses at night because he's some Corey Hart fan.'

Ryoko frowns. 'I don't get it.'

'For crying out loud,' Craig says, giving me a less than amused look. 'No one listens to eighties music, dude.'

'Everyone should listen to the eighties. It was the peak of civilization.'

'Oh, don't start.'

'Just saying.'

'Night-vision lenses,' Craig says, turning back to Ryoko. 'Things go dark in here, and security gets instant cat-eyes.'

'Really?'

'Military-grade gear, very hard to come by.'

'I want a pair of those.'

'No you don't,' Craig says. 'They damage optic nerves if you use them too much, give you retinal cancer. Kinda like those augmented-reality glasses did before they were all pulled off the market.'

Ryoko casts another glance at the bouncers. The sunglasses have been either put away or pushed up on their crowns. I remember back when augmented-reality glasses were all the rage, before it came to light that the eyewear was watching and recording everything for third parties while slowly blinding you at the same time, everyone donning little toxic invasions of privacy that could be exploited. Walking into any establishment while wearing a pair nowadays will get you beat the fuck up in NYC.

'Can I get you good-looking kids another round?' Craig asks.

We both nod and Craig fetches us more tequila. I check the time on my Liaison and see there is a notification about a person of interest in proximity. The link shows me Phineas is in the area, at a restaurant only a couple blocks away. I message him to come meet us if he's free. The message I get back says he's on his way.

Ten minutes later I'm surprised to see Phineas enter the front doors of the Rochester with Nikki, the receptionist, in tow. He spots us instantly and leads her by the hand through the crowd. Ryoko greets both of them with a hug and kiss. Nikki looks happy to see me, much to my surprise. I embrace her. She tells me I'm looking good. I must admit that she is too. Whatever tension there might have been between us before seems to have evaporated.

I order a round of shots for everyone as Ryoko and Nikki indulge in some chatter. The girls have always gotten along well. The smiles between them are plentiful and genuine. Phineas saddles up next to me at the bar and leans over, speaking in a lowered voice, answering my question before I even ask.

'Nikki needed a night out. She's taking Miller's death pretty hard.'

'I think we all are.'

'I got talking to her after I saw you and Baxter this morning. She was awfully fond of the guy.'

'Yeah,' I say. 'He was always real sweet to her.'

Phineas nods. 'A real gentleman.'

'Did they have a thing going on?'

'More of an unspoken thing . . . an off and on kind of thing.'

I risk a glance at Ryoko. 'I know the type.'

Our tequilas arrive and we fire them back in unison. Phineas orders beer chasers, making them Miller Genuine Draft for old times' sake. I picture Miller leaning against the bar with a bottle of the stuff in hand, bullshitting all the girls, saying his family owned the brewery and that he was heir to the company fortune. He always got us laughing with that stunt. We gave him shit about it more times than I can remember.

'I didn't think you'd be out on the town tonight,' Phineas says. 'What with your gig tomorrow.'

'It's not a gig I give a shit about.'

'Who you got a session with?'

'Does it matter?'

Phineas looks to the ceiling and says nothing. I watch as Ryoko puts a sure hand on Nikki's hip, her thumb hooking into the belt loop of the girl's jeans as they talk and laugh. Nikki responds by twirling a finger in Ryoko's dark hair, telling her how much she likes the feel of it, asking her what kind of product she uses. Craig delivers the MGD and Phineas raises his bottle high.

'To a good friend, colleague and trailblazer,' toasts Phineas. 'It's Miller time!'

We clink bottles and chug. Conversations continue. Lots of laughs, plenty of smiles, the odd touch here and there. As more people enter the bar we find ourselves squashed together, bodies pressed up against the bar. Another round of drinks and things get more affectionate.

'It's starting to get crowded in here,' Ryoko says.

'We could move on to somewhere else,' Phineas says, checking the time on his Liaison. 'What are you guys in the mood for?'

Nikki throws back another shot. 'I'm in the mood for some loving.'

Phineas scans the room for prospects. 'See anything you like?'

'Yeah, you guys,' Nikki says, giggling and pointing at the three of us.

Ryoko doesn't hesitate. 'I'm game.'

She downs her shot, then leans over and plants one on Nikki, fingers sliding up the girl's neck and grabbing a handful of her hair. Phineas and I watch as their tongues dart in and out of each other's mouth. Some jackass behind us hollers at the sight like a frat-boy. We both turn and tell him to grow the fuck up. He is quick to quiet down.

'I don't even think they need us,' I chuckle.

Phineas turns to me with a broad grin. 'You interested a little group hug, mate?'

'Let me settle up.'

I throw back my shot and catch Craig's attention with a wave, signalling for the bill. He sends the tab to my Liaison and I try to pay it from my account. Craig is quick to come over with an apologetic look on his face.

'It's not going through,' he says.

'What?'

'It says the transaction failed.'

'How the hell is that possible?'

All at once the panic comes. I can feel it welling up in my chest, the anxiety over just the possibility of somehow being broke. Childhood memories flood my head. The bounced cheques, maxed credit, even the counterfeit money that came into play at one point. I'm struck by a memory of my mother standing at a supermarket check-out lane and arguing with the cashier, ashamed that she's being forced to leave groceries behind yet again because the debit card wouldn't go through.

'The blackouts screw up all kinds of stuff,' Craig says. 'I've had a couple problems already tonight with customers trying to pay.'

'Shit, just put it on my credit card then.'

I pass him my card. Craig rings it through on a terminal and frowns. He tries it two more times without any luck.

'Oh, you've got to be kidding,' I say, patting my pockets. 'Jesus, I don't have any cash on me, Craig.'

I look over my shoulder at my companions, Ryoko and Nikki still kissing, Phineas watching, as entertained by it as they are. The thought of asking any of them to cover the bill, especially Ryoko, is disheartening. I check my accounts and credit via my Liaison and find both have a temporary suspension notice on them. After firing off an angry message to my bank, I consider asking my roommate for a favour. Craig is intuitive, beats me to the punch.

'Don't worry,' he says. 'I got you covered tonight. You can pay me back later.'

'Really? Are you sure?'

Craig laughs and waves me away. 'Like you're not good for it, buddy.'

I thank him and turn back to my friends, only to find a stranger standing before me, the unexpected sight making me jump. The brunette is about my age, skinny, wearing too much make-up. She stares at me with nothing less than hatred, lips pressed together so hard they whiten. Before I can speak, she throws her martini in my face and shoves me hard against the bar.

'What the hell, lady?'

'You *bastard*!' she screeches.

I watch as she winds up. Before I can duck the punch, Phineas's hand shoots out and grabs the woman's forearm, stopping her in mid-strike.

'Easy now, honey,' he says, looking at me with increasing worry. 'What's the problem here?'

'What's the problem?' she spits back. 'What's the *problem*?'

The question is rhetorical. Clearly, I'm somehow the problem. The woman wriggles out of Phineas's grip and pushes him away, giving herself another opportunity to attack. She comes at me with both hands, fingers curled into claws like she's ready to rip my eyes out. I raise my palms, bracing for her this time, but Ryoko slips between us. With cat-like reflexes she deflects the woman's assault, ensnaring one of her arms in a kimura before spinning her into the bar with a bang. The woman writhes next to me, her eyes ablaze as Ryoko twists the arm up her back and pins her against the countertop until security arrives.

'Call the police,' the woman shrieks. 'Arrest this man!'

A bouncer takes over Ryoko's armlock and glances at Craig, who gives him a quick shake of the head that says there is no need to involve the police.

'Get her out of here,' Craig orders.

The woman struggles ferociously in the bouncer's grip, making him work to keep her subdued. Ryoko and Phineas step forward to offer assistance, but are waved off.

'I got it from here,' says the bouncer and begins hauling the woman away.

She doesn't go easily. The bouncer has to lift her off her feet to make any progress. She kicks wildly, one of her stilettos stabbing into his shin, making him yell and drop her. As soon as she touches the floor she's out of his grip and running at me again. I catch her by the wrists as she hurls her body at mine.

'Lady,' I protest, holding her firmly, our faces close enough to kiss. 'I honestly have no idea who you are.'

Her eyes search mine frantically. I can see it, the sudden amazement and curiosity in her prying pupils. It's clear that she has looked into my eyes before, stared into the windows of this soul while I wasn't home. Her expression softens, somehow realizing from the look on my face that I really don't know who she is.

'You don't know what you've done,' she whispers.

Then she is gone, pulled off of me by Phineas and Ryoko who throw her to another bouncer as he emerges from the surrounding crowd. There is no more fight left in the woman as she is escorted to the front door and tossed out of the joint. Craig signals us over to the bar and nods toward the rear of the Rochester.

'You guys are more than welcome to leave out back,' Craig says. 'Might be a good idea to avoid that one out on the street.'

Everyone is in agreement. We make our way through the kitchen of the Rochester and exit into the cool air of the back alley, all of us strangely turned on by the mix of drinking, flirting and unexpected violence. Our breath is heavy as we walk and talk, though no one speaks of the woman who attacked me. We all know situations like that arise sometimes, come with the territory. Ryoko and Nikki exchange expectant, aroused looks between themselves and us. Both girls' nipples are hard against their shirts. I have to adjust the crotch of my jeans. Phineas is all smiles. Out on the street, Ryoko is quick to hail a cab for us.

'Whatever happened back there,' Nikki says, eyeing Ryoko and fanning her face with a hand, 'that was freaking *hot*.'

Phineas pulls me aside for a second before we get into the cab. 'Hey, you took an HIV vaccine, right?'

9

The four of us are flopped on the sofas in my living room, naked bodies beaded with sweat, air smelling of sex and perfume, limbs only recently untangled after nearly an hour tied together. Down-tempo lounge music plays through the apartment. Nikki's breath still comes rapidly, a lingering effect of her recent orgasms. Ryoko stretches like a cat and licks her lips, still tasting the sweetness of skin on skin, pleased that she had everyone right where she wanted. My tongue aches in the best possible way, my groin even more so. Phineas rests his head on a pillow, staring up at the ceiling with a grin. The level of pleasure experienced was mind-blowing, but it doesn't hide the fact that it was also escapism, our way to try and outrun personal demons for a mile or two.

I make my way to the kitchen, find some cognac and pour everyone a nightcap. I don't want to think, don't want to let any of my worries weasel their way back into my head. Ryoko runs her fingers up and down our receptionist's milky thighs. Nikki sighs and playfully kisses Phineas's rope-like muscles. She grabs my ass as I serve her drink, squeezing me in appreciation. Ryoko slides a hand up to cup Nikki's breast, her thumb stroking her nipple. They both groan affirmatively, eyes widening, twinkling with deviancy. Everyone's still in the mood, although we're almost too tired to do much about it. Nikki rests her head on Phineas's chest, her tongue flicking its way down to his abs.

'What time will your roommate be back?' Phineas asks, twirling Nikki's blonde hair in his fingers.

'Not until dawn,' I say. 'But we should call it a night soon. I have to get *some* sleep.'

Nikki wants to say something, but her mouth is suddenly full. Phineas moans. Ryoko sips from her tumbler and watches, a sly smile on her face. She gives me that look, inviting me so she can perform as well. I go to her without hesitation. Soon, the girls are spreading the taste of cognac all over us. Then Phineas and I are both on our knees, dripping liquor on them, licking them thank you and goodnight as the ambient music plays on.

Outside my apartment the activity on the street is still boisterous. Men and women catcall to each other. Cab drivers pip or lean on their horns. Thumping music from car stereos ebbs and flows up and down the blocks. Once in a while there is an angered shout or pained shriek, preceded or followed by brittle things breaking. A car alarm goes off, then another. Two gunshots ring out. Minutes later the wail of a siren sounds. New York has always been the city that never sleeps, but it's becoming the city that never stops to take a breath. Oxygen deprivation leads to brain damage. You can hear the increasing insanity outside my window almost every night. Exhausted, unable to indulge in each other any more, we lie about and listen, fully aware that our world is worsening. Deep down, I think it terrifies us all. Knowing Craig's Glock is in the apartment provides me with some small measure of comfort.

The thought of my impending gig with Winslade creeps into my mind and I urge everyone to drink up. The girls curl up with their cognac on the sofa, sleepy-eyed and speaking low. Phineas rises and walks over to one of the windows, stretching, yawning. He looks out onto Tompkins Square Park and smirks at the shocked people on the street who glance up and notice his naked black body framed by the pane of glass. It isn't long before he turns his attention to something that makes him squint into the dark. An unimpressed grunt follows.

'See something you don't like?' I ask.

Phineas downs the contents of his tumbler. 'Drones.'

'They're here almost every night now.'

'I swear the only true privacy I have any more is when I'm Husking, when I'm under and dreaming.'

'Shit, our clients enjoy more freedoms than we'll ever know.'

Phineas grunts again, more disapproving than the first time. He slips away from the window and sits back down beside Ryoko and Nikki, who are already drifting off to sleep. I watch them with envy as their eyelids droop and their heads loll. It's me who needs sleep most, yet I'm wide awake. I fetch the cognac and pour myself and Phineas a second helping. We don't say anything for a while, lost in our own thoughts. When Phineas finally speaks, it snaps me out of a trance I wasn't aware I was in.

'You all right, mate?'

I shake my head. 'I've been better.'

'What's on your mind?'

'Just thinking about the woman back at the Rochester.'

'Yeah, I was too. It happens every now and then, running into our recent pasts like that. Some woman came up to me at a restaurant in Brooklyn a couple months back, crying her eyes out, asking me how I could be so heartless.'

'Can't help wondering what I was involved in,' I say. 'What role I played in whatever happened to her . . .'

'Could have been anything, mate. You know how kinky or cruel clients can be.'

I swallow hard. 'She screamed for the police, man. She cried for my arrest.'

'Hell, maybe you flashed her in the park,' Phineas chuckles. 'Maybe you took naked pictures of her and posted them online. Maybe you screwed her out of her life savings. Who knows? You can't burden yourself with it.'

'Why can't I?'

Phineas looks me square in the eye. 'Because it wasn't *you*.'

We Husks pass this excuse around like a joint. *It's not you, it's them.* That's our motto, our mantra, our rationale to make sure we're never on the hook for anything. It's what I told Ryoko yesterday. The same thing I'll tell another Husk tomorrow or the day after. For the first time I begin to wonder how I can get out of this business. I fantasize about Ryoko and me making an exit, escaping from the likes of Baxter and Winslade and Ichida and Navarette.

'You're in love with her, aren't you?' Phineas says softly.

'Huh?'

Phineas is looking between me and the woman I realize I've been staring at for the last minute. A woman I trust so much that I've just shared her with two other people, a woman who deep down I know only I belong to. I can't hide anything from Phineas, and I don't try.

'Yes.'

Phineas looks at me for an almost uncomfortable length of time. In the persisting silence I feel exposed. *Love* is one hell of a dirty word in our line of work. Most people's opinions don't mean shit to me, but his does. Phineas's lips finally split into a wide, knowing grin.

'I think she might be in love with you too, mate.'

He leans over and knuckles my bicep, making me grin in return. Nikki stirs from slumber and looks at us with squinty eyes.

'What time is it?' she asks, rubbing her face.

'About time I took you home and put you to bed, my dear,' Phineas says, pulling his pants on.

'I'll call you a cab,' I say.

They dress in the near dark while I order a ride. Ryoko opens her eyes long enough to say goodnight before falling asleep among the pillows. Nikki and Phineas both bend down and plant kisses on her cheek. I walk them to the front door and hug them both. Outside, we hear the wail of another police siren.

'Stay safe you two,' I say, finishing my cognac, feeling a swirl of tiredness.

Phineas puts on his coat. 'Tell me, who are you Husking for today?'

'Between us,' I mumble, 'it's Winslade.'

Phineas stops, shooting me a distasteful glance, his coat hanging awkwardly on his shoulders. Nikki gives me a watered-down version of the same expression, her hands frozen midway on the zipper of her jacket. They share a nervous look between them.

'I've heard some stuff about that guy through the grapevine, Rhodes,' Phineas says. 'I think you and I should have a chat in London later this week.'

I nod, too tired to talk any more. They leave without another word. As I lock the front door I hear my Liaison ping and check the screen. It's an automated message back from the bank that says the suspensions on my accounts have been lifted. I breathe a sigh of relief as I gently pick up my sleepy Ryoko from the couch and carry her to bed.

IO

'Wilhelm Winslade,' I mutter.

The deep breath I take does little to calm my nerves. On the varnished oak door before me is a solid gold placard engraved with the number thirty-six. My client owns the whole floor. I'm standing at the entrance to a penthouse on Central Park West with a heavily armed guard either side of me who have been my escorts from the moment I set foot in the building. Both are decked out in the latest body armour. They're not packing personal-defence weapons like the Vector. No, these guys have fully outfitted assault carbines with drum magazines to lay down extensive suppressing fire if needed, enough to repel a small citizens' uprising. Winslade must be worrying over what is growing outside his window. Half his investments are helping to hollow out the middle class. The other half is tied up in weapons manufacturing and defence contracting. The people who hate him most fit the profile of the average disgruntled civilian, and his death was never announced to the public.

One of the guards raps on the door. We wait a minute. Time to reflect, think my own thoughts before I get taken for a spin. When I awoke this morning Ryoko was already gone. My heart sank. The plan was to make her breakfast in bed, get her to stay another hour or two so we could talk, mindless chatter, heart to heart if possible. More time alone with her seemed imperative. In her presence there had been fewer flashbacks, fewer unnerving thoughts. I still have that weight on me, pressure from an unknown source, but Ryoko eased it somehow. The girl has a habit of sneaking out the back door after an overnight, a habit I'm trying to break. A note was left on the kitchen counter. Said she will miss me while I'm gone and that we need to talk when I get back. It was signed *Love Ryoko*, something she's never done before in our history of leaving notes. The thought makes me smile, even as the penthouse door opens to reveal a wiry man in a shirt and tie who tries his damnedest to smile back.

'Mr Rhodes,' he says with a French accent, the smile re-forming into a sneer of sorts. 'Good to have you back.'

'It's a pleasure to be back.'

We're both lying, and we both know it. Renard is the man's name, the only one I know him by. He serves as Winslade's butler, assistant and personal bodyguard all rolled into one. As he receives information through his earpiece, my eyes are drawn to his shoulder holster. There it hangs, the gun, the prototype weapon that destroys living tissue in such a way as to haunt my dreams. I know 'M-6 Rapier' is stencilled on the gun barrel, and its presence alone is enough to invoke fear in those who recognize it. Even the security guards give it a nervous glance. To a guy like Renard it is merely an accessory, a tool, something to aid him in his tasks. I'm no science geek, couldn't tell you specifics, but I know that gun shoots a whole new kind of bullet technology, advanced cartridges filled with corrosive chemicals and projectiles, firepower that carves a smooth and sizeable chunk out of an unfortunate target.

'Come in,' Renard grumbles, dismissing the guards with a nod. 'Time is money and Mr Winslade wishes to waste neither.'

I sincerely hope the Rapier, with its state-of-the-art munitions, is slowly giving Renard inoperable cancer, feeding some tumour next to his heart, if he even has one. I enter the penthouse, Renard ushering me ahead. You do not walk behind this man. He keeps rear guard at all times, never takes his eyes off you for more than a second.

'I trust you have been keeping well?'

The inquiry is about my personal health, the quality of me as a product, not my wellbeing. I look around the luxurious living space. It's twice as big as Navarette's place in Las Vegas, adorned with three times the wealth. Old Money lives here, and lots of it.

'Well enough,' I reply.

My response does not impress Renard. He picks up a tablet from a desk and types into it. I stroll the massive living room, inspecting the military antiques on the walls, Renard always close behind. I feel his eyes on me constantly. It makes me feel cheap and criminal, like some kind of shoplifter. I'm a Husk, the ultimate whore, not just a gigolo. For my services I expect to be treated with a certain amount of respect, maybe even a little class. It's a lie I tell myself a lot. Old Money has no regard for anything except its own interests, no matter what is said or done. Renard appraises me, sees something he doesn't like, approaches with a hand held out.

'A moment, *s'il vous plaît*,' he says, reaching toward my throat.

'Certainly.'

He removes my necktie, shaking his head at my pathetic attempt at an Eldredge knot, making *tut tut* noises as he undoes it. I watch as he drapes it over his own neck and effortlessly ties the knot correctly before handing it back with a look of contempt.

'There,' he says. 'Better.'

As I don the tie my eyes are drawn to a framed photo of Winslade shaking hands with the former President of the United States, closing the deal that made him his last billions by supplying the Defense Department with the EMU, or Escalation Military Unit, an eight-foot-tall odd-looking bipedal drone that specializes in walking, running and killing on rough terrain. Initially meant for warzones grown too treacherous for conventional soldiers, EMUs now roll off assembly lines en masse to be sent out ahead of platoons in order to cripple and demoralize the enemy before an offensive. I pick the picture up, looking past the two powerful men at the remote-piloted machine in the background.

'Please put that down,' Renard says.

I do it casually, but carefully. 'How have you and Mr Winslade been keep—'

Renard puts one finger to his lips to silence me, holds another against his earpiece before typing something else into the tablet. Feeling unwelcome, I walk through sliding glass doors and step out onto the penthouse balcony to look out over Central Park. The Occupy Movement below is unmistakable. The Great Lawn has become an enormous scab among greenery, the field a mingling mass of disaffected and disenfranchised. Incessant protest marches flow in the park's concrete veins. Organized chants rumble in the air. OCP was a smart move. Back in the day, Occupy Wall Street annoyed employees of the financial district more than anything. But this new location is too close to home for the one per cent. Every wealthy weasel and rich bitch living around Central Park look out of their window every day to see a swelling resistance, reminding them just how much they are pissing off the majority of the country. There are fewer surveillance cameras in the park too, putting facial-recognition software at a disadvantage. Aerial drones don't like to operate much in daylight either. It's a perfect place for social disobedience, handy for criminal elements like Integris too. Renard clears his throat loudly and I re-enter the penthouse without hesitation.

'He will see you now.'

Renard points down the hallway. Unaccompanied, I make my way to Winslade's room. I feel relieved not having Renard, or his weapon, at my back. Relief is short-lived, however. At the end of the hall is a reinforced stainless-steel door that slides open for me. The room is poorly lit as I enter, window curtains closed as always. In one corner lies a silver-skinned server system housing customized virtual worlds. On the other side of the room, before a large fireplace, a darkened figure sits in an over-stuffed throne of a chair, deathly still, enough to be my client's corpse. I gulp, feeling a knot plumb my neck.

'Hello, Mr Winslade,' I manage.

In the quiet of the room I hear the subtle whirring of machinery as the robot turns its head to regard me. The polished eyes glint as the silicone-composite face remoulds into something that vaguely resembles being pleased. Painted lips pull back to reveal teeth made of rare ivory. Regardless of how many times I see it, the smile freaks me out. As with most robot technology, no matter how lifelike it may look, it still doesn't look real.

'Good day, Mr Rhodes,' Winslade replies in a replica voice that sounds inhuman to me. 'Please have a seat.'

I sit in the vacant chair beside his and try my best not to look at him. He leans closer, his movements slow and deliberate. The soft clicking and humming of his prototype body, one he is very unsatisfied with, bothers me. From the corner of my eye I see his head tilt as he examines me through those silvery lenses he calls eyes. The cold fingers of his manufactured hand rise and stroke my cheek awkwardly, trying to feel what they cannot.

'I have missed you, my boy.'

My boy bothers me even more, makes me feel like I'm an item owned. I want to pull away from his touch, but that would be bad for business. Reluctantly, I lean into his hand, feeling the metal skeleton underneath the soft materials impersonating muscles and sinews. The hand cups my chin and turns it toward him. His eyes don't blink. They never do. I try not to appear uneasy. The machine staring absently into my face is supposed to resemble Mr Winslade when he was in his thirties. To me it just looks like a wax sculpture come to life. The fake smile falls away. Features become blank, expression erased.

'I don't like that scratch on your cheek,' Winslade says.

'Sorry,' I reply, swallowing hard. 'I was hoping to have more time to heal properly before my return.'

The blank look maintains. 'No matter. I require you now.'

Winslade peels back a layer of pseudo-skin from his temple to reveal an input jack. His head bobs up and down, ushering me to proceed. I take out my Liaison and start the Husk sequence. Winslade holds out a hand. I plug one cable into my Ouija and place the other in his smooth upturned palm. Robot eyes stare at it, the rest of him completely still. For a moment I think he has shut down.

'Pity,' Winslade remarks suddenly. 'Only one day this time.'

I nod as if I agree, even though I don't. Winslade plugs the cable into his head as I retrieve my pillbox and select a red one for a twenty-four-hour session.

'See you tomorrow, Mr Winslade,' I say, and swallow the pill.

Soon a sleep tunnel opens and I'm sliding backwards into the emergence of night, watching as the world before me grows smaller. My thoughts become sluggish, slipping into stasis. A figure passes in the gloom, travelling in the direction I have come from, moving toward earthly existence. It does not acknowledge me. My last controlled thought wonders where Winslade will go with my body.

I settle down in the recesses of my mind, cocooned by

the dark for what seems like ages, unmoving, unthinking. When the dreams finally come they are vivid, like memories playing on a movie screen. Most of them are of Miller. I recall the first time I met him, in a private booth at a restaurant in Greenwich Village where he touched on the aspects of my new profession, explaining Husk life and protocol. I see him and Tweek taking potshots in the Solace offices, ribbing each other relentlessly until they both break into fits of laughter. I watch Miller chatting with Nikki at the reception desk, complimenting her clothes, her hair, making her blush with well-timed charm. His death seems so distant, impossible even. There is a most unnatural sense of immortality about the man. I call out to him and he turns my way. The image on the screen becomes pixilated, images and sounds breaking down. His face becomes haggard, sullen. His skin turns pallid, mouth widening to shout something that never comes. As the screen burns up I swear he's an animated corpse.

It is then that I notice Miller sitting in the dark with me. Abstract shadows cover most of his face, cast from things unseen by light that does not exist. A sliver of sun reveals the stubble on his cheek he always grew to give him that rugged look which made him so desirable to others.

'What are you doing here?' I ask.

I have a responsibility to be here.

His voice, it makes a connection, reveals a truth that has been eluding me. The voice in my head that's been talking back recently sounds eerily similar to Miller's. I don't know why I haven't noticed it before. We sit in silence, me unsure what to say, him unwilling to give me a clue. I slowly realize this is not completely Miller, only a piece of the man. I reach toward him, but my hand never seems to get any closer.

'Is there something you want to tell me?'

The head nods, but he says nothing. Muffled sounds come, speech straining against a gag. Shadows retreat, revealing the mess that was formerly Miller's face. The skull is bashed, opaque fluid leaking from his hairline. Eyes are closed, criss-crossed with scars. Lips are sewn shut. Ears have become melted lumps of skin. There is a ragged hole behind one of them where Tweek removed the Ouija. Despite the damage, I can see past it, see the beauty lying beneath it all. Miller is still handsome to me, still someone worth coveting.

'Jesus, what happened to your face?'

He can't talk. The stitches are pulled tight. I feel something in my hand and look down to find my fingers curled around a pair of silver scissors. I reach for Miller and this time manage to grab him by the shirtsleeve. I pull him close, hug him with one arm.

'Hold still.'

I work the scissor blades between the stitches sealing his lips, carefully snipping each one from right to left. His mouth pops open, dust and a dead smell expelling with a bad breath that has been held for far too long.

'You need to be more careful,' he says, gasping. 'Life is sacred.'

'I'm trying to be more careful.'

Miller shakes his head, unsatisfied with my answer. 'Ignorance was bliss, but I still knew. I still figured it out.'

'Figured what out?'

'Where I went, what I did.'

Miller raises a hand and pulls the cut string through the holes around his mouth. I watch as he dangles them over his tongue and eats each one.

'You need to retrace your steps,' he says, chewing, licking perforated lips.

Suddenly he's distracted, attention drawn to something unseen out there in the black. For a moment I get the feeling he has forgotten about me completely. His mouth moves ever so slightly. I have to strain to make out what he's saying.

'You've been given a sign,' he mutters. 'And all signs point to . . .'

'What?'

'Can't you read the signs?'

'I don't understand.'

Miller turns a horrible grin on me, scarred eyelids straining open to reveal milky white over his soothing blues.

'You need to wake up, sleepwalker.'

There is a creaking sound, a door opening at the opposite end of a large, quiet room. I get the distinct feeling that something else now shares our space. Confirmation comes with the sound of approaching footsteps.

'I have to go,' Miller says, beginning to crawl away on his hands and knees.

'Wait,' I say, reaching after him. 'I need you to tell me more.'

I watch as the soles of his feet slide off into the dark, shuffling sounds of movement fading. I want to reach out again, try and hook a piece that can pull me away too, but I already know it will be futile. He calls back to me only once.

'You have to go now too, sleepwalker.'

The footsteps stop directly behind me. The breathing I hear is rapid, rasping. I don't turn to look. I don't want to look. A heavy hand drops on my shoulder, cool to the touch. In the next second I know it is also my hand. Then, for a few moments only, I become one with this entity and hate myself.

I have no doubt my body is sprawled as I re-emerge. All four limbs seem cast away from my centre, draped over whatever I'm sitting on. A hand grips my shoulder, pressing me into cushions and steadying me. The fingers of another are pulling apart my eyelids, holding them open. I paw at whoever has me pinned.

'Get off of me,' I whine.

'Relax,' Renard says, checking my pupils. 'I'm not going to hurt you.'

He checks the other eye and grunts, satisfied. The pressure on me is suddenly lifted. I sit upright in the same throne of a chair my mind went dormant in twenty-four hours before. Fresh clothes feel soft on my skin; expensive loungewear that isn't mine. One of the data cables is still plugged into my head, connecting me to the silver-skinned server system beside the fireplace. I unplug it eagerly, feeling relief as the proboscis pulls out. Vision is a bit blurry, but I see the robot sitting in the other chair where I last saw it, head slumped forward, eyes staring at its lap, seemingly deactivated.

'Apologies,' Renard says, typing on his tablet. 'But I had to restrain you.'

'Why?' I ask, rubbing my face. 'What was the problem?'

'As Mr Winslade was trying to extricate, you began struggling . . . You almost pulled the damn cord out.'

He gives me an unimpressed look. I give a perplexed one in return. What he's describing almost never happens. Client upload and download times are normally calm, uneventful, someone slipping out of a stilled body through a fibre-optic cable. One mind exits while the other re-emerges, barely enough time for a hello and handshake.

'Just what the *fuck* was that all about?' Renard snaps.

I see it now, the anger in Renard's eyes. If I had ripped that data cable out during his employer's defection from my head, there might have been serious consequences. I've heard stories about partial transference; interrupted transmissions to and from a Husk that turn both clients and whores into demented halves of their former selves. It's one of the reasons secure hard-lines are so important.

'I don't know,' I admit. 'It's never happened with me before. There might be a problem with my Ouija.'

'See that you get it fixed then.'

I look at the robot, still shut down for all I can tell. 'Where's Winslade?'

'Returned to one of his worlds for the moment,' Renard says. 'He'll be with us shortly.'

I watch Renard take a cable from the server and plug it into the robot's temple. On top of the server is a piece of tech I recognize from Tweek's control room, a small device in a cobalt-blue shell. I lean forward, trying to get a closer look. A sudden sharp pain in my side makes me flinch and give up. I glide my fingers over the spot, worrying it might be a cracked rib. The need for sleep weighs heavily on my eyelids, though I'm not nearly as exhausted as I am after some of my other clients. I would even wager that Winslade's given me a decent nap somewhere in the twenty-four-hour period. So far there haven't been any drugs during sessions with him, never any viruses or infections to worry about. I haven't had one STD from the man. All evidence points to him living a pretty clean existence through me.

'Coffee?' Renard asks, taking note of my tired eyes.

'Please.'

Winslade is a considerate client, I'll give him that. After his contracts I reawake showered and groomed, freshly shaven, even manicured. Cologne and creams are spread on my skin. What injuries I may have acquired have been tended to. I'm always in new clothes that he lets me keep, jewellery too on occasion. There is a gift presented to me every time we part ways.

I can just make out the sounds of the robot reactivating, circuitry flushing with electricity, hardware and software rebooting with a subtle crackling. The head rises, but the eyes don't move. Startup typically takes a minute. Renard hands me my coffee. My eyes drift to the Rapier sleeping in its sling under his arm. I wonder how quickly he can draw it when he has to.

'Were there any other problems?' I ask, taking a sip.

He doesn't give me an answer. No one ever does, really. Don't know why I bother asking. I lock eyes with him and find them cold and unsympathetic, the kind that regularly bear witness to what most people never could. In an instant I understand there are things I can't be privy to, can't understand. I will never know how the world of the one per cent works, the rules and reasoning that govern them, if any at all. My Ouija clicks and for a second I glimpse something that could haunt me for a life if only I could remember it past the fraction of time it takes to see it. My flinch does not go unnoticed.

'What's wrong with you?' Renard asks.

'Nothing,' I lie. 'I'm fine.'

I turn to the robot, startled to see Winslade looking back at me, pseudo-smiling through that painted silicone mask that passes for a face.

'How are you feeling, my boy?'

'Not bad,' I say, but the discomfort from my injured side is obvious.

'How are the ribs?'

'Hurt like hell,' I say, forcing a chuckle and wincing involuntarily. 'Jesus, did I get hit by a car or something?'

'Took a little tumble on the ski slope, I'm afraid. I flew to Aspen for the day.'

'Good times?'

Winslade's smile widens, as do his eyes. 'Oh, you should have been there.'

The silvery lenses fall on the steaming coffee in my hand and Winslade's rubbery face readjusts to the most disapproving look it is capable of making.

'Renard,' Winslade says. 'Fetch us something a little stronger, please.'

Renard goes to the liquor cabinet and pours us both

some Louis XIII. He hands one crystal goblet to me and places the other in the robot's hand. I take a generous sip of the expensive spirit, tasting perfection on my palate, hoping it will help numb my pain. Winslade brings the goblet to the robot's mouth, clattering glass off ivory teeth, spilling cognac down the silicone chin. Renard ignores it, as does his employer.

'How do you like the cognac?' Winslade asks.

I study the amber fluid in my glass. 'It's exquisite.'

'Then, please, take a bottle with you.'

Renard reaches for the liquor cabinet's lower shelf and retrieves an unopened bottle of Louis XIII, which he presents to me. I'm almost speechless.

'Oh my God.'

'There is no God, my boy,' Winslade says with a chuckle. 'Only gods among men.'

I run my fingers over the crafted crystal glass. 'Mr Winslade, I . . . I couldn't possibly accept this.'

'Think nothing of it.'

'Thank you.'

'You are most welcome. And please know I require your services again soon.'

'Sure, sure,' I reply. 'But unfortunately I'm booked with other clients for the next several days.'

'I'm aware,' Winslade says.

'Oh.'

'I have spoken with Ms Baxter already,' Renard says to me. 'Arrangements will be made for when you return from the UK.'

Renard gives me a look and gesture that suggest it is

time to be on my way. I rise from my chair and the robot rises as well. Winslade walks me to the front door with shuffling steps, Renard following close behind.

'Until we meet again, my boy,' Winslade says, extending his hand.

I shake firmly. The cold, fleshy materials make me want to pull away, but I don't dare. Renard hands me a bag containing my original clothes and opens the penthouse door. In the hallway I am received by the same two heavily armed brutes that brought me up the day before. Renard shuts and locks the door the second I've stepped over the threshold. The relief I feel in escaping my client is railroaded by a sudden spike in the bad feeling I've been carrying around. My head spins. My gut churns. The guards usher me into an elevator and take me down to street level, where they practically toss me out of the building.

On the sidewalk outside, I fall to my knees and vomit.

The Percocet is pleasant. A bottle of beer in my hand is cold, sweating, though I don't drink from it. The antacids I downed might have calmed my stomach, or maybe it's because I feel safe stowed away in my room. Lights are dimmed, the windows open. My half-naked body is propped on the bed feeling a cool breeze coming in. No pain for now. Don't need any discomfort to remind me who I am tonight. I'm certain of myself for once. How long this feeling will last, I don't know, but I'm going to try and get it to stick around. It's all I have to keep me company tonight.

Ryoko didn't pick up her phone this evening. Called twice, left one message, didn't want to seem desperate. Honestly, I could really use her right now. She must be on a gig. Baxter probably convinced her to return to work with some big payday. I figured out Phineas is in a session. Craig's out on a date somewhere. Clive's incarcerated. Miller's dead. Baxter will have Nikki and Tweek pulling overtime down at Solace with the company's recent handicapping. Getting some hang time in with the few people I call my friends are opportunities I can no longer afford to miss, but I'm missing each and every one of them tonight.

I take to my bottle, wash the Perc in my stomach with

beer and get a surprising second kick. The plan after Winslade's session was to simply get my ass home, swallow a sleeping pill, and pass the fuck out. Then I got needy for human contact, a bad case of being lonely with nobody available. Now I'm starting to think getting high is a better idea. Want another Percocet, but left the damn things on the kitchen counter with my Donormyl. Screw it. My buzz is far too good to get out of bed. It's clear I won't be retrieving anything that isn't within arm's reach.

I grab my Liaison and bring up Miller's last messages to me. Cue the first one, watch it again. I still feel guilty over him getting killed while covering my gig. If it wasn't for the painkiller, I'd probably cry like a bitch.

'. . . give me a call when you get this and you've got a little free time on your hands . . .'

Free time seems funny to me. So much of mine has become billable. I'm a walking hourly rate most days. My dead friend doesn't seem quite so dead to me, like in my dreams. When I see his grinning face it makes me smile. I'm almost positive that'll he'll answer a call if I place one. It must be the drugs. Might as well delete his number from my contact list, but I just can't bring myself to do it. I watch the first video over and over, expecting him to say something different each time. He never deviates, but I'm positive his physical reactions differ slightly, a smile comes sooner, or a laugh comes later. Jesus, it *must* be the drugs. I play the second message; find myself fading in and out as Miller speaks.

'. . . just letting you know that I'll be covering one of

your regulars . . . Baxter's orders . . . client is awfully adamant that they have a rental this weekend . . .'

Who the hell was it? I've got almost a dozen *regulars*. Can't help but think about one in particular though, tomorrow's client, Mr Ichida. He's definitely a customer that doesn't like to go without. I'm pretty sure he spends more time in rented bodies than in his virtual worlds.

'Take care, stay safe, we'll talk soon,' Miller says.

Famous last words. I think.

I close the video, contemplating love and loss and those I hold dear. My fingers start to dial a number I haven't called in a while, and probably wouldn't if I was feeling level-headed. The phone rings repeatedly. My sister doesn't pick up. I let it go to voicemail, just so I can hear the sound of her voice. In soft, confident tones she tells me that she isn't available right now. Says she's sorry she missed my call. She urges me to leave a detailed message after the tone. I hang up before the beep. Five minutes later I do exactly the same thing, with the same results. The third time I leave a timid message, asking her to call me back when she can, getting cut off before I finish speaking. There's so much I should say, so little time. I'd get bummed out if I didn't feel so damn amiable right now.

The Percocet makes the lights and bed and breeze seem extra soft. My isolation starts to become enjoyable, but it is soon interrupted by the sound of Craig coming home. I hear him open and shut the front door, move about the place, putting his stuff down, turning on the HG. It isn't long before he's standing outside my door. The knock is quiet, his voice low.

'Buddy? Are you in there?'

I say nothing, too high to function properly, too numb to care. My fingers curl into the blankets as my roommate tries the door handle and finds it locked. He's silent a moment, then mutters a string of profanities. I hear him walk to the kitchen, picture him spotting my pharmaceuticals on the counter, picking them up, growing pissed. Don't need this right now. He's back at my door in less than a minute, knocking harder, voice raised.

'Hey man, everything all right?'

I want to call out, tell him I'm fine and leave me the hell alone, but it just feels like too much work. My toes seem worthy of being stared at. The room feels like a sealed jar, the open window a hole poked in the lid for air. I'm an insect, a beautiful butterfly in relapse, cocooned and carefree. More knocking comes. I let Craig hammer and yammer away, hoping he'll just get fed up and leave.

'Damn it, Rhodes, say something or I'm breaking this door down.'

The grunt I give in response is feeble, practically inaudible. Craig pauses, then throws his weight into the door, to no effect. I listen as he messes around with the lock, trying to slip a credit card or something past the latch. That doesn't work either. Once again he rams the door. With great effort I force myself out of bed to save him the trouble, unlock the door and open it wearing the angriest look I can muster.

'Why the hell are you trying to break down my door?'

'You weren't answering,' he says, holding up two prescription containers, my Percocet and Donormyl.

'Found these in the kitchen, man. You back on this shit again?'

'No, I'm not back on that shit again,' I moan. 'I had a rough day earlier and just had a Perc to help take the edge off, that's all.'

He shakes the drugs in my face. 'You mix these two together and there's a hell a good chance you'll end up taking the *big sleep*, buddy. You know that?'

My eyes widen when I realize he's right. The combination could have been lethal, and I most likely would have slipped them both later. Stupid me, I hadn't even given it a thought. Still, I meet Craig's comment with some righteous indignation and a hint of apathy.

'What the fuck, man, are you on suicide watch or something?'

'I don't know . . . am I?'

'No, you're not,' I say. 'I had a lapse in judgement, nothing more. And I'm not abusing that stuff in your hand, believe me.'

It's a half-truth, since I can only vouch for the half I know about. I try to keep my backyard as clean as I can between clients shitting in it. There were some problems with painkillers in the past, but I'm not dependent on them any more. The Percocet doesn't like me standing, so I sit down on the bed. Craig looks between me and the drugs in his grip, unconvinced by my claim. He soon notices the bruised ribs and a look of pity replaces his annoyed scowl.

'You look like shit,' he says, sitting down beside me and pointing at my injury. 'You get that from Husking?'

'Yeah, I went skiing apparently. Took a tumble on the slopes.'

'Looks like you rode the moguls on your belly.'

'Feels like it too, trust me.'

We sit side by side at the foot of the bed, staring ahead; two men too tough in the face of adversity to look each other in the eye. Craig turns the prescription bottles over and over in his hands, pills clicking and clacking inside them.

'How did your date go?' I ask.

'I'm back early. How do you think it went?'

'Sorry, man.'

'Ah, I didn't dig her that much anyway.' Craig shrugs and laughs. 'Hey, you got that money you owe me from the other night?'

'Crap, I completely forgot.'

'Don't sweat it. You can get it to me whenever.'

My ears open into echo chambers. Capsules of altered consciousness and lack of consciousness crash against the plastic. The pills are starting to sound like maracas in my head. I want my high to stop. The sound grows, becoming rocks banging around in oil drums rolling down hills behind my eyes. Everything seems so unbelievably fucking loud all of a sudden. I put a hand on Craig's forearm to stop the shaking. I want to confide in someone, confess all that's been bottled up.

'Look, I owe you an explanation about those pills,' I say, still staring ahead. 'You know I'd never hurt a fly, let alone myself, right?'

'Please, don't,' he replies. '*You don't need to do this.*'

That last sentence, sick and scared, not Craig's voice. My heart stops. The air suddenly seems coppery, pricked by the scent of something bleeding. It is no longer my roommate sitting next to me, but I dare not look directly at the altered shape. From the corner of my eye I see a head of red hair and green irises sunken in a thin face of pale skin. I feel like crumpling under its accusing stare, curling up in a foetal position until whatever is nearby gets bored with me and leaves of its own accord. More unnerving is what is mixed with my fear. There is recognition. This thing beside me is not foreign.

'Craig?' I manage.

The thing doesn't reply, merely cocks its head and leans closer, baiting me to look. Panic spikes in my chest. I refuse to turn my head and come face to face with it.

'Craig?!' I yell.

'What?' he exclaims. 'No need to yell. I'm right beside you, for fuck's sake.'

I risk a glance. The visitor is gone. It's Craig and Craig only, looking irritated over my inexplicable outburst. I eye the Percocet in his hand, wishing I'd lain off the stuff. Sleep is clearly needed, and plenty of it.

'Give me my Donormyl, dude,' I say, grabbing for the sleeping pills. 'I need to get a good night's rest.'

'Hold on, when did you take the Perc?'

'About an hour ago.'

'Okay.' He checks the bottle's instructions, then the time on his Liaison. 'You can have a sleeping pill in a few hours, but not before. I'll hold onto these until then.'

'Oh, you bitch.'

'Yeah, yeah, call me whatever you want, but you'll thank me tomorrow when you actually wake up for work.'

Knowing what's in store tomorrow, I most likely won't.

13

The corporate environment is undeniably cold. It's as if I'm not even here. None of the staff have glanced my way as they go about their work. It feels strange, since I'm used to being noticed, used to catching people's eye. The secretary, buried in paperwork, said to take a seat ten minutes ago. She hasn't looked up from her desk to acknowledge me since. The couch is comfortable, but low to the ground, putting my knees higher than my ass when I sit, making me feel awkward. The magazines stacked on the coffee table are mostly of the business variety. There is a copy of last month's *GQ* that I thumb through, perusing pictures of how a man ought to pose and dress and wear his hair in this day and age. A couple male models look like perfect specimens, would undoubtedly make good Husks if they possessed the right mindset.

I'm to meet Mr Ichida here, at his company's headquarters. The floors are so polished they're practically reflective. Employees hurriedly walk back and forth with their inverted doppelgängers underfoot, places to go and people to see. Most of the walls are made of glass, giving me a clear line of sight across the offices. Opposite from where I sit is a large boardroom, two opposing teams of lawyers sitting at either end of a long black table. Sharks in an aquarium come to mind, primed to feed. I can't hear what is being discussed, but the atmosphere seems tense. In a corner of the boardroom stands a dark-skinned man with strong arms crossed over his broad chest. His dimpled chin juts out in contemplation as he listens attentively to the legal battle going on. I catch him glancing at me a few times and soon recognize the face. It's Chase Jackson, former football player cum film and TV star. Bit of a barbarian if you ask me. Haven't seen or heard much about him in the media since he got busted on a DUI with a hooker and an eight-ball of coke in Malibu several years ago. It was pretty much a career-ender. How he's come to be employed by Ichida, I have no idea.

I'm bored out of my mind sitting and waiting, so I get up and pace around, watching as things in the boardroom heat up. A couple lawyers stand and point accusingly at one another, voices raised. Chase Jackson remains cool and collected, holds up a hand and gives a short speech that calms everyone down a bit. A brief discussion ensues and minutes later the lawyers rise and leave together. The two primaries continue squabbling as they exit the board-room. One, obviously the counsel for the defence, is far more confident than the other.

'. . . until you have something other than circumstantial and hearsay, I'd advise you and the SEC tread very carefully on this matter.'

The prosecutor turns on him angrily. 'Don't push me, counsellor. This charade has gone on far too long now. And furthermore, I'd say it's about time Mr Ichida himself attended these hearings in person. Wouldn't you agree?'

'Not possible,' the counsellor replies. 'His current ailing health forbids it.'

'A video conference then. Surely he can manage that?'

The counsellor considers, gives a slow nod. 'I'll see what can be done.'

I have to hold back a snort of laughter. That video conference will be a CGI mock-up of Mr Ichida. The man died almost three years ago, some kind of undiagnosed wasting disease. The prosecution team leaves the offices while the defence team lingers behind. Chase Jackson confers quietly with the counsellor, a knowing smirk on both their faces. I feel awkward, like I'm in the wrong place at the wrong time. My gut says I shouldn't be here. I check my Liaison to make sure I have the correct details for the appointment. When I look up Chase is approaching me.

'Good afternoon,' he says, extending his hand.

'Likewise,' I say and shake firmly. 'I have an appointment with Mr Ichida at two o'clock.'

Chase smirks and tells me I'm looking well in Japanese.

'Mr Ichida,' I say quietly and give a little bow. 'My apologies.'

He chortles, turning his head to glance at his counsellor. 'No apology necessary. How were you to know?'

I tilt my head and look for the tell-tale sign of a Ouija. The scar behind his ear is big and ugly, a piss-poor instalment, semi-pro at best. I withhold the look of contempt that is itching to present itself. In fact, I'd like to punch Ichida's rental right in the teeth. We Husks regard hacks like Chase Jackson as little more than used condoms. They've come on the scene in recent months, washed-up

118

or disgraced celebrities in dire need of cash who have somehow caught wind of the business and approached lower-tier outfits with offers to freelance. Clients can walk around town with a well-known face if they want, get the experience of being instantly recognizable, formerly famous. Not exactly low-key, but some Post-Mortems are giving it a whirl, enjoying all the attention and adoration for a day or two. I don't like having my territory encroached on by those who are past their prime and can only milk their heyday.

'Chase Jackson?' I say, looking him over. 'Are you a fan, Mr Ichida?'

'American football, American movies,' Ichida says, grinning. 'I'm like a god out on the streets of New York.'

'I'll bet.'

I double-check the time on my Liaison. We're running late. Tomorrow I have planes to catch, people to be. Tight schedules are as important to me as they are to my clients, and I don't want to be clocking any overtime between them.

'Our appointment was for two,' I say, figuring Ichida is eager to transfer. 'Where would you like me to prep for the session?'

'Walk with me,' he says.

He gives a nod to his counsellor and marches off. I follow him through a set of glass doors that lead to a private elevator. We step inside and Ichida punches in a security code on a keypad to activate it.

'There has been a change of plan,' he says, hitting the button for the rooftop.

'Oh?'

'I would like you to accompany me back to one of my residences first. There is something I need before we begin. Due to a hectic schedule, I have mistakenly over-booked Mr Jackson here and have to extricate earlier than anticipated. I would prefer to download and upload in the comfort and safety of my own home.'

Like changing clothes, I think. 'Of course.'

Ichida is a heavy user of Husks, has a frequent rotation going on, using several different companies to facilitate his constant need. He uses so many of us digital whores that he's practically the baton in a relay race. The elevator takes us up to the roof, where Ichida's private helicopter is already prepped and waiting.

'Where are we going?' I ask as we board.

'The Hamptons.'

We take off and gain altitude quickly, flying directly over Central Park. Below I see a broken brown and black blotch spread over the green fields. From a bird's eye view, the Occupy Movement looks like bacteria growing in a petri dish. Suddenly, the face of Chase is right beside mine, eyes turned down, seeing what I see.

'Preposterous,' he says. 'Allowing a perfectly good park to be ruined like that.'

'Looks like someone took a shit on the lawn down there,' I mutter.

Ichida laughs and slaps me on the back far too hard, palm banging off my spine. I withhold a wince. Clients really don't know their own strength when piloting a body. A brief silence ensues, the size and significance of

Occupy Central Park capturing our full attention as we pass above it all.

'If only Tatsumi were here to see this,' Ichida muses.

'How is your wife these days, sir?'

'Dead.'

I swallow, tug at my collar. 'I had no idea. I'm terribly sorry –'

'Don't be.' He holds up a hand, shaking his head. 'We decided on assisted suicide just last week. She went Post-Mortem with a successful transfer.'

'Oh, wonderful.'

Little is said for the next twenty minutes of the journey. The chopper travels quick and direct along the shoreline, descending as we enter Long Beach airspace. I watch the buildings and roads below go by in a blur, thinning out and becoming sparse as we near our destination. In no time we're touching down on the helipad of Ichida's Hamptons home. The beachside estate is massive, ten acres, enclosed inside a twelve-foot reinforced wall that a tank would have trouble getting through. Inside those walls I see security guards, dogs, cameras everywhere. No sooner have we disembarked the helicopter when it takes off again, heading back in the direction of Manhattan. Ichida leads me inside the mansion, where we soon find ourselves in a spacious living room that is minimally furnished and particularly organized, Japanese style.

Very feng-fucking-shui, I think.

'Would you care for some tea?' Ichida asks.

'Please.'

I don't notice her straight away, but standing perfectly

still near a doorway is a pretty white girl done up as a geisha. She looks at me with only her eyes, seems a little on the young side. Ichida offers me a seat and says something to the geisha in Japanese more complicated than the few customary phrases I know. She returns something halfway between a nod and a bow and exits. Through the windows I notice workers setting up tables and tents on the lawn.

'Having a party?' I ask as we sit down.

'I'm hosting an event tonight.'

'Business or pleasure?'

'A mixer of sorts, let's say.'

'I trust you've been enjoying the services of Solace Strategies?'

'Enjoying them more than your competitors,' Ichida says with a smile, looking at his hands and taking in the last of being Chase Jackson. 'Which is why you end up getting most of my business.'

'I'll take that as a compliment,' I say, faking a smile that fools him. 'When was the last time you used a Solace Husk, if you don't mind me asking?'

Ichida's eyes narrow, give me a sideways look. I play it off like I'm scrounging for small talk. Treading lightly on this subject is paramount. Need to keep things casual, stay clear of thin ice. Don't want to bring any heat from Baxter for gossiping with a client. What I'm trying to find out is if Ichida used Miller recently, particularly the night he died.

'I'm not entirely sure, Mr Rhodes,' Ichida replies finally. 'I rent so often that things can become a bit of a blur. I'd have to refer to my appointment schedule.'

'No, no,' I wave him off. 'Just making conversation,

Mr Ichida. I want to make sure you're completely happy with me and my company, that's all.'

'Rest assured that I am most satisfied, Mr Rhodes.'

The grin he gives me tells me he's recollecting some prior enjoyable instance of being me. There is a tinge of deviancy in it that makes me a little angry and ashamed at what he or I may have done. The geisha returns with a tray balancing a teapot, cups and a small silver container. Seconds later another geisha appears, this one the same skin colour as Chase Jackson, carrying a metal briefcase. Both girls act with the utmost care and obedience, but they look at me with eyes that tell me they don't want to be here. Ichida plucks the container from the first geisha's tray as she places it on the coffee table. I watch him open it and take out a small white pill, an Ejector I'm sure, or some variant. The other girl opens the briefcase and takes out a laptop, which she sets down and plugs into a terminal under the table. Ichida sits very still as she runs another cable from the computer to his head and carefully plugs it into his Ouija.

'Mr Rhodes, you will have to excuse me while I vacate Mr Jackson here and return to my system for a short period of time. I'll be ready for upload soon.'

He swallows his pill with a sip of tea. Things like the Ejector are not to be used lightly, but I've learned that billionaires pretty much do whatever the fuck they want, whenever they want. Lower-tier outfits aren't as stringent with the rules, let clients bend them, even break them sometimes. Over the next minute I watch Ichida lose consciousness, only to see the mind of another emerge. The real Chase Jackson is soon back, blinking rapidly in the light, looking at me like he's never seen me before.

'Who you?' he grunts.

'Just another player in the game, Mr Jackson,' I say.

The geisha checks results on the laptop screen until she's satisfied, then gently unplugs the cable from Chase's head. I can't help but stare at him, my irritation at this minor leaguer growing. He slowly sheds his grogginess, doesn't like the glare I'm giving him.

'What you looking at, boy?'

'An amateur, clearly,' I snarl. 'Who do you work for?'

'Huh?'

'What outfit do you Husk with?'

Chase lets out a deep and unsettled laugh. 'Who the hell is you to be asking me something like that?'

'Just answer the question.'

'Fuck you. Don't need to tell you nothing, man.'

'Let me guess . . . you're linked up with Eternity Executive, right?'

The sneer and middle finger he shows me says I'm correct. He gets up and starts to walk away, though it's pretty obvious he doesn't know which direction to go.

'Mr Jackson,' the dark-skinned geisha says, beckoning him toward a door. 'This way, please.'

He looks at her irritably and complies. I watch him march for the door, my mouth opening, unable to resist.

'Hey, Jackson, stick to making B-movies. Oh, and don't drink and drive.'

Point taken, I think. Chase's shoulders tense, his jaw flexes. For a moment I think he might come back and take a swing at me, but he leaves the room without another word, the second geisha following close behind. The first geisha watches me with slight irritation as I sip my tea and have a chuckle to myself.

'Please do not start fights in this household, sir.'

I shrug apologetically. 'How long do you think Mr Ichida will be?'

She ignores the question. 'Tatsumi Ichida is currently taking tea as well and wishes to meet you before the session, Mr Rhodes. Please allow me to take you to her.'

'Tatsumi? Having tea? But I thought … uh … I thought she was …'

'Mrs Ichida procured her own rental yesterday and has already been uploaded. She is waiting for you in her chambers.'

'Oh,' I say. 'Lead the way.'

She guides me out of the living room and through a great hall that is in the middle of being set up for some kind of masquerade. Among typical party preparations of booze and food, there are things I can't help but notice: bowls of condoms, bejewelled masks hanging on the wall, bondage gear and sexy costumes laid out on tables. Several cameras on tripods are set up around the huge room.

'Wild night ahead?' I remark.

The perturbed look the geisha shoots me does not fill me with confidence. We soon find ourselves in Tatsumi's wing of the mansion, evidenced by the collection of Japanese cartoon and doll paraphernalia that litter the rooms we pass through. Tatsumi was a fan of Hentai in particular, almost to the point of obsession. Sculptures and renderings of girls getting fucked every which way by all kinds of men, monsters, and machines seem to be everywhere I look. I'd met Ichida's wife in the flesh a few times, a diminutive woman in her late fifties. A very strange and bitter lady as I remember, more than a bit eccentric too. Her make-up would always be overdone, professionally, in an attempt to make her resemble female characters from the Japanese anime she adored so much. As the geisha leads me into Tatsumi's private chambers I'm not sure what to expect, but what I find makes me sick to my stomach.

Tatsumi's room is painted various shades of pink and blue. A trio of tiny, fluffy dogs come running at me, yipping and yapping around my ankles. Framed pictures of cartoon characters cover the walls. A woman with silky black hair sits in the middle of the room with her back to me, painting Kanji on a canvas. She slowly turns around as I announce myself. One look and I have to halt the cry of shock that wants to come, flex every muscle in my body to stop myself from recoiling at the sight of her.

'Is everything all right, Mr Rhodes?'

The girl I'm in love with, my sweet Ryoko, is Tatsumi's Husk. She's dolled up in some manga style that looks hideous when interpreted in the real world. Her complexion is horribly pale, mouth seeming small with a thin application of red lipstick. Oversized cartoon eyes are painted on her eyelids, looking doleful and alien. Feeling repulsed by Ryoko is one of the most unnatural experiences I've ever had. She sips her tea and looks me up and down.

'Everything is fine, Mrs Ichida,' I manage. 'It's just that I only learned of your recent assisted suicide a short time ago.'

Tatsumi's smile is demure. 'Oh, that.'

'Congratulations on a successful transfer. I had no idea you were even ill.'

'Ill?' she chuckles. 'No, I was perfectly healthy for my age.'

'Oh?'

'My death was pre-emptive. Unlike my husband, I don't particularly enjoy existing in this world any more. Real life bores me. It always has. I much prefer worlds of my own creation.'

'Fair enough. But why the Husk then, if I may ask?'

Tatsumi gives me a bored look. 'As you might have noticed, we are having an event later on this evening. I am to co-host the night incognito with my husband, who will be uploaded to you. Also, I thought it might be good to get out and about a little. I'm told that it is good for Post-Mortem wellbeing.'

She rises from her chair and approaches me, hips swaying sensually. I try not to flinch when she runs her fingers through my hair, looks me in the eye with Ryoko's pupils. There is a glassy instability in her irises, addict-like. Seen it before on other Husks while on the job, a look that suggests the client is having trouble differentiating virtual reality from actual reality. The dark-skinned geisha enters the room carrying the laptop that Mr Ichida downloaded onto. She presents the computer to Tatsumi, who places it on her dresser and beckons me over. From my pillbox I take a red pill for twenty-four hours, start the Husk program, and hand over my Liaison. Tatsumi plugs one cable into the laptop, then slings her arms around my neck, pulling me close, pointing the proboscis of the second cable at my eyes as she looks into them again.

'Y'know, out of all of my husband's rentals, it was the Rhodes model I always liked best.'

She kisses me, tongue forcing itself into my mouth like an eel, the feeling of my love's lips foreign and frightening against mine. I inhale the faint smell of Ryoko, buried under a pungent jasmine perfume. Tatsumi gropes me and I go with it, faking pleasure like a porn star. The pill makes me drowsy. She kisses harder. Her fingers feel for the lump behind my ear. Reluctantly, I let her plug in the proboscis and feel myself start to slip away.

14

It's raining in London on my day off. Go figure. Twenty-four hours to myself couldn't have come sooner. The gig with Ichida just about sidelined me. For the first time I question how much longer I can do my job. Exhaustion in my line of work isn't new, but this is different, fatigue that burrows down to my bone marrow. It feels as if I'm treading close to a total burn-out in mind, body and soul. I couldn't have done a gig today if someone held a gun to my head. Too many of these sessions back-to-back could kill me if I'm not careful, adding yet another headstone to the Rhodes family plot.

Most of my family is dead. My older sister succumbed to breast cancer in her late twenties when I was a sophomore in college. My dad went by way of an aneurism soon after graduation, my mother of a broken heart not long after that. My younger sister and I are all that's left, and we don't talk much. I've only spoken to her a handful of times since we buried our parents. Last thing she said to me was that she wanted to be cremated if I was the one between us that ever had to make a decision for the other. All I know for sure is that she's a whore now, an authentic one, with an official Madam, has a respectable client list and charges a lot per hour for her precious time.

I sit in a pub licking my wounds and nursing my sore

head with a cold pint. Even the bartender said I looked knackered. A couple pretty English girls have chatted me up, but my conversational skills, strained by exhaustion, leave much to be desired. They must think I'm high or maybe a bit mental. Flew into Heathrow last night, took a black cab into the city and checked straight into a hotel, where I slept for thirteen hours straight. When I did finally wake it was from some dream that had me covered in sweat. No recollection once I wiped the sleep from my eyes. I've been roaming the city since then, trying to remember. It's a welcome distraction actually.

There is a message on my Liaison that has been bothering me, sent yesterday by Ryoko, giving me an update on Clive's detainment in Paris. There was an attachment that I opened on my flight. I had to stifle a cry of shock at what appeared on screen. Ryoko forwarded me three photos of Clive's second-degree burns that she'd somehow managed to acquire from the Parisian police. His face looked horrible, red raw and blistery, skin weeping fluids. He's lost the use of his right eye. I can't stop staring at the pictures. Have to fight back tears. Seeing such beauty reduced to wreckage breaks my heart. Clive didn't deserve this.

The vomiting is bothering me too, these semi-regular rejections from the pit of my stomach. I was sick once on the flight over, chucked again before I went to sleep. Wanted to throw up this morning while taking a mist, but managed to hold it back. No nausea or gut pain. No food poisoning or flu. If anything it feels like the worst kind of nervousness, a case of the butterflies turned into locusts.

At the hotel I managed to hold down my continental breakfast for twenty minutes before it ended up splattered in the sink. Only in the last half-hour have I started to get my appetite back. Looking at the pub menu, I notice that none of the meat dishes denote their source. This means all the meat is lab-grown. I've eaten the stuff countless times before, but now the thought of it makes me uncomfortable.

Chelsea versus Arsenal plays on every oversized flat-screen in the pub. Seems like an important match judging by the clientele's reaction to the game. I try to watch, but I can't get into it. I'm too distracted by anything and everything and nothing at the same time. All I want to do is get drunk, but for some reason I can't even get a buzz on. I hammer back my pint and order another. Chelsea scores a goal and the place goes nuts. Two minutes later Arsenal pulls one back and shuts everyone up. A minute later I'm not even watching any more. My Liaison provides me with the NYC news instead.

A local politician caught with his hand up his secretary's skirt is the top story of the day. The violent spree of cab robberies I'd heard about earlier has escalated too, with two more drivers found shot to death in their vehicles, riddled with armour-piercing rounds that went straight through their bullet-proof partitions. Two more Manhattan women are reported missing. The first one is Annabel Colette, a blonde 22-year-old rich kid from the Upper East Side. The picture they show of her, relaxing on a yacht with a glass of champagne and a snobbish smile, screams *spoiled brat* to me. Judging by what I see around her neck and on her fingers, the girl has expensive taste in jewellery. Footage of her father, some Wall Street fat-cat in a suit with his arm around a sad, but stoic, blonde trophy-wife, tearfully pleads for her safe return. Something tells me the girl would put up a hell of a fight. Whoever is holding her has their hands full, I'm sure.

The second one's name is Clarice Patton, age twenty-three, an aspiring actress and model. The photo is of a sultry blue-eyed brunette with a mischievous grin. It seems to me like she has more than a touch of the *bad girl* in her. I figure she might have snuck off to LA all starry-eyed to party it up and get discovered. I imagine her taking one for the dream team while friends and family worry back home. I can picture her with panties round her ankles on a casting couch, a strong hand clutching her throat in an aggressive act of erotic asphyxiation as she whimpers and wheezes for the chance at a role. I picture this so clearly, like I'm experiencing it from both first-person and third-person perspectives, as if I'm somehow standing in a corner watching myself go gonzo on this poor girl.

Although no ransom demands have been made, cops aren't coy about trying to tie both women's disappearances into Occupy Central Park. At a press conference a police captain states that he suspects Integris may be involved in these recent Manhattan snatchings. He seems damn sure of himself, the contempt in his voice unmistakable when referencing to the group. The faction's long list of alleged crimes includes kidnapping, and the NYPD claim they are on top of the situation. The smug smile I feel taking over my face can't be helped. Our United States . . . just like

Mexico, just like Brazil, just like Columbia or fucking Ven-ezuela now. I called it days ago, knew the lower classes were getting desperate enough to hijack the family mem-bers of our society's elite. North America, South America? Ghettos or favelas? Shit, there's no difference now. We're just like every corrupt, poor, overpopulated country we ever looked down on. Our missing Manhattan girls are just the newest promissory notes in one of the world's oldest and most popular crimes.

After the anchor reports an eleven-car pile-up on the Brooklyn Bridge, he releases the identity of a body found in the meat-packing district: Dennis Delane, the missing dude from a couple days ago. Police are ruling his death a homicide. Beaten beyond recognition is what the anchor says. When Delane's photograph takes over the screen, I hitch in my breath.

Seen that guy before, I think. *I know him.*

You wouldn't forget him easily, with his frizzy red hair, green eyes and thin face. Looks like a bit of a creep to me. No matter how hard I try, I can't place him. He seems like a threat to me somehow, a person of interest who could make my life difficult. Seconds later Delane's image is gone. Live footage follows, showing a decrepit alleyway, police-taped and crawling with cops, blue tarp covering the corpse that peeks out from behind a row of garbage cans. I'm no detective, but I'd say his body was dumped.

Thrown away like trash.

As I stare at my pint, the thought eats at me. Another goal is scored and the pub erupts into applause. A woman's shriek rises above the shouts of men. It is one of

133

excitement, but its pitch and duration trigger something chilling in my head. I've heard this shriek before, I think. I turn to the bar, looking for the screamer. She's standing by the draught taps, both arms stretched over her head, squealing with delight as she looks at the screen.

The vision comes in a flash, a woman's bare arms stretched up over her head. I remember turning to look into a large lens, watching something as it watches me. A red light glows on top of it. For the first time I can retain the information and I'm instantly panicked by it.

Seconds later I'm dialling Tweek in New York. I don't expect him to answer, but thankfully he picks up after the second ring. His voice sounds unimpressed.

'I assume you're calling me about another problem, Rhodes?'

'Why do you say that?'

'You Husks tend not to call me for any other reason.'

'Sorry, Tweek,' I say. 'But my head is getting worse.'

'How bad?'

'Fuck, bad enough for me to be calling you about it.'

'Are you getting enough rest like I told you?'

'Goddamn it,' I hiss. 'A good night's sleep or two is not going to fix this. This is something else. Something in my head is . . . malfunctioning.'

There is a pause on the other end. I hear sounds of Tweek rummaging around, drawers opening and closing, things clattering on a desk. I don't know if it was what I said, or how I said it, but I can hear concern in Tweek's voice when he finally replies.

'Okay, okay. As soon as you get back, come straight in.

I'll take a closer look, try some different things. See if we can't get to the bottom of it.'

'What should I do in the meantime?'

'Relax. Meditate.'

'I'm in a frigging bar, man.'

'Then get drunk. Numb your head, slow your brain activity.'

'Trust me, I'm trying.'

'Try harder.'

He hangs up and I down the rest of my pint. Need another, but the bar is packed. As I get up I suddenly feel the drunkenness that seemed to have been eluding me. One misstep and I've hip-checked some guy's chair, bumping him forward into the pint he's drinking. I hear him choke on the lager; watch it spill in his lap. Three other guys at his table bitch and moan, giving me shit. Their accents are harsh to my ears.

'You stupid fucking prat.'

'Jesus, I'm so, so sorry.'

The guy rises from his chair, wiping his chin. 'You will be.'

'Looks like you've pissed yourself, Roy,' laughs one of his mates.

Roy isn't laughing. He gives me a shove. The volume of the pub's patrons gets halved. Heads begin turning in our direction. I raise my hands, indicating that I want no trouble of any sort.

'It was an accident, man,' I say. 'I'd be happy to pay for another pint.'

He shoves me again. 'Another pint isn't gonna fucking dry me off, now is it?'

The second shove is on my bruised ribs and it hurts, a lot. I open my mouth to apologize again, try to smooth things over. An apology isn't what comes out, much to my surprise.

'Ah, get fucked.'

'Eh?' Roy's eyes widen. 'What?'

That wasn't me, I think, my eyes widening as well. *That wasn't me at all.*

Maybe it's the drink working my lips. Roy's hands are already balling into fists. Another apology is in order. I go to speak again and realize my mouth isn't mine. I catch my reflection in a mirror on the wall. My lips are pulled back in a cruel smile.

'You deaf as well as thick?' I say. 'I said get *fucked.*'

The pub goes quiet. Roy takes one look at his mates and then takes a big swing at me. I duck it easily and get inside his guard, sinking a vicious knee into his crotch, doubling him over with a squawk. Palming the back of his head, I smash his face into the table twice, busting nose and teeth on the varnished wood. One of his hooligan friends jumps out of his seat and grabs me by the throat. I return the move, kicking his ankles out from underneath him with a sweep and slamming his head down hard next to Roy's. His neck bends at an ugly angle with the hit, but I don't hear it break. The lack of a snap disappoints me.

The two others get up and come at me. The first one swings wide and I sidestep his attack, nudging him in the ribs hard enough to send his bulk crashing into another table. The second one gets two body shots in before I break a pint glass in his face and dropkick him into the mirror. Just before the glass shatters, I see my reflection. I look like I'm poised to fight a dozen men. My breath is coming in heaves. The smile on my face tells me I'm enjoying it all far too much.

'Oh my God,' a nearby woman gasps.

Moans and cursing come from the men on the floor. I look around the pub. Everyone's eyes are glued to me, wide and horrified. I straighten my clothes, open my wallet, drop more money than I owe on the bar. There is blood on my hands, transferring to the banknotes I lay down. For a single moment I'm reminded of something all too similar, but I forget it in a second.

'Sorry,' I say to the bartender.

He says nothing, just looks back and forth between me and the four I've beaten up. The patrons part for me as I walk hastily through the pub and out into the drizzle. On the street I break into a run, splashing through puddles, putting some distance between me and the bloody scene I've just created.

That wasn't me, I think again. *I wouldn't have done that.*

Two blocks away I stop running and slip into an old telephone box to catch my breath. The blood on my hands makes me feel like vomiting again. I need more rest, need to get in another ten or twelve hours' sleep back at the hotel. I suddenly want to call Phineas. I know he's in London, though I suspect he might already be in session. Speaking into my Liaison, I leave a message for him instead to pick up when he's done.

'Need to have that chat soon, my friend,' I say. 'Pick a place and make sure you call me when your job is done.'

Sick and muttering, I roam the streets of London in the rain until I find an entrance to the Tube and descend. For an hour I ride the Underground aimlessly, crammed in my seat, hypnotized by the tunnel lights flashing outside the windows. Being below ground is comforting somehow, the train carriage packed with mute passengers pressed in around me, the closest thing to a cocoon I can manage. Eventually I feel good enough to make my way back to my hotel and I crawl into bed. Soon I'm sleeping like the dead, dreaming about one of the worst periods of my life, when me and my family hit rock bottom.

15

Rock bottom for my family happened when my parents tried to get their kids into modelling. It all started with some slick guy in a suit coming up to us in an outlet mall one day, praising my folks for having such beautiful offspring, saying we all had that 'star quality' about us. After laying on the charm, he gave us his card, said he was a talent scout for a top modelling agency, talked on and on about fashion royalty, designer labels, lifestyles of the rich and famous. The promises were plentiful, the suggestions lucrative. Mom and Dad fell for it hook, line and sinker. They emptied their savings account into headshots and demo reels, outfits and shoes, paying agency fees up front. The twinkle in my parents' eyes made me eager to please them. In all honesty, both my sisters and I salivated over the prospect of wealth and success for little more than donning new clothes and posing for photographers. The agency told us to be patient, said they were setting things up, and that they would be in touch.

Nothing ever came of it. No gigs were booked. In fact, the phone never rang once. Weeks went by with no contact. Frustrated, my mother called the modelling agency one day, only to discover the number was out of service. She went to their office and found the place gutted and abandoned. The con men had moved overnight. Hundreds of suckers had been caught in the scam, fleeced by these assholes. My family was back in the shit, broke and without prospects. It almost destroyed us. Precious little held the unit together after that. Years later, with all those savings gone, there was no way to pay for my older sister's cancer treatments when she fell ill. She eventually died because we'd bought some magic beans. That is all I dream about throughout the night, the guilt of it ravaging my slumber.

Late the next morning a kindly old man in a tweed jacket arrives at my hotel in a Rolls-Royce Phantom. He is polite and charming and asks only that I call him Phillip. He takes my bags and drives me out to the countryside of Kent, where his employer resides. We chat for the whole ride. I find myself chuckling at his pithy little jokes. I wind down the window, taking in the rural sights and smells. Low rolling hills rise and fall in all directions. Little crops of cobblestone houses appear along the roadside nestled in plots of lush, damp vegetation. It's peaceful out here. I find myself nodding off periodically, only to be stirred awake by Phillip's ramblings. He goes on at length about Mr Shaw and his family, clearly fond of his employer. I can't help but like him, strikes me as a good sort, sweet and sincere. What's more, he doesn't carry a weapon of any kind.

From what Phillip tells me, Mr Shaw seems like he will be a breath of fresh compared to my usual clients. When we enter the wrought-iron gates of the sprawling country estate, I'm charmed by what I see. Manicured gardens and well-kept grounds peppered with objects from bygone eras: birdhouses and baths, trugs and gnomes. It's kind of cute, this penchant for old things, antiquities abounding. It seems far removed from the modern world, frozen in time outside the city limits. We pull up to the front doors of a massive ivy-covered residence, and I realize how lonely it all feels despite the allure. The place appears unguarded, though I have no doubt there are multimillion-pound security systems in place. I think Phillip may be the only human inhabiting these private acres.

Phillip opens the car door for me, but does not retrieve my bags from the trunk. With a beckoning hand he leads me into the manor. I follow him through the halls of the great house until we come to a cozy lounge with a long bar along one wall. On the floor, in the centre of the room, is an HG unit twice the size of the one I have at home. Phillip picks up a box from a side table and opens the lid to reveal a row of Cohiba Esplendidos.

'Would you care for a Cuban, Mr Rhodes?'

Most definitely, I tell him. Phillip cuts the ends of two, hands one to me and strikes a match. I lean into the flame, sucking on the cigar.

'It's still a challenge to get these in the States,' I say, puffing thick smoke.

'I know.' Phillip grins and lights his. 'It's tragic really.'

I stroll around the lounge, enjoying my smoke, taking in the peaceful air of the place.. Not a typical day on the job. I envy Clive for having had this client as a regular. The dull throb in my ribs soon reminds me of my other clients and my role.

'Um, will Mr Shaw . . . ?'

'He will be with us in a moment,' Phillip replies. 'And he's very much looking forward to meeting you.'

As if on cue, the HG unit activates. It takes a few seconds to warm up before a three-dimensional body blooms in the centre of the room. The hologram is that of a man around Phillip's age, bespectacled and smartly dressed in a maroon blazer. Shaw greets his butler with a warm smile and kind words before his eyes drift over to me.

'Mr Rhodes, I presume,' he says, and chuckles. 'I'd shake your hand, but you know how it is.'

'I know how it is, Mr Shaw.'

'Please, do sit down,' he gestures to the chairs and sofas around the room. 'Can I have Phillip get you anything? Coffee? Tea? A fine whisky maybe?'

'Whisky,' I say, remembering to dull my mind. 'Definitely.'

'Phillip, would you be so kind as to bring our guest something that would complement his Cohiba?'

'I've got just the thing.'

Phillip goes to the bar and brings back a whisky, neat. I take a sip and discover it's even more enjoyable than Winslade's cognac. Shaw watches me as I drink and smoke in turn, pleased that I'm pleased. I notice when his smile begins to fade.

'I must say I'm very saddened to hear about Clive.'

Suddenly the cigar and whisky don't taste so good. 'We all are, Mr Shaw.'

'I'm told the Parisian police understand that he was, in fact, attacked first.'

'Yes and he will be pleading self-defence to that fact,' I reply. 'The law firm representing him is nothing short of the best. I'd say there's a good chance he will be found not guilty.'

Shaw's eyebrows rise. 'And if so, will he be returning to work?'

'I don't think so. His face . . . his face was too . . .'

The eyebrows lower. 'How bad were his injuries?'

'Bad.'

'Surely some reconstructive surgery is not out of the question?'

'It won't be the same . . . *he* won't be the same. Plastic surgery doesn't constitute perfection, Mr Shaw. That's what our clients pay for.'

Shaw shakes his head. 'As I told your boss, Baxter, I would be more than happy to hire him regardless. He was a positively wonderful rental.'

'That's very kind of you, but a Husk can't get by with just one client, and others won't share your point of view.'

Not the answer Shaw wants to hear. After a pause he accepts the reality of the situation with a grave nod. His eyes look into mine, or at least I think they do. I wonder if he actually sees out of them and, if so, how.

'A pity,' he says.

I take another drag on my Cohiba and chase it with whisky. A cigar suddenly materializes in the hologram's hand. Shaw raises it, looks at it with a wry smile, then holds it to his lips and takes a puff. The graphic of smoke he exhales doesn't drift very far. I'm sure I see it become pixilated. Shaw sighs.

'Not nearly the same.'

Phillip seems saddened by the sight. I get the sense that these two men, despite being employer and employee, shared many a drink and smoke over the years in this very room. I finish my whisky in another two gulps.

'I'm ready if you are, Mr Shaw.'

'Indeed, Mr Rhodes. Please have a seat.'

I settle into an overstuffed armchair near the HG and take out my Liaison. The Husk program boots up, cycling algorithms. Shaw gives Phillip a nod, sending the butler to the bar, where he fixes himself two more drinks, one for him and one for my client, who is minutes away from having a mouth again. I plug one data cable into a jack on the HG unit and carefully inspect the proboscis on the other.

'May I ask your intentions?'

Shaw shrugs and smiles. 'I can give you my whole itinerary if you'd like.'

'The Cliff's Notes will be fine.'

'Basically, I'll be spending this afternoon with my grandchildren, posing as their new tennis instructor. Tomorrow and the next day, I'll be looking after my wife at the Carrington Nursing Home.'

The look I give Shaw amuses him. I don't know what I expected him to say, but I didn't expect that.

'Seriously?' I ask with a smirk.

'Perfectly serious,' he replies. 'Is there a problem?'

'No. It's just that I thought . . . I thought you'd . . .'

Shaw is the one who smirks now. 'You thought I'd be booked for some skydiving or rally car racing? An orgy perhaps, with prostitutes and platters of cocaine?'

Phillip guffaws, spilling his drink a little, turning Shaw's smirk into an amused grin. I can't help but blush as I insert the proboscis into my Ouija.

'No, Mr Rhodes,' Shaw says, gesturing to the cigar still in my hand. 'After life has ended, all some of us want is just a little taste of it now and again.'

16

For the first time I don't dream. Somehow, in my unconscious state, I recognize the absence of it. It strikes me as odd. My lucid dreams often serve as crude yardsticks of my Husking. I don't – *can't* – remember any of the sessions I'm hired for. I can only remember the dreams I had when I was under. What passes for my usual dormancy is an indefinable block of lost time, duration unknown. Could have been minutes, could have been months. There is nothing, except this thought that I know I'm experiencing nothing. This awareness of what is missing is alien to me, consciousness in an utter dead zone with almost nothing to contemplate. If I didn't know better, I'd say I was at peace.

Suddenly, I'm brought back to life, emerging into myself as the newfound residue of foreign cognition starts to slip from my brain. Soon the squatter is gone, leaving out the back door as I enter the front, vacating my head for only me. It takes a little longer than usual to come to my senses. My eyes are returned to me first, vision blurry. Shaw's hologram stands before me as I sit, talking apparently. Not sure if he's speaking to me or someone else. Can't understand a word he's saying. Computing my surroundings feels like a chore, though I start to recognize the cigar lounge. I try to say something, but my mouth won't do as it's told. Only two words come to mind.

Brain damage.

Phillip leans over me and holds a fist under my nose, pressing the webbing of his thumb to my nostril. I inhale smelling salts off his skin, snap awake, look up at the hologram. The 3D image is not a bespectacled old man any more. The head has red hair and a thin face. The eyes looking back at me are green and angry.

'What –'

I blink and Dennis Delane is gone, the image of Shaw standing in his place. My shudder is involuntary, drawing the attention of my client and his butler. I see the unease on both of their faces.

'How are you feeling, Mr Rhodes?' asks Phillip, his pitch high with nervousness.

'Not sure,' I say, wiggling fingers and toes.

'You seemed to have considerable trouble returning to us.'

I try to rise from the overstuffed chair I'm in, but the connected proboscis tugs at the side of my head, keeping me anchored.

'Here,' Phillip says, reaching toward my Ouija. 'Let me help you.'

I flinch and pull away. 'I got it, thanks.'

Phillip backs away, hands held up in apology. An awkward stand-off follows, everyone frozen for a few moments, unsure of how to proceed. I disconnect the proboscis and gather enough of my own thoughts to realize the prospect of brain damage is growing unlikely. Despite the

147

grogginess, my body feels surprisingly good, well-rested and respected. This experience is new to me.

'How did everything go?' I ask.

Shaw pauses. 'To be honest, Mr Rhodes, I think I preferred Clive.'

'Why? What happened?'

'Nothing happened. Either you don't suit me, or I just don't wear you very well.'

Clients can have any number of reasons why they don't think a Husk is suitable for them. I'm not buying Shaw's, however. I've never asked much of my clients in the past, but I press for some answers.

'Something must have happened,' I snap. 'Spit it out.'

My curtness surprises even me. Shaw and Phillip exchange a glance that I don't particularly like. I turn my attention to Phillip, wondering if he might spill something. The butler is well trained, knows his place in matters such as this. He purses his lips and wanders off to the bar, where he fixes a drink, leaving me to face Shaw alone. The hologram takes off his spectacles and cleans them with a handkerchief.

'What happened was I spent all of yesterday looking after my beloved wife, just like I told you I would . . .'

'How is she?'

'She's old, Mr Rhodes, and probably doesn't have much time left on this earth. My wife is one of the few people who knows I'm dead, unlike my company's board members and stockholders, whom I no longer meet in the flesh. Despite my best efforts, she has expressly wished not to join me in this so-called afterlife. I still try and sell her this snake oil though, because I miss her terribly and can't bear the thought of her gone. Yesterday, I found myself losing patience with her, something I have never done before. If I didn't know better, I'd say you were rubbing off on me.'

'How do you mean?'

'I sensed something pushing back while we were in session, felt as if there were echoes of you in there coming out.'

Not of me, I think, but say nothing.

'I'll wager I'm not like most of your other clients, Mr Rhodes.'

'No, you're not.'

Shaw replaces his glasses and the cigar materializes in his hand once again. He raises it, turns it in his fingers, analysing the image with disappointment, if not outright distaste. His sensing of someone twice removed, a seed within a shell, a dream within a dream, has me worried.

'I know this isn't real,' he says, wagging the cigar at me. 'I'm cheating myself at the end of the day, but I'm no fool.'

My response seems ruder than intended. 'What are you then?'

'I'm scared, Mr Rhodes.'

'Scared of what?'

'For starters . . . a man like *you*.'

'Me?' I say. 'You don't know anything about me.'

'And that makes you all the more frightening.'

Phillip comes back from the bar and hands me a glass of Scotch, his intuition correct. I grab for it gleefully. Shaw watches as I gulp it down in one go.

'You see, Mr Rhodes, it's the little things in life I've always loved; a good book, a decent cigar, a respectable Scotch. My personal favourite is a good night's sleep and a long lie-in.'

'I was wondering why I feel so well-rested,' I say, forcing a smile.

Shaw does not smile back. 'There was no good night's sleep with you, Mr Rhodes. I can assure you.'

'Pardon?'

'In all my living days, I never had nightmares like the ones I had the past two nights while in session with you.'

His words bore into my gut, hollow it out. Shaw is the only client I've had that has used me like a decent human being and because of it I somehow feel exposed, naked, on trial for crimes I haven't committed. This man has caught wind of the nest of worms writhing in my head and he doesn't like it. I don't like it either.

'Nightmares? Of what?'

'I wish I could tell you,' Shaw replies. 'I can't remember a single detail, only the awful panic and anxiety they left me with. Whatever dreams may have come, they were the most terrifying things I've experienced in a long while.'

Shaw leans forward, fingers stroking his chin, holographic eyes narrowing to slits behind his glasses as he stares at my hairline.

'Just what on earth is going on up there, young man?'

'Goddamn Winslade.'

I don't know why I muttered Winslade's name exactly, just felt like the right person to bitch at in the moment, the right guy to blame. Mr Shaw's hologram straightens suddenly, brows creased with concern, a new interest in his eyes.

'Mr Rhodes, I believe you just mentioned the name *Winslade*.'

'No, I didn't,' I say.

'Let me clarify,' Shaw replies, his eyes scanning back and forth. 'I've just reviewed the recording, and you did, in fact, say *Winslade*.'

'So?'

'This wouldn't be Wilhelm Winslade, would it?'

I swallow hard. 'What does it matter?'

'Is he one of Solace Strategies' clients? Is he a client of yours?'

I start to rise from my chair. 'Sorry, Mr Shaw, I'm not at liberty to discuss the company's confidential –'

'Sit *down*.'

Shaw's anger catches both Phillip and me off guard. I drop back down in the armchair and grip my knees nervously, feeling like a child in trouble. Shaw sees this and his demeanour softens.

'I'm sorry. Please, answer the question.'

'Yes, Mr Winslade is a client of Solace, and a client of mine.'

He seems disappointed by my answer. Phillip looks absolutely horrified by it. Silence descends. After a few moments Shaw gives Phillip a certain look. The butler interprets it correctly, takes his drink and leaves the lounge, shutting the door behind him. I feel abandoned. For some reason I want another living, breathing human being in close proximity as I'm forced to talk to this ghost in the machine.

'Do you believe in God, Mr Rhodes?' Shaw asks.

'I'm not sure,' I reply, growing uncomfortable. 'Do you?'

'Yes, but, more importantly, a man like Winslade doesn't. If anything, he believes he is a god among men.'

'I get that impression from him.'

Shaw hesitates, collecting his thoughts. He stares at the bar, licking his lips, no doubt wishing he could have a stiff drink. As more and more seconds go by it becomes evident that he is lost in these thoughts.

'When did you start?' I ask, breaking the silence.

Shaw looks up. 'Start what?'

'Believing in God.'

'Oh, after I died.'

God talk makes me feel either annoyed or anxious, a reflection of how I wrestle with the idea on a regular basis. I don't know where Shaw's going with this, and I don't much care, but I decide to play along.

'I've always wanted to believe,' I say. 'Asked for some kind of revelation plenty of times, but never got a thing in return.'

Shaw chuckles. 'You want God to connect to you, but you've got it the wrong way around. It is you who must connect to it. A soul, like all life, is meant to grow. It has to expand, has to reach out and try and touch what lies beyond its grasp.'

'How do you know?'

'Because I lost that ability to grow. When I turned Post-Mortem I didn't just digitize, Mr Rhodes, I dehumanized. When you do that, when you leave behind what you once were, you finally understand what made being human so special, so . . . *spiritual*, for lack of a better word. Tell me, have you ever picked a lock, Mr Rhodes?'

'No . . . have you?'

'Plenty,' he says with a wry smile. 'My first career, so to speak, was that of a common burglar. Post-war England had very few employment opportunities for young men leaving school. I made ends meet in my own foolish ways for a while. Eventually I was nicked and detained at Her Majesty's pleasure. The stretch inside gave me plenty of time to think and turn my life around.'

Like some lounge act magic trick, a flame forms on the tip of his index finger, which he puts to the tip of his hologram cigar.

'I understand now that there are some answers you're just not allowed to have when you're alive. It's the questions that keep us moving, questions that make followers out of us.'

Shaw takes a long drag and then blows the smoke out into perfectly formed rings that simply erase themselves after drifting a few feet.

'Faith is naturally elusive, Mr Rhodes, a gift that turns people into perpetual-motion machines. We chase our beliefs constantly, in religion, in science, in love and life, into the future. Faith propels us forward as much as it holds us back. Everyone wants to be given the key, but that's not how it works. It's more like picking a lock. We're all novices. You have to work at it, jimmying tumblers, applying correct pressure, setting teeth until it all happens to line up just right and suddenly click. But you can't see what you're working toward. That's the rub. You can only do your best to feel it out. And you never know when it's going to come together. You just keep trying until it does. For some it can be quick, others can spend a lifetime. Some never manage it at all.'

A key, the old kind with puzzle-piece teeth, materializes in Shaw's hand. He looks it over with affection. I'm sure it is a replica that unlocked a special something at one time or other in his life. My mind conjures up a picturesque cottage in the countryside where he and his wife might have spent summers together, a place where great memories were made. The thought is vivid and moving. I wonder if some residual recollection of Shaw's has been provoked in my head.

'It was only after I died that I realized,' Shaw continues. 'I finally had hold of that key. A key I could tell others about. The problem is I think the door no longer exists for me. I have now become part of something woefully . . . unnatural. With the very same key I've locked myself out of that which was ready to welcome me, the next mystery so to speak. Instead, I'm trapped here. This uploaded consciousness we're prone to calling immortality is not what I'd call an achievement. It's more of a manufactured limbo, barely a pass mark that allows things to continue with dismal mediocrity. I'm not sure how long I'll stick with it, to be frank.'

'Why?'

'Because we're not supposed to go on indefinitely,' Shaw replies. 'I know this now, but there are others who don't believe it, won't accept it.'

'You mean Winslade?'

'Wilhelm was a machine long before he was uploaded to one. I met him in the flesh many years ago in regard to business ventures with our shared capital. He was no innovator, no entrepreneur. That man made his fortune in hostile takeovers, liquidations, forced mergers, whatever could mine the most profit. Typical of our breed. Our appetites can be limitless. Our horizons seem endless. Remember, Mr Rhodes, people like us could have anything we wanted in life ... some of us still have that expectation, even in death.'

Phillip enters the lounge and places my packed bags near the doorway. The keys to the Rolls-Royce Phantom jingle in his hand. Shaw, forgetting momentarily that he has been returned to phantom form, begins to offer me a handshake. Once he realizes the mistake he drops his hand with a look of embarrassment. I stand and hold my hand out, beckoning him to shake. The wry smile returns as he reaches out to me again. We fake a gesture of farewell, graphics overlapping flesh, both satisfied by the action. Those holographic eyes look into mine, holding me in place better than a physical appendage ever could as his projected pupils search my own made of matter.

'You'll understand if I don't rent you again?'

'Of course,' I reply.

'It's nothing personal.'

'Quite all right, Mr Shaw, I could do with fewer clients right now, to be honest.'

I approach Phillip and bend down to retrieve my bags. As I rise the butler slips a Cohiba into my shirt pocket for the road and gives me a reassuring pat on the shoulder. It's nothing personal, the sharing of brains and bodies between living and dead.

No, I think. *Nothing personal at all.*

'Mr Rhodes?'

'Yes, Mr Shaw?'

I turn back to see my client standing in the middle of the room, looking doleful, one hand raised in a warning of sorts. His holographic image flickers once, twice.

'Remember, there is a vast difference between those that seek to live for ever, and those who are simply too scared to die.'

17

My last evening in London consists of nursing a drink in the Red Lion pub and doing as little as humanly possible while waiting for Phineas to show. I sit by a window and stare out at the street, my forehead pressed against the cool glass. It's raining again, an unending line of anoraks and umbrellas shuffling past in the slick grey. Everyone appears faceless, moving at a uniform speed, skins drained of colour. Garbage and recyclables are piled on the pavements, awaiting collection, their stink encumbered by the rotten weather. This place, like every city, is so damn overcrowded, saturated with people and the waste they produce. My mind keeps replaying snippets of what Shaw said earlier. His words are starting to seem obvious now.

'We won't get it until we're dead,' I mutter.

We're almost there, I think. Mass depression must be the first step toward our species' extinction, a collective lack of giving a fuck about the future that in effect cancels one. It's already beginning, new diseases and disruptions, fresh war and famine, news reports clocking death tolls higher than the day before. The four horsemen are out of the starting gate, but most people aren't watching this last race. All bets are off. There is too little left to gamble with. Maybe it's not a bad thing. As mass killers of everything else, perhaps we deserve a taste.

Every day I see more examples of how awful we treat the majority of everything we come into contact with, how inhuman we can be when it suits us. We're like locusts, consumers that can't help themselves, predisposed to eat each other out of house and home. How many more of us can our world handle? All I want is to make enough money to insulate myself against the inevitable, get me and Ryoko someplace safe by the time everything goes to total shit.

But no matter how much I make, it never seems like enough.

When I was a kid, I formulated some incorrect ideas about earning money. Anyone on a TV or movie screen, those motherfuckers had *made it* in my opinion. Didn't matter if they were playing a bit part or offering a clownish bleached grin for a toothpaste brand. Any face on a concert poster, any chiselled body on an advertisement, any mouths delivering lines to cameras, I assumed those people didn't have to work another day in their lives. Figured their houses and cars were paid off, debts settled, money in the bank that would never run out. The pedestals they were on, heights above the average person, kept the cash coming somehow.

This consumed me, the idea that there was a loophole in the system, certain jobs that you only had to work once or twice to reap eternal benefits from. Star in a movie, drop an album, pen a book, get a million hits on a viral video and for ever collect on bountiful residuals. Check your bank account every few days just to see the cash stack up for that one important or popular thing you did. I believed being the centre of attention for even fifteen minutes of pseudo-fame could be milked for dough and dates for the rest of whatever. That spelled *contentment*. I was convinced of its reality, a defining moment from where you never looked back. Money for nothing and your chicks for free.

I remember when I woke up and stopped believing this bullshit. It was winter, unending days of no snow, but bitter cold. I was seventeen and desperately looking for a part-time job, wandering from store to store with copies of my resume. Getting hired before a Christmas season was supposed to be easy, but I was learning different. Automated cashiers were taking over everywhere. Most stores were looking to downsize. Even a good-looking white kid with a high school education couldn't get jack shit for minimum wage. All up Broadway I tried with no results. When I hit 14th Street I wandered into the market at Union Square, browsing stalls until I saw something that made me stop. A puckered, pissed-off face glowered at customers from behind a table of novelty hats. The face was familiar, something celebrity about it. As I stared, a cute tattooed chick manning another booth nearby flagged my attention with a little wave. She was three or four years older than me, with a tongue ring, selling someone's homemade puppets.

'Recognize him?' the girl said.

'I think so.'

'That's the lead singer from Red Rum Runners.'

'What's he doing here?' I asked, dumbfounded.

'Being a douche-bag, thinking he's superior to everyone else.'

'Didn't his band just get nominated for Best New Artist?'

'Yep. And look where it got him.'

I guess my look of disbelief amused her, because she let out a deliciously evil giggle and beckoned me over with a finger.

'Believe it, cute stuff. When the Rum Runners aren't on tour, this is where you'll find him, broke and brooding.'

It took me a while to digest the fact that this rock star was working like a chump once he stepped away from the spotlight. The girl looked me up and down, told me I could hang out with her, asked if I wanted a puppet. I set my sights on a plush werewolf, but I had no money. She gave it to me regardless, said I could work it off in other ways. After she closed up we went back to her place to smoke dope and fool around. Beth was her name. She was broke like me, beautiful too. She was my first love. That girl showed me how to get more out of my young life than anyone else.

We screwed almost every night for two months in her dingy little apartment. She called me her *no strings attached*. I called her my *sock puppet*. Drunk and high, we would devise plans to get rich and famous so we could leave our hardships in the dust. Music, modelling, acting, it didn't matter, as long as it let us dabble with lifestyles of the rich and famous. Beth was determined to do something, anything, that would get her royalty cheques for the rest of her life. Easy money, she called it. It might only take a single leaked sex tape. She said we'd do it together. It was our escape plan.

Then one day I showed up at her apartment and found it abandoned. Not even a note left behind. Went to Union Square and discovered the puppet stall was gone. Poked around, but no one seemed to know a thing. The Red Rum singer gave me a bemused look when I asked him if he'd seen Beth at all. After a long pause he told me he hadn't seen her since she'd left his apartment two nights ago. I asked what the hell she was doing in his place and he responded with a sly smile. I glanced around at the other vendors, the little community of mostly young men. There were smirks on almost half the faces. The realization of how many of them Beth may have had behind my back began to dawn on me. Strangely, I didn't feel jilted, but when the lead singer gave a derisive chuckle I turned back and decked the prick. He went down, out cold, knocking over his table and chair. Next thing I knew I was running, hoping my right hook had left him unable to sing for a while. Back home I called Beth repeatedly but her phone was disconnected. I never heard from her again. Being left in the lurch like that, it broke my fucking heart.

A couple years later I got into a cab in Brooklyn and found a headshot and IMDb acting history taped to the back of my cabbie's seat. We got to chatting and he ran down the list of shows he'd been hired for at one point or another, everything from cop dramas to comedy sitcoms. Said he was driving the taxi to help out a friend. Told me it was for nostalgia more than anything, since it was the gig he'd had before the acting career took off. Driving cabs kept him grounded, he said. Good for the soul, he said. He liked helping people out, getting them to where they needed to go, good karma and shit, he said. That was before he pressed me for any possible connection to the entertainment business. The man wanted a gig . . . anywhere . . . for anything . . . It was pathetic. He was clutching at straws. The desperation in the car was like humidity. His eyes bothered me, the way they wobbled in their sockets when he spoke of his chosen profession.

It was sitting in this cab, looking out the window and wanting out as my driver prattled on, that I caught sight of Beth again. She was standing on a corner in front of a backlit bus shelter advertisement, looking much different from how I remembered her. As we drove by, my feelings came bubbling back up, flooding me with anxiety, drowning my heart. The infatuation and rejection, all of the crippling love and hurt I'd previously felt pervaded every inch of me. In an instant I threw cash at the cabbie and told him to pull over.

I ran back to Beth, calling her name, eyes fixed on the girl wearing the black miniskirt and heavy mascara. When I finally reached her it took her too long to recognize me. There was no joy in Beth's face when the penny finally dropped, just indifference. She had gained weight. There were bags under her eyes. Thick make-up almost camouflaged the cold sores. The old bruise on her cheek dusted with rouge was more noticeable. Her first words to me were nothing more than a curse under her breath. She told me to beat it, that she was working and I was fucking it up by being around.

'Working?'

'Yeah.'

'You're a *whore* now?' I asked, realizing the point of her attire.

Beth looked at me, glassy-eyed and nonchalant. 'We're all whores now, kid.'

The words hung on her lips, making me step back, the truth as offensive as the open sores caked with foundation and lipstick. The girl I had been in love with was alien to me, little more than a silhouette before the glowing advertisement. In a nearby store window, flat-screens flickered images of those types I'd misinterpreted: newscasters, weatherpersons, late-night infomercial hosts. I looked at Beth, the one who'd been a dreamer like me, determined to make that *easy money* for life. That's when I finally understood. We're all just slaves to the system. It's only the people you never see that get all that never-ending wealth.

'Scram, man,' Beth said. 'You're scaring away my customers.'

And just like that, I grew the fuck up. The juvenile longings bending me out of shape simply stretched and snapped. This was adulthood, with all its bleak realities and petty problems. Beth was showing it to me, drawing back the curtain. I hated her for it. I wanted to hug her and hit her at the same time. She repulsed me, yet there was an erection swelling in my jeans. If she wanted to be trash, I would use her up and throw her away like trash. I opened my wallet, watching her hungry eyes flick to the bills I withdrew.

'How much?' I asked.

My question was supposed to shame her. It was supposed to give me a sense of superiority. Beth's mouth bent into a cool smirk instead, her eyes flashing viciously with a level of experience I could barely comprehend.

'For what you have in your wallet you can barely get a handjob. Find an ATM and add thirty to it and I'll suck you off. You wanna put it in my vag or ass, it'll cost you double.'

All I could manage was a whimper.

'But if you wanna call up a friend with some dough,' Beth continued in a soft voice as she licked sore lips, 'I can swing you a real sweet deal on a three-way. It's my specialty.'

The delicateness with which she placed that sour cherry on my cake was horrifying. I felt blood drain from my face, strength slip out from behind my knees. My stomach cramped. Her laugh was cruel.

'Go home, kid.'

I turned and walked away, never feeling so small in all my life. By the time the tears welled up in my eyes I was running. I ran all the way home, locked myself in my room and cried. Then I dropped my pants and masturbated, thinking of Beth, imagining all the other people who had shared her, passed her around and fucked her rotten ass. When I came it was the biggest orgasm I'd ever had.

Like Beth said, we were all whores now.

Sitting in the pub waiting for my friend, I think about the profound effect that one girl had on me, how anything sacred seemed like snake oil afterwards. When Phineas walks into my field of vision holding two pints, I don't recognize him. His striking features make me think he's some actor, or model or reality TV star gracing me with his presence. When I realize it's my friend and he's just a man like me, I'm dismayed. He looks tired and troubled. I doubt he's had a sleep since his session.

'I didn't know you liked coming to watering holes like this,' I say with a smirk.

'Had to come here, mate. At least a quarter of my misspent youth was having too many rounds in this place.'

Phineas sits, putting a pint down in front of me, looking around the rough old establishment with reminiscence in his eyes. This is the world he clawed himself out of; vicious cycles of binge drinking, dole money, gang violence and trying to live out one more day. It took him moving across the Atlantic to finally escape it. He seems out of place among its scratched wood and chipped paint now. The sour smell of spilt beer clashes with his cologne. The dull yellow lowlight looks greasy on his smooth black skin. The expression on Phineas's face, however, tells me he couldn't be more at home.

'What time is your flight?' he asks, taking a sip of lager.

'Got a few hours yet.'

'How was your gig?'

'Good for me. I was used for something other than life's excesses for a change.'

'And the client was happy?'

'That's another story,' I reply. 'How was your gig?'

Scowling, Phineas unbuttons his silk shirt and opens it to reveal a long ragged scratch, almost a gash, between his

165

pectorals, glistening with some kind of ointment. Whatever medicine he's spread on it won't stop it from scarring. We both know an injury like that will have an effect on his stock price.

'Damn, how'd you get that?' I ask.

'I didn't ask,' he replies. 'But I'll be filing a complaint with Baxter about it.'

'Might piss off your client if you do that.'

'Bugger the client. They broke the rules. Don't care if they hire me again or not. We've got more than enough customers clamouring for us right now.'

'True.'

'Speaking of clients ... let's go back to your most recent one for a minute.'

I shrug. 'I don't think he was very happy.'

'Why?'

'He said he preferred Clive.'

'Who was the client?'

I look around the pub, checking my proximity for a threat that probably doesn't exist. I lean closer to Phineas, lowering my voice so no one can overhear. I must be getting paranoid.

'A guy named Shaw. Heard of him?'

Phineas nods. 'Made his first billions investing in those commercial desalinization units, got a second helping on the new industrial markets out of Europe. You said he treated you well?'

'Seems like it. I woke up refreshed, rested, and without injuries.'

Phineas puts a hand to his chest. 'A rarity.'

I drink my lager, feeling my lips press into a sneer as I think about clients like Winslade, Ichida and Navarette. Every bruise and bash I feel in my bones, every cut and tear in my skin, reminds me of the daredevil rag-doll cum-dispenser I am so often to so many people. I want to tell Phineas of my sick head, my glimpses into hellish filmstrips that I can't form into memory.

'It's getting to me,' I say.

'What?'

'The job.'

Phineas takes a long drink, his eyes watching me over the rim of his glass, unblinking as the amber fluid disappears down his bucking throat.

'You know how it is,' Phineas says and wipes his mouth. 'It's all in how we perceive the work and pace ourselves. As long as we know our role and don't rock the boat, we're good.'

'We're not good,' I protest.

'Fuck that, we're great. We're pure-bred, the definite article, perfect specimens. Why do you get hired? So someone can walk in the shoes of some stunning top-shelf Aryan stock, blond hair, blue eyes and all. Why do I get hired? So someone can live vicariously through a handsome black buck, swagger around town with a swinging dick ready to infect folks with jungle fever. We don't judge. We ignore client motives. We take the money and run. What's wrong with that in today's world?'

This reminds me of when Phineas and I first met four years ago, at a corporate event where we'd both been hired as *dates* for two high-ranking cougars in pantsuits who trotted us around like a couple show ponies before taking us back to their hotel room and putting us out to stud. Afterwards, while the women talked shit about our services in the bathroom, Phineas and I counted our earnings and pulled on our clothes in the gloom while he whispered to me about a lucrative new venture he was getting involved in. A week later he introduced me to Miller and I never went back to getting work from my online ads.

'We're a new necessity,' Phineas says.

'We're whores, man,' I moan.

Phineas hates the word. 'We're not whores, mate. We're *Husks*.'

'What's the difference?'

Phineas pauses for too long.

'The only difference is our clients are *dead*,' I say. 'Like some fucking kind of reverse necrophilia.'

My comment darkens the mood and we both take to our beers to offset its sobering effect. Phineas undoes his tie, slumps in his seat, drinks too fast, spills a trickle of lager down the front of his jacket. He doesn't bother to mop it up. Now he's starting to look like he belongs here. I order another beer for him and unexpectedly request a glass of Merlot for myself. Phineas gives me a bemused look over the wine. I take note of the dullness in his eyes. Usually when Phineas drinks, he talks.

'Before I left New York,' I say, 'you said you heard some things through the grapevine, some things about Winslade.'

'Yeah.' Phineas lowers his voice, casts a glance over his

shoulder. 'I didn't want to talk while we were in town. Some walls have ears, y'know.'

'What did you hear?'

'I heard about some of the previous Husks he'd hired.'

'What about them?'

'Well, they ain't around any more, mate.'

New drinks arrive and Phineas takes to his immediately. I swish the wine around in my mouth, wondering what happened to these Husks he's on about. I must look worried because Phineas sees my expression and shakes his head.

'Looks like they just up and quit the business, walked off the reservation without as much as a goodbye.'

'Where are they now?'

Phineas shrugs. 'Fuck knows.'

'Why are you telling me this?'

'Because they were all you at one point, Rhodes, Husking for Winslade and not bloody happy about it, taking session after session until something drove them to quit. And you know how hard it is to quit this business.'

'I've heard.'

'I'm aware of four people other than you that have been hired by Winslade. Three have gone AWOL and one . . . well, one is dead.'

'Dead?'

'That would be Miller.'

I can't contain my shock. 'Miller Husked for Winslade?'

'On occasion.'

'How do you know?'

Phineas grins. 'Pillow talk, baby.'

'Nikki?'

'Our receptionist is privy to some of what's going on internally. Baxter does her best to keep bookings and business airtight, but Nikki gets wind of a few things.'

'Was Miller in session with Winslade the night he died?' I ask.

'That I don't know,' Phineas says, shaking his head. 'But he couldn't have been. The client would have died when Miller did.'

'Right . . . well, what about the other three? What can you tell me about them?'

'Can't tell you much, other than that they weren't Solace employees. They were hires from one of our rivals.'

'Which one?'

'Eternity Executive.'

'Those fucking jokers?' I laugh. 'They deal in bimbos and himbos, wash-ups and hacks.'

Phineas shakes his head again. 'Those fucking jokers supply most of Asia's one-per-cent Post-Mortems with contracts now. EE has that lucrative market cornered. They ain't no joke, son.'

I can't help but think of Mr Ichida and his many rentals. 'Did you ever Husk for Ichida or Winslade?'

'Ichida, yes. Winslade, no,' replies Phineas, sucking his teeth. 'The way I hear it, he doesn't much like *the niggers*.'

I raise my glass to my lips and find it almost empty. Don't remember drinking the wine. I look to the bartender to signal for another when I see something from the corner of my eye. My heart jumps. Seated at the end of the bar, a pale face with green eyes set in a bush of ratty red hair. I know who it is before I flick my eyes over and focus on him. Delane stares me down. Immediately his face distorts, melting into the features of a ginger-haired woman who is appraising me from across the room. I close my eyes, rub them hard. I mutter a curse.

'You okay?' Phineas asks.

'Seeing shit again,' I grumble.

'Come again?'

I wave his question away, trying to quell my growing irritation with these one-second phantasmal visits from some fucker I've never even met.

'Do you know a guy named Delane?' I ask. 'Dennis Delane?'

'No,' Phineas replies. 'But why does that name sound familiar?'

'His body was found in the meat-packing district a few days ago. Police think something foul.'

'Yeah, I remember it. Dumped in some alley?'

'That's the guy.'

'Why are you asking me about him?'

I look Phineas straight in the eye. 'I'm seeing him everywhere.'

'What . . . like on the telly?'

'No, like visions, hallucinations.'

Phineas just stares at me, one finger stroking his pint glass, unsure of what to say. Finally he clears his throat and straightens.

'Well, you said before you were having problems with your Ouija —'

'It's not the fucking Ouija,' I snap. 'This *isn't* technological. It's biological, or psychological, or . . . or . . .'

'Or what?'

'Metaphysical? Spiritual? Christ, I don't know.'

I start running a finger around the rim of my wine glass, an old habit of mine, creating a constant hum. Phineas watches me with suspicion as the hum grows louder.

'I'm not sure of much right now,' I say. 'But I'm growing convinced that what's happening to me has something to do with Winslade.'

Phineas taps a fingernail against his pint glass, his thoughts racing with mine. He looks almost angry with me. I wish I'd shut my mouth. My friend is growing more worried by the minute. I'm still spinning my finger around the rim of my glass when Phineas holds up a stopping hand.

'Why are you doing that?'

'Doing what?' I ask, continuing.

'That,' he says. 'With your glass.'

'Don't I always?'

'No, you don't,' he says sharply. 'That's what Miller always used to do.'

The hum stops. I look down at my finger stalled on the rim, unable to shake the feeling of familiarity. I've done this a thousand times, I'm sure of it. When I look back up Phineas is shaking his head, looking even more worried than before.

'Rhodes, you need to track down these other Husks that have gone underground, find out why they walked. You need to get some answers.'

'Where do I start?' I groan.

'Talk to Nikki, see if she can shed some light. Pull her aside tomorrow when you have a chance, tell her you need some leads.'

'Tomorrow?'

Yeah, tomorrow.' Phineas gives me a confused look. 'Miller's wake?'

I hadn't gotten the memo.

18

Black suits and ties darken the men attending Miller's wake. The women are only slightly more colourful. The room is mundane, everything brown or cream-coloured, lit by fake candlelight and electric lanterns, reminding me of the days I buried my older sister and parents. A solemn procession of Miller's immediate family makes its rounds, greeting those that have arrived. Nods and handshakes mostly, occasionally a hug. I watch people break into tears around me. I see stoic faces refusing to speak, lips quivering. Postures are either resolutely rigid or slumped in dismay. It feels like old film to me, everything looking dull and drab like the first colour movies, back before they got it right. I'm surprised by the numbers in attendance. Miller was a popular guy. Well loved.

My dead friend had predominantly Irish heritage. There are beer and whiskey at the wake, helping to mould the overall mood. I'm thankful for it as I mingle with a Guinness in hand. I need to stay numb, keep some stability in my head. The drink scatters unwanted thoughts, cockroaches running from the light, back into the cracks forming in my psyche. More than a dozen other Husks pepper the wake. I give each one a nod or quick handshake as I cross the room to where Phineas stands. The casket in the corner is closed. Phineas tells me the lid was open earlier, that the mortician did a great job reconstructing Miller's head, but the family took one look and wanted it shut. I wish I could lay eyes on my friend again, look upon him one last time and see if he appears at all like he does in my dreams.

'What's the official story?' I ask.

Phineas looks around the room, leans in and lowers his voice. 'Accidental prescription drug overdose, a lethal combination of sleeping pills and painkillers.'

I swallow, thinking about Craig chewing me out over my Percocet and Donormyl, thinking how this cover story could end up being the coroner's report for my ass if I don't exercise more caution.

'Does his family know the truth?' I whisper.

'The truth? Of course not.'

'Well, they must know he died from head trauma and not an overdose.'

'No idea,' Phineas shrugs, sips a whiskey. 'They're sticking to the story though.'

Through the crowd I spy Tweek standing alone in a corner, wearing an ill-fitting suit and bow tie. He stares at the floor, arms hanging loose at his side. I collect a stout from the tray of a passing server and go to him.

'How are you feeling?' I ask, offering the pint.

'Fine, I guess.' Tweek's eyes glance at me through thick-rimmed glasses that don't hide their redness. 'More importantly, how are you feeling?'

My silence tells Tweek all he needs to know. He accepts the pint and takes a sip, wrinkling his nose up at the strong taste.

'Gross,' he says.

'The Irish aren't known for watering down their beer.'

'Your head –' Tweek points to his temple. 'Is it getting any worse?'

I swallow, give a single nod. 'I really need your help, Tweek.'

'Well, I can run a more in-depth diagnostic if you'd like, try some –'

I grab him by the arm and pull him further into the corner, making sure our backs are to the crowd to block other eyes and ears from our conversation.

'No,' I whisper. 'I need to find out what my clients are doing with me in session. That's the root of the problem. That's what's driving me crazy.'

Tweek looks at me, his expression somehow both surprised and expectant at the same time. There are conflict and pity in his eyes.

'Just what do you think it is I can do for you?'

'I'm thinking maybe you can supply me with one of your E-33s –'

Tweek chokes a little, eyes bulging. 'You're asking me for an *Ejector* pill? Are you nuts, Rhodes?'

'I will be if I don't do something soon.'

'Which client are you suspicious of anyway?'

I don't answer. These walls might have ears. Tweek stares at me, then at someone approaching behind me. Before I can turn to see who it is a hand falls on my shoulder and squeezes.

'Gentlemen,' Baxter says. 'How are we holding up?'

Tweek says nothing, taking a reluctant gulp of Guinness. I hold mine up and force a grin for my boss.

'Booze at a wake should be mandatory,' I say. 'Lightens the mood, makes for a proper send-off.'

Baxter smiles, snagging a neat whiskey from another passing tray. She throws back a mouthful, turns and surveys the huddled groups of dark suits and boring dresses. When she turns back she is no longer smiling.

'Did I interrupt something?' she asks.

I don't miss a beat. 'We were just shooting the shit, boss.'

'Shooting the shit,' Tweek concurs.

'It's a real tragedy, this Miller business,' Baxter says and tips her head toward Tweek. 'I expanded Tweek's R&D budget last week, see if we can't finally develop some kind of failsafe component for you guys in the field. Make sure this kind of thing never happens again.'

'You think that's possible?' I ask.

'Sure it's possible. Don't you think so, Tweek?'

Baxter gives Tweek a most peculiar look, one that speaks to him in the silence between the question and answer. Tweek's too meek with his response.

'It's a big project, lots of complicating factors, but I'm sure I'll develop something that's applicable in due time . . .'

On the far side of the room I see Ryoko enter with Nikki in tow, their faces long. Even dressed in conservative funeral attire, they still look stunning. The sight of my love is bittersweet. The memory of her all painted up in Tatsumi's strange tastes, exaggerated and clownish, makes me go cold. I have to hold back a grimace, remind myself that it wasn't her that day, just her shell filled with a stranger. The girls scan the room, looking for friendly faces. Phineas spots them and gives me a glance, signalling to come join him.

'Please excuse me.'

As I walk away Baxter and Tweek start discussing something in a secretive tone that makes me suspicious. Ryoko sees me approaching and begins to lead Nikki by the hand through the crowd. After a few steps Nikki pulls on her arm as Miller's coffin comes into view. She anchors herself, shaking her head at Ryoko, lips quivering. Phineas and I quicken our step, realizing how hard she is working to keep from falling to pieces.

'Hello, ladies,' Phineas says, positioning his body in front of Nikki so it blocks her view of the casket. 'First things first, let's get you a drink.'

Phineas leads us to the little bar and orders for everyone. I need another drink in order to warm up to Ryoko. We're into the whiskey and before I know it we're all getting tipsy, chuckling at our shared memories of the man in the box. For some, our laughter eases the room. For others we're an irritant. Eventually something in our chat strikes a chord with Nikki and we watch her tear up, smiling hard to stop from crying outright. Phineas pulls her aside and holds her tight, allowing me a moment alone with Ryoko.

'I missed you,' Ryoko says.

I smile, though I can feel how weary it must look. 'Missed you too.'

'How was England?'

'Easy gig.'

Ryoko cocks her head and examines my face, putting a hand on my cheek, fingertips stroking my skin. My eyelids flutter, grow heavy. I lean into her touch.

'You're tired.'

'I'm always tired these days.'

She turns my head and glides her index finger behind my ear, over the small protrusion of the Ouija. I find myself looking into the sad blue eyes of Nikki as she rests her head on Phineas's chest. Ryoko's lips part and pause. I know what she's going to ask.

'No, I'm not all right,' I say before she speaks.

Nikki hears this and comes to me, arms outstretched, head nodding. I embrace her and hold her tight, our lips next to each other's ears, the smell of whiskey on our breath. This is still the safest way to communicate with another person in the modern world.

'I need some information,' I whisper.

'I know.'

'I don't want to get you into trouble.'

'I can take care of myself.'

I hold Nikki even tighter, as if it might somehow protect her from the shit-storm I could be bringing her way by discussing such confidential matters.

'Winslade's previous hires,' I say. 'What can you tell me?'

'Phineas told you what company they worked for?'

'Yes.'

'Three of their employees filed company complaints against Winslade. They all reported post-session problems similar to yours, and repeatedly requested other assignments, which were denied.'

'Do you know who they were?'

'All I've got is names. Brad Garrison, Cameron Tate, Kirk King.'

She repeats them and I commit the names to memory. 'What happened to them?'

I feel a shiver run through her body. She glances around, checking to see who might be within earshot. Her voice becomes husky as she brings her lips even closer to my ear.

'Rumour is they all eventually suffered mental breakdowns. Then they disappeared overnight. That's all I know.'

Nikki releases me, straightens my jacket and tie like that's what she was doing all along. I lean forward to ask more of her, but she concludes our conversation by pressing a finger to my lips. I push past her touch and press for one last answer.

'Was Winslade Miller's last client?' I whisper.

'Only one person knows the answer to that.'

Nikki stares. I think she's looking at me at first, but then realize she's looking past my head. I turn slowly, giving a nod to a couple other Husks as I do. From the corner of my eye I see Baxter looking in our direction. Nikki surreptitiously slips something into my jacket pocket.

'There's something on my Liaison you need to see. It's too risky to send.'

She turns back to Phineas as I excuse myself and make my way to the washroom. Baxter watches attentively as I go, does not smile back when I offer her one in passing. Inside the men's washroom there isn't a soul about. I promptly lock myself in the nearest stall. On Nikki's Liaison screen a video recording is set up to be viewed. I hit 'play'. The video is a message from Miller. He, too, is in a washroom somewhere. His eyes are confused, his movements erratic, speech slurred. At first I think he's drunk.

'Nikki? Nikki? It's me . . . Something's wrong. Call Baxter. Call Tweek. I . . . I think I'm long overdue here. You need to bring me in for download immediately.'

Miller puts his palms to his eyes, pressing hard, fingers raking his hairline. A thin line of drool escapes his mouth and hangs off his bottom lip. Suddenly, he stands straight and looks at the Liaison camera with curiosity. The intoxication is gone. So is the stress. What replaces it is an assured, if not irritated, persona. The video ends just as someone opens the door to the men's room. Whoever it is takes a few steps inside and stops. I hold my breath, stay absolutely still. There is only silence. I wait for this person to walk over to a urinal or enter a stall, maybe go to the sink to wash up. They simply stand and listen, long enough for it to be uncomfortable. After a minute I tire of playing church mouse, mock flush the toilet and exit the stall to see who it is. There is no one waiting.

I go back to the wake and scan the guests, wondering who it was that followed me in. It could have been anyone. Hell, with all the Husks about it could have been anyone *masquerading* as anyone. I try not to dwell on it as I reconvene with my friends. We're engaged in conversation when Miller's immediate family finishes talking to an older couple nearby, spots our little group and approaches. Mother, father and two brothers share an uncanny resemblance to the dead man. Mrs Miller leads her boys to us, the matriarch no doubt.

'Bless you all for coming,' she says, smiling weakly.

'My condolences, Mrs Miller,' I reply.

'Thank you, young man.'

'Your son was a wonderful person and dear friend,' I say and feel my throat tighten. 'He always looked out for me.'

'You're too kind,' she replies. 'How did you know my son?'

'We worked together.'

'In what capacity?'

'Uh, business consultation . . . at Solace Strategies.'

My answer darkens the mood. Mrs Miller's face becomes pinched. Frowns descend on the faces of the men. I'm sure they suspect the company had something to do with Miller's demise. Next to me Ryoko, Phineas and Nikki stand frozen, saying nothing. A few other Husks throw nervous glances in our direction. Baxter walks over cautiously and stops a little ways away. Tension grows in the ensuing silence. I open my mouth and begin floundering, knowing I'm digging myself a hole.

'I'm so very sorry. It's tragic. Such a terrible, untimely thing to happen . . .'

Mrs Miller bares her teeth. 'You mean this prescription drug overdose bullshit?'

'Pardon?'

'It's all a lie, you know.'

'Excuse me?' I say. 'Mrs Miller, I don't know what you're talking about.'

182

'Business consultation.' Mrs Miller glowers at me. 'I know what you high-finance types are like. I know what kind of lives you lead, what drugs you got my boy hooked on.'

Her eyes tear up, convinced by this lie she thinks is the truth. I'm only relieved that she's got it all wrong. Mrs Miller looks me up and down with disgust.

'All of you big-spending, fast-living, hard-partying fools . . . and now my son is dead because of it.'

She turns and walks away, disappearing into the gathered crowd. I'm left to face Miller's father and brothers. They do not look impressed. The dad takes two steps forward, close enough for me to smell the liquor on his breath.

'High finance,' Mr Miller whispers. 'I know what you really are.'

His displeased expression turns to anger. He flicks a glance at my friends, then boss, then co-workers. I see him tense up, the look in his eyes weighing the pros and cons of a decision he has yet to make. Then they become resolute and I see the punch coming.

Not the face, I think, but do nothing to avoid it.

His fist catches me clumsily on the edge of my jaw and sinks into my neck. The old man put some weight behind it, but it's not the worst punch I've taken in my time. What it symbolizes though hurts plenty. I'm sent sprawling, my fall partially broken by my friends. When the back of my head hits the floor things go black for a bit. In the dark I hear raised voices, swearing and cursing, a series of small crashes. Sounds of a fight starting rise above the ringing in my ears, followed by the sounds of its diffusion.

I open my eyes to see Baxter standing over me. She bends down, face leaning in to examine the spot where I was struck.

'Ah, shit,' she says.

'Shit what?'

'That's going to leave a mark.'

'How bad?'

'Bad enough for business,' Baxter says, helping me up. 'You're booked with Winslade again tomorrow.'

Looks like I'll be missing Miller's funeral.

My headache is decidedly above average. The old man had a surprising right. I guess I deserved it. After all, it was my gig that Miller was covering when he died. I sit in a corner of the room with my head hung, staring at the floor, pressing a bag of ice to my jaw. Most people have left the wake. A few stragglers hang about, people I don't know who talk in low voices, mostly about the fistfight earlier that laid me out. Could use another drink, but the booze has been cleaned up and packed away. Phineas and Nikki left about ten minutes ago. Ryoko is still around some- where, gone to see if she can find some aspirin for my throbbing head. I figure I've got about fifteen minutes before the funeral home director shuts this little lingering party down.

Somebody slips quietly into the wake, the last latecomer. I don't bother to look up, just watch his shoes cross the floor and stop before Miller's casket. By the time I raise my eyes the man has turned his back to me and bowed his head. Even from behind, I recognize the guy.

'Clive?'

Clive turns around slowly, looks at me with one eye. Bandages cover the left side of his face from chin to brow, reaching back as far as his ear. At the edges of the dressings I can see raw, swollen skin. I rise from my chair, cross the room quickly with arms open wide.

'Oh my God, Clive, what are you *doing* here?'

I hug him tight. The embrace he gives in return is weak and tentative. I stand back, look him over, trying to determine how salvageable my friend is as a product. When I ignore what's on the left, his right still looks gorgeous. He's got the side profile of a pretty boy that causes people to stop and stare. Clive's baby blue eye wells up with tears, his bottom lip quivers. He puts a hand on Miller's casket to steady himself.

'I had to come and pay my respects.'

'Of course, of course,' I say. 'What I mean is how the hell did you get here?'

'The client paid my bail, and happens to have friends in high places. I flew back from Paris yesterday.'

'Oh.' I nod vigorously. 'Why didn't you come earlier? You just missed everyone.'

'I didn't really want anyone to see me, Rhodes. Not like this. Not after what happened. I need time to get my head right.'

A tear spills down his cheek. He wipes it away slowly, careful not to touch his bandages. The strangeness of this encounter becomes more evident. Last time I saw this man he was no killer. I still don't know how he could have committed such an act. Maybe I'm not the only Husk destabilizing around here. Maybe we all sail over the edge if pushed too far. I want to reach out and hug him again, tell him not to worry and that everything will be okay, but that would be doing my friend a disservice. I place a hand on his shoulder instead.

'Sure, I understand ... Jesus, it's just so good to see you. I had no idea you were released from custody. Did you check in with Solace?'

'Yeah, I had a meeting with Baxter as soon as I got back. That's how I found out about Miller. Right before I was told our company will no longer be requiring any of my services.'

'She fired you?' I ask, acting shocked, knowing it was inevitable.

Clive hangs his head in shame. 'She didn't use those words, but yeah, pretty much. I mean, look at me, Rhodes. I'm no use to Solace now.'

'Stop it, you still look stellar. Those injuries can totally be fixed.'

'You think so?'

'I know so.'

Clive gives a nervous smile, runs an effeminate hand through his hair. 'I've got my first round of reconstructive surgery tomorrow, some initial skin grafts. Doctors say there is a chance they could restore sight in my right eye too. If it all goes well I reckon I could be top tier again.'

I give the biggest grin I can muster, one that masks the wince that is starting to come at his optimism. He'll never be top tier again. He's an athlete with a permanent injury now, one that will cripple him in every game he tries to play. But Clive's a friend. The least I can do is pretend to believe these lies he's propping himself up with. I clap him on the back and nod in mock agreement.

'That's great news, man, really great. Look, if you need some work in the meantime, my roommate could probably hook you up with some bartending gigs.'

'Actually, I've already signed up with someone else.'

'Really? Who?'

That shameful look returns. 'Eternity Executive.'

'Those guys? Really?'

'Had an interview first thing this morning. They hired me on the spot. I'm definitely taking a pay cut, but I need the work. These medical bills are going to put me in the red pretty quick.'

'Hey, it means you're still a player in the game,' I say, feigning enthusiasm. 'You gotta do what you gotta do, right?'

'Guess so.'

There is a moment of unwelcome silence. I can't stop glancing at Clive's bandages. He notices every time. Tiny light yellow is spotting in places on the white dressing, pus or fluids starting to seep through. Clive turns his head, keeps it that way, showing me a bigger portion of the perfection he once had.

'When do you start with EE exactly?' I ask.

'Right away. I'm going back to their head office this afternoon for my orientation and security clearance. They're going to profile me as an option for some future clients. Once the plastic surgery smoothes out these new wrinkles, I'll be ready to go.'

'So you'll have access to the company starting today?'

'Yeah,' Clive replies, a little suspicious. 'Why? What's it to you?'

'I might have a favour to ask.'

19

The frozen gel pack pressed to my neck does little to ease the pain as I sync my Liaison to the HG in the living room. The balm Ryoko applied to the swelling before she left my apartment is making my face numb, but the cold feels comforting. I've spent the last few hours trying to find information on any of the three employees at Eternity Executive via the net, but have come up empty-handed. The curtains are drawn to every potential window into their lives, past and present. In a world where practically everyone's existence is on record, the absence of theirs is concerning. The hollow feeling in my stomach is growing, slowly expanding into a miniature black hole, coring my guts and sucking everything I thought I once knew into oblivion. I wonder if this is what being shot in the stomach with a Rapier feels like, minus the unbearable pain.

Back at the wake, Clive came and went before Ryoko returned with the aspirin. She never saw him, and I didn't mention his visit. My friend was adamant that I not tell a soul he was back in town, told me he wasn't willing to face anyone until he'd at least got through a couple plastic surgeries. He said I owed him that much. I'd have to agree. Getting the guy to do some snooping for me at Eternity Executive after all he's been through was a dick move on my part. Clive refused outright when I asked, but I leaned on him, harder than I should have, and the boy broke. Just minutes ago I got a message from him saying he scored some hits on the names Nikki supplied me. He's included attachments on two of the former employees: Brad Garrison and Cameron Tate. According to Clive, no information is available on Kirk King.

I open the attachments, confidential company records, and examine Brad Garrison's first. A holographic of the man in nothing but his underwear pops up. Even I'm surprised by his looks. Blue eyes, blond hair, freshly shaven face of a cherub. His body is absolutely ripped, a Husk of high quality indeed. All his information is there: age, attributes, employment history, nightclub and gym affiliations, hobbies and tastes. I read his arrest record, noting that he'd been busted for prostitution several times and drug possession twice when younger. That Baxter undoubtedly has similar files on all Solace Strategies employees is not lost on me.

I skim the records until I see something of interest: a log of requests and complaints from Garrison to the company directors. The dates on them are more than a couple years old now. All entries were logged over the course of several months, spaced a week or two apart.

Brad Garrison (314-A68):
Request full medical evaluation: Request granted.
Complaint filed: Abnormal post-session stress.
Request technical evaluation: Request granted.
Complaint filed: Unacceptable post-session injuries.
Complaint filed: TC-87 'Ouija' malfunctioning (unconfirmed).

Request psyche evaluation: Request granted.
Request reassignment: Request denied.
Request additional personal days: Request denied.
Complaint filed: Abnormal post-session stress.
Request sick leave: Request denied.
Request reassignment (re: Wilhelm G. Winslade): Request denied.

What follows is a record of infractions by Garrison and disciplinary actions taken by Eternity Executive. His behaviour required an increasing attitude adjustment according to his superiors. A stint in rehab was ordered for alcohol and narcotics abuse. He was put on probation after failing to show up for sessions with Winslade. EE came down on him hard for his refusal to work, forced him to do the gigs. The threats they made were empty, scare tactics, but according to what I'm reading it seemed to keep Garrison in line for a while . . . right up until he was suddenly and unceremoniously let go.

I can find no reason why the company dropped him. After the termination of his contract, the trail goes cold. There is a phone number listed for Brad, but I find it no longer in service when I call. His mother is listed as his next of kin, currently residing in New Jersey. An old land line is provided. I place my bets and punch the digits.

A woman picks up, voice gravelly and curt, speaking in a southern accent with a matter-of-fact tone. I talk in my friendliest manner, introduce myself with a fake name, address her as Mrs Garrison, tell her Brad and I used to work together way back when, tell her I'm calling to see how my old buddy is doing these days.

'There's been no change in him.'

'Would it be possible to speak with him?' I ask.

'What?' she says. 'Brad . . . Brad isn't available.'

'Do you know when he'll be back?' I ask. 'It's most important that I talk to him sooner rather than later.'

'Back?' She sounds confused. 'He's never left. But you can't talk to him. You won't get anything out of him.'

'Pardon?'

'He's still in a coma.'

My pause is long and unsteady. 'What happened?'

I shudder as the woman feeds me the same lie every PR agent and publicist states for the unglamorous and untimely death of every A-lister, rock star, celebrity and socialite, the same lie we touted for Miller today.

'Accidental prescription drug overdose.'

'Oh.'

'Hey, where did you say it was you worked with Brad?'

I hang up quickly, frightened by what she's told me. Cameron Tate's file is next, and I open it with trepidation. He's another looker, tanned and muscular, a blond as well. After scanning through his unremarkable profile, I find the log of his requests and complaints. What's listed before me looks eerily similar to the problems Garrison reported. It also looks like Eternity Executive took Tate's complaints more seriously than those of his co-worker. The company's follow-up is more thorough, detailed reports instead of dismissive memos, video recordings of meetings and evaluations. There are several on file. I play the first one, watch as Tate sits at a table across from two men in lab coats. Another man in a charcoal suit paces the room irritably, asking questions. Cameron does not look well.

Suit: 'Why are you continually requesting reassignment?'
Tate: 'Why are you continually denying me?'
Suit: 'Because there are no grounds for it.'
Tate: 'No grounds?'
Suit: 'Medical and technical evaluation came back clean, Cameron.'
Tate: 'But my goddamn psyche evaluation didn't.'
Suit: 'Those results are inconclusive at this time.'
Tate: 'OK, fine, but my anxiety and depression sure as hell aren't. I'm at my wits' end here.'
Suit: 'Cam, you don't even know why you're upset. You complain about these post-session problems, yet you can't tell us a goddamn thing about them.'
Tate: 'What does it matter? Just bench me, for Christ's sake! Winslade can have any other frigging Husk he wants.'
Suit: 'Winslade doesn't want any other Husk. Winslade wants you.'
Tate: 'Look, I'm telling you, that client is —'

The video becomes pixilated, starts to glitch. Soon the picture and audio stutter, skip, stop. I try to play it again from the beginning, but the whole thing breaks down before my eyes. I've tripped something. There is a security measure at work here, a virus embedded in the files that is designed to eat the information if its programming becomes suspicious of unauthorized access. I attempt to play the other videos, but find each of them in the process of being deconstructed and erased. I go back to Tate's profile and commit some things to memory before the pages burn up. The virus works fast, sentences flickering and disappearing as I try and read. I scroll down and set sights on Cameron Tate's notice of termination. The last words I manage to take in before everything disintegrates are *mentally unfit* and *Bellevue Hospital Center.*

The HG goes blank. Seconds later I'm flying into a rage, an unexpected tantrum that both fascinates and terrifies me. White-hot anger sparks violent urges that are uncharacteristic. My fingers tear into a nearby pillow and rip the stuffing out. My Liaison almost finds itself pitched across the room. I want to choke the living shit out of someone. I want to make someone pay.

When I finally calm down I get back on the net and visit the Bellevue Hospital Center website. I poke around until I find myself reading up on its newly renovated and expanded psychiatric wing. No individual patient information is available, but my suspicions are strong. Running on instinct, I grab my wallet, throw on a jacket and leave the apartment.

At the nearest ATM I withdraw a thousand dollars cash and stuff it into an envelope. Then I hail a cab and tell the driver to get me to Bellevue Hospital pronto. As we speed through the streets of New York I notice more of the city's ignored and avoided inhabitants. People yelling at nothing, men in rags running from invisible monsters, women with too many layers of clothes wailing at things unseen and pitiful. These poor folk, I think, minus their medication, lacking the money and means to get fixed. I see so many characters that should probably be locked inside the walls of the very place I'm headed to. Then I realize that their mental states are perfectly acceptable in a world gradually going insane. We're all losing it a little. Places like Bellevue are just microscopes focused on a sliver of the evolving brain disease which escaped the lab decades ago.

Twenty minutes later I'm at Bellevue Hospital Center, standing outside the ivy-covered red brick towering over me like some fortress of old built out of concrete and crazy. Patients arrive here at least one card short, but the stress alone of being committed in a place like this undoubtedly burns others from their decks. I enter the front doors, careful to avoid the reception desk, and meander through the halls. My reconnaissance of rooms and personnel is uneventful until I pass by a break room and spy a portly orderly standing before an old-school vending machine. He looks bored and broke as he peruses the confectionery. I note the electronic pass card clipped to his belt and decide to approach him, fishing change out of my pocket. The orderly hears the jingling of coins and looks over his shoulder at me.

'No rush,' I say. 'Take your time.'

'All yours,' he says with a sigh and steps aside. 'Forgot my damn change today.'

'Yeah, I hear you. I hardly ever have coins on me these days. You almost never see these old machines around. What are you having?'

'Huh?'

'I got you this time,' I say. 'What'll it be?'

'Coffee Crisp.'

I buy myself a Big Turk and select a Coffee Crisp for my new friend, who watches the steel spirals turn until both chocolate bars have fallen to the trap door below. He looks hungry. I retrieve the bars slowly to further whet his appetite. When I place the Coffee Crisp in his sausage fingers the orderly is all smiles.

'Gee, thanks, man, I owe you one.'

'I might have to call you on that.'

He chuckles and peels back his candy wrapper. 'I'll be sure to keep change on me then, case I see you around.'

'Maybe you could help me now actually . . .'

'Yeah?' His mouth is already full of wafer and chocolate. 'What's up?'

'I'm looking for someone, a patient that's been committed here I think, goes by the name of Cameron Tate. You know of him?'

The orderly stops chewing, lips frozen in an angle of distaste. His eyes regard me coldly, unblinking. Eventually he gives a shake of his head and raises a hand, index finger pointing back the way I came.

'Reception is down the hall, buddy. You can state your business there.'

I look over my shoulder, and then back at him. 'Yeah, I don't really wanna go through official channels if you know what I mean . . .'

'You Tate's family?'

'No.'

The orderly shrugs. 'Then I can't rightly help you.'

After a pause I pull the envelope of cash from my

jacket and open it toward him, running my thumb slowly over the collection of hundred dollar bills inside.

'Okay, what about wrongly helping me then?'

The orderly stares at the grand in my hand and swallows the last of his chocolate bar with a gulp, licking sugary brown smears from fingertips in earnest. I hold out my unopened Big Turk to him.

'You can have this too.'

'What do you need?'

'A little information,' I say. 'I just need to speak with him.'

The orderly hesitates, looks around, then takes the money and chocolate and stashes it in his pocket, telling me I must follow his every instruction to the letter. He leads me to an empty office where he grabs a tablet off the wall and finds me a visitor's pass in a desk drawer. I clip it to my jacket and follow the orderly through security doors, up flights of stairs and down sterile hallways. I expect to hear shouts and wails from the incarcerated, but the psychiatric wing is practically silent. Only our footsteps on the hallway tiles and the buzz of fluorescent overhead lights can be heard. The orderly tells me the dope the patients get is stronger than ever, everyone sleeping like a baby or tranquilized like a beast. Eventually we come to a locked door with a small window. It is among many of the same, but on a placard below reads the name 'Tate, Cameron'. I look inside and view the padded cell. A solitary figure lies strapped to a bed in the corner, wrapped in what appears to be a backward coat.

'A straitjacket?' I say. 'You still use those?'

'For some patients, yeah.'

'Aren't those a little, well, outdated?'

'Whatever works,' the orderly says with a shrug. 'Cam's partial to self-harm when his antipsychotics wear off and his limbs are loose. He needs to be restrained.'

'Self-harm?'

'He suffers from a kind of xenomelia, foreign-limb syndrome, except it's more than just his limbs. The jacket stops him trying to remove parts of his body, like pulling out fingernails or ripping out hair. He's tried to break off fingers and toes too. There are also occasional attempts at self-enucleation.'

I shake my head and frown. 'In English, please.'

'He tries to tear his own eyes out.'

I swallow hard. I can feel sweat beading on my forehead. Cameron Tate used to be like me, was of a like mind. He once gave himself over to those that I do now. I have too much in common with this lunatic, an affinity with the root cause of his diagnosis. Whatever truth lies inside that room, within that patient's cranium, could eventually drive me mad enough to be committed to the cell next door, or worse. The thought terrifies me. That void over the edge of sanity, the one we become aware of when suffering from fever, the one we are wise not to look into. It's beckoning. Take a peek. Look just long enough to see the outline of a new horror wriggling in the dark and take from it a fresh fear that will haunt half of your remaining days, reminding you that your old nightmares were never even close.

'When was he admitted?' I ask.

The orderly brings up his tablet and checks. 'Mr Tate was brought to Bellevue just over a year ago after he suffered a series of psychotic breaks.'

I gesture for the tablet. 'Mind if I take a look at his file?'

He hands it over reluctantly and makes sure to hover close as I read. On the admittance report a familiar name is listed as one of the contacts: Kirk King. No address, no email, just a phone number provided. I try calling, but no one picks up. No message service either. The orderly gives a loud sigh, making a grabby motion with his hands, impatient for the tablet's return. I hand it back without a word.

'So, do you want to see the patient, or what?' he asks.

I nod. The orderly unlocks the door with his pass card and ushers me inside. I hesitate, reluctant to go any further, which is met with impatience.

'You don't need to worry. I've never seen Tate be a threat to others, but I'll be in there with you anyway. You got five minutes.'

'I'll be fine alone.'

'No way, pal,' the orderly shakes his head. 'Not part of the deal.'

Cameron Tate is asleep when we walk into the room. The orderly clears his throat loudly. Moments later the patient is wide awake, looking at me with unease. His eyes are watery and grey, his button nose has been broken multiple times. I know he was handsome once, but the scars and scratches around his sunken eyes and cheeks have negated that. There are bruises on his forehead, probably from Tate bashing himself in bouts of self-injury. The pallid skin of his face is a canvas displaying the ugliness within leaking out of every pore like watercolours. I look upon the effects of his inner torment and outer brutality with wonder.

'Who are you?' he asks.

I glance at the orderly. 'My name isn't important, Mr Tate.'

'Are you another doctor?'

'No, I'm not. Let's say I'm a friend of a friend, some-one we mutually know.'

'Who?'

I ignore the question. 'How are you feeling?'

'I don't want any more pills,' he says, cringing. 'No more pills. I won't eat them. You can't make me.'

The orderly puts on a soft voice. 'Now, Cameron, they're for your own good.'

'I don't like them. They put me in a fog, obscure the truth.'

The orderly rolls his eyes and gives a snort. He's heard all of this before, probably can recite Tate's ramblings from memory.

'What truth is that?' I ask, the question directed at either man.

The orderly shrugs. Tate looks around the room, seeing or sensing things I cannot. He pushes against his restraints, testing their strength and resiliency. His voice becomes agitated, pleading.

'Please untie me.'

'You know we can't do that, Cam,' says the orderly.

'Please, quickly, I have to pull out my teeth.'

I grimace. 'Why do you have to do that?'

'Because these aren't my teeth,' he says, as if this should already be clear. 'This isn't my tongue either.'

I exchange a look with the orderly who merely raises an eyebrow. Tate's talking, and that's good. I feel I should play along, try to soothe him a bit before I get to my point.

'Your teeth are yours alone and they are just fine, Cameron.'

'Please,' he says again. 'They're not mine. They have to go. I can't keep what isn't mine.'

'Well, what is yours then?'

'My voice, I think,' he says. 'My breath, my blood, my heart, my soul.'

He repeats *my breath my blood my heart my soul* several times, eyes fluttering and then closing. When they reopen, Tate regards me strangely, as if seeing me for the first time, like I haven't existed in the room for the last two minutes. I wonder if I'll have to go through our introduction again for his benefit. Five minutes with Cameron Tate suddenly seems like a fraction of the time I'll need to get anything out of this poor man.

'Who are you?' he asks.

I take a deep breath. 'I'm ... currently in the line of work you used to be in, Cameron. I'm here to ask you questions about a former client of yours named Mr Winslade.'

His body writhes under the straps, trying to burrow into the mattress. His chin wobbles. I watch as tears well up in his eyes.

'Mr Winslade?' he asks.

'You remember him don't you?'

'Remember him?'

Tate makes a noise, something between a snort and a snicker. I see his restrained arms squirming under the straitjacket, watch as he bares clenched teeth, pushing air through them in a hiss. His head lolls away from me, turning toward the wall.

'Do I remember Winslade?' he whispers.

Both the orderly and I lean closer, intrigued. We hear a whimpering giggle, a little trembling precursor. His face suddenly snaps around, eyes glaring at me as he explodes.

'I am fucking Winslade!'

His screams send us reeling. They won't stop. I back up out of the room, stumbling and shaking, the orderly scrambling behind me for the door so he can trap the shrieks inside the soundproof space before anyone is alerted. Once we're in the hallway he slams the reinforced steel shut, cutting off Tate's anguished cries.

'What the hell was all that about?' he pants.

I say nothing, trying to process what just happened. Inside the padded cell I faintly hear the incoherent cries of Cameron Tate, now full of pain as well as rage. The orderly takes an old smart-phone out of his pocket and holds it at the ready, threatening to make a call if I don't comply.

'Mister, I'm gonna go out on a limb here and say you've overstayed your welcome at this point.'

'I'm sorry, please just let me ask him –'

The orderly holds up a finger to silence me. 'All the chocolate bars in the frigging world ain't gonna get me to let you back in there, buddy.'

I hold up my hands. 'All right, just show me the way out.'

21

The next day I vomit before I get to Winslade's residence.

I'm walking through Central Park, dragging my heels, hoping to God some cancellation call might come in the half-hour remaining before the session. I go so far as to offer up a mumbled prayer of sorts, asking a higher power for relief. I make my way west, sidestepping stragglers of the Occupy Movement. Through the trees the sight of my client's penthouse brings on a wave of nausea. My chin cramps, commits to the impending puke and I'm running, looking for a good spot to be sick. Nowhere seems appropriate. I lean over a hedge, heaving soupe de jour and filet mignon in the dirt. People passing by regard me with disgust as I spit up the last of it, trying to avoid getting any on my clothes. I look for somewhere I can wash my lips and chin. There is nothing around. I buy a bottle of water from a falafel vendor and douse my face over a patch of grass, rinse my mouth, carefully scrub a splatter of puke from my necktie that is topped with another horrible attempt at an Eldredge knot I'm positive Renard will give me shit over.

No fountains operate in the park any more, or anywhere in the city for that matter, due to water shortages. I remember playing in them when I was a little kid. It was cheap entertainment, wading in the cool shallows, splashing my unimpressed sisters while my parents watched until we grew hungry. A hot dog and a Coke in the park were something I relished, until my older sister told me what they were made of. Mashed cow heads, she said, left-over snouts and ears and assholes and hooves. And the caramel colouring in my cola, she said that would give me cancer. A couple offhand comments killed the fondness for ever. I changed to chicken dogs, until I was told they were moulded from the puréed sludge of beaks and bone marrow. Not even the veggie ones were good. My siblings took great pleasure in telling me the soy would one day give me tits.

But I'm not here to reminisce. The Occupy Movement is the real reason I'm wasting time in Central Park. I want to get close, hear and feel the growing discontentment, see what's got my clients so spooked. Scattered over the grass are people from all walks, a fat slice of anywhere America, their one commonality the right to protest what they perceive as injustice. Under bridges groups gather, making signs and slogans, organizing impromptu marches along the footpaths. They look weary, but their collective anger perpetuates their movement. They are the other kind of husks: those gutted by reality, left empty by our leaders, discarded by democracy. They're not attractive, not physically fit, not easily marketable. But they are the majority, the ones who believe they have the power to make change. The rumble of the Great Lawn hits your ears long before it comes into view. When it does, your jaw drops.

It's a fifty-acre tent city out there, thousands of protesters gathered together as small-scale parades make their way around the perimeter. Almost all wear hats or hoods, sunglasses and upturned collars, making it difficult for the few cameras in the vicinity. Each of the Great Lawn's eight baseball diamonds is packed with people who thin out toward the outfields. Makeshift headquarters operate at each home plate. As I walk between the tents I hear pirate broadcasts coming from old transistor radios. The signals are surprisingly clear. Most of what I hear is repeats from earlier. I spent half an hour sitting at the foot of my bed this morning in a daze, dialled in to the frequencies, trying to remember the importance of my dreams and forget the anxiety of my nightmares. Three cups of coffee so far today and I still don't feel awake.

Around the edges of the lawn the police presence has grown in proportion to the protest. Officers stand rigid as the more relaxed citizens give them a wide berth. I'm surprised to see a pair of stationary EMUs positioned under some trees, bodies painted black with NYPD denoted in white on their appendages, outfitted with riot control equipment instead of weapons and munitions. Their lens-like eyes scan back and forth over the crowd so slowly it is barely perceptible. The drones act only as sentries for the moment, but the cops are obviously worried enough to be bringing in the heavy gear. Winslade made another killing when he was contracted to manufacture drones for law enforcement.

At one of the nearby baseball diamonds, on a small podium built over home plate, a buff bearded man steps up and greets the crowd with a megaphone and a sign that says *Our Contract With America Is Broken.* The crowd erupts in applause before he's even spoken a word. When he addresses everyone his deep, amplified voice commands even my attention. The self-righteousness is hard to ignore.

'Ladies, gentlemen . . . and now the children of our United States. On this historical land around us lies a truth so large that it can no longer be ignored. Right here is where a new history will be written. We are the epicentre of how most Americans feel about their country. We are not a minority, or a fringe, or a few detractors that can be downplayed. We are less divided than our so-called superiors want us to be. We unite in peaceful protest to their detriment. For they know divided we would fall. This, above all else, is what we need to remember. They keep telling us this country is not in a depression, but I tell you I've never felt more depressed –'

I hear nothing more. Between the shifting bodies, I catch sight of red hair and green eyes among the drab clothes and hooded heads. One person is turned my way, the only occupier not watching the man with the megaphone. It is Delane, and he is staring at me. His pale face is unimpressed, a death mask of displeasure. He backs away, gradually enveloped by the crowd. I start after him, pushing through the protesters packed around me. Delane's retreat seems effortless as I fight through the people. In the sea of bodies he simply goes under, taken by a current and resurfacing periodically, just long enough for me to get a bead on him and continue pursuit. He makes it to the north end of the Great Lawn, where the protesters are sparse. I'm about thirty yards away when he flashes me a strange smile and steps behind a tree. When I get there he is gone. I circle the tree, but find nothing, wondering if there was ever anything to find in the first place. He looked so real this time. And it wasn't just a glimpse I caught either.

Someone pushes paper into my hand. I look up. The Hispanic man giving me the flyer seems familiar. He points to the advertisement, an upcoming appearance by some international guest speaker I've never heard of. He tells me it's important I go. The guy's eyes draw to slits, reciprocating the look I'm giving him. It takes me a minute to place this person. The moment I realize who he is, he recognizes me in return. It's the poor son of a bitch I bought breakfast for at Harbinger's the other week. We don't say anything at first. When he finally does speak there is emotion in his voice.

'That meal and money kept me going for three days, my friend.'

I shrug. 'You looked like you needed it.'

'More than you know,' he says with a tired smile. 'You have my thanks. I was getting desperate, quite literally.'

'It was the least I could do, quite literally.'

'Yeah, well, it went a long way. The world needs more men like you. You're one of the good guys.'

'Maybe I'm not as good as you think.'

'I don't buy it,' he says with a chuckle and extends his hand. 'Javier.'

I shake firmly. 'Rhodes.'

A pack of cigarettes I'd bought earlier comes to mind. I pull them from my pocket and peel off the cellophane.

A long time ago they were instrumental in helping me cope with stress. Starting up that old habit again isn't a good sign, and breaking another rule for healthy Husks is bad for business. Ask me if I give a shit any more. I take a cigarette and offer the packet to Javier.

'Smoke?'

His eyes light up. 'Don't mind if I do.'

Javier takes the pack, pulls out a cigarette, and goes to give it back. I hold up a stopping hand, shake my head.

'Keep it.'

'You sure?'

'Very.'

I put the lighter to my cigarette before passing it to Javier. He takes a deep drag, holds it in, looking me up and down. Nearby, I overhear a couple protesters passing by, talking about the police and Integris in hushed voices.

'Well, you certainly don't look a victim of unregulated capitalism, my man,' Javier says, expelling smoke.

'Not yet.'

'Said the same damn thing myself a few months ago, back when I thought I had a home, some job security and a few solid investments.'

I nod. Javier, as with so many others, likely got cleaned out from the ongoing aftershocks of the second housing market crash. Makes me feel glad I never bought into all that property ownership bullshit when condos made of second-rate glass and Chinese steel were going up everywhere over at an unsustainable rate. I haven't really been paying attention, but the speech from the podium behind me has grown louder and angrier, as has the crowd's reaction. I sweep a glance over the Great Lawn and turn back to Javier.

'It's gotten so big,' I say. 'This is crazy.'

'You wanna know what's really crazy?' Javier says and nods toward the guy spewing vitriol through his megaphone. 'The organizers have already been contacted by a few big conglomerates about corporate sponsorship.'

I laugh. 'This revolution is brought to you by . . .'

'There really is no such thing as bad publicity.'

'So, are you part of all this?'

'Kind of,' Javier coughs, heavy on the lung butter. 'I'd say it's more like I've got no place left to go.'

He turns and spits, hand shielding his mouth, trying to make it as polite as possible. The gob that lands in the grass is discoloured enough for me to wonder about his health. I check my Liaison. It says I've got less than ten minutes to get to Winslade's for upload. Javier points to the pile of flyers in his hand, then motions to the one he gave me.

'This speech is happening in less than an hour onstage over there. I recommend you check it out.'

'Sorry, I've got somewhere I have to be.'

Javier shrugs, unaffected. 'Guess I'll see you around the neighbourhood then.'

'You look like shit,' Renard says.

'I'm getting that a lot lately,' I reply.

He leans against the doorframe, peering at my Eldredge knot. '*Mon ami*, when will you learn to tie a tie properly?'

'Is it that bad?'

He sighs and steps aside. I walk through the penthouse door, leaving the two guards in the hallway. One of them now has an automatic shotgun slung across his back in addition to his other firepower. Security has doubled since my last visit, more armed personnel stationed in the building's foyer. I noticed even the doorman was packing a sidearm. Renard shuts the door behind me and follows close behind as I walk into the living room.

'You are late as well.'

'I got held up,' I say. 'It wasn't easy getting through Central Park with all those protesters about.'

I can feel Renard staring at the back of my head. I don't need to see his face to know the look of dissatisfaction he's giving me. When he speaks his tone is accusatory.

'What were you doing in Central Park?'

Irritation swells in me, one part incensed by his question, one part guilty over it. The response that I'm thinking in my head is suddenly ejecting from my lips.

'What?' I snap, turning on him. 'You got something against a fucking stroll in the park now?'

Renard's eyes widen, his jaw flexes. Clearly nobody has spoken to him like this in a long time. I hold his angered gaze before my own slides down to the Rapier at his side, making me wish I'd shut my mouth. Before he can reply, we hear the soft whirring of machinery and the sound of approaching footsteps. I turn to see the robot shuffle into the living room, rubbery face stoic. When the silvery eyes fall on me, the visage tries to reform into a look of concern, as fake as the question that follows it.

'Is everything all right, Mr Rhodes?' Winslade asks.

'I'm fine,' I lie. 'I just had to work my way through those squatters in the park.'

'Yes, I find them quite irritating as well.'

Winslade walks to the leather couch in the centre of the room and motions for me to sit. I comply, watching as he takes the seat opposite me. A data port sits on the coffee table, connected to a terminal nearby. On top of the terminal I spy the small cobalt-blue device, two small red lights glowing on its side. I jerk my thumb toward it.

'I've been meaning to ask you what that little blue thing is over there.'

'A new toy,' Winslade says, ignoring it. 'Nothing important.'

'And none of your business, Mr Rhodes,' Renard chimes in.

Winslade holds up a hand. 'Renard, please. This man is our most welcome guest. He may ask any question he likes.'

I give Renard a sneer. 'Thank you, Mr Winslade. I appreciate that.'

'The device in question is just a new piece of technology that I've put some money into researching and developing. Unfortunately, I'm not at liberty to discuss the details. It is company policy to keep information confidential on product development. I might upset the shareholders if I say much more.'

There are no tells on a fake face, no ticks or twitches or giveaways, no way to know if a robot is lying or not. His airbrushed lips peel back from his ivory teeth in a truly inhuman smile.

'Is that enough of an answer?'

'More than enough, Mr Winslade, thank you.'

The lenses scan back and forth over my face, up and down my body. 'I hope you don't mind me asking again, but are you all right?'

Anxiety plumbs my stomach. Pressure puts a knot in my throat. I'm not even remotely okay. I look at an old silver-plated .45 automatic displayed in a glass case on the wall. I picture putting the gun to my temple and think about how much relief could be attained if I took my mind outside my head for a moment. The idea doesn't even register as suicidal until I realize I haven't thought like this since the time between my father's death and my mother's impending one.

'I've been working hard as of late, that's all.'

Winslade nods, says he understands, then cocks his head at me. The lenses fix on my neck and do not move.

'Oh my, how did you get that bruise?'

'It's from another client,' I lie. 'I apologize.'

'Unacceptable,' Renard says. 'I'll file a complaint with Baxter immediately.'

'No, do not,' Winslade replies. 'I do not wish to cause trouble for my boy here. I'd prefer to rent Mr Rhodes with a blemish or two over any of the other options.'

I try to smile. 'I'll take that as a compliment.'

'It is the truth. I am very much looking forward to our session. A mere day of your services is nowhere near enough. In fact, I find even three days together somewhat disappointing. Not with you, you understand, simply the allotment of time.'

I shrug. 'It's the maximum, and for good reason. Anything more and serious problems start to arise.'

'Oh, I'm aware. Would you care for anything before we begin?'

'Thank you, but no. I'm ready when you are.'

'Very good.'

I reluctantly boot up the Husk program and plug into my Liaison. Winslade reaches forward and takes the other data cable. From my pillbox I fish out a red pill that will put me under for twenty-four hours. My mouth is dry and I have trouble swallowing it. One goes down like a golf ball. As I watch the program sync on screen, my Ouija clicks and I'm hit with a flash of brutality, eyes rimmed with mascara, wide and terrified, looking into mine. This I try to remember as the edges of my world begin to blacken.

'Wait . . .' I mumble. 'Stop . . .'

'We're well past that now,' says Winslade.

22

At first I dream of sex. Young girls come to me in the dark, soft and supple, high-schoolers and university sophomores pressing their naked bodies against mine. I'm licking them, sucking them, riding them, fucking them as they moan, groan, squeal. They are all one in the same; straddling, bucking, bending over before me. Their eyes change colour as I look into them, short hair growing long and refashioning in my grip. Breasts swell and shrink, faces morph, skin turning different shades as tattoos and piercings appear and fade. These girls are all familiar, though I can't remember any of their names. I revisit every page in the history of my little black book for moments at a time, revelling in these days gone by when I indulged for pleasure and not payment.

Before I was a Husk I was a whore. Something in my past planted the seed of it long ago, but university is where it actually started. It began at pub nights and frat parties, me nursing the only beer I could afford, hoping some girl might offer to buy me a drink or two. One night I got an offer I couldn't refuse. Some sassy rich bitch named Patricia, whose advances I'd been deflecting for a month, appeared in front of me at a kegger and drunkenly proclaimed she'd pay outright to take me back to her dorm for a good fuck. With all the student debt I'd amassed, it was an easy decision. She came once and paid me a hundred bucks before passing out. When we woke next morning, I was informed that we could hook up in the same fashion anytime, for the same rate. I took her up on the offer. Patricia had wealthy brat friends too, and had no qualms about offering my ass up to them. Pretty soon I had a semi-regular rotation going on. The girls ranged from hot to not, but I couldn't argue with such easy money. I needed it. Soon after graduation I fell into escorting. The fast cash that came in made the student loan payments on time, kept the creditors satiated while I tried and failed to find real and decent jobs.

It is Patricia atop me in my dream now, hips gyrating in a reverse cowgirl, her breath coming in short hitches. I rest my forehead between her shoulder blades and watch her ass grind on my lap. She arches, throws her head back, letting long hair dangle in my face as she bucks and rides. I lean back for a better view. As we near orgasm her pale skin begins to change, growing pink, then seemingly red with sunburn. She arches more and more until her inverted eyes are looking into mine, until it appears she can bend no further. She's squealing with delight. I'm close to being uncorked. A few more thrusts and I begin to erupt. Her skin suddenly becomes maroon and wet, blood smearing on my body wherever she touches.

'What have you done?' she cries.

I'm coming inside her when the squeals turn to screeches. Horrified, I hear a crunch and watch as her neck breaks, causing the back of her head to hit her spine. Then I'm screaming, trying to push her off me, still tethered to the hellish vessel. More cracking sounds come, shoulders splintering and vertebrae snapping as she folds inward, oozing fluids, her body compacting, crumpling, tearing until she is a tangled mess of shredded skin and crushed bone draped over me.

Shrieking, I watch as the mess melts into an indistinct pile of slurry meat that could be any questionable order from a butcher's backroom.

'Jesus, shut up already,' a voice behind me says.

I stop screaming and whirl around to find Miller standing in a recess of my mind, most of his face enshrouded by the dark. Below his chin are a shirt and tie topping off an expensive grey suit. I realize it was the one he was buried in. He steps forward, shadows peeling away from his head. A Miller more like the old one I knew appears. He's been repaired, looks much better than the last visitation.

'What are you doing here?' I ask.

'You wanted to see me one last time, remember?'

I remember looking at the closed coffin at the wake and thinking it. Miller gives me a tentative smile, though his face looks brittle, as if too much expression might strain and break the skull under his skin, undo the careful work that's been done.

'You Husked for Winslade,' I say.

Miller looks sheepish in light of my accusation. He adjusts his tie, straightens his jacket. I wait impatiently for him to answer while he fidgets with his cufflinks. When he speaks he avoids eye contact.

'He liked being me, but he didn't love being me. What he really loves is being *you*.'

'Yeah, I'm getting that impression.'

'How was my wake by the way?' Miller asks.

'Your dad got drunk and punched me in the face.'

'Wish I could have been there to see it. Did they say how I died?'

'They told everyone it was a prescription drug overdose.'

'Well, that's better than the truth.'

'What is the truth?'

'The truth is for you to find out.'

Miller sits down beside me and lights up a cigarette, brightening our pocket of night with a surprising orange glow. I look down at my lap. It is empty.

'What was all that?' I ask, my hands feeling the space where Patricia had been.

'The girl?' Miller exhales smoke. 'She was your first gig, the start of your career. She was the beginning of you as you are now.'

'What just happened to her?'

Miller looks around at the darkness beyond the reach of his ember. 'What happened was a forecast, or a broadcast, or maybe a report of the weather outside. Some kind of perspective, I think. Beyond this cocoon awful things are transpiring. Part of you is already aware. It has been eating you up inside, sickening your sense of self. Your consciousness and Winslade's consciousness are becoming more connected the more you share body and mind, just like it happened with me.'

'I don't understand.'

'You will if you want to.'

'I want to, but what am I supposed to do?'

Miller takes a heavy drag and flicks the remainder of his cigarette into the dark, the light of its ember trailing, a tiny shooting star in this inner space between waking and dreaming, living and dying. I watch it trail off into nothingness. It hits the ground, sparks and rolls, coming to rest at someone's bare feet. In the glow I see fingers pinch it, lifting the cigarette to a new pair of lips. The ember glows brighter with inhalation and I see Dennis Delane's face. The cigarette is passed on. Next, I see Tiffany Burrows bathed in orange. Another pass and it is Clarice Patton. Each face that appears in the dim light is that of some missing woman reported in the last while. They all watch intently as Miller turns and blows acrid smoke in my face that vaguely smells like cooked meat.

'Like I already told you, sleepwalker . . . It's time for you to wake up.'

When I awake I'm restrained. My re-emergence is slow, but panicked. Again my head feels like a writhing nest of hot worms, the squirm of them pushing against the back of my eyes, lashing my optic nerves. I struggle until my vision clears and I can comprehend what's going on. I'm tied to a chair in Winslade's living room. Renard stands before me with arms crossed. In one of his hands is a pearl-handled switchblade. My first real thought is that I'm about to be interrogated, or tortured.

'What's going on?' I ask.

'Safety first,' Renard says. 'I'm not taking any chances with you.'

'Untie me,' I demand.

'Once you calm down, I will.'

'Let me go!'

Another voice speaks. 'Patience, Mr Rhodes.'

To my surprise the robot walks into my line of sight, awkwardly holding an old-school straight razor. Winslade approaches me, blade held out in front of him. It looks as if he's pointing it at my neck. I'm convinced this will be one of the last images I ever see.

'I do apologize,' Winslade says. 'But due to the unpredictability of your last re-emergence, we thought it best to limit your movement this time.'

Renard and the robot kneel before me and saw away at the ropes tying my wrists and ankles. As soon as my right hand is free I raise it to my ear to pull the proboscis from my Ouija, only to find it absent. Renard must have already unplugged me, which is against the rules. It's clear in the contract. Husks are responsible for their own gear. As Winslade cuts through my ankle restraints, I notice the cobalt-blue device in his other hand. The ropes fall away and I stand.

'There,' Winslade says, rising.

He reaches forward with mechanical hands and slowly straightens my clothes like a father readying his son for a recital. I come very close to recoiling from his touch. My body does not hurt like before, but my head is one giant exposed nerve. I don't bother to ask how the session went. I don't care. All I want to do is get away, back to whatever I can call my own life.

'I would like you to stay for lunch, Mr Rhodes.'

I shake my head. 'I don't think so, Mr Winslade.'

'Please, I insist.'

'I'll have to take a rain check. Perhaps next –'

'It wasn't a request, you idiot,' Renard snarls.

I shoot Renard a glare. 'Excuse me?'

'You heard me.'

I turn back to Winslade, expecting him to reprimand his uncouth subordinate. The robot simply stares back, lenses cold and calculating.

'Renard is correct. It was not a request.'

The meal of roast pheasant threatens to fly out my throat as I walk down Central Park West, though I try hard to keep it marinating in the pool of champagne at the bottom of my belly. Nausea waxes and wanes in my nose and neck. I attempt to walk in a straight line, my pace erratic, bumping into tourists who don't know enough to get out of a staggering man's way. I'm berated in different languages, given all sorts of rude gestures. Even a challenge to fight is proffered. The looks I get, people must think I'm drunk or high or crazy. What I actually am is no longer comfortable in my own skin. Fantasies of cutting it off and peeling it away invade my head. I want to shed it, leave it in the gutter, start anew.

Lunch with Winslade has left me feeling rotten and restricted. As he sat at the dining table and watched me consume the food he could not, he informed me that I would soon become his one exclusive rental. Once he and Baxter finished negotiating the new contract, I would have one client and one client only. Winslade said he didn't want to waste time with other Husks. Said he only cared for me. With the new deal my services would no longer be available for other clients, but exclusivity would pay handsomely. Hearing this, I almost choked on my food. Protesting would have been pointless. Winslade wasn't making a request. He was a fortune teller dictating my fate through dollars and demands. My next session with him will be the commencement of this new exclusivity. The thought of it fills me with nothing but dread. I call Baxter. She picks up on the first ring, seems to have been expecting me.

'What can I do for you, Rhodes?'

'We need to talk,' I say.

'I trust your session with Mr Winslade went well?'

I suck my teeth and hold my tongue a moment, annoyed by the question. All Baxter ever cares about are the goddamn clients.

'I can tell you my lunch with him afterwards did not.'

'Why's that?'

'Because he just informed me of the new exclusivity deal you two are drawing up behind my back.'

Baxter grunts. 'I thought you'd be pleased about that.'

'Pleased?'

'Of course,' she replies. 'A deal that gives you only a single client to schedule, one who has been very generous so far and treats you exceptionally well, not to mention a significant increase in your pay . . . what's not to like?'

'What . . . what if I don't want the gig?'

'Pardon?'

'I should have a say in whether or not I do this.'

Baxter's voice hardens. 'Your contract with Solace Strategies stipulates that you take the gigs and clients I book and go when and where I tell you to go. It doesn't say anything about you having a say in these matters.'

'Well, I don't want to be Winslade's fucking one and only.'

'Well, that's just too bad.'

'Fine,' I spit. 'What if I want out, Baxter? What if I quit?'

'If you want out now, I promise you'll walk away with nothing.'

'What?'

'I'll freeze your accounts, cancel your credit.'

'You can't do that.'

'I can't?' Baxter laughs. 'The other week, when you were at the Rochester and all your cards didn't work . . . did you think that was just some fluke error?'

'What?' Her words are like a slap in the face. 'You did that? Why?'

'To remind you what it's like to be penniless. That day in my office, after your first session with Navarette, I found your attitude bothersome. Fancy you, telling *me* when *you* feel like working. You were getting out of line, starting to think for yourself. That's bad for business. You don't give me orders. I give the orders. Temporarily suspending access to your funds was just a little reminder of who is in charge here, Rhodes.'

'You rotten cunt —'

'Hey,' Baxter snarls. 'Do you have any idea how fucking hard it is to get and keep a client like Winslade with our competitors constantly nipping at our heels? Clients like him come to us for the very best in service and quality, and they're willing to pay shitloads for it. You're the service and quality he wants. It must be delivered. Solace Strategies give their clients what no one else can. That's *what we do.*'

'But —'

'No buts. Do your job. Take the gig. Everyone wins.'

Baxter hangs up. Another wave of nausea washes over me. Direct sunlight amplifies it and I stick to walking in the shade of trees. In the distance I hear chanting from protesters in the park. I sit on a bench and try to calm my nerves with deep-breathing exercises. I remember Tweek's advice and start mediating. The skin on my scalp slackens. My muscles go rubbery. I start to get a grip. Eventually my sickness subsides. I'm grateful for it. I have dinner plans later with Ryoko that I don't want to break. Nearby, the subway entrance seems inviting. The need to get underground comes again, a desire to descend into the cool dark below the city and burrow away from sun and sky. Sleep on the train comes easy to me, coffined in boxes of glass and metal and plastic. I resign myself to a few hours of this burial in transit that will allow me enough rest to rise again.

Before I go underground my Liaison notifies me of an incoming message, marked high priority. It's from Clive. He's managed to dig up something on Kirk King, our man who wasn't there before. The message is one sentence, the only lead he can give me.

Kirk King: bartender @ Las Iguanas Bar & Grill. Las Vegas, Nevada.

23

'What's next?' Ryoko asks.

She doesn't take her eyes off the menu. I skim the wine list, wanting none of the brands available, throwing glances her way. She's controlled as usual, her emotions tricky to gauge. Her Japanese half acts as her anchor, a culture of calm instilled by her father during her strict upbringing. It serves as Ryoko's restraint against feeling too much of anything. I think I'm the only one who has ever truly seen the heart she keeps caged and curtained. The restaurant I've taken us to is her favourite, although this is no date, at least not officially.

'I'm in Las Vegas again tomorrow,' I say. 'Just for a day.'

'Same client as last time?'

'Yeah.'

She looks up and again I'm hit with just how exquisite Ryoko looks, far too beautiful to be out with the likes of me. I've cleaned up pretty well under the circumstances, but still feel ugly among her and the other clientele. The handsome man I'm used to being has stepped out, leaving behind a haggard, tired twin. The weight of slack skin pulls on my face. The bags under my eyes seem the size of scrotums. I feel like I'm sitting under spotlights everywhere I go now, all my marks and bruises on display. Something in my expression makes Ryoko reach across the table and stroke my cheek with the back of her hand. She cracks a smile.

'You still look like shit, y'know.'

I lean into her touch, kiss her fingers. I want to put them in my mouth, feel her painted nails on my tongue. Her hands are smooth and soft. She wears jewellery on them, though there is nothing on her ring finger. That small circumference of relationship real estate seems attainable for the first time ever.

'Ryoko Rhodes,' I say. 'Has a nice ring to it.'

Ryoko blushes. 'What did you say?'

'Nothing, just thinking aloud.' I change the subject. 'When's your next gig?'

'No bookings. I'm taking a hiatus, despite Baxter's protests. You should think about doing the same. You look like you need it.'

'I do.'

'So take some time off then. Let's me and you get the hell out of here, go someplace nice and sunny for a while.'

'The both of us?' I say, warmth spreading in my chest. 'Really?'

'Yeah.' Ryoko shrugs. Her smile is shy and sweet. 'We've never taken a holiday anywhere together before. It's about time, don't you think?'

'If it's all right with you . . .'

The look Ryoko gives me says it's more than all right, that I should know better than to ask. I feel like an idiot. Running away with her has been a constant thought on the backburner, a fantasy never given much credence. The fact that she's suddenly placed it within reach leaves me momentarily speechless. Then I think about my earlier phone call with Baxter. Ryoko knows what I'm going to say before I do.

'I can't.'

'Can't, or won't?'

'Ry, there is nothing I'd love more, believe me, but the boss has me locked in for a while. There's too much demand for me right now.'

'There won't be soon,' Ryoko says, looking at the bruise on my neck. 'The wear and tear on you is starting to show plenty. Jesus, you've even got a few grey hairs now.'

'What?'

She reaches over, plucks one from my temple, shows it to me. 'See? You're getting too much mileage on you. I can't believe you're still on a first-call list. Clients are going to start dropping you soon, you know that?'

'It doesn't matter.'

Ryoko frowns. 'And why doesn't that matter exactly?'

I want to tell her about the impending exclusivity with Winslade, the fact that I will be a highly paid one-man show who will soon be off the market. I want to tell her how shitty that makes me feel. I digress instead.

'All this Husking, all these gigs ... I don't feel like myself any more, Ryoko.'

'The work gets to us sometimes, follows us around. You're just thinking about it too much, babe.'

'No, this is different,' I protest. 'I feel ... dirty inside. It's as if the sessions are leaving residue behind, guilt or shame or sadness over things I can't understand, fear and anxiety from memories I don't actually possess. They're emotions without origins, coming in waves. It's creeping me the fuck out. I wish I could explain it.'

Ryoko leans forward. 'Try.'

'My clients ... they're infiltrating and appropriating me, as always, but after some of my sessions ... I'm not sure the client is fully extricated. I'm not sure they leave me entirely or something –'

Ryoko holds a finger to her lips. My voice has been steadily rising. Nearby customers cast wary looks our way, some with frowns of disapproval. Even the waiter knows to keep his distance from our table at the moment. Ryoko lays her hand on mine and squeezes gently.

'Calm down, relax. You're getting all worked up.'

I rub my temples. 'God, I feel like I'm going to hell.'

'Like you're falling to pieces?'

'No, like *damnation*,' I say, shooting her a look. 'But condemned by someone else's actions, not my own. I feel like a fucking patsy.'

Ryoko sits up straight. She chews her bottom lip and stares at me, her pupils searching mine, checking the windows of my soul. We don't break eye contact for what seems like an eternity. Eventually she speaks in a slow and soft voice.

'Did I ever tell you about the time I ran into you while you were on the job? Last year, not long after we began ... hooking up?'

I shake my head. Ryoko tucks her hair behind her ears as her eyes grow reminiscent. Her voice becomes whispery, cautious.

'In a city the size of New York, it was a total fluke. I mean, what were the chances? I had the night off, didn't know where you were at. Me and a couple girlfriends hit the town and at one point ended up in some upscale cigar lounge. We were drinking and smoking and shooting the shit when I suddenly heard your voice. I turned around to see you, leaning against the bar, laughing with some petite brunette. When you turned to the bartender to order a drink I caught your eye. You gave me a smile, like you recognized me. I smiled back and you beckoned me over. I was sure it was you, Rhodes, positive of it.'

'It wasn't me though.'

'No, and it took me a minute to figure that out. Who-ever was renting must have suspected that I already knew you, because they played along, led me expertly. After some small talk I noticed a deviancy in his eyes, *your* eyes, that was completely unlike you.'

'When did you know for sure?'

Ryoko smirks. 'Our code word.'

I nod. Our code words were never pet names for each other, never meant to be cute or playful. This was their purpose right from the start.

'When I called you cheesecake, you called me eye-candy. You tried to slip your hand around my waist, grab my ass. That's when I knew it was time to leave. You said I should stay, have a drink with you, see where the night would lead. When I wouldn't, your client showed his true col-ours. You told me not to be such a stuck-up bitch, that I didn't know what I was missing out on. I told you to go to hell. You grabbed my arm, said a two-bit slut like me should consider myself lucky I was even allowed on the premises.'

'I'm sorry.'

'Why?' Ryoko shrugs. 'It wasn't you. That's what I'm trying to say. You would have never said those things to me. You've never been anything but sweet to me. You're a good man. I know that with all my heart.'

'I just want to be your man,' I say.

That's a tough request, even I know it. Her eyes moisten and she averts her gaze, looking back down at the menu. I say nothing. The waiter comes. Ryoko orders a tonic for herself and I order a glass of Shiraz, even though I don't care for the stuff. By the time she looks back up at me she is completely composed. I reach across the table and take her hand in mine, massaging her palm. No words are needed. We stay that way for a long time, our moment interrupted only when the waiter returns and delivers our drinks. Ryoko takes to her tonic, but I don't drink from my glass. Instead I catch myself running my finger around the rim, creating a hum, same as Miller used to do. This does not go unnoticed by Ryoko, who gently pulls her hand away from mine as she watches, feeling uneasy over what she's witnessing.

'What do you want to order?' she asks.

'Shit,' I chuckle. 'I haven't even looked yet.'

My stomach rumbles with hunger, not sickness. I peruse the menu, suddenly feeling like I want to sink my teeth into flesh. The red-meat dishes listed before me spring saliva in the back of my mouth: New York strip steak, sirloin, T-bone, roast beef, veal and lamb cutlets. I want it all. As I read on I notice that nothing denotes the meat as organically sourced; no free range, no natural growth, no farms mentioned. This means all the meat is lab-grown. My Ouija clicks and for a second I see the torsos of cattle and swine, suspended in fluids, grown quickly and without limbs or heads for easy harvest. The word *harvest* bothers me and I examine the back of the menu. At the bottom in small print is *Locally Grown by Modern Harvest NYC Inc.*, one of the many companies Winslade owns.

I cackle involuntarily at *locally grown*, the play on words designed to fool people so they won't realize their dinner is being built cell by cell in science labs a few miles away in the meat-packing district. I lose my appetite completely, don't want to eat anything by Modern Harvest for some reason. I don't want Ryoko to either. She puts her menu down.

'I think I'll try the beef stroganoff . . .'

'No,' I blurt, placing my hand on hers. 'Don't order that –'

Behind Ryoko's head, a well-dressed man in his forties enters the restaurant with a young woman on his arm. I'm speechless as I stare. The girl is beautiful, blonde hair and blue eyes, dressed in an exquisite outfit that makes most men's, and a few women's, heads turn. I hold my breath. The restaurant host greets them and leads her and the obvious client across the restaurant. She does not notice me sitting in the corner as they pass by. A complete professional, her attention is fixed on the man footing her bill. It's been more than two years since I saw her in the flesh. The less we see of each other, the less we're reminded of our shared past.

'Wow, she's stunning,' Ryoko says. 'Do you know her?'

I nod. 'My sister.'

'Your sister?' Ryoko's eyes widen, face growing worried. 'Oh my God.'

'Yeah.'

They slip into a booth within my line of sight and the man orders martinis. In no time they're chatting away, frivolous conversation, the man smitten, my sister pretending to be. They down their drinks quickly when they arrive. Ryoko and I watch, saying little to each other. It isn't long before the client slips out of his seat and heads for the washroom. An insistence grows in me, an urgency to speak with my sister while I have the rare opportunity. Without a word, I rise from my chair and approach the booth while she's occupied with her Liaison. She doesn't look up until I'm seated across from her. Must have expected her date because the fake smile she's wearing drops into a very real scowl.

'Oh, for fuck's sake . . . what are you doing here?'

I look back at Ryoko. 'I'm on a date.'

My sister looks over my shoulder at Ryoko and gives a small, demure smile. Ryoko responds with a nod and equally small wave.

'Your girlfriend?'

'Working on it.'

'You shouldn't leave her waiting. It's impolite.'

She wants me gone. I expected as much. My sister has never liked coincidences, doesn't believe in them. But this feels like a turn of something fateful to me. I stay seated, and just like that we're back to our old catty ways.

'You know what else is impolite, sis? Never returning any of my calls.'

'You don't need to call me. Ever.'

I sigh. 'Look, I worry about you sometimes.'

'Well, you shouldn't.'

'How hard is it to take a couple minutes out of your day, pick up a phone and call me back?'

'What's your problem? I *just* saw you, for crying out loud.'

'Pardon?'

'I saw you the other week,' she throws Ryoko an unimpressed look. 'You and that freak bitch both.'

'Sorry, when and where did you think you saw me exactly?'

She throws up her hands. 'In the Hamptons, at the crazy Japanese mansion . . . saw you at the damn sex romp that night where you were trying to be the life and soul of the party.'

'That . . . wasn't me.'

'What are you talking about? Of course it was you. We argued in front of everyone, for Christ's sake. I told you to get the hell out of the main room when all those guys wanted me to –'

'Stop,' I gulp, feeling sick. 'I was on hire at the time. I was . . . Husking.'

'You were what?' My sister's eyes widen with disgust. 'Oh, my God.'

I curl my lip. 'Don't look at me like that.'

'You're . . . *Husking?*'

It's like she vomits the word over me. With a sneer she

leans back, away from me, knocking back a mouthful of martini to drown her distaste. I'm insulted that she, of all people, is feeling uncomfortable around who I am and what I do.

'Jesus,' I groan. 'Don't even try getting on your high horse. You're no better.'

'I beg to differ,' she says. 'At least I don't let *dead* people fuck with me.'

'Don't do this. I'm only trying to be here for you.'

My sister glares at me, sending a chill across the table. I wasn't there for her when I should have been. I didn't know how to be. She was eleven, I was twelve. Barely old enough to understand what was happening when he snuck into our room one night while my parents were hosting a party downstairs. He was a friend of our father's, someone with money who had lent my folks a significant amount when they needed it most and never asked for repayment. In his eyes, the donation entitled him to something. He chose two kids as compensation. He abused us only the one time, mumbling threats of harm if we told, turning us into our own conspirators as the muffled sounds of music and mingling came from downstairs. My sister got it worse. She was the favourite. After I'd warmed him up with my hands, he made her finish him off with her mouth. As per his instructions I watched, terrified, huddled on my bed in the gloom of our shared room, listening to his grunts and groans staggered between my sister's quiet sobs. When he was done he left us in the dark and returned to the party as if nothing happened.

My sister and I never told anyone, never spoke of it. We didn't know if our parents knew or even suspected. All we did was drift further and further apart, ashamed to look at each other, too scared to say anything. We slept in the same room for years after, every night both of us lying in our beds staring at the ceiling until sleep took over and the nightmares came. Sometimes I would snap awake in the small hours of the morning to the sound of my sister crying. I wanted to go to her, hold her tight and tell her I would never let it happen again. But I wasn't there for her. I was barely there for myself. By detaching from my own flesh and convincing myself that my body was of no real importance, I dealt with the abuse. At the same time I formed a perfect mindset for the world's oldest profession.

'Please,' I say. 'Just give me a chance . . .'

My sister leans back, crosses her arms over her chest. 'You better go. Your dinner's getting cold.'

'No it isn't. I haven't ordered anything yet –'

A heavy hand lands on my shoulder, making me jump. I look up to find a displeased look on the face of my sister's date.

'What do you think you're doing, pal?' he asks.

'I'm just finishing up, won't be a minute.' I turn back to my sister. 'Call me soon? Please?'

'Hey, who the hell are you?' he barks.

I shrug out of his grip. 'Don't worry, man. I'm nobody.'

'Well, nobody better get out of my damn seat and leave my woman alone.'

'Your woman?' I sneer, incensed by his comment. 'What do you mean *your woman*?'

The man leans in, grabs me by the scruff of the neck, holding me firm as he brings his lips to my ear and whispers. 'I paid a lot of money for her tonight, asshole, so that means she's mine.'

My Ouija clicks and for a moment the man holding me morphs into the one who abused us. It is now his hand on my neck, immobilizing me, making me do his bidding. Despite all my visions in recent days, this is the first time I've hallucinated someone from my own recognizable past. I feel another crack form in my psyche, another stumbling step toward insanity. Terror and anxiety flood me. I picture Cameron Tate strapped to his bed in the nuthouse. The image threatens, angers, teases me all at once, telling me my time is coming. Heat from the rage that flares inside reaches the surface of my skin almost instantly. I see the look of surprise on the man's face as he feels the temperature change beneath his grip.

'You don't *own* us!' I scream.

I deliver a vicious elbow to the man's head, resulting in an audible crack that sounds stereophonic to my ears. He staggers back, holding his face, blood seeping through his fingers, nose or orbital bone broken. I slide out of the booth and launch myself at him, sending the two of us crashing to the floor. He gets three punches in before I overpower him, each one connecting with my head. Before I know it I'm straddling him, my fists raining down, delivering blows to the soft body inside the expensive suit and enjoying every second of it. By the time two waiters pull me off the man is begging for mercy, face bloody and battered and swollen. I try to walk away, but stumble into a table and collapse. My sister races to her client's side just as Ryoko comes to mine.

'Jesus fucking Christ,' my sister snarls, looking at Ryoko. 'I don't need anyone defending my honour.'

Ryoko picks me up off the floor, starts pulling me toward the exit. 'I don't think that was what he was doing, honey.'

Ryoko and I lie on my bed, fully clothed, our chests rising and falling with slow, unified breaths. My left eye is bruised and my lip is split from the restaurant fight. She strokes my head, holds me close, telling me over and over not to worry, telling me the past can't hurt me any more, saying all the things I should have said to my sister years ago. I'm haunted by the idea that I might have been able to change our paths, alter our futures, but I know better. Our histories define us until our dying days, written already by the purveyors of fate, snickering at our belief that we make our own destiny.

Whores aren't born, they're made. This much I know. There are no skeletons in our closets, just shattered bones and dried marrow, crushed skulls that never speak. You can't be in this business without them. Fear is something you run toward or run away from. Husks and hookers embrace it. We thrust our dicks back into torment, spread our legs and allow invasion until it no longer threatens or frightens us any more. We make it our bitch, relieving it of any power it once had. Ryoko has secrets, Phineas and Clive have secrets, Miller had secrets, some piece of the past, maybe only minutes in duration, but powerful enough to change the course of their lives. Only Ryoko and my sister know of the night that cancelled any bright future for me, leaving a darker road in its place, the night that dictated my path regardless of where I thought I was going.

It is here, lying in bed with our heads on the pillows, that I finally tell Ryoko that I've completely fallen in love with her. Her eyes glisten. She swallows hard. Her lips kiss mine, but don't smile, don't reciprocate the words I've spoken. I run my fingers through her hair and she responds by telling me the real reason she has stopped Husking.

Ryoko is pregnant.

24

When I land in Las Vegas I've got a few hours to kill before my session with Navarette. Make-up and sunglasses cover most of my black eye, but my split lip is obvious. Outside McCarran the same limo driver awaits. He reaches for my bag, but I hold on to it. He shrugs and opens the back door, glancing at my injuries. I slip onto the leather seats and pull out my Liaison, rechecking the message Clive sent me: *Kirk King: bartender @ Las Iguanas Bar & Grill. Las Vegas, Nevada.*

I search the name of the bar and discover it's just north of the old Stratosphere Hotel and Casino at the end of the Strip, a block away from the Clark County Marriage Bureau, where all brides and grooms get licensed to wed. Good business is all about location, location, location. I figure Las Iguanas nailed it, making some coin serving up liquid courage to all the poor penguin suits prepping themselves for a fast, cheap ceremony. The driver's voice comes through the car intercom.

'Where to, sir?'

'Take me to the Strat,' I say.

I hear the driver snort with laughter through the partition before his voice comes through the speaker again. 'Did you just say the Stratosphere?'

'Yes, is that a problem?'

'No problem, sir . . . it's just that no one goes to the Strat any more. It's about to go the way of the Sahara.'

'Yeah, well, I wanna hit some low-stakes blackjack for an hour.'

'Low stakes?' I hear the driver laugh again. 'That's definitely the place to go.'

We drive the length of the Strip slowly, stuck in rush hour traffic. I lower the tinted window so I can view the casinos and tourists in all their bright, gaudy, ill-advised glory. The Nevada heat is more oppressive than ever, sun cooking everything in sight. I drink a beer from the minibar to keep my mind numb. On top of the bar lies my per diem in an envelope, but I leave it where it is. There is a small pull-down mirror in the ceiling of the car, and I check my split lip and black eye, wondering if my marred looks will anger Navarette or Winslade.

Fuck them. I was already entertaining the idea of skipping on Navarette's booking. Now I commit to bailing. Winslade's opinion means less and less to me every hour, and what do I care? He's going to practically own me soon anyway, able to slip in and out of his paid slave whenever he wishes. I don't want to give it another thought, but half my mind is fixated on my future with him. The other half is stuck on Ryoko's pregnancy.

Conceiving wasn't in the cards, as far as she knew. There had been damage done to her in the past, when Ryoko was a teen, episodes of sexual violence that she never talks about. Years after it happened she began experiencing abdominal pains. Doctors examined her, drew conclusions and prescribed pills. The verdict was she'd never bear children, which is why she never used birth control on or off the job. This pregnancy is happening against all odds. She wants to keep the baby, though she has no idea who the father is. All the Husking she's done in the last little while provides her with an array of possible donors, men she can't recount meeting and having sex with. She's getting a DNA test in the coming days to determine if I'm the dad. She's confident it will come back positive. I'm not so sure.

And I'm not sure how I feel about it either. Not quite numb, more a suspension of shock. When she broke the news in my apartment I said nothing. We just lay there. She waited patiently, but I couldn't reply. The situation was an impossible one. My head wouldn't process it. My mouth wouldn't work. Blue coloured the ensuing silence, trace amounts of tension and dismay added to every second that slipped by. Minutes felt like hours, felt like each and every one of those times Ryoko failed to make a return on my professions of love. When she finally rose from the bed and stood tall and proud before me, I knew she'd go it alone if need be, but I could see how bad I'd hurt her with my silence. By the time she left my place, I still hadn't said a word. I don't know what I'll say to her next time we meet.

Never gave kids more than a passing thought really, gave even less consideration after I got involved with Ryoko. Whether we should bring children into this world is a question every generation asks itself, but I think the concern is undeniable now. The future holds little value for those we send into it. They're going to inherit a shithole, a system of unending struggle and strife, a place of greater greed, violence and scarcity in all things. How on earth do I keep a kid safe in a world going to hell? How would I protect them from the likes of some of my clients and their companies? From being kidnapped and killed by organizations like Integris? From the kind of predator who abused my sister and me? My mother and father were good people, good parents, and look how their offspring turned out. The odds are so stacked against new arrivals now that it's barely worth considering. The world's a meat grinder, waiting for the hopes and dreams of the young to mature just enough for the slaughter. Ryoko's kid doesn't stand a fucking chance. I don't know if I want this child to be mine. I don't think I want the responsibility. I don't think I can give it a good life.

The limo pulls up to the Stratosphere. As I get out I grab the per diem and pocket it. The driver tells me he will wait in the car, reminding me that I've only got a couple hours until my appointment at the Emerald City. Inside the Stratosphere Casino I find an empty seat at a blackjack table and play a dozen hands, losing almost all of them, wondering if the limo driver is casing the joint and keeping an eye on me. Eventually I catch sight of him sitting at a slot machine on the other side of the pit, glancing occasionally my way. When his attention is distracted by a voluptuous waitress I give him the slip, snaking through the casino crowds and exiting out the rear of the hotel, where I head straight for the Las Iguanas Bar & Grill.

The air is warm and still outside, skin of the sky beginning to bruise with early-evening light as I pass rows of cracked concrete buildings, half of them with windows boarded up. Las Vegas goes from shiny to shitty real fast. A block away from the Strip in any direction is a shock for most tourists. It takes all of ten minutes before I'm standing outside the saloon-style doors of the dive where Kirk King supposedly works. Las Iguanas is splashed across its exterior, red paint faded to pink. Old southern rock belts out of cheap speakers inside. Through the windows I see the glow of neon beer and liquor signs, casting weak silhouettes of a few shaggy customers within. One of those shadows comes lumbering toward the door, opening it with rubbery arms, stink of booze wafting out with him. He almost falls onto the sidewalk as he passes. I slip inside before the door swings shut.

There are two shifty men and a weary-looking woman in the bar. No one speaks. They all look up and give me a once over before refocusing on the drinks in their hands. I seat myself at the far end, away from them, next to the ancient jukebox. The bartender's back is turned as he counts money in the till. He wears cargo shorts and a black T-shirt. I already know it's Kirk King by his physique. He's slim and fit, still possessing the well-toned body of a Husk.

'Hey, bartender,' I say. 'Could use a drink down here.'

King turns and looks at me, sizing me up. One eye is pale blue, the other milky white. A thick scar cleaves his eyebrow and cheekbone above and below the sightless orb. He makes his way down the bar to where I sit and doesn't smile once.

'Name your poison,' he says, checking out my threads. 'And know we only take cash here.'

'All right, give me a Maker's Mark, double and neat.'

He snatches the bottle of bourbon off the mirror-backed shelves behind the bar, peering at my black eye and split lip in the reflection as he undoes the cap.

'You all right?' King asks. 'Looks like someone did a number on you.'

'You should've seen the other guy,' I say and grin. 'Looks like you're no stranger to a scrap yourself.'

King's nostrils flare. 'I've had my share.'

He pours my order cautiously, his one good eye flicking between the tumbler and my hands on the bar. It seems wise to keep them where he can see them. I think about wading in cautiously, but I'm low on patience and running out of time.

'Slow night?' I ask, looking around at the few customers.

'Yeah,' he replies. 'But I like slow nights.'

'Mind if I ask you a question or two?'

He hands me my drink. 'About what?'

'About your former career with Eternity Executive.'

He must have already figured, because the sawn-off shotgun is out from under the bar and pointed over the top of the counter at me, real subtle like. The other customers don't even notice.

'I got nothing to say, pretty boy,' he whispers. 'Think you should knock that bourbon back real quick like, and be on your way.'

'I just got here,' I say, my arrogance and annoyance oblivious to the gun. 'Came all the way from New York.'

'And if you leave now, you'll get out of here in one piece.'

'We need to talk, King.'

The fact that I know his name does not improve the situation. King bares his teeth and cocks the hammer back on the scattergun.

'Dude, I don't know who the hell you are, and I don't want to, plain and simple.'

'I can't leave until we discuss a few things.'

'Why the hell would I want to talk with you about any of my business, current or former?'

'Because it's about Winslade.'

I've caught him off guard. King straightens, cocks his head and looks at me for what seems like a long time. He scratches at his arms, his neck, fidgets with his clothes, every action agitated. His expression seems angered, but his good eye looks woeful. I can't tell if he wants to hug me or hit me. Finally he stows the gun back under the bar.

'Lemme guess, brother,' he says, snatching my bourbon up and swallowing it down. 'He's your client now?'

'Yeah.'

King wipes his mouth. 'You have my condolences.'

'What I want from you is some insight.'

'Insight?' King snorts. 'Best thing to do is get the fuck out, hightail it while you can. That's my advice.'

'You know it's not that easy.'

King glances around at the dilapidated bar and its shoddy customers. He touches his fingers to the scar over his white eye. I can only imagine how good his life was before he quit Husking.

'Yeah,' King sighs. 'I do know.'

'But you still managed to get out . . .'

'Let's not go there.'

'. . . because of something to do with Winslade . . .'

'I said I don't want to talk about it.'

'. . . and not just you, but others too.'

King pours a glass of bourbon for me and another for himself. 'I wouldn't say the others got out exactly.'

'How well did you know Cameron Tate and Brad Garrison?'

My question hits another nerve. King gives me a look that says I'm very close to crossing the line and getting thrown out of his bar. I give him an apologetic look in return, sorry for asking him to exhume what he's been trying hard to bury. King stares into his glass, swishing the spirit around.

'I assume the bad dreams have started?'

I nod. 'The worst.'

'Are you getting the flashbacks too? Those vicious visions that leave you feeling sick to your stomach with guilt and repulsion, like some kind of fucking post-traumatic stress disorder from a war you were never shipped out to?'

I nod again.

'And you can barely remember anything about them afterwards. Am I right?'

I swallow hard, my fingers fidgeting with my glass and coaster. Beads of sweat form on my forehead. King notices all of this and flashes me a smile that looks more like a wince.

'It only gets worse, brother,' King says and fires back his bourbon in one gulp. 'It'll either drive you mad or make you dead.'

He pulls out a pack of smokes and puts a cigarette between his lips, offering me one at the same time. I accept and he lights both with a trembling hand. With his other hand he takes down the *No Smoking* sign pinned to the wall behind him.

'Garrison was one of the first at Eternity Executive to Husk for Winslade, and quickly became the guy's favourite. After several months of smooth sessions Brad started to report some issues, but nothing that the bosses would sideline him for. They don't care about their employees. All they care about is how much profit they can make off a Husk before he or she becomes an unviable product, before we get too old or too beat up to be sellable. By the time Winslade wanted exclusivity to Brad, his condition was rapidly deteriorating. Eternity ran all sorts of tests, but couldn't come up with anything solid. I mean, shit, there are so many potential factors. We're talking about a disciplined form of brain damage here . . . artificially created, digitally regulated, drug-controlled splits in our fucking psyche, for Christ's sake. We're the tip of the spear on a new frontier. Who knows what the short-term and long-term effects will be?'

'I think I'm starting to get an idea,' I say with distaste, though it has just as much to do with the stale tobacco I'm inhaling.

'Brad was too.' King takes a long drag. 'Then he had some accident while on hire and ended up in a coma, resulting in his termination. Winslade tried out a few other Husks before settling on Tate, who he took a real liking to. That didn't turn out well either. By the time Winslade started renting me, my bosses at EE had noticed a pattern, but no one bothered informing me because –'

'Because you're compartmentalized and forbidden to discuss business, even among your own colleagues, same as me and my company.'

'Which outfit did you say you were with?'

'I didn't.'

'You're well-trained,' King snickers and shrugs. 'They're all the same anyway.'

'So why Windslade? What is it about him that affects us so much?'

'Never got that far into figuring it out. Every now and then I'd hear rumours of similar post-session problems happening with Husks at other companies, particularly the shabbier ones, but it was all just bits of black-market gossip from sources you could never fully trust. When things started getting weird with Winslade, I tried asking around, but couldn't get anything out of anyone. The only exception was Tate. He was the one who thought he had things all figured out.'

'How so?'

King's laugh is bitter. 'You can't trust a word that guy says. Cameron's a lunatic now, a certified one.'

'I know. I visited him in Bellevue before I came to see you.'

This was something King wasn't expecting, and the revelation rocks him back. His manner becomes evasive, guilt and regret eating at him. It's clear to me that he hasn't been to see his old co-worker in a long time.

'How's he holding up in there?' King asks.

'Not good.'

'Yeah, I figured. It was me who helped get him admitted to Bellevue, y'know.'

'I know. Saw your name attached to his file.'

'Did you manage to get anything out of him?'

'Only that he didn't believe his body belonged to him, and that he thought he was Winslade himself.'

King sighs and seems to crumple against the bar before me, head hanging, shoulders going slack, as if he's fighting off a spell of fainting. At first he just moans. When he finally does speak it's into the countertop.

'Before he broke, Cameron kept telling me over and over: *Husks are houses, clients are ghosts, and what transpires between us and them is a haunting.*'

'A haunting?'

'You know what a haunting is in actuality?'

'What?'

'Unfinished business.'

King twitches involuntarily, mumbles something. He's far from the cool, collected individual who first poured me my drink. It's becoming more evident that he has a few screws loose, despite his acting skills. His blue eye and white eye shift back and forth as his fingers drum on the bar counter. He's remembering things he doesn't want to, growing more agitated, as if he's getting ready for something to go down.

I draw my finger across my eye. 'Did Winslade do that to you?'

'Winslade? Nah, I did this to myself.'

'Why on earth would you . . . ?'

'Because clients want pretty young things, perfect people . . . you know that. If you don't look the part, you don't take the stage. And I didn't want to be in the show no more.'

King retrieves a couple beer bottles from the fridge under the bar and puts one in front of me. He pops the cap on his with his teeth, nicking his lip in the process, not caring in the slightest. I watch blood seep to the surface under the upturned bottleneck as he takes a long swig.

'So you blinded yourself?'

'Worked like a charm.' King gives me a wink with his good eye. 'In the land of the blind, the one-eyed man is King.'

'There's got to be a better way.'

'Nope.' King shakes his head. 'The problem is you can't quit on clients, it's they who have to quit on you. People with that much power and influence have full access to all your data, your accounts; every last dirty little secret about you. They can control your life with keystrokes and commands if they want. See, a guy like Winslade . . . once he takes a shine to you, it's over. You're his property as far as he's concerned, you're his boy. By contract he owns you. He'll rent you over and over again until you're all used up . . . or worse.'

'Worse?'

'Winslade has a bad habit of trying to push Husks past the acceptable limits. That's how Garrison ended up in a fucking coma. Winslade rode him more than eighty hours in their final session, broke the guy's brain.'

I shiver. 'One of my co-workers at Solace got killed

that way. A client kept him for over three days, pushed him until he had a psychotic break and went suicidal. I can't prove it, but I think the client was Winslade.'

'So you're at Solace Strategies, eh?'

'Did I let that slip?'

'Nice work if you can get it, man . . .'

'I think we both know better.'

Silence falls between us. I think about Ryoko and the baby, the money that I'll no longer be able to provide them if I quit Husking. King finishes his cigarette, polishes off his beer, watching me intently the whole time. I down the rest of my bottle and ready to leave. King leans over the bar, lowers his voice, winks again with his good eye.

'Brother, if you want, I can give you something that will really help you out with this Winslade situation of yours.'

'You can?'

'Yeah, I keep it in the backroom. C'mon, let's go get it.'

King tips his head and beckons me to follow. He leads me to the back of the bar and down a hallway to a small office where he ushers me inside ahead of him. I'm barely through the doorway when he tackles me to the floor. He's on my back, fighting to keep me restrained. The surprise in the backroom is a switchblade apparently. It springs open in his hand, and I watch as he brings it close to my face. King outweighs me and uses the extra pounds to great effect, locking me down. I manage to slip an arm and throw an elbow back into his chin, but it doesn't faze him. He grabs my hair and picks my head off the floor, turning it just enough so I can see him. The determination in his one good eye is obvious.

'Hold still, you fucker,' he growls. 'And I'll make this quick.'

The knife comes within an inch of my eye, blade skimming lashes. I reach up, my hand gripping a handful of King's hair on his blindside, then wrench downward, pulling his face into the floorboards with a crunch, knocking out one of his teeth. It's enough for him to lose his hold on both me and the knife and I capitalize on it, shoving him off and getting to my feet. He tries to rise, but I deliver a front kick to his face, sending him crashing into a pile of boxes. He groans and spits something. More teeth clatter on the floor. Breathless, I back away, heading for the door. King puts his fingers in his mouth, locates which teeth are gone, and smiles, satisfied, pleased that he's been made even more unattractive. He sees me moving toward the door and holds up a stopping hand as blood dribbles over his lips and down his chin.

'Wait a second, brother,' he pants. 'Let me explain.'

I see his hand creeping towards the switchblade on the floor nearby. I turn and run, bolting down the hallway and out to the bar. King howls after me.

'You don't understand,' I hear him shout. 'I was just going to cut you up a little, shave down your appeal. I'd be doing you a favour!'

25

I book a room at a cheap motel next to a drive-thru wedding chapel and pay with cash. My attempt to avoid being bothered by anyone or anything doesn't pan out. I watch ten minutes of NYC news on the flat-screen. A story about another missing girl in Manhattan that upsets me. As the police accuse Integris again in connection with her disappearance. To my surprise, the news goes on to report that one of the previous missing girls, Annabel Colette, has contacted her family claiming to be alive and well, but has refused to cooperate with them or police in regards to her current whereabouts. Cops are confident that Integris has her held somewhere in the city, and make some reference to the girl possibly having Stockholm syndrome at this point.

The last story I see reveals Chase Jackson has been arrested outside a Brooklyn nightclub for attacking a former girlfriend and her fiancé. Details on the incident are sketchy. I can't help but wonder if it was Chase at the time, or if it was a client who committed the assault. He had it coming either way. Amateurs are always getting themselves into trouble. I shut off the TV and lie back on the bed. In no time my Liaison pings; a text message from Clive. My gut tightens when I sit up and read it.

Eternity Executive just found out I was siphoning confidential company information and fired me.

I call him back immediately. He picks up on the first ring.

'Clive, I'm so sorry –'

'You *asshole*, Rhodes,' he says, voice breaking. 'Do you know how badly I needed that job? Do you have any fucking idea? *Do you?*'

'I'll make it up to you. I'll make it right.'

'How? Tell me how you're gonna make this right.'

'I'll . . . I'll figure something out.'

'Don't . . . just do me a favour and fuck off. I don't want you to make my life any worse than it already is.'

'Clive, give me a chance to fix this. I won't let a friend like you down.'

Clive's laugh is bitter. 'Oh, shove it, pal. With friends like you, who the hell needs enemies?'

He hangs up. I try to call him back, but he doesn't answer. I feel like shit, want to cut myself off from outside interference. For the first time since purchasing it, I turn my Liaison off, take the battery out, and leave it on the nightstand. I count out all the money I have and leave the room, angry over the trouble I've caused, determined to win Clive a small fortune to help him out and say I'm sorry.

Walking past the motel pool, I glance up at the early night sky and stop. The sun has fallen below the horizon, orange and red light struggling to stay afloat in the west as dark encroaches from the east. The first emergent stars overhead are mesmerizing out here in the desert.

Their light reaching me – some of it travelling from sources already long dead, origins snuffed out by the definitive black of the Universe. I'm awash with uncertainty. What was the point of them? The cremation of whole galaxies, resulting in a thick sky of ash, it's all I need to realize the sheer insignificance of who and what I am. I've never felt so small or alone. Looking up begins to get me unbearably down.

Then I hear a high-pitched shout that breaks me out of my mood. It comes again, followed by a low laugh. I look over to where the motel tennis courts lay and see a man and a young boy pretending to swordfight with their rackets. A memory suddenly strikes me, one that is not personally mine. There is warm sun and flowery smells. A tennis racket is in my right hand. I'm on a court, fending off my giggling grandsons as they pretend to be heroic knights. I am full of joy, blessed by these two boys whom I am very fond of and miss dearly. This brief recollection is a glimpse of Mr Shaw's session, part of the itinerary he told me about. As quickly as it comes, the sweet memory begins to slip away. I try to hold on, grasping at it in my mind's eye, but another blooms in its place. I am reading a book to my beloved, but bedridden wife, a partner I don't ever want to part with. She smiles weakly at me as I take her wrinkled hand in mine. There is still starlight in her old eyes, twinkling at me the same as the first day we met. She is not long for this world. The great love of Shaw's life reminds me so much of Ryoko it's akin to déjà vu. Then she is gone, and I realize I've sunk to my knees on the concrete.

I stare at my hands. Things line up inside my head, turn as one, click into place. A moment of clarity is unlocked. I turn my gaze to the night sky, all that darkness up there, any measure of it harbouring new twinkles yet to come. I could be looking toward the birth of a star and never know it, something that might grow to be one of the brightest lights in the Universe. The possibilities seem endless. Mine or not, maybe I can give this baby a decent start. Maybe I can give it a good life. The least I can do is try my luck.

With a few grand in hand I begin working my way south on the Strip, stopping in at various casinos, hitting up roulette and blackjack tables, on a mission to try and make things right. At the Wynn I get onto a winning streak in a craps game that bolsters my confidence and eases my worries. The oxygen pumped into the casino air invigorates me. All caution is thrown to the wind. I begin to think there's no need of Solace Strategies, or Winslade, or the services I provide for high prices. King's advice to get out seems plausible. I actually believe I could make my nest egg through gambling. It's foolish, I know, but I start to bet big.

My luck throughout the course of the night proves otherwise. My betting becomes uncharacteristically reckless. My strategies are all off. I don't feel in control of what I'm doing. A rollercoaster of risky wagers plagues me in the Monte Carlo. I manage to win enough back to almost break even at the Bellagio, but the Mirage damn near cleans me out afterwards. By 2 a.m. I find myself at a low-stakes table at the Hard Rock, dangerously low on cash, playing with my last couple hundred. At the roulette table I bet half on black, only to end up seeing red. I pocket my last c-note and avoid the ATMs. Baxter may have frozen my accounts for fucking off on Navarette, and I don't want to be traced anyway. Go big or go home; that was the plan. I'm definitely going home.

Frustrated and ashamed, I play nickel slots just so I can snag free drinks from cute waitresses while I flirt to forget my foolishness. More than ever, I don't feel like myself. Ryoko doesn't even cross my mind. Neither does the baby. It's like I'm operating in a daze, my brain made of clay and moulded by another's fingers, my eyes made of glass and fogging up. A redhead babe with a Texas accent starts talking to me real friendly like, her manner mischievous and confident. I'm taken in by the firm tits and ass barely contained in her skimpy uniform. She's good to me, makes sure I never have an empty glass in hand. In no time I'm tipsy, speaking suggestively to her. She tells me her shift ends within the hour and asks if I happen to be staying at the Hard Rock. I confess that I'm booked into a shithole near the Stratosphere. She doesn't care, says it's been a long-ass night and she'd sure like to have someone get her off after she gets off, if I'm down with the idea. I hit an eighty-dollar jackpot on my slot machine and tell her I am.

A half-hour later we're in my motel room, pulling off clothes, groping and tonguing the bare skin that is revealed. All the lights are on and I find myself staring at the girl's tight, tanned body as she pulls off her jeans and thong in one motion. She pins me against the wall and grinds against my hardness. I try to kiss her, but she won't have any of it. Giggling, she puts a hand on my chest and pushes off. I watch her crawl onto the bed where she strikes a pose, back arched, ass in the air.

'You like what you see, stud?'

I should, but I don't. Seen in the soft light of cheap lamps, her red hair is suddenly upsetting. The shade seems identical to that of a man who haunts my waking dreams. I think about Dennis Delane, think about the distressing newscast I watched earlier when I checked in. The girl on the bed isn't impressed by my lack of response. She pulls a condom and a packet of lube out of her purse and places it at the foot of the bed with one eyebrow raised.

'So . . . you gonna come over here and fuck me, or what?'

The girl gets back on all fours, reaches under and caresses, moaning, readying herself. She rests her head on a pillow and wiggles her ass, waiting patiently for me to penetrate. Something comes over me. My clay brain gets sculpted by foreign thought processes as arousal trumps my fear. I grab the condom and roll it on, smother it in lube. I come to her, slowly sinking the tip of my rigidity into the tightness of her asshole. She lets out a gasp, looks back at me with surprised eyes that show a hint of worry.

'Oh, so that's how you wanna ride tonight, cowboy?'

I nod. She accepts, licking her lips as she turns and presses her open, moaning mouth into the pillow, reaching back under to stroke the both of us. We start slow, but soon enough we're screwing with a strong steady rhythm. She comes once, twice, her cries muffled, body tense. She grabs my hand and makes me spank her, buttocks rippling with each hit as I slip in and out. Another minute passes and I find my fingers creeping over her throat.

'Uhhh ... fuck, fuck,' she pants. 'Yeah, yeah, right there, just like that.'

I palm her windpipe and apply pressure, fucking her harder as my fingertips sink into her jugular. I feel her vocal cords vibrate as she whimpers in my grip.

'Uh, uhhh, harder, *harder.*'

I double my efforts, listening to her climax again, feeling her writhing against me. I'm so unbelievably hard, but I feel like a voyeur, like I'm watching some kind of POV porn. I tell my hand to ease up, but my grip ignores my command and tightens. The girl starts struggling for air, breath coming in wheezes. Her face begins to turn the same colour as her hair. I stare at my fingers curled around her neck. A spectator now, trapped in my own body as it becomes a shell inhabited by a predator. The vehicle is on autopilot, the action is muscle memory. I'm just strapped in for the ride.

'Stop,' I mutter.

'Tighter,' the girl gasps, eyes rolling up into her head. 'Harder.'

My body obeys her words over my thoughts. I try willing myself flaccid, but my erection is engorged to the limit. The thrusting won't slow. The grip won't relax. My Ouija clicks and for a second I see the truth in all its awful iniquity. The revelation is gone before I can commit it to memory.

'Stop,' I say aloud.

'Don't. Stop. More.'

'Please stop.'

'No,' she manages. 'More. Coming. Again.'

I feel her coming hot and wet on my cock and I almost burst into tears. 'For Christ's sake stop!'

Wait,' she gasps, throat bucking as I crush it. 'Stop. Stop. St—'

And then she goes limp, body flopping like a rag-doll getting pumped by my sweaty, flexing body. My cry of shock returns control of my body back to me and I'm flipping her over, shaking her, searching her wrist for a pulse. Before I can try and resuscitate her, she comes to, sucking in all the air her lungs can manage.

'Oh, wow,' she says hoarsely. 'I think I reached nirvana.'

I almost collapse with relief. 'Thank God.'

'Did you come?'

I don't answer. She catches her breath, pulls off my condom, and immediately attempts to go down on me. I demand she stop. She looks up in confusion, then sees my face and quickly becomes concerned.

'What's wrong, sweetie?'

'What?' I say. 'Are you fucking kidding me? I almost *killed* you.'

'Just blacked out a little is all,' she says. 'It ain't no thing. You knew what you were doing.'

I hold my hands up, look at them. 'How do you figure that?'

She shrugs. 'You did last time.'

I stare at her. The girl's eyes are all recognition. She knows me, we've done this before. She reaches out to touch me with long, painted fingernails and I lean away.

'You need to leave,' I say. 'Now.'

'What?' she laughs. 'Baby, we're just getting started.'

'No, we're not. Please go.'

'Aw c'mon, sweetie, you done gone and broke me in now —'

'I said get the fuck out!'

She recoils from my outburst and scrambles to collect her clothes from the floor. Half of them are on by the time she gets to the door, where she turns and shoots me an unnerved look.

'Y'know, you're starting to fucking scare me.'

I drop my face in my hands, holding back tears, pushing palms against the eyes that have seen such horrible things when I haven't been home.

'I'm starting to scare myself,' I whisper.

When I disembark the jet at JFK, I put the battery back in my Liaison and turn it on. Within minutes a call comes in from Baxter. I ignore the ringing for as long as I can, knowing she'll ream my ass, knowing her questions will remind me of the night I'm trying hard to put out of my mind. When she calls three times in as many minutes I finally give in and pick up.

'Yeah, boss?'

Her first words are explosive and indiscernible, sounds like she's ready to kill someone. I have to hold the Liaison a few inches away from my ear.

'Goddamn it, Rhodes, I've been trying to get hold of you since last night. Where the hell are you?'

'I'm back in New York,' I say.

'New York? You're supposed to be in Las Vegas right now you son of a bitch. You're *supposed* to be in session with Mr Navarette.'

'I wasn't up to the job this time, boss. I was burnt out, too sick.'

'You can't fucking do this to me, Rhodes,' Baxter shouts. 'Do you have any idea how much damage control you dumped on me with this stunt?'

'All part of your job description, isn't it?'

'Get your ass back to the office. *Now.*'

'Yeah, that ain't gonna happen.'

'I beg your pardon?'

'Not a priority,' I say. 'Got some personal stuff to take care of first.'

'Don't toy with me, boy. You get back here within the hour, or else –'

'Or else what?' I snap. 'You'll do what exactly?'

'I'll . . . I'll . . .'

'You'll do nothing, that's what. You wanna know why? Because I'm your fucking golden boy, Baxter, and I'll be bringing home Winslade's big nuggets real soon. So back the fuck off, leave me the hell alone, and let me do my thing while I still can.'

Baxter lets out a long, aggravated breath and says nothing. I tell her to wait a minute, put her on hold, let the lady mull things over while I type *Dennis Delane NYC* into my Liaison and cross-reference my search. In no time I turn up a viable address and switch back over to the boss.

'So, do we have an understanding?'

'Yes,' she replies curtly. 'Anything else you want to spring on me at this time?'

'Oh, absolutely,' I say. 'If you really expect me to go through with this exclusivity contract with Winslade, I'll only do it on one condition.'

'Which is?'

'You rehire Clive.'

'What?'

'You rehire Clive,' I repeat. 'Call him up and tell him you made a mistake letting him go. Tell him he's back with Solace Strategies at full strength with full pay, effective immediately.'

'No, no,' Baxter laughs. 'I don't think so.'

'You better start thinking so.'

'Fine, I'll give it some thought.'

'Not good enough. When our conversation is finished, you call him and give him his old job back. I want him back on your books by the time I come into the office to sign your damn contracts.'

'Clive is damaged goods,' Baxter protests. 'I mean, Jesus, the guy is a fucking fire sale with all those burns on his face. And he's half blind as well, for crying out loud! What good is he to me?'

'He's getting cosmetic surgery. Doctors might save that eye too.'

'Rhodes, our company doesn't provide anything less than *perfection*.'

'Don't feed me that bullshit,' I moan. 'You were the one who recently told me that clients were willing to forego perfection in order to have their demands met. Besides, you're understaffed at the moment and my availability is about to become zero. It's a goddamn win-win for you, Baxter.'

For once I've got the bitch by the balls and she knows it. I savour the moment, enjoying the long and frustrated pause from her, knowing I'll never have a taste of it again. When she finally speaks, her tone is something I've never equated with her. For once Baxter sounds defeated.

'Okay. I'll rehire Clive ASAP.'

'Good. I believe we're done then, yes?'

'Fine,' she says, and clears her throat. 'Now, when will you be coming in?'

'I'll come in when I'm good and ready,' I say and hang up.

Two out of three Husks I located were better off dead, and the third wanted to cut my eye out of my head after a few drinks. Dennis Delane seems to be the only decent lead I have left, but he's a corpse. Regardless, I take a cab to his old address in Greenwich Village to see what I can find. After all that's happened, I'm more than willing to dig up a body.

When I get to his apartment building on Charles Street my gut tells me I'm onto something. A girl with a bag of groceries is unlocking the front door as I approach and I offer to hold it open, disarming any suspicion she might have about me with an easy smile. Once inside I slip past her and climb the stairs to the fourth floor, where I find apartment 402, Delane's former residence. I try my luck and knock on the door. On the other side I hear footsteps and a cough. I turn my face away from the peephole.

'Who is it?'

'NYPD,' I say, making shit up as I go. 'Detective . . . Shaw. Just need to ask you a couple questions pertaining to Dennis Delane.'

The muffled voice sounds annoyed. 'I already told you guys everything I know.'

'We're investigating new leads. It will only take a few minutes of your time.'

'All right, hold on a second.' There is a pause, then the sound of two locks disengaging. The door begins to open. 'What is it you wanna –'

The dude on the other side is young, early twenties if that. His pimply face looks tired and unhappy when he first sees me. When we make eye contact he realizes I'm not the cop I claim to be. His expression turns to one of outright fear.

'Oh, shit.'

I barge through the door before he has a chance to slam it in my face. He backs up quickly, eyes wide, mouth agape. There is a baseball bat in a nearby corner that he sets his sights on, but I put myself between him and the weapon as I shut the door behind me. Then I grab the bat for good measure, so he knows I'm not messing around.

'C'mon, don't hurt me, man,' he pleads. 'Take whatever you want.'

'I'm not here to hurt you,' I say, holding up a hand. 'And I'm not gonna rob you either. Who are you?'

'I'm nobody, just a student at NYU, man.'

'And I'm not a cop, okay?' I motion with the bat for

him to take a seat on the couch. 'I'm only here to ask you a few questions. That's all.'

The kid sits, hands clasping his knees. 'Yeah, no shit you're not a cop, man.'

'Five minutes of your time, that's all I want, then I'll be on my way and you'll never see me again, all right?'

The kid nods, but I can tell he doesn't believe a word I'm saying.

'What's your name?' I ask.

'Burke.'

'Okay, Burke.' I walk around the small apartment. 'And you were Delane's . . . what exactly?'

'Roommate. We were both at NYU.'

'Do you have any idea who killed him?'

Burke just stares at me.

I shrug. 'Okay then, do you know anyone who might have been involved in the circumstances surrounding his death?'

Burke keeps staring. His mouth looks like it wants to speak though he forms no words. His eyes shift back and forth, looking for a way out.

'Where'd Delane go the night he disappeared?' I ask.

His voice is barely a whisper. 'He said he was going out for a pack of smokes and never came back.'

There are framed photos all over the apartment, old-school style, done with camera and film and developed in a darkroom. None of them are any good really. There are more than a few of Delane, his erratic red hair and thin weaselly face making him the opposite of photogenic. One picture in particular grabs my attention. It's a photo of Delane with his arm slung around a blue-eyed blonde bombshell with high cheekbones and a foolish smile. I've seen this girl before, on TV and in my nightmares.

'You a photographer?' I ask.

Burke swallows hard. 'Trying to be.'

'This picture you got here of this girl,' I say, holding up the photo. 'Who is she?'

'That's Tiffany,' he replies, looking sick. 'Tiffany Burrows.'

'And Delane knew her?'

'Of course, Delane . . . *loved* her, man. He'd have done anything for her.'

'Did she love him too?'

Burke stalls, which I interpret as the negative. Even though his hands clutch his knees, I can tell they are trembling. They leave sweaty marks on his pants.

'Tiff only liked hot boys,' Burke says finally. 'Dennis was stuck in the friend-zone. He followed her everywhere though, dragged me along half the time too.'

'This Tiffany Burrows, she went missing, right? Supposedly kidnapped by that extremist group with the Occupy Movement? She still hasn't been found?'

Burke shoots me a vicious look, suddenly growing a pair. 'Yeah, and Dennis was the one who reported her missing. He went straight to the cops when he found out she didn't come home, and he told them *exactly* what we saw.'

'Okay, give me details.'

'Huh?'

'Explain it to me.'

'C'mon,' Burke moans, suddenly looking like he might cry. 'Why are you fucking with me like this, man?'

269

'I'm not fucking with you,' I say, my voice rising. 'Tell me what you saw already, damn it.'

'W-w-we were the last ones to see her,' Burke stammers. 'We were there that night when she left the club. We saw her get into a cab with . . . with . . .'

'With who?' I demand. 'Who the hell did she get into the cab with?'

Burke looks at me perplexed. 'She got into a cab with *you*, man.'

26

On the elevator ride up to Solace Strategies, I'm consumed with a desire to play the role of the detective I claimed to be back at Delane's apartment. I need a break in the case. Connecting the dots is taking too long. Exclusivity for Winslade starts tomorrow. Baxter will no doubt make me sign the contract today. My personal freedom will be curtailed in exchange for more money than I could hope for, and more mental anguish than I have ever known. Winslade will maximize usage, put a premium on seventy-two-hour jaunts. This I'm sure of. Before I know it I'll be a highly paid prisoner with limited yard time. Something drastic needs to be done.

I've also got to find out exactly who is on my side. I put my trust in Ryoko and Phineas, Nikki too. Anyone else, there are doubts about. The elevator door opens to reveal Nikki sitting behind her reception desk. She reaches for the phone out of habit when she sees me, but stops, fingers hovering over the receiver. I shake my head subtly.

'Don't announce me,' I whisper. 'Is Tweek in?'

She nods and waves me over. I step off the elevator and scan the offices. No sign of Baxter. I slip over to the reception desk and squat beside Nikki. She hugs me, lips brushing my earlobe, speaking in hushed tones.

'The boss is furious over you ditching your session in Vegas. You're in big shit.'

'I know.'

'I took Dante's call when you didn't show up for your appointment. Navarette is threatening to take his business elsewhere, and sue us over breach of contract. What happened out there?'

'I decided to follow up on one of those leads you gave me.'

'Which guy?'

'Kirk King.'

'Did you find him?'

I nod. 'He filled in a few blanks.'

'What about the other two leads?'

'The other leads,' I say, 'are alarming.'

I stand, start heading for Tweek's control room. Nikki calls after me.

'I just spoke to Clive by the way. Baxter rehired him. I thought you should know.'

'Is that so?'

'He wants you to know he appreciates what you did.'

'Me?' I say over my shoulder. 'I didn't do anything.'

'He says he owes you one.'

I smile to myself and keep walking. Tweek emerges from the doorway of his control room and stops cold when he sees me. He looks a little nervous. I continue towards him and he retreats back into his room, beckoning me to follow. When I enter he tells me to close the door and pull the blinds.

'You've gone and pissed off Baxter bad,' Tweek says. 'I

heard a few things smash in her office earlier. I'd wear a helmet when you go in to see her.'

'I'll deal with Baxter later,' I say. 'You're the one I need to see right now.'

'Is it about what we discussed before?'

'Yes.'

'You want me to run some more tests?'

I shake my head. 'Not exactly.'

Tweek crosses his arms. 'Then what, exactly?'

'I need one of your Ejector pills.'

'That again?' Tweek's eyes bulge. 'You're kidding me, right? This is a joke?'

'It's not a joke.'

'No.'

'No what?'

'No, I won't give you a fucking Ejector, Rhodes,' Tweek says, shaking his head in disbelief. 'I don't think you really understand what you're asking of me.'

'I'm gonna level with you here, Tweek,' I say, putting a hand on his shoulder. 'I'm out of options. I know what I'm asking for is a tall order, but I'm about to walk into Baxter's office, where I'll basically be blackmailed into signing an exclusivity contract for Winslade. And you know how that's going to work out for me, don't you?'

Tweek swallows hard. 'The same as it worked out for Miller.'

'I frigging *knew* it. I knew Winslade was in session with Miller when he died.'

'Yeah, I suspected it too.'

'How'd you find out for sure?'

273

'With my skills?' Tweek says, looking bemused. 'You have to ask?'

I don't. This new confirmation strengthens my resolve. I pull up a chair and sit down, partially out of tiredness, partially to make myself look small and vulnerable before the little lab rat. I need to play on his sympathies.

'Miller wasn't the only one, Tweek,' I say. 'I tracked down some of Winslade's former Husks from Eternity Executive. Turns out he wrecked them all, ended up putting two in the hospital and drove another one underground. Each of them suffered the same traumatic post-session shit that I've been experiencing.'

Tweek adjusts his glasses. 'I still don't know why you need the Ejector . . .'

'I have to find out where Winslade is going with my body,' I say. 'I need to know what's he's doing.'

'Why?'

'Because I need to know the truth.' I take a deep breath. 'A woman named Tiffany Burrows went missing on a night Winslade was renting me. I found a witness who identified me as the last person she was seen with. Her whereabouts are still unknown. She's one of the women I see in my flashbacks and dreams.'

'You're sure of this?'

'Positive,' I say. 'I think Winslade kidnapped her. I think he's keeping her somewhere, and I've got this horrible feeling she's not the only one. The hallucinations I've been having, the nightmares, I'm recalling moments from Winslade's perspective, scraps or leftovers from his sessions.'

'Residual memory,' Tweek replies, stroking his chin.

'Pardon?'

'It's only theoretical, the idea that trace amounts of a client's previous computation can sometimes stick around after a session is over, acting like echoes in the Ouija. To be honest, I didn't even believe in it until I took a closer look at your last test results. What's your plan exactly?'

'I'll use an Ejector to bring me back mid-session and find out where he's taking me. Maybe I can find some clues, get some closure.'

'And this is the only way?'

I nod. 'Winslade's security is world-class. There's no way anyone can get near him from the outside. The only way I'm going to get any answers is if it's an inside job.'

Tweek considers a moment, nods affirmatively, then walks to the wall and takes down a framed charcoal sketch of Albert Einstein. Behind it is a wall safe with a touchscreen. He keys in numbers and presses his thumb against the screen for fingerprint recognition. When it opens, Tweek reaches inside and rummages around. It isn't long before he withdraws a small white pill pinched between his thumb and forefinger.

'Rhodes, the E-33 was developed for emergencies,' he says. 'It's only to be used in extreme cases when a Husk's consciousness needs to be brought out of its dormant state prematurely. Less than three minutes after administration the effects of your twenty-four- to seventy-two-hour pills are completely neutralized. So, when exactly do you think you're going to have an opportunity to take this?'

'I was hoping that ingenious little brain of yours could help with that part.'

Tweek gives me a sheepish grin. From a cabinet he retrieves a small plastic tub and picks out what looks like a transparent blue jellybean. He brings it back to his desk, where he takes a scalpel to it. I watch as he carefully makes an incision into the jellybean and pushes the white pill inside the slit before sealing it with a glue-like substance.

'I'm encasing your Ejector in a strong gelatin layer to time-delay release. It will take your stomach acid approximately six hours to eat through the glucose compound and get to the drug. Calculate your window of opportunity and ingest accordingly.'

Tweek examines the gelatin carefully to ensure it is completely sealed, and then hands it to me. I place the Ejector in my pillbox.

'I'll swallow it as close to upload as possible.'

'There's another problem,' Tweek says. 'You won't be doing this in a controlled environment. You won't be plugged in to transfer Winslade out before you come back. You're going to emerge while he is still active.'

'Meaning what?' I say, but already know.

'Meaning there will be two personalities vying for control. Our brains aren't designed to cope with something like that. You'll go mad, Rhodes. I mean absolutely psychotic, and quickly too.'

'I'm already going mad.'

Tweek pokes me in the chest, hard. 'Rhodes, I'm not fucking kidding here. You'll end up just like Miller, but in a matter of minutes not hours.'

'So if I go through with this, it means I'm dead?'

'Not necessarily.'

Tweek clears the clutter on his desk and sets to work under the swing-arm magnifier. With his tablet he uploads something onto a tiny USB key and then patiently fixes a proboscis to the end of it.

'Listen carefully,' he says, delicately placing the key in a small plastic case. 'When you re-emerge, the very first thing you do is stab this into your Ouija. I've installed a Husk program on it. Once it connects it will automatically sequence and download Winslade off of you, safely storing him on the drive in less than a minute.'

'That'll piss him off.'

'He'll go into stasis, won't even know what's going on.'

Tweek hands me the key and I place it in my pill-box alongside the Ejector. He holds out his hand to shake mine. I give him a bear hug instead, making him squeak.

'Time to see the boss,' I say. 'Sign my life away.'

'Wait. Before you go, I have something to show you.'

He beckons me closer and activates his HG. Diagrams and details, numbers and codes, blossom before us. Tweek points to them, but it's all Greek to me.

'Upon further examination I found something in the test results I ran on your Ouija. I discovered these sliver-like oddities in the digital interface, trace amounts of data signatures, lines of code. It took me a while to isolate them. They were active, interactive, *evasive* even, their behaviour almost like brainwaves.'

'Yeah?' I reply. 'And?'

'They aren't yours, Rhodes. They're . . . Miller's.'

I'm lost for words.

'It's incredible,' Tweek says with growing excitement. 'Somehow Miller left something of himself behind in you. It must have piggybacked its way via Winslade. It's absolutely crazy. I've never seen anything like it. I have no idea what it means, can't decipher the lines of code with my gear. It's all inaccessible.'

To your technology, I think. *But not my biology.*

'I see him, Tweek,' I say. 'He visits me in my dreams, when I'm comatose. We talk. He tells me things.'

Tweek simply stares at me, jaw slack. Miller was leaving me interactive messages somehow, in real time, a phantom in file format defying known natural law to provide me a trail of bread crumbs. I remember what King told me about Husks being homes and clients being ghosts. Jesus, I'm turning into one big haunted house.

'What does he say?' Tweek finally manages.

'He tells me it's time to wake up.'

Tweek lowers his eyes to the floor, dumbstruck. We sit in silence for a minute, feeling the weight of the whole situation, knowing just how much shit we might be getting ourselves in to. I check the time on my Liaison.

'All right,' I say. 'I've got to go see Baxter.'

Tweek lifts his head. 'Rhodes?'

'Yeah?'

'You've been in contact with former employees of Eternity Executive, right?'

'Right.'

'So . . . you didn't get that pill or key from me. Blame someone else. Understand?'

I nod. 'Thanks for doing this for me, Tweek. I owe you.'

'I'm not doing this for you, Rhodes,' Tweek replies, shaking his head. 'I'm doing this for Miller.'

27

To say Baxter chewed me a new asshole would be an understatement, but it still didn't go half as bad as I expected. She'd had time to calm down. The focus was on professionalism and punctuality, nothing more. Exclusivity with Winslade comes with plenty of cons, and Baxter was careful not to add insult to injury. When she slid the contract across her desk, I simply stared at it. When she slid the pen across for me to sign, I stared at her. She took pains to remind me that I could cut loose and start from square one with not a penny to my name if that's what I wanted. She added that finding employment might be difficult without a reference from her. That and the fact I'd be blackballed wherever she or Winslade had an ounce of influence, which was damn near everywhere. It didn't take much more arm twisting for me to put pen to paper.

It's 8 a.m. on the morning of my session with Winslade. I'm sitting naked on the edge of my bed, looking out of the window over Tompkins Square Park. The aerial drones are staying longer every day now, pushing their luck in the early light. I slept alone last night, all fourteen hours of it. Ryoko left a message on my Liaison at some point, but I haven't listened to it, haven't called her back. I don't want to tell Ryoko the things I'm about to do, don't want her involved in any way. My pillbox lies open on my nightstand and I flick glances at the Ejector lying among my coma pills. The USB key turns in my fingers as I mentally commit the importance of its immediate integration into my Ouija upon re-emergence. It has to be my first thought the second I get my bearings.

I put the key back in the pillbox and consider my timing. Winslade wants a long jaunt, a seventy-two-hour session to start the new propriety. I don't feel sick any more, just drained. I fail to go through any of my usual routines. No exercises. No beauty care. No hearty breakfast. I drink a beer, smoke a cigarette, laze the fuck around. I don't bother shaving or brushing my teeth. I don't apply make-up to my injuries. The only thing I do is take a long mist and try to soak in the tepid spray. Afterwards I dress like shit, old jeans and my CBGB T-shirt, slip my feet into worn sneakers. What does it matter anyway? Winslade will have me dressed in one of his slick suits minutes after he takes me over.

I'm about to leave when it hits me that I haven't seen Craig in days. Opening his bedroom door a crack, I peek in and see him sprawled on his bed, forty-ounce bottle of Jack Daniels almost empty on his nightstand. He looks peaceful, snoring away in his boxers. I fight the urge to wake him and recount everything that has happened. He's another person I trust, but don't want to involve. I sneak to his nightstand, open my wallet and leave more money than I owe him for the night he covered me at the Rochester. Craig doesn't even stir as I leave the apartment.

Outside the air is cool and damp, sky overcast. The neighbourhood looks sapped of colour. Even the green of Tompkins Square Park seems more of a sickly grey. I walk through the square, watching rats and squirrels of equal size dart across the pathways. I buy a coffee from a vendor and have another cigarette. People scurry on the street toward their destinations, shoulders slumped, eyes cast to the concrete underfoot. As I flag down a cab on Avenue A, one person in particular catches my attention. It is Javier, rooting through a garbage can across the street at the bus stop, wearing an Occupy Central Park hoodie. I expect he's waiting to transit down to the protest. He watches me with dull eyes, face expressionless. I wave, beckoning him to come catch a ride with me, but he makes no show of recognition. His unresponsiveness suggests he's drunk or high. Still, I get the feeling he has been watching me for some time.

The cab drops me off at Central Park. My session isn't until noon. More than two hours to kill. I make my way to the middle of the park and find a grassy spot under an oak tree where I can look out over the entire Great Lawn. The sea of protesters is incredible. They idle in a giant mass, some standing, others sitting, none of them moving much in the grey morning light. Every fourth or fifth person has a coffee or cigarette in hand. More than a few sneak sips from hip flasks or beer cans in paper bags. The scent of marijuana is in the air. I'm positive the protesters have grown by another twenty per cent since I was last here. It isn't long before agitation begins to swell inside their ranks. They grow more audible, arguments and accusations against the status quo breaking out. I keep my eyes open for Javier, expecting him to show up any moment, intending to buy him a coffee or hot dog or something to help him out. He's nowhere to be found.

I chain-smoke, filling myself with nicotine to keep myself awake, not giving a shit about the damage I'm doing to the lungs I don't consider mine any more. By the time the bearded man takes the podium and starts addressing the crowds with his megaphone, I'm already walking toward Winslade's place and swallowing the Ejector. A call comes in on my Liaison. It is Renard.

'Do not be late today, Mr Rhodes.'

'I'll be there in ten minutes,' I reply and hang up.

Renard slams the penthouse door behind me and looks me over, opening his mouth to give me shit about my appearance. I hold up a finger and give him cut-eye.

'Save it, man,' I say. 'I've had a rough couple days.'

'Unacceptable,' he mutters.

The robot, alerted by the sound of my voice, emerges from a doorway and walks toward me. We meet each other in the centre of the living room, where Mr Winslade embraces me. Inside his arms of metal and silicone I feel frigid. The robot's eyes glide over my new split lip and black eye. I touch the injuries lightly with my fingertips.

'I apologize in advance for the wear and tear you see, Mr Winslade.'

'Apology accepted,' the robot says. 'May I ask what happened?'

'It's just from other clients,' I lie. 'Clients who haven't been as . . . considerate and respectful as you, sir.'

The robot seems to smirk. 'Well, you won't have to worry your head about that any more, now that you've signed the new deal.'

I'd like to tell Winslade I didn't have much of a fucking choice in the matter. I'd like to tell him that he alone is the main source of my worries. I want to tell him to go to hell, but I don't. A forced smile comes instead.

'I'm looking forward to our new arrangement.'

'You are mine and mine alone now,' the robot says with a hideous grin. 'My boy, this is truly a wonderful day.'

'The first of many.'

'Fix us a drink, Renard,' the robot snaps. 'To celebrate.'

We walk to the leather armchairs and sit. Soon Renard serves us both a priceless Scotch. I sip from my tumbler and watch as the robot pretends to sip from his. When I've downed mine, I take out my Liaison and Renard begins preparing Winslade for upload. Once I connect to my Ouija, I open my pillbox and select a green seventy-two-hour pill lying beside the USB key in its case. My first and most important emergent thought repeats over and over in my head as I look Winslade in the eye and see myself reflected in his silvery lenses.

'Let's dance,' I say and swallow the pill.

At first there are no dreams, only dark. I simply wait. Everything feels like it is in real time. Minutes go by, then hours. Eventually a spark shows against the black. Miller's face appears in the glow of his cigarette ember. There is a rumbling sound, agitation permeating the night around me. I feel instability rushing through the air, coursing through my body. Miller approaches, stopping inches from my face.

'What's happening?' I ask.

'You're finally waking up, sleepwalker,' Miller says, placing his cigarette between my lips. 'I suspect you're about to see what I feared all along.'

I inhale deep, sucking in the acrid smoke. The blackness around me ignites, burning white hot, the void irradiated.

The absence of colour is spread before my eyes. Soon I'm seeing starbursts on white that start to dissipate the pale fog. I'm closing in on my own perspective through a tunnel of sleep, sliding toward a porthole at the end that grows larger with each passing second. It is a familiar feeling. I'm a slumped passenger awakening in the backseat of a car, sitting upright, watching the road from behind the driver of the vehicle. As I move forward, my sight expands and presses up against the porthole until the convex glass becomes my own eyes. An attractive raven-haired girl lies beneath me on a bed, biting her lip dreamily. One of her wrists is handcuffed to the bed frame. My nostrils fill with the smells of sex and sweat. I am naked, as is she.

I start to reconnect with parts of my body, but control none of it. I feel my hips rocking rhythmically, plunging myself into moist warmth. My erection is beyond hard, beyond aroused, almost Viagra-worthy. My ears are returned to me next, hearing feminine moans and sighs.

My fingers squeeze breasts, grip ass, scratch nails down soft young skin. I reach toward the girl's mouth, thumb caressing lips before being sucked. Then my hand slips down to her throat, palm pressing against her jugular, feeling the young woman's quickened pulse. I try to pull away, resulting only in a flinch. Instantly I'm aware of the other awareness. Winslade knows I'm here. Our thoughts intercept one another. He is displeased. We become one.

We begin to fuck the girl harder and she starts to come. The sex is rough, but from what I can tell it's consensual. Instinctively I understand Winslade is speeding up whatever he has planned now that I've crashed the party. His thoughts race through our shared consciousness, but I can't understand, can't grasp them. He keeps our eyes on the climaxing girl while our right hand strangles her in an act of erotic asphyxiation. Our left hand reaches under the pillow beside her head, fingers curling around something cold and metallic. Deeper thrusts come now, slow and deliberate, causing the girl to close her eyes and throw her head back in orgasm. To my horror Winslade pulls a straight razor out from under the pillow and flicks it open over the girl's throat. I can't stop any of this.

Don't do it, I think and these words escape my lips. *Tell the girl to run.*

Control ... I have it for a moment. Suddenly concerned, the girl opens her eyes and they immediately fall on the razor held below her chin. She hitches in breath and screams, her trapped wrist straining against the handcuffs. I scream too.

'Go! Get the hell out of here!'

But she can't. What little control I have slips away. I'm just a spectator again. Her free arm flails, striking me weakly as my hand pins her neck to the mattress. I watch helplessly as Winslade raises and readies the razor. Using sheer willpower I try to wrestle control of it away from him. He stalls his strike, fighting back, blade suspended above the squirming girl as our two minds fight over the use of one body. Opposing intentions collide inside our head. Somehow he manages to shuck me off, sending my thoughts spinning. He brings the blade down in an arc just as I recover enough to launch my consciousness at his. The hit feels solid. His grip loosens, arm flinches, screwing up the accuracy of his strike. It still connects, catching her on the left side of her neck, blade sinking into skin, though nowhere as deep as Winslade wanted. In the following moments I regain more control. For the next minute we know each other's thoughts completely. I see what he has done and who he has harmed.

With great effort I force him to throw the razor across the room, hearing it clatter off the wall. The girl keeps shrieking beneath me, bleeding profusely under my withering grip. I release her and she rolls over, trying to crawl away on the bed, her one free hand clutching her throat to stem the flow of blood. I sweep terrified glances around the bedroom, over the upscale decor. It's an apartment of some sort, sparsely furnished and windows covered. There is a digital camera on a tripod nearby with a red light glowing atop it. The lens is pointed at the bed.

287

My clothes lie in a heap in the corner of the room. I suddenly remember what was supposed to be my first and most important thought.

The key, I think, panicking. *Connect the damn key.*

My instinct is to help the girl, but I won't be good for shit if I end up having a psychotic break in the next few minutes. I get off the bed and stumble to the corner of the room, Winslade fighting me every step of the way. I rummage through my trouser pockets until I find my pillbox. A few of my coma pills spill out as I open the lid. When I lay my eyes on the USB key inside Winslade becomes enraged, understanding at once my intention to remove and capture him. He begins throwing himself against the confines of my skull. The meat and matter of my brain will start tearing soon if I don't get him out.

All my focus and determination are needed just to slip the key out of its case. Between my finger and thumb, the miniature drive feels too delicate, too pathetic. I bring it up to my head, pointing the proboscis behind my ear, trying to stab it into my Ouija. Three inches from my skin, it suddenly stops. I can't move it any further. Winslade's response is violent, both in mind and body. He briefly reveals more memories of the brutality he's inflicted on others, harm he wishes to do to me as well. I recognize Dennis Delane cornered in an alley, refusing to come quietly, telling me I will pay for what I've done. He manages a single cry for help as I launch a savage attack, beating him beyond recognition before finally strangling him with my own hands. I hear a police siren sound nearby, see Delane's lifeless body being dragged and dropped behind a dumpster by Renard, evidence that couldn't be properly dealt with in the heat of the moment.

My hand is flung far to the right and smashed against a dresser. The proboscis snaps on impact, the key drops to the floor. I wail with despair, certain we will now go mad and perish together. Winslade doesn't think so. He turns my head, sets his sights on an object on the nightstand. There, beside a lamp, lies the cobalt-blue device, red lights glowing on its side. He forces me to walk toward it. We stumble and fall, writhing on the carpet like the girl on the bed. Winslade makes me crawl, forces me to reach up and grab the device. I mash my thumb against the button repeatedly and feel it buzzing in my hand. The frequency with which it vibrates seems attuned to a frequency within my skull, igniting a splitting headache. I scream, palms pressed to my eyes as I roll around on the floor, feeling unimaginable pressure. Just when I think the bones in my face and forehead might crack, the headache dissipates. Winslade slips away with it. The lights on the side of the device are now green and blinking.

The girl's shrieks have weakened into sobs behind me. I crawl back to the bed, pull myself onto the bloodstained sheets. She kicks at me feebly, eyes bulging, breathing shallow, everything from her chin to stomach red and wet. I reach toward her and she recoils.

'I'm so sorry,' I wail. 'Please forgive me, I wasn't myself.'

'Bastard,' she croaks, eyelids fluttering.

'Don't worry, keep calm. I'm going to free you. I'm going to call an ambulance.'

There are towels on the floor and I grab one, giving it

to the girl and telling her to put pressure against the cut on her neck. I don't know how bad the wound is, she turns away, won't let me look. I stumble over to where my clothes lay and root around until I find my Liaison. Tapping the touch-screen with my bloodstained fingers, I bring it back to the bed and dial 911. When I look up the girl isn't moving.

'911,' the automated voice says. 'What's your emergency?'

I roll the girl over. Her open eyes meet mine, glassy and unmoving, the light gone out of them. Deep down I know this isn't the first time I've looked into the eyes of the dead.

'What's your emergency?' the voice repeats.

I hang up quickly. The newly deceased girl sends shivers down my spine that turn into tremors. I sit on the edge of the bed and cry uncontrollably. When my tears are all used up I cover the girl's naked body with a sheet and begin searching the apartment. I want to release her so badly, but I can't find the handcuff key anywhere. I'm looking under the bed when a call suddenly comes through. The screen says the caller is Renard.

Panicking, I immediately shut off my Liaison and remove the battery. Before I know it I've pulled on my clothes and cleaned myself up, running on instinct and adrenaline. Pulling back the curtains and looking out the bedroom window, I realize I'm somewhere in the meat-packing district. In the bathroom I find the victim's handbag and stuff the cobalt-blue device inside, throw Winslade's straight razor in there after it. Next I disconnect the digital camera from the tripod and examine it.

There is no hard drive, no memory card. The red light on top is part of a transmitter attachment, actively sending the footage offsite for safe storage. I turn the camera off and bag it before escaping the apartment.

28

I know Tweek will be working late at Solace Strategies. He's a creature of habit with zero social life. On the elevator ride up, I regret using the retina scanner and keypad downstairs to access the building. There will be a log of my entry. I have to be more careful, and not just for my sake. Nothing in the handbag provides me with the identity of the victim, though a handful of Winslade's recent thoughts have been committed to memory in the brief time we shared. I remember her now from the session. I met the girl at a restaurant, charmed her with martinis and compliments before convincing her to come back to the apartment. Recollections of Delane play on my mind too, the young witness Winslade murdered with my own hands.

By the time the doors open on the top floor I've formulated a short-sighted half-assed plan. The first person I see is Nikki, also working late, stuck at reception and dealing with our current short-staff problem. She looks up from her desk, surprised to see me standing there holding Winslade's straight razor in one hand and the woman's handbag in the other.

'What are you doing here, Rhodes?'

'Is Baxter in?'

Nikki shakes her head. 'No, she left for the day.'

'Get up,' I order, looking around the empty office,

noting the location of the security camera directed toward the elevator. 'You're coming with me.'

'Pardon?'

'You heard.' I walk toward her, holding out the razor. 'C'mon, move your ass.'

'W-w-where are we going?' she stammers.

'We're going to the control room.'

She's frozen with fear. I grab her by the arm and hoist her out of the chair, waving the blade menacingly. Pushing her in the direction of the control room, I feel a sliver of Winslade slither through me like a parasite. This is something he would do, I think, a way he would act. Nikki walks ahead of me, glancing back at the blade in my hand. The sound of our voices alerts Tweek and he emerges from his doorway holding a cup of coffee.

'Rhodes? What's going on?'

'You,' I say, pointing the razor at him. 'Turn the fuck around and get back in there.'

He complies without another word. I shove Nikki through the doorway after him and shut us inside the office, locking the door behind me. When I turn back to them I'm all apologies.

'I'm so sorry, you guys.'

Nikki is furious. 'Just what the hell was all that about?'

'That?' I say, folding the razor and pocketing it. 'That was an act for the security camera out front.'

'What? Why?'

'Because I don't want you two to get in any trouble,' I say. 'As far as anyone out there will know, I came in here and forced you both at knifepoint.'

Nikki and Tweek stare at me as I clear a space on Tweek's cluttered desk. They both take a curious step closer when I open the handbag and reach inside.

'Forced us to do what, exactly?' Tweek asks.

I pull out the digital camera and lay it on the desk. 'I need you to trace the outgoing signal on this camera.'

Tweek looks it over. 'Why?'

'Because Winslade used me to murder someone an hour ago,' I say. 'He cut a girl's throat in an apartment over in the meat-packing district.'

There is stunned silence. Nikki holds a hand to her mouth, places the other on the desk to steady herself. Tweek's face pales. He sits down, head lolling, looking as if he's going to be sick. Neither of them knows how to respond.

'Who was she?' Nikki finally manages.

I shake my head and turn away, uncomfortable with making eye contact.

'No idea,' I say. 'But this camera was set up in the room, recording the whole thing and transmitting the footage offsite. I need you guys to find out where it was being sent, and I need it done quickly.'

'Wait a minute,' Nikki says, looking back and forth between Tweek and me. 'How is it that you aren't in session with your client right now? Can someone please explain?'

'Before the gig, I swallowed an Ejector so I could re-emerge mid-session and find out what Winslade was doing with me during his rentals –'

'Uh, Rhodes?' Tweek interrupts, shooting me a nervous look. 'Where exactly is Winslade now?'

'I don't know.'

'What the hell do you mean, you don't know?' Tweek says, beginning to panic. 'Do you not have him stored on the drive I gave you?'

I reach back into the handbag and pull out the cobalt-blue device. Tweek gasps when he sees it. Nikki looks even more confused than before.

'What's this?' I ask.

'Oh shit.'

'Oh shit what?'

Tweek scratches at his neck, furrows his brow. 'If my theory is correct, that thing is some newfangled wireless transmitter, designed to sync with the Ouija, built specifically to transfer large amounts of data in seconds.'

'Yeah, well, Winslade used it to check out before I could do anything.'

Tweek snatches the device from my hand and takes it to his desk. Under the swing-arm magnifier, he turns it in his fingers, examining it closely.

'Winslade's done this before,' Tweek says. 'He jettisoned himself minutes before Miller died in that club. That's how he managed to survive without being plugged into a terminal when Miller perished. I think as long as Winslade can pick up a strong enough Wi-Fi signal, he can jump out of a Husk and hitch a ride online back to his server with the push of a button.'

'I've seen this thing before,' I say, pointing at the device. 'Last week you had one right here, in this office.'

· Tweek opens a desk drawer and pulls out the thing I'm talking about. He holds it next to the one he took from me. They look identical.

'This is some cutting edge shit Winslade has been developing. Mine is the one the police found next to Miller's body. Baxter claimed it was company property and managed to retrieve it. She brought it in for me to examine, made me keep quiet about it. I've been trying to reverse engineer it ever since. I haven't managed to get very far. It's too damn advanced.'

'So, what does it mean?' Nikki asks.

'It means Winslade is on the loose and is most likely looking for me,' I say. 'It means I don't have much time. Tweek, can you find the location of the footage?'

'I can try.'

He carefully separates the transmitter from the camera and connects it to his tablet via a pair of cables. The HG starts up, holographic numbers and codes appearing before us, hacker programs working to break down the security measures in place.

'Someone sure didn't want this signal traced,' Tweek grumbles.

Nikki and I watch patiently as he runs a decryption algorithm to reveal the signal, tracking the transmissions to their destination. A minute later a ping sounds from his tablet, indicating success. Tweek looks at the screen and his jaw drops.

'Holy shit,' he says. 'I don't believe it.'

'What?'

'It must be an error.'

'What's an error?' I press. 'Where does the signal lead?'

'This . . . this can't be right.'

'What can't be right?'

Tweek looks up with worried eyes. 'Rhodes, this transmitter was sending the footage back to Solace Strategies.'

My legs go wobbly, weak in the knees. I feel light-headed, have to pull up a chair and sit down. Nikki leans forward and looks at the tablet in Tweek's hands.

'No, no, no,' she whines. 'There must be some mistake.'

'There's no mistake,' Tweek says, reviewing the results again. 'It most definitely came here.'

'Access it,' I say. 'Show it to me.'

'I can't,' Tweek mutters, typing into his tablet. 'It's not available on our office network. It isn't even on the server system.'

'Where is it then?'

There is a long pause as Tweek checks, then double-checks, the information. When he finally speaks his voice is trembling.

'It was sent directly to Baxter's personal computer.'

I try to rise, wanting to see the evidence on Tweek's tablet for myself, but my burgeoning shock plunks my ass back down. Mouth goes dry, headache starts. Sweat breaks out over my body. I notice Tweek and Nikki starting to sweat too.

'Can you break into it?' I ask, voice hoarse.

Tweek swallows hard. 'I don't think I want to.'

'Please, Tweek.'

Without another word he recommences hacking, remotely connecting to Baxter's hard drive from the control room. Results take longer this time, causing Tweek to bitch and moan under his breath as he tries to outsmart the computer's security while at the same time cover his tracks. We wait until we hear the tell-tale ping from his tablet.

'Whoa,' Tweek says, recoiling from the screen.

'Whoa, what?'

'There's a whole collection on Baxter's comp.'

'Collection?'

'I've found a whole damn catalogue. I'm putting them up on the HG now.'

Tweek brings up a selection of videos on the Holographic. They begin playing randomly side by side in high definition, some kind of stats listed beneath. They're no longer than thirty seconds or so in length, quick shots cutting to different angles, edited like porn movie trailers. Each features a Husk from Solace Strategies, and every one of them is horrifying. The revelation is more than I can take.

I see a naked Husk approaching a crying child clutching its blanket on a four-poster bed. I watch a Husk in a skin-tight white latex outfit strangle a naked man tied to a velveteen throne. I witness a Husk beat a middle-aged woman senseless with a baton, then begin having sex with her unconscious body. I close my eyes to a Husk who is about to do something horrible with a car battery and jumper cables to terrified cats and dogs in metal cages. I recognize each of the Husks perpetrating the crimes: Phineas, Ryoko, Clive, Miller, and more.

When I open my eyes again I see a Husk standing over a terrified teenage girl, ripping her blouse and gripping her hair, forcing her to say dirty and demeaning things that bring tears to her eyes. It takes me a moment to realize who this Husk is. When I finally do, I'm watching myself handcuff the girl to a bed against her will. I beat her so viciously her crying soon stops. I tcar my eyes away, unable to look any more at this CCTV footage from Hell, unable to watch myself committing the damning act.

'Holy shit,' Tweek gasps, eyes skimming from video to video. 'Is that you, Rhodes? Is that Phineas there? And Ryoko?'

'Turn it off,' I moan.

'Oh my God,' Nikki whines, hand held to her mouth. 'This is unbelievable.'

I risk another glance at the footage. For one second I see my sister kneeling among a group of naked men wearing colourful masks. It's from the party Ichida threw at his mansion, the same one he rented me for.

'For God's sake *turn it off*!' I scream.

Tweek closes every video except one. Together, in silence, we focus our attention on the newest recording in the catalogue as it begins to play unedited and uninterrupted. We watch as I bring the raven-haired girl into the room. We watch me seduce her, strip her, have sex with her. We watch as I handcuff her to the bed, then strangle and slit her throat. Then we watch as I almost lose my mind.

'How many of these videos are on Baxter's drive?' I ask.

'Dozens,' Tweek croaks.

'What the fuck is she doing?' I shout. 'Why is she keeping them?'

'Keeping them?' Tweek replies, bringing up the other

videos again and pointing to the stats listed below them. 'Look at the numbers and names at the bottom of each one. Those there are prices and those are bidders. This is an auction, Rhodes. Baxter is *selling* them.'

'And for hell of a profit too,' Nikki says, leaning into the HG and peering at the names. 'I recognize some of those user handles. They're Solace Strategies' clients. This is some kind of private file-sharing network they're all logged into.'

'Solace Strategies gives their clients what no one else can,' I whisper. 'That's what we do.'

'Huh?'

'Something Baxter said to me the other day,' I say, pointing at the videos. 'Now I get it. All of this, it's our boss giving clients what no other company will.'

Nikki gulps. 'Jesus . . .'

'I need a copy,' I tell Tweek. 'Of everything.'

'What are you going to do with it?'

'I'm not sure,' I reply. 'But it's evidence I can stop Winslade with.'

Tweek shakes his head. 'All it proves to anyone else watching is that you and the other Husks are guilty of crimes you didn't actually commit.'

He's right. How would I convince anyone that the man murdering the girl in the footage isn't actually me? How could I explain that the villain in each video isn't in control of his own actions, is just a puppet on a string? How would I begin to tell the authorities about an underground consortium of digitally enhanced prostitutes that have dealings with the world's wealthiest deceased?

'I'll figure something out,' I say. 'I'll try and get –'

We freeze. A three-note electronic chime sounds at the reception desk. I hold my breath as Nikki shoots me a terrified look.

'Someone's downstairs,' she says. 'Someone wants to be let in.'

We hear the chime sound another two times, loud and impatient. Tweek turns on a flat-screen on the wall and checks the front door's security camera feed. I see Renard's stoic face looking into the lens. The two security guards from Winslade's penthouse flank him, both dressed in civilian garb. Inside Renard's jacket I see the butt of his Rapier in its holster.

'Shit,' I say. 'That's Winslade's attaché.'

Renard presses the button a fourth time, keeping his finger on it. The chime plays over and over in the office. I turn to Nikki and Tweek, who both look at me petrified.

'Don't let them up. They don't know if anyone's here.'

'Um, Rhodes?' Nikki says, pointing. 'I'm not sure that's going to stop them.'

I turn back to the screen. One of Renard's men has plugged a handheld device into the retinal scanner beside the door and is beginning to bypass security.

'We don't have much time,' I say. 'Tweek, copy those files.'

Tweek just stands there, eyes glued to the flat-screen, watching Renard and his men working to get through the front door.

'Tweek?'

'I can't.'

'What do you mean, you can't?'

'It's not going to work, Rhodes. Every one of these files is locked up tight. They're just previews, all part of the auction system. Each video is for sale to members of the network only, and they must be purchased to be attained.'

'Can you find a way around it?'

We watch as Renard and his men deactivate Solace Strategies' security system. They're through the door and on their way to the elevator.

'Not with the time we have left,' Tweek says. 'You're going to have to find another way to take Winslade down.'

Nikki grabs my arm. 'You have to get out of here right now.'

She's right. If I stay any longer I risk everyone's safety more than I already have. I take out my pillbox and pluck out a twenty-four-hour pill. I break off a third of it and drop the piece into Tweek's mug of coffee to dissolve.

'Each of you needs to drink half of this,' I say, stirring with my finger. 'It will render you unconscious for several hours. They can't know that you helped me willingly with any of this. When you eventually come to, just play dumb. Tell Baxter and Renard that I forced you to surrender your computer access before I knocked you out. You know nothing more.'

'They just got in the elevator,' Tweek says, still looking at the flat-screen.

'How are you getting out?' Nikki asks.

'Fire exit,' I say and hold the tainted coffee out to her. 'Now drink.'

Nikki takes the mug and holds it to her lips, drinks down half of the lukewarm liquid. Tweek holds his hand out and she passes it over before sitting down on the floor. He looks at the remaining half uncertainly, then back to Nikki who is already starting to pass out. I stuff the camera and wireless transmitters into the handbag, sling it over my shoulder and take the razor blade out of my pocket. I risk another glance at the videos playing on the HG and feel my stomach churn. Ryoko is engaged in an unspeakable act, something which makes my blood run cold.

'Shut it all down,' I say.

Tweek nods, turns everything off with a few keystrokes, then tips back the mug and finishes the coffee in two gulps.

'Good luck,' he says, removing his glasses. 'And be careful out there.'

He slumps over his desk as I exit the control room. Quickly, I make my way across the office floor to the fire exit on the far side, where seventeen flights of stairs await. As I slip through the door I hear the elevator ping over by reception. Its doors open only seconds after the fire exit shuts behind me.

I start running.

29

I clear the building without incident and head straight for the 34th Street subway entrance, checking over my shoulder the whole time. Avoiding cameras and hiding in crowds become my first priorities. Underground feels like the only place I can think straight. I ride the train for over an hour, trying to figure out what to do next. No good comes from it. All I want to do is contact Ryoko, but I don't dare turn on my Liaison. I'm positive it can be traced, certain that calls will come in from people I don't want to hear from.

I stare at my hands. How long has this been going on? How many people have I hurt? How many have I killed? At a loss, scared out of my mind, I finally get off the train and find an old payphone at Grand Central Station. I reluctantly dial Ryoko. She picks up after the second ring.

'Hello?'

'Sugarplum, it's me,' I say, unable to disguise the desperation in my voice. 'It's Rhodes.'

'Cheesecake? Where are you?'

'I shouldn't say.'

'Are you all right?'

'Not even a little bit.'

Ryoko pauses, lowers her voice. 'Phineas has been calling me, said he's been trying to reach you all evening. He sounds a little freaked out, but won't tell me anything. Baxter has tried to call me a few times too, but I haven't answered.'

'Good,' I say. 'Don't talk to Baxter. I'll get in contact with Phineas.'

'What's going on, baby?'

'I can't talk over the phone, sweetheart. Need to meet you in person.'

'Sure. Where?'

I pause, wondering if anyone is eavesdropping. The only way to play it is to play it safe.

'Meet me in a half hour outside the restaurant where I ran into my sister.'

'Okay . . .'

'And Ryoko?'

'Yeah?'

'Make sure you're not followed.'

I hang up and collect my thoughts, thoughts that dance around Phineas. It takes me a minute to formulate a decent plan. I pick up the receiver, dial his number. He picks up after the first ring.

''ello?'

'Phineas, it's me, Rhodes.'

'Rhodes, Jesus, I've been trying to get hold of you. Where are you?'

'Can't say. Not over the phone. It's not safe.'

'What the hell is going on, mate? Baxter's been calling me non-stop trying to find you. She says it's important, says it's an emergency. Did you lose your phone or something today?'

'I lost a lot more than that,' I say.

'Meaning what?'

'My innocence and ignorance for starters. I've uncovered something real big and real bad at Solace. Need to meet you face to face and tell you more. It involves us Husks and we need to figure out what to do about it.'

'Okay, now you're scaring me.'

'You should be scared, my friend.'

'Where and when do you want to meet?'

'I'm on my way now to link up with Ryoko. Meet us in two hours at the hotel where you and I first met on the job, that time we were hired as escorts for those two cougars. Remember it?'

Phineas grunts. 'Remember it well, mate.'

'Go now,' I tell him. 'Book a suite with cash, text Ryoko the room number only and wait for us to show. Make sure you're not followed.'

'Consider it done,' he says and hangs up.

A light rain falls over the city. Ryoko is already standing under an awning outside the restaurant when I get there. As soon as I reach her I throw my arms around her and hold tight, press my face into her neck. The tears come easily, despite my efforts to hold them back. The collar of her jacket soaks them up as I cry.

'It's all right,' she says. 'Tell me everything.'

Sniffling and sobbing, I spill my guts. The only thing I leave out is the worst act I saw her commit on video. The one I can't bring myself to admit I witnessed.

*

An hour later we get into a cab and tell the driver to take us to the Algonquin Hotel. As the cab speeds through the wet streets of New York we hold each other in the back-seat. I keep looking at Ryoko, expecting her to look shaken and stressed by the things I've told her, but the looks she gives back are cool and composed. She tells me we will find a way out of this together. Halfway to the hotel Ryoko's Liaison pings and she checks the screen. Phineas has sent her a number: 314.

We arrive at the Algonquin and wait in the lobby for the elevator. As I stand there I can't shake the feeling of being watched. A mew comes to my ears and I turn to see the hotel's resident cat curled up on a seat nearby. This guardian of the underworld fixes its slit-pupils on mine, holding my gaze until the elevator arrives. It meows again as the doors open. Upon entering the elevator I glance over my shoulder to see the cat sit up straight, staring at me like I'm prey. It paws the air, a wave hello, or possibly goodbye. The doors close and I'm left feeling disconcerted about the brief encounter. The cat's eyes play on my mind as we ride up to the third floor and find room 314. Ryoko raps on the door. Phineas is quick to open it.

'Come in, come in,' he urges, ushering us inside. 'Thank God, I was beginning to worry about you two.'

'You weren't followed?' I ask.

'Not to my knowledge,' he replies. 'I tried to make it difficult to tail me if anyone was trying.'

Phineas locks the door behind us. The room he's rented is small, claustrophobic. Ryoko takes off her coat and sits on the edge of the double bed. I pull up a chair from the desk in the corner and plunk myself down, dropping the handbag to the floor.

'You guys all right?' Phineas asks. 'All this cloak-and-dagger stuff has got me more than a little spooked here.'

'We're safe for the moment,' Ryoko replies.

Phineas nods. 'So . . . can you tell me what's going on exactly?'

'My God,' I say, running my fingers through my hair. 'Where do we start –'

I look to Ryoko and stop. She's looking at Phineas with concerned eyes. Then I see what it is that is bothering her. Two of Phineas's fingers are broken, secured with splints and taped up in clean, white bandages. The injury is recent.

'What happened to your fingers, man?' I ask.

'Careless client,' Phineas replies, brushing off my question. 'Said it was hang-gliding mishap.'

'Hang-gliding?'

'That's what I was told.'

I look at his broken fingers again, can't help but think he's full of shit. Something else doesn't seem right. Phineas's accent sounds odd, fluctuating between Cockney and something else. I realize he hasn't called me *mate* once since I've arrived. I get up from the chair and take Ryoko's hand in mine.

'Let's go down to the lobby and get a drink,' I say. 'I could use one after what I've been through today. We'll find a quiet table and I'll tell you everything.'

'What's wrong with this room?' he asks.

I laugh. 'No booze for starters.'

'There's some in the minibar.'

'I think we need a proper drink.'

I start for the door, leading Ryoko behind me. Phineas steps into our path, reaches inside his jacket and pulls out a Beretta M9. He aims the gun at stomach level.

'Please, sit back down.'

'Phineas? What the hell are you doing?'

His accent completely dissolves, changing to American. 'Your friend Phineas isn't home right now, Mr Rhodes.'

The smile Phineas gives us is one I've never seen before on him. Ryoko and I sit back down on the bed, our eyes fixed on our friend being used as a trap. I piece it together. They must have got to him soon after I called. He managed to hold out for the first broken finger, but the second one caused him to confess. Phineas keeps the gun trained on us as he brings out his Liaison and makes a call using speaker phone. Renard's voice answers on the other end.

'Yes, Mr Winslade?'

'He showed up at the Algonquin,' Phineas says. 'I've got him.'

'On my way, sir,' Renard replies. 'ETA less than ten minutes.'

Phineas hangs up and looks me in the eye. 'This will all be over soon, my boy.'

I hold his gaze. There is a difference in those eyes. I can see it, that deviancy Ryoko mentioned over dinner, the eyes of an impersonator, an imposter. The unwelcome guest is looking out of those windows to Phineas's soul, moving behind the reflection in the glass, a visitor whose fondness of me knows no bounds. Before I know it, I'm standing up and taking a step toward him. He cocks the hammer back on the Beretta, raising it to eye level.

'Stay, boy.'

I shake my head. 'You won't kill me, Mr Winslade.'

'Maybe,' Phineas says, turning the muzzle of the gun toward Ryoko. 'But I will most certainly kill your woman.'

'Don't you *dare* point that at her.'

'I'm willing to comply, Mr Rhodes, if you'll be so good as to sit back d–'

All the lights in the room flicker once and then go out, a rolling blackout temporarily painting the suite pitch black. Whether it's a touch of fate, or stroke of dumb luck, it's my only chance. I lunge at the spot where I last saw Phineas and crash into him. The gun goes off, muzzle flash lighting up the interior in a single strobe, the round going into something soft. I hear a gasp. When the lights come back I'm struggling on top of Phineas, trying to keep the gun from pointing at me. I look up and all I see is Ryoko and blood.

'No!'

She slumps back on the bed, arms wrapped around her torso like she's shivering. I can't tell where she's been hit. My fists beat on Phineas beneath me in a blind rage. He defends himself poorly, but I fail to see his arm swing up to my head. The butt of the Beretta slams into my temple, sending me sprawling. I land on my back and he's on me in seconds, straddling me, bringing the gun around.

'Time's up,' he pants. 'You've become more trouble than you're worth.'

A moment later I'm staring down the hollow black eye

of the barrel. Phineas pulls the trigger just as I grab the muzzle and shove it aside. The bullet misses my head, grazing my ear, deafening me in the process. With all my might I wrench the gun out of Phineas's grip and toss it. The next instant his hands are closing around my throat. His contorted, angered face hovers over mine. Saliva seeps through his bared teeth and drips onto my cheek. The ringing in my ears hardly lets me hear what he's saying, sounds like he's speaking through thick glass.

'The only good witness is a dead witness.'

The grip feels inhumanly strong, denying me air instantly. I claw at him, but can't pry his crushing fingers from my neck. I feel the fight in me weakening as I struggle. The edges of my vision begin to blacken. With one last effort I strike upwards with my knee and catch Phineas in the balls, hard enough to knock him off. He rolls over, manages to get to his knees, a defeated look on his pained face. I roll over and crawl toward the gun. Phineas reaches for something in his jacket, going for a back-up piece I figure, maybe even a Rapier. As my hand curls around the Beretta's grip I hear Phineas make a strange noise.

I spin around and bring the gun up, aim it right between Phineas's eyes, eyes that in a sudden flash display confusion and horror. He starts to raise a hand, the one with the broken fingers. His other hand starts to pull something out of his pocket.

'Rhodes, mate –'

But I've already pulled the trigger. Phineas's head rocks back, a splatter of dark, meaty red exploding out the base of his skull. The eyes, eyes that are his now, roll back to show only whites. A cobalt-blue device slips from his fingers onto the floor with a clunk, green lights blinking on its exterior, signifying a successful transfer.

'Oh God,' I croak. *'No.'*

Phineas's body crumples to the carpet, twitches once, then stills. The smell of cordite fills the air. Ryoko moans on the bed. I get up and stumble over to her, stuffing the Beretta in the waistband of my pants. She's been hit in the arm, bullet gone through and through. There's blood everywhere. I help her to sit up.

'We have to leave, now.'

Ryoko nods, her eyes falling first on Phineas's body, then the cobalt-blue thing lying beside him. She says nothing, rising from the bed and reaching for her coat as I grab the handbag from the floor. I lead her out of the room and down the hall to the elevator. On the way down I use my necktie as a tourniquet to tie off her bleeding arm before draping her jacket over her shoulders to hide the injury.

At the ground floor the elevator doors open on a frantic scene. The lobby of the hotel is chaos, reports of gunfire sending people into a panic. Hotel security calls for calm, reassuring guests that the police are on their way and that the hotel is safe and secure. Ryoko and I slip by unnoticed in the confusion and head for the entrance. We're halfway across the lobby when I see Renard and his two goons enter through the front doors. Quickly I turn away, but he spots me within seconds.

'You!' he shouts. 'Stop!'

Ryoko and I start to run. Renard reaches inside his

jacket and draws his Rapier. From the corner of my eye I see him level it at us as we duck among a crowd of hotel guests and employees. I hear the Rapier discharge twice and watch as a round takes off a bellhop's head beside me. The second round hits someone unseen, making them shriek with pain. Maybe Renard is being overzealous, or maybe Winslade will take me dead or alive at this point.

Two hotel security guards draw their weapons and begin shooting, turning the lobby into a battleground. People scream, fleeing in all directions. Others hit the floor. Ryoko and I are among them, dropping behind a sofa. I peek out to see Renard's men take cover behind pillars while he sprints toward us. The Algonquin's cat scampers across the floor and collides with his shins, sending him tumbling to the floor. The Rapier slips from his grip and is sent skittering across the tiles. He gets to his hands and knees, cursing aloud, searching for his lost weapon. I stand, draw the Beretta and point it at him. He looks at me, defenceless, frozen to the spot. I pull Ryoko toward the rear of the lobby, keeping the gun trained on him. Near the doorway I pause long enough to fire three rounds that miss Renard completely, but make him dive for cover, where the security guards keep him pinned.

We escape toward the back of the hotel, heading through the dining room and kitchen, hearing gunplay continue behind us. Everything is an electrified blur, sights and sounds soaked in adrenaline, rapidly passing to the beat of our thudding hearts. Eventually, I crash through an exit door and drag Ryoko into the rancid air of a back alley where dumpsters and garbage cans are scattered about. We stop for a moment, trying to catch our breath, casting nervous glances behind us. I hold Ryoko's chin in my hands, make her look me in the face.

'We have to split up,' I say.

She shakes her head. 'We have to stick together.'

'They're after me, not you.' I look at her arm. 'You've lost a lot of blood. You need to get that taken care of.'

My eyes inadvertently lower to her stomach, to what is beginning to grow within. She won't go to the hospital. There are many private practices in Manhattan where money ensures confidentiality. Ryoko knows how to take care of herself. We dash further down the alley and cut through another, looking over our shoulders for any sign of our pursuers. We finally stop in a darkened alcove. I slip the clip out of the Beretta, make a quick bullet count, slam it back in and hand the gun over to Ryoko. She takes it reluctantly, giving me an unimpressed look as she tucks it in the back of her pants.

'Eleven rounds left,' I say. 'Use them if you have to.'

'You need protection too,' she protests.

'Don't worry, I got a plan. I know where I can get a gun.'

'You do?'

I nod, not even sure if it's a good plan, but it's the best I can think up under the circumstances. I lead Ryoko out to the street and around the corner, where I flag down a cab. She grabs my hand, squeezes it hard.

'I'll contact you as soon as this is settled,' I say. 'Lie low and wait for my call.'

'I will,' she replies. 'And Rhodes . . . ?'

I turn to her as she slips a hand around the back of my neck and pulls me close. The kiss is tense and long, her lips trembling slightly against mine. Next thing I know she's getting into the cab and leaving me standing on the sidewalk. Once the car door closes, the window rolls down.

'You make sure you come back to me in one piece,' she says.

I nod again, look her in the eye. 'I love you.'

She only mouths the words back and turns to the cabbie. Whatever she says makes him pull away from the kerb with a screech. I cross the street and walk southwest for a while until I come to a discount tourist store near Times Square. Inside, I buy a memory card for the camera, and a cheap knapsack in which I stuff the lady's handbag and all of its contents. At another store I purchase an NY hoodie and ball cap. I put them on as I venture out again, brim pulled low, hood over my head to conceal my face as much as possible from the CCTV cameras and their facial-recognition software.

As I walk the streets, the horror and guilt over accidentally murdering my friend tie my intestines in knots, making me hunch over and moan aloud. People on the sidewalk cross the road to avoid me, assuming I'm some drunk or lunatic. I can't get the thought of Phineas out of my mind, the image of his eyes changing a second before I put a bullet between them. The only silver lining, is that Phineas died never knowing the horrors he'd committed, would never be haunted by it. I figure there must be peace in that, for him, and maybe a little for me too.

Ryoko would have called me crazy if I'd told her where I was planning to go. It's the only place I know of where I can get my hands on a gun. In the unending Manhattan lights I try my best to stick to the shadows as I make my way back to my apartment in the East Village on foot.

30

In the dark, I sit on a bench in Tompkins Square Park and watch the front door of my building from a distance. Everything appears normal, but I look for irregularities, people out of place, stationary when they should be moving, maybe someone on the street or in a car casing the entrance to my home. For a long time I wait, uncertain. Eventually two girls sit on the stoop and smoke cigarettes, laughing aloud at each other's jokes. I'm so focused on them that I don't notice the dark figure approaching through the trees and bushes on my right. By the time he's upon me, I have barely enough time to react.

'I thought I recognized you,' he says.

I close my fist, readying it as the man sits down beside me. He turns his head and I'm relieved to see the unshaven face of Javier. He holds out his fist. I pound it with the one I was about to strike with, getting a whiff of bourbon and body odour as I do. In his other hand is a bottle of Jim Beam.

'What are you doing in the park at this time of night?' he asks, taking a swig. 'Don't you have a nice warm bed to go to?'

I shake my head. 'Not sure it's safe to go home right now.'

Javier laughs. 'Girl trouble?'

When I don't laugh in return he infers correctly that it's nothing so trivial. He looks to where I'm looking, squinting to see anything that might give him a clue as to what's bugging me.

'It's been quiet, tonight.'

'Not for me.'

'Drink?' he says, offering the bottle.

'I'll pass,' I reply, though I could really use a shot of the stuff.

'Suit yourself. Are you on duty or something?'

'Just staying vigilant.'

'What is it exactly that you do for a living?' Javier says, looking me over with suspicion. 'If you don't mind me asking?'

'It's complicated,' I say.

'Yeah,' he chuckles. 'Ain't everything in this world?'

'You ever heard of Husking?'

'Husking?' Javier considers a moment. 'You mean the rumours you sometimes hear about those downloadable hookers for the rich?'

'It's kinda the other way around, but yeah.'

'Thought that stuff was all science fiction?'

'It's not science fiction,' I say. 'Hey, can I still get in on that drink?'

Javier hands me the Jim Beam and I get some liquid courage in me, feel the bourbon burn all the way down to my writhing guts. I've waited long enough, haven't seen anything to be concerned about. I hand the bottle back and stand, slinging my knapsack over my shoulders.

'Gotta grab something from my place,' I tell him. 'I'll be right back.'

'I'll be right here, man.'

Five minutes is all it should take. I make my way through the park and cross the street to my stoop. The two chuckle-heads don't even look at me as I weave past them and let myself into the building. Three flights of stairs and I'm at my apartment door. Before I can pull out my key, I notice the scratched and splintered wood around the doorknob. The lock is broken. The door is closed, but has evidently been kicked in at some point. I push it inward to reveal darkness beyond.

Every light in the apartment is turned off. Stepping inside, I try my best to negotiate the dark, peering through the gloom for any sign of trouble. I tread carefully across the living room until I'm able to flick the main light switch on. The apartment is illuminated, revealing everything in its usual state. A window to our fire escape is open, letting in a cool breeze. I circle the living room cautiously, listening and looking for any sign that someone may still be here. On the coffee table is a pair of night-vision glasses Craig must have brought home from the Rochester. I swipe and pocket them. My roommate's bedroom door is closed. I call his name as loud as I dare and approach. No response. The Glock is most definitely in there. Carefully, I turn the doorknob and open the door. The scene inside makes me whimper.

'Oh, God.'

Craig lies slumped on the bed in his boxer shorts, dead. His eyes are open and glazed, staring at the ceiling. In the middle of his chest is a hole the circumference of a tuna can, cut almost perfect, cauterized on impact, not a trace of blood; the kind of damage made by an M-6 Rapier at close range. I can see bed sheets through the wound on the other side. On the floor in front of Craig is his open gun case, the Glock missing from it. Two magazines are discarded nearby, bullets scattered around them. He must have been trying to load it when the assailant broke in and shot him. I'm about to turn and run when I hear the front door of the apartment open with a bang behind me.

'Don't fucking move.'

I freeze, my hands held where they can be seen. 'I'm unarmed.'

'I don't care. Make one wrong move and I'll core you like an apple.'

'Whatever you say, just don't shoot.'

'Turn around slowly.'

I do as I'm told. Two men stand in my apartment door-way. I recognize both as members of Winslade's security detail. Each has a Rapier trained on me.

'Get on your knees, now.'

I drop to my knees. The guy doing the talking holsters his weapon and reaches for his Liaison to make a call. There is a sudden shattering sound as liquid and glass explode over the head of the goon standing in the door-way. He drops to reveal Javier standing behind him in the hall, the neck of the broken bourbon bottle gripped in one hand. The first goon reaches for the gun inside his jacket, but Javier lunges forward, stabbing the jagged remainder of the bottle into his shoulder, causing him to yowl with pain. Javier and I both tackle the guy to the floor, pinning him with all our weight, working to keep him subdued. I drive my fist into the back of the man's head, knocking his face off the floor. His struggling lessens enough for me to shoot Javier a quick look.

'What the hell are you doing here?'

'Saw these two assholes follow you into the building. Thought there might be some trouble.'

The guy underneath me tries to say something, but I deliver another rabbit punch and silence him. I look up again at Javier, only to see the second operative starting to get to his feet behind him.

'Watch out –'

The goon stumbles forward and throws all of his weight at Javier's back, knocking him into me and both of us off the guy we have pinned. Our advantage is lost in seconds and we find ourselves grappling with an assailant each. The guy that was below is now on top of me, trying to draw his gun. Javier and his opponent wrestle madly for control of the other Rapier. Amid grunts and shouts one of the weapons suddenly discharges. I watch as a streak of projectile and propellant shears my enemy's right arm off above the elbow. I kick the screaming amputee off me as Javier throws his attacker over the couch. The goon loses his grip on the Rapier when he hits the ground. We hear it clatter across the floor and come to rest on the far side of the room. The operative is on his feet in seconds, scrambling toward it. Javier and I glance at each other. No time to stop him. All I can do is hit the lights.

'Fire escape,' I say, looking at the open window nearby. 'Go.'

I flick the switch and the apartment goes black, leaving our attacker to search blindly in the dark for his weapon as we scramble out the window. By the time we're two floors down I hear the Rapier fire from above, sending rounds streaking past us in the night.

'Quick, get to the park.'

Javier kicks the latch, releasing the last ladder to the sidewalk. We practically slide down, then race into the traffic crawling along the street, using slow-moving cars and trucks for cover as we make our way across. Rapier rounds slam into the vehicles and concrete around us, causing mayhem, becoming less accurate as we distance ourselves and disappear into the dark of Tompkins Square Park.

31

'Christ, who were those guys back there?' Javier asks as we slip into a cab on 10th Street. 'And what the hell kind of pieces were they packing?'

I shake my head. 'You don't want to know.'

'Yes, I do.'

'You don't want to get involved, trust me.'

Javier throws up his hands. 'Well, fuck, I'm already involved now, aren't I?'

I say nothing. The cab driver watches us warily in his rear-view mirror, already regretting picking us up. His voice wavers slightly when he speaks.

'Where to, sir?'

'Take me to Washington and West 13th Street,' I say. 'And step on it.'

Javier and I sit in silence, watching the nightlife slip by our windows, letting the adrenaline drain from our systems as we try and digest what went down back in the apartment. He must be so confused, so scared. A part of me wants to tell him everything, but I don't say a word. Guilt over getting Craig killed doubles down on the remorse I already feel over Phineas. I don't want anyone else's blood on my hands.

'Why are we going to the meat-packing district?' Javier finally asks.

'*We* aren't going anywhere,' I say. 'Tell me where you want to be dropped off.'

'There's nowhere to drop me off. You know I ain't got any place to go.'

'Then you should probably get out at the next corner.'

'Well, I don't want to hang out on street corners no more either.' Javier shrugs and tries to smirk. 'Sorry, you're stuck with me, man.'

'Javier . . .'

'Look, when I was at my worst you bought me food, gave me money,' Javier continues, looking me in the eye. 'Hell, you even donated your smokes. You're a good man, Rhodes.'

'I'm not.'

'Bullshit.'

'I've done some things I'm not proud of.'

'Haven't we all? Everything's shades of grey, man, now more than ever.'

'Shades of grey,' I mutter.

'Shades of grey,' repeats Javier, looking down at his dirty hands. 'Good and bad, right and wrong. They're just compass points. No one travels in a straight line. Life's never as simple as we think it should be. There is darkness between the stars in the heavens, and even the fires of Hell shed light.'

He's stone-cold sober now. I don't know what he's reciting, but his wisdom surprises me. I mull it over, feeling the truth, reconsidering my own recent stance on the stars. Javier is far sharper than I originally gave him credit for. Having the guy at my side suddenly feels reassuring. Still, I don't want him involved in my problems.

'If you don't get out of this car, Javier, I can't guarantee your safety.'

'Safety has been an issue for a good while now, my friend. I have a chance to repay my debt, help you out with your little problem. And shit, I got nothing to lose. So, I'll ask again. Why are *we* going to the meat-packing district?'

'I have to follow a lead . . . the only one I have left.'

'And what are you hoping to get out of this lead?'

'Evidence, leverage, truth . . . take your pick.'

I take the digital camera out of my knapsack and check it over, relieved to find it wasn't damaged in the apartment attack. I insert the memory card I bought near Times Square and power it up. The camera is state of the art, too complicated for the likes of me. All the menu options and their abbreviations on the screen start to give me a headache. After five minutes of my dicking around with it, Javier holds out his hand.

'Do you even know what you're doing with that?'

'Not really.'

'Give it here.'

I pass him the camera and he handles it like a pro, scrolling through menus and changing settings, seeming to know all the ins and outs.

'Bought one just like this months ago,' Javier says. 'It was the first thing I pawned for rent money when I lost my job.'

'What was your job?'

'Worked in advertising. I came up with campaigns to convince the masses to blow their money on products they didn't need, selling crack to consumer addicts that couldn't help themselves.'

'What kind of products?'

'Things like this,' Javier replies, holding up the camera before handing it back. 'All the latest and greatest gear, only to be replaced with new versions every six months. Advertising is a horrible, cutthroat business. Getting good at it . . . I'd say it's the closest thing to selling your soul.'

'I know the feeling,' I mutter. 'How'd you lose your job?'

'How do any of us lose our jobs? They're taken away.'

'You got a wife, kids?'

'Had a wife, she went soon after the job.'

'I'm sorry.'

'Don't be. For richer or poorer wasn't a vow she took seriously. And kids . . . ?' he snorts, shaking his head. 'Who in their right mind would want to bring a kid into a world like this? What future would they have?'

'You have a point.'

'Losing my job was a relief in a way. Getting fired from all that soul-crushing shit did me some good.'

'I only wish I could get fired from my job.'

Javier eyes me. 'Look, I don't know much about Husking, my friend, but the rumours I've heard make it sound very unappealing.'

'We all have our price, right?'

Javier nods and says no more. A few minutes later the cab pulls up to the corner of Washington and 13th, dropping us off in the meat-packing district, the last location I remember after fleeing the session in a panic earlier. I look around, trying to get my bearings, anticipating some sense of recognition. I had been too terrified to commit much to memory before. Ran blind out of there and didn't look back, didn't think to stop for one second. Returning to the scene of the crime would be the last thing anyone would expect me to do, my one and only advantage. I try to retrace my steps, try to remember where I'd escaped from. Slowly some sense of familiarity returns.

'What's the plan?' Javier asks.

I start walking west. 'We're gonna follow my gut.'

My pace quickens, Javier jogging intermittently to keep up. Instinctively I know where I'm heading. Within ten minutes I find myself standing in front of an old six-storey, brownstone building. It is the one I ran from hours earlier, I realize, the one I left the murdered body of a young woman inside. Strangely, it feels more familiar than that. I've been here many times before. The upper floors look like they may be lofts or apartments. The first three floors are leased out to a business. The company name is displayed in large silver letters on a black sign over the main entrance: *Modern Harvest NYC, Ltd.*

Winslade's other major business venture, producing much-needed lab-grown meat for increasing human demand, proudly made in the USA. He's got plants in every state. I read the name over and over again, resisting the shivers that want to come. Javier looks back and forth between me and the sign.

'Modern Harvest? You hungry or something?'

'This is the place,' I say. 'We need to get inside.'

The front entrance features reinforced doors with key-pad access and security cameras. We avoid it and circle the building, looking for another way in, making our way around back. Both of us freeze when we turn the corner. There is a white company van parked in the alley, pulled up to a set of double doors even though it's the middle of the night. Parked in front of it is a brand new Cadillac CTS, black with silver trim. We wait a minute, looking for any sign of activity. Dumpsters and bins line the alley, stinking of rotten meat, flies buzzing through the stench. Only one security camera covers the back entrance, hanging loose on its hinge, broken a long time ago. Javier and I move cautiously down the alley and approach the vehicles. Both are empty, but the keys dangle from the ignition of the van. I move to the back door of the building and try the handle. It's locked.

'Shit.'

Javier pulls me aside, looking at the second-storey windows. 'I've got an idea.'

We retrace our steps back along the alley to a dumpster positioned under a fire escape. He climbs onto it and motions for me to do the same.

'Gimme a boost,' he says. 'I think I can reach the ladder.'

I climb atop it and brace myself as I lace my fingers together for his foot. He steps into my hands and I lift him just high enough to reach the bottom rung. I watch as he pulls himself up, then releases the latch and lowers the ladder for me. We quickly find that all the windows adjacent to the fire escape are locked. Javier takes off his coat, holds it against a pane, and kicks in the glass with a subtle smash. No alarm sounds. Whoever is already in the building has turned off the security system.

'After you,' Javier says.

I slip through the window, careful to avoid the broken glass, Javier following close behind. Near darkness inside. My eyes take a minute to adjust. In the gloom I see a large open office space, outlines of cubicles stretching from one side of the room to the other, tiny lights on desks from computers blinking in their sleep. In the far corner is a glowing red exit sign. We cross the room and find it leads to a stairwell. Inside the stairwell a sign denotes each floor of Modern Harvest NYC, Ltd.

3rd Floor: Laboratories, Research & Development
2nd Floor: Offices
1st Floor: Production, Shipping & Receiving

Javier and I take the stairs down one flight to the factory floor.

Most of the lights are turned off on the production level. In the gloom the place looks fucking creepy, one part aquarium and one part slaughterhouse, something dreamed up in the mind of a mad scientist. We walk cautiously down rows of large glass vats, cloned headless and limbless pig or cow carcasses suspended in each, growing imperceptibly in green-tinged amniotic fluid. We watch stomachs and sides expand and contract with breaths fed from oxygen tubes connected directly to tracheas. The feeling of déjà vu comes in a wave. I realize I've seen this all before, more than in my visions and nightmares. My gut churns as I look at these living, breathing, brainless meat-bags waiting to be used.

I can relate, I think.

We pass a temperature-controlled section of the floor where large glass partitions have been erected. Inside chicken breasts and lamb shanks are slowly being printed on stainless-steel slabs by industrial 3D printers feeding genetic code into base stocks of proteins and fats, building dinner portions cell by cell. The areas cordoned off beside it feature the headless bodies of cattle in long lines being fed nutrients and hormones intravenously, their udders permanently connected to milking machines. The air is damp with a fine spray descending from nozzles in the ceiling. The stench is almost unbearable, ammonia and flesh and something else that smells like medicine. Javier retches. I hold my hands over my nose and mouth and continue on.

Suddenly we hear a loud whirring and grinding, some kind of machinery activated at the far end of the building. The noises squeal and stop, squeal and stop. We approach in silence, advancing on a brightly lit back corner of the warehouse, trying to stay hidden among shadows and production equipment. Soon we hear voices of men talking. I recognize the French accent instantly.

'Son of a bitch,' I mutter.

Renard and his two enforcers come partially into view, hunched over something laid out before an ominous-looking mechanism. A wide concrete pillar blocks most of my view, but I can make out enough as they move about. They wear white coveralls, rubber gloves, face shields. Red is smeared on both them and the metal surface of the machine they're working at. When Renard and his men step back, Javier and I both have to stifle a cry of shock.

The naked body of a young woman lies on a steel slab, her face turned out way, dead eyes staring past us. There is a deep, dried cut in her neck. It's the girl Winslade used me to murder in the apartments above. The men move to the left, disappearing behind the pillar. The girl's body slides away with them out of sight. Whirring sounds start up again. The pitch soon becomes a squeal, then falls off. This repeats over and over. I can't see what's happening, but I dare not try for a better look. On the far side of the pillar I notice automated meat processers and grinders in operation. I realize the sound I'm hearing is that of a bandsaw, the kind used for sectioning meat. Everything comes together in an instant. This is how Winslade disposes of his victims, feeding the evidence of his crimes to the unsuspecting people of New York City. My client regards the population as little more than livestock. He's a case of affluenza gone critical.

'Hurry up and finish,' Renard tells his men. 'There are other loose ends we need to take care of.'

He's talking about me no doubt. I take the camera out of my knapsack and hit record. The pillar blocks too much of the view. Javier's position a few feet away allows him a better angle. I flag his attention, slide the camera carefully across the floor, motion for him to pick it up and film. He raises it and begins capturing the crimes, watching it all on the display with wide and frightened eyes. I realize I'm turning him into more and more of an accomplice and regret it. Among the whirring there is a loud grating followed by a sudden clunk sound. A chunk of something bloody goes skidding across the floor, disappearing under a table. Renard swears aloud. Javier covers his mouth, makes a whimpering sound. I watch as he lowers his face to the floor and pukes, trying his damnedest to keep it quiet. The stink of it wafts up, threatening to make me throw up as well. I choke it back and signal Javier to record more of the evidence while it's relatively still in one piece.

'Christ,' he whispers, wiping his lips and chin, unable to look at the display any more. 'This is insane, man.'

'Insanity doesn't even begin to describe it.'

'Is this what you were hoping to find?'

'It'll do,' he replies

Javier leans toward me, hands the camera back. 'We need to get the fuck out of here, like right now.'

'Just one minute more. That's all I need.'

Renard and his men walk back into my line of sight, searching for the piece that escaped. I slink away, focusing the camera on their faces, making sure I get the company logo painted on the wall in the background. When I feel I've got all the damning evidence I need I turn the camera off and stuff it back in my knapsack. Keeping my eyes on the enemy, I reach out and tap Javier on the shoulder.

'Okay,' I whisper. 'Let's get out of here –'

Renard suddenly turns in our direction, lifting the visor of his face shield and sniffing the air, catching the scent of Javier's vomit. His expression hardens. I watch as he reaches into his coveralls and draws out his Rapier, flagging to his men with his other hand.

'Something is wrong,' he says. 'We may have a breach.'

His men remove their face shields and draw their weapons. Renard signals them to investigate the factory floor on the left and right while he takes the middle. The three of them fan out, advancing slowly. Javier and I melt into the shadows, keeping tabs on their progress as we retreat through the rows of vats to the back of the building. Their white coveralls make them easy to spot in the gloom. Just when I think we're going to get out without being detected, all hell breaks loose.

The first Rapier round rockets past my head and shatters a vat behind. Glass and fluid and meat flood out, sweeping me off my feet. I hit the ground hard. Javier picks me up from the floor as Renard shouts orders to his men and squeezes off two more rounds. Another vat explodes, then another.

'Run,' Javier shouts.

We sprint through the rows, dodging in and out so our attackers can't get a bead on us. More rounds go off, destroying the surrounding equipment, punching holes in suspended carcasses as they blow through the tanks. Javier and I manage to make it to the rear of the building in one piece. As we burst out of the back doors and into the alley my eyes fall on the van parked nearby.

'Get in the van,' I yell to Javier, pointing. 'The keys are inside.'

We wrench open the doors and jump in. I crank the ignition, floor the gas pedal. Renard crashes through the back door behind us and raises his Rapier, levelling it at us as we take off. Three rounds rip softball-size holes in the side of the van as we speed down the alley.

'Goddamn it,' I seethe, smacking the steering wheel with an open hand. 'We're like fish in a fucking barrel.'

'We need guns,' Javier pants. 'I know where we can get them.'

'Where?'

'Occupy Central Park.'

'What?' I skid onto the street with a screech and accelerate. 'You're kidding?'

'There's a core group of protesters who call themselves Integris, a real diehard faction, armed and ready. They've been sneaking in weapons for days now, anticipating an attack by the NYPD.'

Something doesn't sit right with me. 'How the hell do you know all that?'

Javier swallows, says nothing. I shoot him an accusatory look and begin to repeat my question. He is quick to cut me off.

'Okay, I'll level with you,' he says, throwing up his hands. 'I'm not really part of the movement.'

'What are you then?'

'An informant.'

I could punch the motherfucker. 'You're a goddamn *snitch*?'

'I don't know what I am!' he yells back. 'All I know is I'm poor and sometimes starving and I feed the cops information about what's going on inside OCP when I need the money bad enough.'

'So, you get paid to report on the occupiers?'

'The occupiers, Integris . . .' Javier shoots me a nervous look. 'And you.'

I almost hit the brakes. 'Me?'

'You were brought to my attention as a person of interest.'

'By who?'

Javier throws up his hands again. 'Fuck, I don't know. I never deal with actual people. They email me targets and give me links where I can send back results. The information I collect is uploaded for retrieval. I don't know names, I don't see faces. I make a report, send some photos, and money is released to my account.'

'So, you've been spying on me this whole fucking time?'

'No,' Javier snarls. 'I haven't told them a thing about you for weeks now.'

'Why?'

'Because they got you figured all wrong, man,' he replies. 'They must think you're some sort of criminal, some kind of threat, but I know you're not. Like I said, you're one of the good guys, man.'

Javier's no fool. I believe what he's telling me. I also believe that whoever was looking at me as a person of interest had me figured right, marking me as a murder suspect, a possible kidnapper and killer of young women in Manhattan. I check my side mirror, see nothing behind us.

'All right,' I say. 'You said OCP's got guns?'

Javier nods vigorously. 'Those Integris guys are armed to the fucking teeth, ready for war. Any police brutality that happens against the movement is going to be met with some fierce opposition, I can tell you that.'

'And they'll hook us up?'

'I know the people involved. I can get us both a piece.'

We speed down 14th Street, run two red lights and make a hard left on 8th Avenue. My driving skills are shit, and I hit the horn to warn people out of my way. I try to weave in and out of traffic, but end up jumping kerbs and sideswiping cars. I expect police sirens and lights to go off behind me any minute, but they don't. Javier looks in his side mirror, then over his shoulder and out the back windows.

'That Cadillac is back there,' he says. 'They're gaining on us quick.'

'How close are they?'

'Just drive faster.'

I floor it, pushing the van as fast as it will go. The Cadillac races up behind, rams us, trying to force us off the road. They try to come alongside, but I use the van's bulk to keep them at bay.

'Keep going,' Javier shouts. 'We're almost there.'

The chase through the concrete jungle is a blur until we reach Central Park. As I enter an intersection I hear the screeching of tyres. Then everything goes black with the force of sudden impact.

32

When I regain consciousness I don't know where I am or what's going on. Javier is shaking me hard, yelling in my face. Nothing registers. Sights and sounds warp around me. I smell gasoline, burnt rubber. It isn't until Javier slaps me across the cheek that things snap into focus.

'C'mon, move it, man!'

He pulls at my shirt. I stumble out of the wreckage and fall to my knees, looking around wildly. A crowd has begun to gather. We're on the edge of Central Park, near the Pond. The side of the van is crushed, front crumpled into a tree, loud hissing coming from the engine. Multiple vehicles are strewn about, some on the sidewalk, others on the grass and road. All have shattered windows and dented bodies, results of collision. Fifty yards away I see the black Cadillac CTS rolled on its side in the street, bashed to shit, Renard and his men struggling to get out.

'What happened?' I gasp, grabbing my knapsack from the front seat.

'We ran a red light, caused a clusterfuck of a crash,' Javier replies, pulling me to my feet. 'It bought us time though.'

We escape into Central Park, stumbling and staggering as we go. I look back to see Renard and his men freeing themselves from their vehicle, readying for pursuit. I try to quicken our pace, but become more aware of the injuries we've sustained in the crash. Mostly cuts and bruises, although Javier has a limp he's trying to walk off unsuccessfully. As we advance further into the park I pull Javier away from the illuminated pathways and into the shadows.

'Stick to the dark,' I say. 'We have an advantage.'

From the knapsack I retrieve the night-vision glasses I swiped back at the apartment. When I place them over my eyes, the surrounding night is instantly bathed in a soft green glow.

'Cat's eyes,' I say, turning to Javier and tapping the specs. 'Follow me.'

I lead Javier past the Wollman Rink and onto Bethesda Fountain. The presence of sleeping protesters grows as we progress toward the Great Lawn. They grumble and bitch as we run between them and disturb their rest. Behind we hear Renard angrily shouting orders to his men. They're hard on our trail, but we manage to stay one step ahead.

Near the boat house shots are fired. Rapier rounds splinter through tree trunks, kicking up dirt around us. People scattered about in sleeping bags and blankets begin to rise up in a panic, screaming and shouting. The spooked crowds start running in all directions, crying for help, allowing us to give our pursuers the slip. By the time we make it to the masses at the Great Lawn, Occupy Central Park is wide awake and alert. Javier and I slip in amongst the thicker crowds and slow down, keeping an eye on the police officers running to the scene, alerted by the sound of screams and gunfire. I look back, see Renard and his men stop at the edge of the lawn and put their weapons away before wading into the crowds to look for us.

'Okay,' Javier says, taking me by the elbow. 'Now you follow me.'

He leads me through the closely packed people to a large orange tent inside one of the baseball diamonds. A tall, muscular guy guarding it stops us, but then lets us pass when he recognizes Javier. Inside the tent a bearded man stands at the centre holding an open gym bag, reaching in and passing out handguns and machine pistols to others who stow them in their jackets and pants. I quickly realize it's the same guy I've seen speaking through the megaphone on the podium, one of the apparent leaders of OCP. I pocket my cat's eyes and Javier takes me to him. Beard Man finally notices me when we're within arm's reach. Before I know it he's pointing a Desert Eagle in my face, hammer cocked and trigger finger itching to squeeze.

'Friend or foe?'

'A friend,' Javier says quickly. 'A friend we can trust.'

I hold my hands out, palms up, keeping cool in the situation. I've had so many guns pointed at me tonight I'm almost numb to it. Beard Man looks me over suspiciously, the sidearm held steady in the grip of a professional. I suspect he's ex-military or former law enforcement. He trusts me about as much as I trust him. The fact that I'm showing no fear irritates him. He presses the cold metal of the gun barrel to my forehead.

'Why did you bring him here?' he asks Javier.

'We need guns,' Javier replies. 'We're desperate.'

'I don't have time for this shit. We all need guns right now. The pigs have started their attack out there.'

'No they haven't. Those shots you heard were meant for me and my friend here. There are mercenaries in the park who want us dead.'

'Mercenaries?' Beard Man looks back and forth between us. 'Why?'

I slowly raise my hand to the gun held against my head and gently push it away, holding the man's gaze. He lowers the gun and lets me speak.

'Because I've made discoveries that can bring down some of the very people you're protesting against. I'm a loose end that they want to tie up pretty bad, because I can't hurt them if I'm killed or captured.'

'What did you uncover?' Beard Man snaps.

'It's a long story,' I say, holding up my knapsack for him to see. 'But I have evidence of it in here.'

'What kind of evidence?'

'The kind that can light the fuse to one hell of a powder keg. Knowledge they will kill anyone to get their hands on.'

'And all you want from me is a gun?' He scratches his head. 'That's it?'

'I just need a piece.'

Beard Man looks me in the eye, trying to determine if I'm a man of my word or absolutely full of it. He must see something reassuring, because he takes my hand and places his Desert Eagle in my palm. From the gym bag he pulls out a Glock and gives it to Javier, who slides back the action and clicks off the safety. Beard Man looks pitifully at the two guns he's donated, and then looks at me with some confusion.

'I'm surprised you don't ask me for more help,' he says, looking around at his armed comrades. 'Do you know who we are? Do you know what it is that we do?'

'I have a vague idea.'

'Look, whatever stories you may have heard about the Occupy Movement or Integris from the media aren't even close to being the truth.'

'I realize that.'

Beard man grabs me by the elbow. 'Do you even know who *I* am?'

Honestly, the guy's a mystery to me. And I'd like to keep it that way. This is a whole other world I can't afford to wade into right now, and picking sides seems like other people's problems. Saving my own ass is my priority. Sticking my neck out any more will certainly get it broken. For a moment I consider giving him the evidence, donating it to the cause, letting him run with it. Then I remember what happened with Phineas and Craig, not to mention the fact that this man just held a gun to my head and the faction he's aligned with is pretty much regarded as a domestic terrorist organization.

'No, I don't know who you are,' I reply, stowing the gun inside my jacket. 'And I don't much care. There's no reason to endanger anyone more than I already have.'

'You're sure?'

'I can take care of myself.'

Beard Man nods respectfully, though he is clearly disappointed. The fact is I don't trust him or Integris any more than I trust the men hunting me at the moment. He steps back just as a beautiful young blonde sidles up to him and curls one hand around his bicep. In her other hand is a gun. Even though she leans into him affectionately, her eyes are fierce, newly protective. It takes me a moment to place her. Annabel Colette, one of the kidnapped Manhattan women whose disappearance I wasn't responsible for, is actually standing here before me, alive and well. The police were right. She's a victim of Integris, not a victim of mine. Except she doesn't look like a victim at all.

'Hey, wait a minute,' I say, nodding toward her. 'Isn't she one of those kidnapped women?'

'She is here by choice now,' Beard Man says, kissing Annabel on the forehead. 'She has seen the light, she understands the truth.'

Stockholm syndrome, I think, glad she didn't fall prey to me. *Lucky girl.*

There is more to it than that though. I can see it in their eyes when they look at each other, behind the anger and the principle. Somehow they've fallen in love, committed themselves to one another as well as the cause. *Till death do us part* seems likely for these two with those guns in their hands. Beard Man points a finger toward the entrance of the tent, telling us it's time for us to be on our way. As Javier and I leave he continues to hand guns out to the gathered protesters. I wonder just how many of them are willing to die for their beliefs.

Outside, I don my glasses as we merge with the crowds of the Great Lawn and walk among agitated citizens, listening to their concerned chatter. Tensions are high.

Worries are growing. The lawn seems to be more illuminated than I remember. Several portable police floodlights
have been activated around the field perimeter as additional officers arrive on the scene in response to the
reported gunshots. Javier and I make our way across the
baseball fields, constantly scanning the crowds for danger,
keeping to areas still bathed in darkness.

Near the eastern edge of the Great Lawn we stop. With
my night-vision I spy Renard behind the police line, con-
ferring with a group of newly arrived men dressed in
plainclothes. More of Winslade's security team has been
called in, most of them guards from his building. They
check images on their Liaisons, undoubtedly of me, as
Renard briefs them. Soon they split up, dissolving into the
crowds to aid in the search.

Thankfully, the operatives move in the direction away
from us. I keep my eyes on Renard, who begins walking
toward the NYPD's two stationary EMUs parked just
outside the perimeter, less than fifty yards from us. With
the police distracted, he sneaks up behind one of the
drones and pulls something from his pocket. At this distance I can tell it is one of Winslade's wireless transmitter
devices. Renard reaches up and connects it to the back of
the drone's head. Within seconds the machine comes to
life, straightening its posture and extending its neck. I
cringe as it tests out its appendages and takes two pensive
steps. Seemingly satisfied, it starts to stalk the crowds
from the shadows, reflective lenses scanning back and
forth over the protesters. Without a doubt I know. Winslade has personally joined in the hunt for me.

The EMU moves south. It isn't long before both pro-testers and police start to notice the eight-foot mech creeping around in the dark. People warn each other of the drone's approach, giving it a wide berth, everyone unsure of what's going on. Eventually a police lieutenant approaches it waving a hand frantically, trying to get its attention while talking to someone on his radio. The EMU ignores him, continuing its search as if he isn't even there.

Javier and I start to move in the opposite direction when a heavy hand grips my shoulder and spins me around. I come face to face with one of Renard's men. The barrel of his Rapier pushes hard into my gut.

'You're coming with me –'

Javier doesn't hesitate. He swings and strikes the enfor-cer on the back of the head with the butt of his Glock. The gun goes off accidentally with the impact, shot crack-ing through the night, muzzle flash giving away our position. As the enforcer sinks to his knees the people around us either run or hit the ground screaming. Police officers, private mercenaries, protesters, they all turn in our direction.

'Into the crowd,' I tell Javier. 'Now.'

We run and catch up with those fleeing, finding cover in their ranks. Nearby, another of Renard's men draws his Rapier and fires at us, the rounds blowing through a woman in front of me, almost cutting her in half. I turn and take aim, pull the trigger twice and down him with the Desert Eagle. When I turn back I see a cop ahead just as he opens up on us with an assault rifle. Javier dodges and returns fire, catching the cop in the shoulder with a round that spins him to the ground. The Great Lawn suddenly erupts in gunfire as armed protesters pour out of the big orange tent, guns blazing, targeting the surrounding police force. Cops fire back, gun barrels spitting fire, unloading magazines indiscriminately into the crowds. People start dropping everywhere, some writhing in pain, others stilled.

Alerted by the commotion, the EMU turns and gets me in its sights. It tries to fight through the protesters and police, spraying tear gas to disperse them, white clouds rolling over the riotous scene. I watch in horror as one man falls in its path and is trampled, the robot's weight snapping his spine like a twig. Central Park descends into absolute chaos.

Javier and I try to escape to the north, sprinting with everything we've got. By the time we reach the basketball and volleyball courts I can hear the thudding footsteps of the EMU gaining on us. I look over my shoulder and see it crashing through the hordes of people, blasting them with its water cannon, smashing them aside with its limbs, sending bodies flying. By now even the police have realized the drone has gone rogue. Cops and armed protesters alike open fire on the urbanized war machine. Multiple rounds ricochet off its metal body, completely ineffective. It keeps coming, growing larger every time I risk a glance back. As we reach the tree line the EMU is upon us, towering over our heads, raising its appendages. There is no escape.

'Rhodes –'

Javier manages to shoot me a terrified glance a second before the right side of his face caves in from a crushing blow. He drops to the grass beside me, dead before he hits the ground.

'You fucking bastard!' I scream, bracing myself for a similar fate.

The EMU's claw grabs me and pins me to a tree, cracking a couple ribs in the process. My night-vision glasses are knocked away and lost. The drone leans forward, its head coming close to my face, reflective lenses searching my uncovered eyes. I can almost see Winslade in there, staring back at me through the technology he's created. I get the overwhelming feeling that he is pleased to have caught me alive. The drone fails to notice as I slowly lift the Desert Eagle up to its head.

'You don't own me,' I whisper.

I pull the trigger repeatedly, emptying the rest of the clip into its face. Sparks fly as one of the lenses shatters. The EMU recoils, dropping me as it staggers backward. I watch it crash half-blind into a park bench and topple over it. Without wasting another second, I get to my feet and run north through the woods in the dark. It isn't long before I hear the EMU wrecking its way through the trees and bushes behind me.

The 86th Street Transverse that cuts through Central Park suddenly appears ahead of me. I run straight into the road without thinking, only to be blinded by the headlights of a truck bearing down on me. The screech of brakes fills the air. I dive forward just as the EMU steps into traffic after me. The truck slams into the drone, sending it hurtling through the air. It crashes to the sidewalk and lies there twitching as the truck skids to a halt.

346

I look up from where I lie and see that the vehicle is an NYPD Lenco BearCat. A heavily armed SWAT team pours out the back and approaches me, assault rifles pointed at my head. I raise my hands to show I'm unarmed. Before I can say anything an officer steps forward with a Taser and fires. Every nerve in my body catches fire before I'm incapacitated.

33

'I need to make a goddamn statement already,' I say again. 'Are either of you idiots even listening to me?'

The arresting officer and the detective trade unimpressed looks before turning their attention back to the paperwork in their hands. They've held me in an interrogation room at the Central Park Precinct for almost two hours. Cops have been coming and going constantly, taking calls and making calls. They keep asking me questions I don't have answers to. Questions about the Occupy Movement. Questions about Integris. Questions about the bearded man and the kidnapped girl and the guns smuggled into the park. I've begged them to listen to more important things I have to say, but no one seems to care. If what's coming out of my mouth isn't in relation to what's going down in Central Park right now, they don't want to hear it.

It's madness in NYC tonight. News of the Battle of the Great Lawn is taking over every website, TV and radio channel. I can hear it every time the interrogation room door opens. It is already being called the worst national tragedy of the century so far. The death toll is still being determined. Mass arrests are being made and will continue throughout the night. The Central Park Precinct has been turned into a giant forward operating base, its sole mission to tackle and finish OCP for good. The detective pulls up a chair and sits across the table from me.

'Who did you say you worked for again, Mr Rhodes?'

'Solace Strategies,' I reply. 'I'm a Husk.'

'Right.' The detective rolls his eyes. 'You're some kind of hooker.'

'You haven't really listened to a word I've said, have you?'

'Well, what I did hear was some pretty incredible stuff, hard to believe.'

'I'm not fucking crazy.'

'I didn't say that.'

'I'm not on drugs either.'

The detective shrugs. 'Sure.'

I sigh, cracking my knuckles in frustration. 'Did you review the footage from the camera that was in my knapsack?'

The detective says nothing. We simply stare at each other across the table, his expression informing me he hasn't bothered to look at it yet. The arresting officer, bored with the situation, finishes filling out his paperwork and leaves the room.

'Do you think I'm lying?' I ask the detective.

'Not necessarily.'

'Then why won't you hear the rest of what I have to say? This could be huge.'

'We're already dealing with *huge*,' the detective replies. 'All hell has broken loose. Our focus right now is the park and the park only. Fact is we don't have the manpower to deal with anything outside of that.'

'Jesus, I'm trying to report a goddamn crime here. Do I have to remind you of your duty to –'

The detective slams his fist down on the table, making me jump. I see it now, the circumference of his tired eyes growing bloodshot, the marks where he's been chewing his bottom lip. He's through playing good cop.

'May I remind you that you're under arrest, Mr Rhodes. You're not here to give statements about shit I don't give a flying fuck about.'

'Fine,' I say, folding my arms and leaning back in my chair. 'Lock me in a cell then until you're ready to hear me out.'

The detective's laugh is cold. 'You sure that's what you want? Because we've got some vicious characters in holding tonight. They'll tear a pretty boy like you up in a matter of minutes.'

I'm about to tell him to go fuck himself when the arresting officer slips back into the room and pulls the detective aside. Both of them cast scowls at me as they converse in whispers that become more and more aggressive in tone. The officer finally raises his voice enough for me to make out the last of the exchange.

'There's nothing we can do. We have to cut him loose.'

The officer leaves again, slamming the door behind him. The detective comes back to the table, but does not sit down.

'You're free to go.'

'What?'

'You made bail.'

'How can that be? I didn't lawyer up. I haven't even used my one phone call yet.'

'Well, someone came through for you. We can't hold you any longer.'

'Who paid my bail?'

'Some friend of yours.' The detective sneers. 'They're collecting your stuff right now. They'll be here shortly to escort you out.'

The detective leaves the room. For a few minutes I'm alone, wondering who is coming to get me. It's the only peace and quiet I've had in days. I slouch in my chair, massaging my sore muscles, examining my cuts and scrapes. My cracked ribs haven't received medical attention yet. Breathing is a chore. The van crash has undoubtedly given me whiplash. I try my best to relax. My eyelids get heavy, exhaustion finally catching up to me. I let my head loll, close my eyes for a few seconds, start to drift off to sleep.

The interrogation room door opens and closes, I hear footsteps approach. God, I can't wait to see a friendly face. When I raise my head and open my eyes, the man is standing on the opposite side of the table with my knapsack slung over his shoulder. He looks intently at me with a single baby blue eye. The bandages are gone, preliminary plastic surgery has been performed on the burns to his face. My saviour is the same man who said he owed me one, although he's the last person I expected to see.

My saviour is Clive.

34

I tie the Eldredge knot perfectly the first time and adjust it around my neck in front of the mirror. The new suit is made to measure. The dress shoes are soft and comfortable and made from endangered alligator. The smell of my favourite cologne pricks my nostrils and makes me giddy. I feel euphoric, despite everything that happened in Central Park last night. Sore muscles and cracked ribs actually make me feel alive. I walk to the fireplace, watch the flames dance in the hearth. The heat feels good on my exposed skin.

In the corner of the study is my old silver-skinned server system, the now permanently deactivated robot crumpled to the floor beside it. I walk over and give the server a pat, still feeling some affection for the person I've committed indefinitely to it. I always was very fond of him. Giving him my old home was the least I could do. Renard knocks on the door and enters.

'Your limo has arrived and is waiting downstairs, Mr Winslade.'

'Very good,' I say. 'We will leave momentarily.'

Renard exits and I turn back to the server with a smile as I hold my Liaison up to my lips.

'It's been fun, my boy. I want you to know that.'

A program I've installed allows me to communicate

with my boy in there, but I mute him to make it a one-sided conversation. I don't care to hear anything he has to say, though I do wonder what he thinks of his new accommodations. It will take some getting used to, no doubt, but I'm sure he'll adjust in time. To be fair, I've given him the option to terminate everything if he proves unhappy with his new situation.

Last night Ms Baxter rented out a Husk named Clive to me, an apparent close friend of Mr Rhodes. Posing as this friend, I was able to earn my boy's trust and lure him out of police custody into the hands of Renard. First thing this morning I had his consciousness digitized and downloaded off of his brain to make room for my permanent relocation.

'I really did enjoy all the time we spent together, but now I'm looking forward to spending some time alone with your woman.'

Silence from the server, of course.

Ryoko is beyond beautiful. The number of things I could do to her seems endless. All I know for certain is that I'd like her to be my first playmate, the one I celebrate with using my new body, the first pulse I feel fading in the clutches of these new hands of mine.

'I do hope Ryoko is a fighter, Mr Rhodes. I hate it when they give up too easily.'

I leave the room and step out onto the balcony of my penthouse to look out over Central Park. The Great Lawn is empty, police tape cordoning off the perimeter. Every last protester has been forcibly removed, only their abandoned personal belongings are left. Forensic teams comb the grass and trees, crime scenes being investigated all over. Occupy Central Park is no more. Last night's incident proved to be the perfect catalyst to clean up that god-awful mess down there. The smile on my face feels grand. I scroll through the contacts on Mr Rhodes' Liaison and find Ryoko's number. I dial it and she picks up after the first ring.

'Ryoko?' I say. 'It's me.'

It's kind of sweet really. She's so happy to hear from me. I listen as she tells me she loves me, and that she wished she'd spoken those words to me before. She tells me she's been so worried. I tell her not to worry any more, that everything has been settled, that I will explain everything to her soon. I provide her with a place and time to meet and she agrees to it. She tells me she got the test results back this morning. I almost ask her what test results, but quickly correct myself and ask what the results were. Her answer astounds me. I'm speechless at first. She waits patiently for my response.

'I'm going to be a father?'

There is a long pause. I can hear her breathing over the line, maybe even crying a little. When she finally speaks her voice is slow and deliberate.

'Aren't you happy, cheesecake?' she asks.

I laugh. 'Of course I am, honey. Why wouldn't I be —'

Ryoko hangs up.

Epilogue

You are no longer yourself. It's not that hard to understand. Emotions feel different in the system, but anger and sadness seem to prevail over the others. Recollections can be strange too. You wonder if you remember things correctly, wonder if memories were copied properly or if aspects were lost in translation. The thought of living this way indefinitely becomes more horrifying with every hour spent inside the server. This isn't immortality. This is a parody of a bad joke, a sequel with no plot that should have never been made. Only by paying for your ticket and sitting through the opening of the performance do you realize how ripped off you are by it all. Others might feel grounded and safe with this result. You only feel anchored and afraid.

You try different worlds; a tropical beach, a sunny valley, a national park, a busy seaside pier. The agony of choice has never been more ironic. Sometimes you see things as they pixilate or glitch, hear sounds that clip and distort, feel things that you know aren't being translated properly by the lips or fingertips that have been devised for you. Your senses run through a thousand microprocessors, your veins now a network of wires. All of it quantifies life, but does not qualify as such. You can't help but feel disconnected. These generated places are prisons, painted to resemble the reality you were designed and destined to leave behind one day. The fraudulence of it all would break your heart if you still had one.

There is one small comfort from everything that has happened. You've left a piece of yourself behind, a signature, an echo. It is purposeful, as much as it can be; a diminutive deterrent trying its best not to be ignored. It will start as an itch or flinch in the flesh, might grow to become a thorn in a side that draws blood with enough persistence. You can only hope it will eventually drive the thief of you as mad as he drove others. You give your blessing to this wisp of your former self that will float through the circuitry of an implant, a microscopic ghost haunting a tiny machine.

The door is still open for the moment, the same door a holographic dead man named Shaw once warned you about when you were technically alive. The same man who told you there is a vast difference between those that seek to live for ever, and those who are simply too scared to die. This door, you can feel it slowly shutting on you. A commitment is needed one way or another. Either stay in the spiritless known, or make promises to further mysteries. The possibilities seem endless. Witness the birth of a star or become the oblivion of one. The decision is time-sensitive in what may be your last conceptualization of time as you have known it. Only two things hold you back. The first is fear. The second is how much you miss her, the one you wanted to spend the rest of your life with. You remember what you called her. You hope it will help save her from harm.

Sugarplum

You'll never be allowed to go back, but there is an opportunity to go forward. Into what, you are unsure. Termination is one command away and you realize she never loved you for your body or mind, the flesh and muscle and matter that encompassed who you were. She loved you for the one thing that could never be detected or defined. She loved you as a matter of faith. She loved you for your soul.

The man who abandoned you in this place said he was on his way to dispatch her. You wonder if the baby was ever yours. The only shred of joy you feel is over the possibility that another piece of you has been left behind. You wonder how long it can survive as part of a slowly dying species. You wish you knew whether the love of your life is still alive or already dead. As much as you want to, you can't find out if she is gone from the real world out there.

But you are.

Delete Post-Mortem Program: Y/N?

Acknowledgements

I owe debts of gratitude:

To my wife and partner in crime, Kara, for believing in me and being my greatest ally when I'm my own worst enemy.

To my parents, Tony and Angela, for encouraging my dreams and raising a storyteller. To my sister, Emma, the best sibling a guy could have.

To my wonderful literary agents Laura Williams and Annabel Merullo, and the amazing team at Peters Fraser & Dunlop: Rachel Mills, Marilia Savvides, Alexandra Cliff. You are all undoubtedly the best in the business.

To Dom Zbogar, the go-to guy who never fails me.

To Peter Sellers for his honesty and for keeping expectations high.

To Rowland White, Emad Akhtar and all the fantastic people at Michael Joseph, Penguin Random House UK, for their great work on this novel.

And to all my friends, family, and fans for their continual love and support. Many Thanks. You make all the difference.

He just wanted a decent book to read ...

Not too much to ask, is it? It was in 1935 when Allen Lane, Managing Director of Bodley Head Publishers, stood on a platform at Exeter railway station looking for something good to read on his journey back to London. His choice was limited to popular magazines and poor-quality paperbacks – the same choice faced every day by the vast majority of readers, few of whom could afford hardbacks. Lane's disappointment and subsequent anger at the range of books generally available led him to found a company – and change the world.

'We believed in the existence in this country of a vast reading public for intelligent books at a low price, and staked everything on it'
Sir Allen Lane, 1902–1970, founder of Penguin Books

The quality paperback had arrived – and not just in bookshops. Lane was adamant that his Penguins should appear in chain stores and tobacconists, and should cost no more than a packet of cigarettes.

Reading habits (and cigarette prices) have changed since 1935, but Penguin still believes in publishing the best books for everybody to enjoy. We still believe that good design costs no more than bad design, and we still believe that quality books published passionately and responsibly make the world a better place.

So wherever you see the little bird – whether it's on a piece of prize-winning literary fiction or a celebrity autobiography, political tour de force or historical masterpiece, a serial-killer thriller, reference book, world classic or a piece of pure escapism – you can bet that it represents the very best that the genre has to offer.

Whatever you like to read – trust Penguin.